LOVE CHAOS

ROOMMATE UP FOR GRABS

UTE JACKLE

He has a constant string of casual hook-ups. She is in desperate need of a break from men.

Making a fool of myself in front of the hottest guy on campus – check

Then getting stuck as roommates with that same womanizer – check

And being completely humiliated by him on the very first night – also check

Why, among all the possible mix-ups in the world, is Luca, who's recently been kicked out by her cheating ex-boyfriend, assigned to a shared dorm suite with the biggest lady-killer of all mankind? Ben Nowak is not only brazen, he is brazenly sexy. He and Luca are like dogs and cats, like fire and gasoline. A real test of her nerves. The jerk seems to think he can do whatever he wants and is badly in need of being taken down a notch. One evening Luca sneaks into Ben's room—a slip-up that sets her heart racing, but for completely different reasons…

This novel has received acclaim from three booksellers as "incredibly funny and captivating."

1

"And you're sure you're not a man?" The secretary, a woman in her late forties, eyed me in confusion as she leafed through her file, all the while wetting her index finger with the tip of her tongue. Her desk was flanked to the left and right by floor-to-ceiling filing cabinets, and next to it stood a sad-looking yucca with drooping leaves like the wings of a depressed hen in a cage. For a fraction of a second, her snooty gaze dropped to my chest, and I spontaneously flinched. From the way she raised her left eyebrow, it was clear that the words *boob job* and *silicone* were going through her head. A faint smirk played around the corners of her mouth, and I had to fight the impulse to cross my arms over my chest. I gulped and pulled myself together. After all, I'd come to the University of Erlangen's Office of Student Housing on a very important mission.

"As you can see, I'm not a man," I replied sullenly. "And yet, your office put me in an all-guys suite." As evidence, I held up the letter I'd received today; my hand shaking terribly. I could hardly believe the awful news this morning when I went to my mailbox and read the letter—and I still hadn't quite recovered, which was why I'd headed over here right away.

"But it says here Luca Vogt," she insisted blankly.

"Yeaaaaah. That's me," I said, drawing out my answer as I tapped my sternum. "My name is *Luca*." This wasn't entirely the truth, but she didn't need to know that. In fact, no one was supposed to know that.

"Oh." She looked up as if she'd just had some sort of an epiphany. "I always thought Luca was a boy's name."

"As you can see…" I gave up. What was the point? I mean, I was standing right in front of her.

She was still smirking at me; tiny creases in her tanned skin formed around her eyes. As a matter of fact, she seemed very fit for her age, which immediately filled me with guilt. As an absolute couch potato myself, I could barely make it up the two flights to my apartment without panting like crazy. To be more exact, my *old* apartment. The one my ex-boyfriend was now living in alone.

"I understand your situation." The lady nodded at me with the angelic look of the Virgin Mary on her face. "Sadly though, all the rooms have already been assigned. Some of the students applied as early as last year."

The way in which she said *last year* didn't give me a very good feeling, but there was no way I was going to move in with a bunch of guys! I'd just as soon join a convent and take a vow of chastity instead. I'd had my fill of men for at least the next couple of decades. Just when I was beginning to seriously contemplate the advantages of becoming a nun, the bearer of bad news went on. "To be honest, you're lucky that somebody's dropped out at the last minute."

"And I'm grateful for that," I lied with a heavy sigh. Behind me I heard a creaking noise, but I didn't let myself be distracted. I thought I'd adopt an extra sorrowful tone instead and leaned over her desk. Maybe playing the pity card would help my case. I spontaneously decided to embellish my breakup story with Ringo just a little bit. It'd really hit me hard when I came home to find him with that bleached blonde in our living room. Especially since Ringo was the first guy I'd taken a chance on a good four years after the worst night of my life. I'd finally given into his advances, but only after he'd chased me for months and months. Woman of his dreams and all that. Yadda, yadda, yadda. What a hypocrite! That was never going to happen to me again!

Tilting my head, I went into full-on attack mode. "Look, it's like this. I really have to move out of my old apartment. My ex had sex on our coffee table—with another woman." My voice was actually breaking, and I cleared my throat. In reality, it cost me a good deal of courage to share this humiliating experience. Plus, this part of the story had honestly happened.

"Why don't you just kick him out?" the secretary suggested indifferently as she studied me over the edge of her glasses. "Let him worry about finding a new place to stay, not you."

"I would, but it's his apartment. I'm the one who moved in with him."

The woman's features softened a little, so I decided to kick things up a notch. It actually felt pretty good to get it all out and off my chest like this. My best friend, Caro, had had enough of an earful the last few days with all my griping about it.

"It all began when I caught him in the bathroom one night… You know…" I made a vague pumping gesture with my hand, to which the office manager gave a hectic nod.

"And then?" she asked with big eyes while I was beginning to sweat bullets. I secretly scanned her face for signs of suspicion, in the hope she was buying my ridiculous sob story. But there was absolutely no way I could live with two guys, not after everything that had happened. I needed a break from men.

"Well, he tried to talk his way out of it. 'Babe, it's not what it looks like'," I said, imitating Ringo's raspy voice. "Yeah, right." I snorted. "I guess he just had his hands full."

She giggled. The pity angle was working better than

expected, and my brain was churning out one horror scenario after another. The woman seemed eager for more, so…

"He actually told me a little 'manual labor' from time to time was good for his immune system, and that he felt like he was coming down with something." I was giving her what she wanted.

"And then?" She was practically hyperventilating.

"He had one of his 'migraines'. I think they were why we kept having so many dry spells." Was she really buying this garbage? With her mouth slightly agape, she was gobbling up every word I said.

"So, I went shopping the next day, hoping to give our love life a little boost, and bought some sexy lingerie and a pair of handcuffs at a sex shop. We even watched a porn film together."

At this, the secretary grimaced in distaste, and I was quick to nod in agreement. Oops, I might have gone too far.

"I know. It's not my thing either," I said.

"Did it help at all?"

I gave a bitter laugh. This was starting to get a little uncomfortable. I hoped I'd never have to see this woman again for the rest of my life. Best to just forget this bizarre conversation ever happened. To wrap it up, I added one last detail. "Well, it seemed to. I got home one day last week and found this blonde bimbo handcuffed to our table with the porn film running in the background." If this wasn't enough to get me reassigned, I didn't know what else to do.

She gasped at me, then added, "I hope she wasn't wearing your lingerie!"

Whaaat? A little doubt was beginning to gnaw at me, like a mouse on a piece of cheese. Had I gone too far in my pathetic attempt to gain her pity?

The woman reached for her puke green coffee cup and took a sip. I could've used some coffee too, preferably laced with something really strong. Sweat dripped from every pore, and my shoulders ached with tension. But it was too late to back out now. I needed to see this through to the bitter end. "No. She was naked, and he was deep inside her." This part was actually true again.

She glanced at my application once more while I held my breath.

"What a creep," she mumbled, turning to her computer and typing furiously.

It felt so good to hear someone else say that. I nodded. She was so right. How could I have been so blind these last two years?

"Hmm, maybe…" she mumbled thoughtfully, rubbing her chin absently.

For the first time in days, I felt a bit of hope pulse through me. She'd bought my story. I was a bad girl, but I didn't care. A new room was as good as mine.

"Yeah, what a creep," a deep voice behind me said. Whirling around, I found myself looking into a pair of midnight-blue eyes; a rich dark blue tinged with black. They belonged to a guy with tousled brown hair. His mouth twitched in an effort not to smile. Where had he come from?

"And you never suspected a thing?" he asked in disbelief. His eyes swept across my chest and lingered there a little longer than necessary. "He obviously didn't appreciate what you have to offer. You're better off without him," he added with a wide grin.

That made the woman giggle. I watched in bewilderment as her hand fluttered in front of her mouth.

"God, you're really naïve, girl. That kind of gullibility only gets you into trouble. Men need to be kept on a short leash."

"Don't take it personally. Every cowboy needs to polish his Colt every once in a while," the guy behind said me, laughing, and I whipped around and glared at him in disbelief.

Oh God, take me now! Not only had he overheard every

word—this horrible little shrew of a woman had obviously goaded me into saying all that stuff with him watching. The rational part of my brain told me to flee, but of course, I couldn't. My gaze dropped to the letter I was holding, and I turned back around to face the secretary without another word. It was better to just ignore jerks like him anyway.

"So, about my application...?" I retorted somewhat belligerently in my exasperation, as this wannabe Casanova shot darts into my back with his eyes. The amusement instantly drained from her face. Evidently, she didn't appreciate being snapped at.

"Unfortunately, as I told you before, it's out of my hands. You can either take the room we offered, or find another solution yourself."

"But... But." My mind went blank. There was nothing more to say, not as long as that jerk was standing there laughing his head off at me. Damn it! He took a step closer, and I could hear him breathing right behind me. I whipped around again and snapped, "Would you mind not breathing down my neck?"

He seemed taken aback. Good.

"Are we in a bit of a bad mood today? PMS?" he inquired with feigned concern. I could only gasp.

"PMS, that's exactly what this is. Primitive Man Syndrome, I believe it's very contagious. Best to keep a safe distance," I replied icily.

This earned me a laugh. I couldn't believe it—he was actually laughing in my face.

"Wow, are you always like this? You really shouldn't be surprised..."

"Surprised about what?" I asked, menacingly, pulling myself up to my full height, and put my hands on my hips. This asshole had just ruined all my plans. Unfortunately, I couldn't create the effect I had been going for since I had to crane my neck all the way back to look him in the face, or I'd have been talking to his chest. On top of everything else, I could feel myself starting to blush. Desperately trying to ignore it, I glared at him instead, ready for a fight.

And it worked! He took a step back and put up both hands.

"Easy there," he said as if addressing a rabid pit bull. "Don't hit me, okay? I'm just here to hand in my application, and I'll be out of your hair so you can keep chatting. Your problems are none of my business anyway." Grinning, he held up his form for me to see, and it read "Parking Space Reservation" in all caps. He gestured at an inbox on the desk marked with the same words.

"Oh," was all I could conjure up. None of this had gone according to my plan, so I forced a smile and pointed graciously at the desk. Meanwhile, the secretary had gotten up and gone to the window to refill her coffee cup.

Beaming at the guy, she said, "Just put the form in the tray, Ben. I'll deal with it right away. I'll see what we can do to get you a spot in the parking lot."

"That's really sweet, Mrs. Weber, thank you," he said, giving her a once-over. "Have you been working out lately?"

She smiled, obviously flattered. "It's nothing. I just do a little jogging in the park, that's all."

How nauseating. What a suck-up! He grinned as he noticed me rolling my eyes before turning back to her. "Well, it shows. You look great. By the way, I'd really love a spot in the first row of the parking garage, so I don't have to walk too far in the mornings. If that's at all possible." His voice dropped an octave, and it sounded like he was propositioning her right then and there. It made me shudder, but she seemed to lap it up. With a swing of her hips, she returned to her desk.

"I think that can be arranged," she said huskily, as if she were channeling Marilyn Monroe singing "Happy Birthday" to President Kennedy.

"Thank you so much—I knew I could count on you." He dropped the form into the tray, and strode past me to the door where he turned once more and smiled right at me before disappearing.

"A very nice young man," the woman remarked while staring at the closed door with a dreamy expression. "You shouldn't get so upset, my dear. Men don't appreciate disagreeable women."

Great, now, thanks to this jerk, I was no longer the poor victim who deserved sympathy, but a cantankerous hag who'd driven her poor boyfriend into the arms of another woman.

Mrs. Weber's smile seemed as fake as the color of her hair. "I think your best option is to move in with the boys for now. Give it a try. I'm sure you'll learn a lot about men there."

I snorted. "You sound like you're trying to sell me a guinea pig! But for your information, I'm extremely allergic to all animal hair. You know, rabbits, cats, men; the whole works."

With a long-suffering sigh, she looked at her watch. "Well, it's time for my lunch break. Either you can take the room for now and I'll give you a call whenever there's another opening. Or, you don't take it and try to find something on your own. It's your call." The way she shrugged and reached for Ben's form made it very clear that she couldn't care less about what happened to me. What was I supposed to do? I couldn't afford my own apartment. I was in my final year here, and staying at Caro's was only a temporary solution. We were literally stepping on each other's toes in her tiny apartment; and there was no way I could go back to Ringo's.

"Alright, I'll take it. But call me as soon as you have something else available. This is only temporary." Could she hear me grinding my teeth?

Mrs. Weber's face glowed like a nuclear reactor spill. She rummaged in a box marked *Keys*, took one out, and held it up. "Please sign here." Then she pushed a list across the desk at me and pointed to a line with my name already printed out in block letters next to it.

After a moment's hesitation, I grabbed the pen from her and signed. My signature was a bit scrawly, but that didn't matter. With that, I stormed out of her office

2

———

O nce out the office door, I paused to take a deep breath. I simply couldn't believe this nightmare. Was I seriously supposed to live with two guys? I nervously fidgeted with the key in my hand until it clattered to the floor. With a heavy sigh, I picked it up, before I marched down the hallway to the stairwell and went down to the lobby.

There, I made a beeline for the coffee machine I spotted tucked away in the corner. I desperately needed caffeine to perk up my defeated spirits. As I headed towards it, I dug out a few coins from my pocket, put them in the slot, and waited. Nothing happened. No cup dropped down, nothing. Dammit, what was going on today? I bent over to look at the spot where my coffee should have been standing; nothing there.

"Stupid thing." I viciously kicked the coffee machine.

"Need some help?" I heard a voice behind me that was now all too familiar. If it wasn't Ben again. Great, just what I needed.

"No, thank you," I growled, but he was already pounding the vending machine with his fist. The entire thing shook, and lo and behold, the cup plopped out, and pitch black liquid flowed into the cup with a hiss.

"Where brute force rules," I quoted as I carefully removed the steaming cup.

"You're welcome," he replied with a smile. "I work at the copy shop across the street, and this is my main source for coffee. I've gotten pretty familiar with Ernie's quirks."

With a great deal of willpower, I forced myself to look up, once again losing myself in the deep blue eyes that would have filled a professional hypnotist with envy. "Thanks." I was trying to at least sound a little friendlier. "Ernie?"

He stroked the side of the machine as if caressing a naked woman. "It's my nickname for her, Ernestine, actually. Machines have a soul too, you know. Since we've started getting along, Ernie always provides me with the coffee I need." He pointed at my cup.

"Ah, so you're a vending machine whisperer." As hard as I tried, I couldn't suppress a chuckle. But he didn't seem to find his commentary the least bit embarrassing.

"Among other things." Ben leaned against the vending machine. "So why didn't you leave earlier?"

"The office, you mean?" I asked, confused.

"Nah. Your ex. You should've broken up with him when he cooked up that dumb migraine excuse." He snorted.

Embarrassed, I sipped my coffee, grimacing instantly. It tasted awful. Did he have to bring up all that BS I'd told the woman at the office? I had no desire to discuss my failed relationship with a complete stranger, least of all with him. The way he said that made it obvious that he questioned my sanity. In all fairness, I had laid it on a bit thick there in the office, but my relationship was a disaster either way. What was there to say? That I'd actually hoped I could salvage my pathetic relationship? That I'd been oblivious? That I had a hard time meeting people and that dating was hell for me? What did he know anyway? He was probably a chick magnet, and had no idea how it felt to be rejected or cheated on. My love life was certainly no business of his.

"Listen, that's private and in the past. Would you do me a favor and just forget that conversation ever happened?"

How cool he looked in his tight black t-shirt and skinny jeans. He was definitely in a completely different league than me. Guys like him usually never even talked to me. Maybe we'd just gotten off on the wrong foot, I thought, and was already mellowing out a little when he delivered the final blow.

"Sex is actually a great indicator for whether a relationship is working or not. It's the tip of the iceberg, really. If things aren't working in the bedroom, you can forget about the rest."

Unbelievable. "Oh, thanks for the analysis, Dr. Freud," I squawked out. I could do without his *professional* diagnosis of my sad sex life, thank you very much. Any spark of attraction that I'd felt for him evaporated in the blink of an eye. "I get it, you're probably a woman whisperer too, right?"

To my dismay, he actually seemed flattered. He put his hand around the back of his neck, and his eyes dropped to the floor as if he were embarrassed to admit to it.

"I guess you could say that, yeah." He was smiling again.

How could someone be this conceited? "Really, you have a girlfriend?"

He leaned in a bit closer. "Why? Are you interested?"

I patted his arm sympathetically. "Keep dreaming, buddy. I was just curious to know if there's a woman out there who can actually put up with you."

"Oh, I could name a few," he said with a wink. "There haven't been any complaints so far. I think all you really need is…"

"All I really need is a guy who knows how to take care of me, right?" I finished for him, folding my arms in front of me. How predictable!

"I was going to say that all you need is a little more confidence, but I like your version too." There was a twinkle in his eye, as if I had just made a pass at him.

"Gotta go." I gulped down the rest of my coffee. As I

tossed the empty cup into the trash can next to the machine, my cell rang. Great timing. There must be a God after all! I could escape without having to waste any more of my precious time with this arrogant moron. I pulled my phone out of my pocket as I walked away and checked the screen. It was Caro. I quickly hit the answer button.

"Hey, Luca. I was just checking to see if you were able to fix things," she declared. On my way here, I'd told her about the letter regarding my living arrangement problem.

"No, there's nothing else available. What a nightmare." Just as I'd put my hand on the glass door to push it open, a now all-too-familiar voice called out behind me.

"Hey, wait up."

"Hold on a sec, Caro." Turning slowly, I lowered the phone and sighed loudly so he could clearly hear it. I was going to get rid of this guy once and for all.

"What?" I snapped.

"You dropped something," he said with a diabolical grin that made me fear the worst. As if in slow motion, he held up a white object between his thumb and forefinger. When I realized what it was, I wished the ground would open up and swallow me whole!

"Looks like I guessed right."

I hissed at him like a cornered cat and snatched the tampon from his hand. Without a word, I turned around and heard him chuckle.

"What? I don't even get a reward?"

3

———

B ack in Nuremberg, I entered the narrow stairway of the building tucked back in the rear courtyard where Caro's apartment was located. With a sigh, I opened the apartment door with the spare key she'd given me and instantly felt at home. I always felt at home at her place. Every wall was painted a different color, and portraits she had done herself hung on every available surface. Caro was an art student and worked several jobs to support herself. We met during my freshman year, at a small downtown chocolate shop where Caro used to work twice a week. Because of my celiac disease, I needed to check all ingredients lists first to ensure that I didn't accidentally eat something containing wheat. Back then, she and I went through all the candy lists together, and soon we realized that we had a lot in common.

She was standing in her usual spot in front of her easel, her black hair tied up into a messy bun, and was in the process of generously brushing red paint on her most recent work. As I deposited my key on the dining table, she turned around, a splotch of red paint on her cheek.

"And? Have you calmed down a bit?"

Snorting, I sat down. "What did I ever do to deserve this...?"

That wasn't a rhetorical question!

Caro walked over and wrapped her arms around my shoulders from behind. "You poor thing."

I turned to look at her. "And then some stuck-up, pretty boy barged right in while I was talking to the lady and ruined my only chance of getting out of this."

"So, what are you going to do now?" Caro sat down next to me. "You know you can stay here as long as you need to."

"Thanks, really. You're the best." I played with my new key. "But I plan to get out of your hair. You and Martha need your privacy." I grinned at her. "Besides, you guys keep me up at night with all your moaning."

Caro slapped my arm. "That's not true! We're as quiet as mice!"

"Yeah, right." I snickered and imitated Caro's breathless gasps. "Oh, Martha! Yes! YES! Oh, my Gawwwd!" With each word, my voice rose higher and higher.

In mock shame, Caro looked down. "What can I say? She's amazing. That girl just knows what she's doing..."

I threw my hands up. "Too much information. Spare me the details please, or you'll make me jealous!" Truth be told, I didn't completely get what all the fuss was about sex. It was my well-kept secret that I had yet to experience an orgasm. I'd never even told Caro that. I was beginning to wonder whether something was wrong with my body.

"Oh, honey." Caro gave me a crooked smile. "There must be someone out there who'd appreciate an awesome girl like you."

"Oh, I'm sure there is." I hastily agreed in order to get her off my case and change the topic. "I just seem to have a knack for attracting only the worst type of guys." I made a square on my forehead with my forefingers and thumbs. "It's like I'm wearing a sign here that says *I heart idiots*. You should've seen that guy I met today."

Caro got up and laughed. "Let me make you a nice Hugo."

"I sure need one!" I called after her.

"Martha and I are going out later. Want to come?" she called from the kitchen. I could hear glasses clinking. "It's Ladies' Night at Desi's."

"Your new bed bunny has really got you wrapped around her little finger, doesn't she?" I teased her. "But I think I'll pass. For better or worse, I need to start taking my things over to that hall of horrors."

"My new bed bunny..." Caro's head appeared in the doorframe. "I like that. Martha really is as cuddly as a bunny." She disappeared again into the kitchen, and her muffled voice asked, "What's the rush? You really don't have to move out right this minute, you know." She quickly returned with two long-stemmed wine glasses containing lime wedges and mint leaves dancing in the stream of bubbles. We toasted one another, and I swallowed down half of my glass in one gulp, the refreshing flavor of sparkling wine and elderflower syrup lingered on my tongue.

"Yeah, I know. But I'll have to move at some point. So why not get it over with today? Maybe I'll luck out, and my new roommates will be a gay couple."

Caro shook her head at me. "You're going to develop androphobia if you're not careful. You'd better snap out of it."

Instead of answering, I shrugged and took another sip as I considered what she'd just said. Were we women at fault if men discarded us like used tissues? Were we unconsciously giving men the OK to go ahead and trample all over our feelings? Had I done that? Ringo sure hadn't put much effort into our relationship towards the end. On the contrary—the harder I'd tried, the less interested he'd seemed.

"I'm not going to be the kind of girl who goes around encouraging guys to treat me like a doormat. I want a man who tells me I have beautiful eyes. I don't need the ones that only care about the way my breasts look naked," I categorically declared and took a last swig of my drink.

"You do have great breasts though," Caro remarked with a grin.

Disregarding her comment, I continued on with my rant. "I want a man who doesn't walk out after a fight. Who doesn't lie to me, or is embarrassed to introduce me to his friends and family. Someone I can talk to, and who will be by my side when times get tough. A guy who I'm everything to. Is that really too much to ask?"

Caro looked at me doubtfully. "Well, you could try asking Santa; maybe he could help you. Do you really expect to find all of that in one single man? Perhaps you've got the wrong idea about what guys are capable of?" She raised an eyebrow. "I'd get three if I were you," she advised dryly.

The doorbell rang.

"That'll be Martha," Caro said jumping up and hugging me before rushing to the door. The two girls returned with their arms around each other.

"Hey, Luca, how's it going?" Martha raised a hand in greeting and sat down.

"Hi, Martha. I'm fine," I answered shortly, getting up. I hadn't had the heart to tell Caro yet, but I didn't care all that much for her new girlfriend. There was just something about her that rubbed me the wrong way.

Standing behind her, Caro ran her fingers through Martha's short, auburn hair. I could see she was having a hard time not ripping her clothes off right then and there.

"Caro says you're moving out?" Martha asked in my direction.

"Yup." I grabbed my glass and slurped the dregs of my Hugo. "It's probably for the best. It'll give you two lovebirds some space."

Martha nodded as if she agreed, and all of a sudden, I felt like a third wheel.

"To an all-male shared apartment, no less." She grinned. "Can you imagine living with five other girls? I'd..."

"Hey!" Caro pulled Martha's head back by her hair and stared into her eyes, upside down. "You'd what?"

"Oh, I'd only have eyes for you."

"Good answer." They kissed tenderly.

"It's only two guys, by the way," I said, interrupting their kiss.

But Martha wouldn't stop. "One for the days, and one for the nights. That works," she said pragmatically. "You straight people have it so much easier anyway. At least men don't always need to talk about their feelings."

"Whaat?" Caro protested. "That's part of a healthy relationship."

"Of course, it is, baby," Martha agreed quickly, stretching out her arms to hug Caro. As Caro nestled against her, I sighed and started collecting my scattered things.

"I'm going to pack up and grab a taxi to take my stuff to Erlangen," I said.

"Oh, I've got the car. I can take you right now if you want," Martha offered before Caro could stop her. Martha pulled her onto her lap and started stroking her thighs. As they sank into a deep kiss, I was suddenly really glad I'd have my own place soon. It was high time I left this love nest.

4

Panting heavily under the weight of a box filled with books, I made my way up to the fourth floor. My new place was one floor higher than my old apartment, and of course, there was no elevator. Go figure. Why hadn't anyone ever told me that filling moving boxes to the brim with books was a bad idea? There it went. It slipped out of my hands and crashed onto the steps as I dropped to my knees, clinging to the railing and trying to catch my breath. My cheeks were throbbing and burning, and I had scraped my palms, which now stung like hell.

"Why are you stopping in the middle of the stairs?" Caro asked from behind me. She was one to talk. In her wisdom, she'd only grabbed my bedclothes, which she was currently balancing on her head.

"I'm done," I panted.

"C'mon, move it." I heard Martha protest from behind her. She was carrying two suitcases as easily as if they were cardboard props, which made sense since she spent half her life at the gym. I obviously needed to start working out myself. Maybe tomorrow, or next week. Some time, for sure. For the moment, I was way too exhausted to concern myself with my lack of endurance. I tried to focus on catching my breath instead, while my heart beat so hard I could feel it in my throat.

"Keep going," Martha urged me on. "I don't have all day."

"I can't," I said, clutching my side. "Just leave me here to die."

"Why don't you take the suitcases, and I'll carry the box instead," Martha generously offered.

What was she talking about? Did she seriously think I could handle two heavy suitcases that weighed at least as much as this stupid box?

"I'm not moving," I insisted, still out of breath. "Just pass me the comforter, and I'll sleep here."

"Luca," Caro said in her sweetest voice. "Only two more flights of stairs to go, come on, you can do it."

Oh yeah? Why didn't she offer to carry the box for me, then? One look at her skinny arms, which were about the size of mine, and I had my answer. I didn't reply.

"Excuse me, can I get by?" asked a deep voice behind us.

"Gimme a minute," I said, peering through both their legs, but I couldn't make out who was standing behind them.

"I'd like to get to my apartment, if you don't mind."

Inwardly, I groaned. Why were students always so impatient? As if they ever actually had to be somewhere.

"Just a minute!" I scrambled to my feet clumsily as if I had just aged sixty years in the past five minutes.

"Would you mind letting me by?" The guy sounded annoyed now.

"Sure." Caro pressed her back against the wall, leaving a narrow gap between herself and Martha. The man ducked under the bedding and squeezed himself between the two of them, then he stopped and said, "Look, we're a sandwich!"

A dozen sirens went off in my head. That amused tone of voice sounded familiar—where had I heard it before? The next instant, I wanted to dive over the railing and throw myself into the (not-very-deep) abyss. What in the world was he doing here, of all places? Was the universe out to get me today? To my horror, my cheeks were burning now, much worse than before.

Then he saw me and stopped. "You?"

To my dismay, he actually sounded pleased to see me.

"Yeah, me." I didn't even try to sound friendly; I didn't have the energy.

"Would you please keep going?" In her charming way, Martha rammed one of the suitcases into the back of his knee. All of a sudden, she was starting to grow on me.

He took two steps at once and landed next to me.

"My bad," Martha said, pretending it was an accident.

He waved it off. "It's okay." Then he looked at me way too intently. "What's the matter with you? You don't look so great."

Yay. Just what I needed—dumb comments from a guy I couldn't stand. My mood instantly devolved from bad to abysmal.

"Charming as always, I see," I said, making a face. With my head held high, I was determined to ignore this jerk and carry my own damn books up those last two flights, even if it killed me—which it probably would. With a groan, I picked the box back up. A stab of pain immediately shot through my back, and I dropped the books again, trying to suppress a yelp.

"You need help?" Ben asked.

I gave him a dismissive wave and rubbed my back. I certainly didn't need his help.

"I'm fine." As I struggled to straighten my back as inconspicuously as possible, Ben reached down, picked up the box as if it barely had anything in it, and asked: "What floor?"

I was too weak to protest.

"Fourth," Caro answered for me, since my mouth couldn't form words. Cocking one eyebrow at me, he started up the stairs with the box. What was that look supposed to mean? It was true that I was being a little ungrateful, but couldn't he understand my issues with him?

He floated up the stairs with Martha and Caro in tow, while I still clung to the railing and pulled myself up the stairs, one hand over the other. I'd probably be spending a lot of time in my room to avoid these stairs. Was this one of the ways people were tortured in the Middle Ages? Right now, I could imagine it all too clearly. I finally arrived on the landing, gasping for breath, while the others waited for me in front of the apartment door.

"Here we are." With an inviting gesture, Ben pointed to a closed door, unsuccessfully holding back a huge grin. He had the cutest dimple at the corner of his mouth, which only made him even more irresistible. In fact, it was a pretty clever camouflage for his nefarious ways.

"How do you know I live here?"

"Well, there's only one vacant room in the whole building, and this is it." For some reason, this was obviously very funny, and his midnight-blue eyes glinted like steel in the sunlight.

"How do you..." I repeated, while a terrible, terrible thought started forming in my head.

5

Every time I felt like things couldn't get any worse, life taught me that yes, they really could. Instead of unlocking the door for me, Ben moved aside and let me fumble with the key. It took a while for my shaking hands to meet with the lock. Regrettably, the key fit. As the door opened, I held on to the irrational hope that Ben would just put the box on the floor and continue to his place further upstairs, but unfortunately, he did no such thing. So, I turned around.

"You can put the box down now. Thanks a lot, goodbye." I could've probably been a little less blunt, but I didn't want to run the risk of Ben misunderstanding me. Maybe he had a hearing problem. He stood in the hallway and looked at me expectantly. Could you get any more presumptuous than that?

"Well? Which part didn't you get? The part about putting my box down, or the goodbye part?"

Snorting, he turned to my friends. "I'm beginning to suspect she's always like this, am I right?"

"Let's just say she's not a huge fan of men in general right now," Caro supplied cautiously, to which Martha added with more candor: "She can sometimes be a little bitchy."

I spun around indignantly. She didn't even know me that well. How dare she judge my character!

I heard Ben heave a sigh.

"I see this is going to be great… May I?" Without waiting for an answer, he stepped past me into the hallway and disappeared with my box through the middle of the three doors on the left-hand side.

"Hey!" I called after him. "Come back! You can't just traipse into someone else's apartment like that!"

This time, he reacted right away and reappeared in the hallway. He took off his gray corduroy jacket and hung it on a hook next to the door with brazen authority. Then he checked himself out in the mirror. Jeez, what a vain…

Wait. My thought from before popped back into my head, the one that I had instantly suppressed.

"Oh God. Don't tell me you live here too, do you?" With my heart in my throat, I waited for his reply. My mouth went dry, and when I saw the expression on his face, there was no need to answer.

"Welcome, new roomie!" He spread his arms wide.

I felt myself deflate, while Martha walked into the apartment and disappeared into the same room to drop off my suitcases.

Caro patted my arm in pity. "You guys know each other?" she asked softly.

I nodded and mechanically pulled the key out of the lock and took a shaky step inside before turning to face her. "He's the guy from this morning."

6

I was still in shock. The four of us sat at the kitchen table, silently eyeing each other. Ben had had the audacity to simply join us. Granted, this was his kitchen too, but he should have realized by now that I didn't really care for his company all that much. He either had abnormally thick skin, or he just didn't care. Probably a bit of both.

"Well." Caro eventually said through the uncomfortable silence. If it had been up to me, the silence could have gone on indefinitely. I certainly wasn't going to give Ben an opening to start talking to us. With a bit of luck, I could spend the following weeks in the apartment without having to talk to him at all. All I needed to do was figure out his schedule and adjust mine accordingly. Maybe I could take night classes. There must be some, and then I could sleep during the day…

"Well." He ran his hand through his unruly hair. Of course, he took Caro's gesture as permission to jump into the conversation.

"Where's your other roommate?" Martha asked, running her hand up Caro's thigh. I was curious to see how Ben would react to a lesbian couple, him being the epitome of ignorance as he was. But his gaze simply brushed over them as he answered in a completely normal voice, "Toby should be here any minute." He stood up and took a beer out of the refrigerator. "You guys want one?"

"Sure." Caro and Martha accepted in unison. For some reason unfathomable to me, they genuinely seemed to like Mr. Full-of-Himself. They must have both been out of their minds.

"What about you?" he asked me.

"No thanks," I declined icily, crossing my arms.

The bottles opened with a hiss, and he set them on the table.

"Because you don't like beer, or because I offered?" he asked.

"Because beer's not gluten-free," I replied haughtily.

They clinked bottles.

"Because it's not what?" He took a swig.

"Gluten-free. I have celiac disease, a food intolerance. No wheat, no rye, no barley, no oats, no spelt."

"Oh, right. Isn't that all the rage in the States now? Why, are you trying to lose weight?" He checked me out.

Caro snorted. I glared at her while Martha kept her eyes trained on her beer bottle.

"Exactly," I replied, simply because it was a waste of time to explain my food intolerance to him. The intolerance I had towards him was a lot worse.

"I'm Caro, by the way." Was my best friend stabbing me in the back now? "And this is Martha. And of course, you've met Luca."

"Ben." He leaned back slowly, and I was already bracing for the anti-lesbian remarks I'd secretly been waiting for. I leaned in, and listened closely for his next words. Soon, the two girls would see what a snake he was.

"Martha," he repeated thoughtfully. "Did you by any chance date Sarah Giebel?"

"I did! You know each other?" Martha was frowning suspiciously, much to my delight.

"I created the home page for the chocolate shop. She had no idea how to do it, so I helped her out. No big deal." He shrugged.

"That was you?"

To my surprise, Martha smiled at him. I'd never seen her smile before. She had certainly never smiled at me. What was going on here?

"Sarah was really happy with your work. The website looks awesome, I have to say. It's crazy how many hits she's getting. And you did it all for free!"

He raised a hand in protest. "Well, not exactly…"

They grinned at each other, then shouted "Chili chocolate for life!" at the same time, clinking bottles as if they'd been friends forever.

That was unexpected. Volunteering to work for a friend. Had I been wrong about him after all? I thought about it for a moment, then shook my head. First impressions were never wrong. The creaking of the front door opening interrupted my useless train of thought, and a dark blond Adonis stepped into the kitchen; a dead ringer for Alex Pettyfer. What was happening here? Had I stumbled into the apartment for the contestants of the Mr. Erlangen contest? I couldn't stand pretty boys.

"Hey, we have visitors! My name's Toby." He gave a general wave to everyone.

The others introduced themselves, whereas I sat frozen. Maybe I could stay at Caro's for another few nights after all. I needed some time to get used to the situation.

Ben pat me on the back. "This is Luca. She's our new roommate."

"Say what?"

"There was some sort of mix-up with her name, and she landed here with us," Ben explained while Toby helped himself to a beer. To my surprise, he seemed to understand Ben's cryptic explanation, and he grabbed a desk chair from somewhere and sat down at the table with us.

"Welcome to our place then. I think it's great to live with a woman; it'll loosen things up a bit. Can you cook?"

That made me laugh out loud. Unbelievable. "Sure! Whenever I'm not vacuuming or doing the dishes, and right after I do everyone's laundry."

He beamed. "Really?"

"Keep dreaming, buddy."

"Oh. Too bad. That would've been perfect… No drink for you?" Toby gestured to the emptiness in front of me.

Oh great, he was just as polite as the other idiot.

"She's doing that gluten thing," Ben supplied helpfully.

Just as he was about to take a sip, Toby put the bottle back down. "Doing what now?"

Ben shrugged. "Some kind of a Hollywood diet."

That was more ignorance than I could handle. My condition had also been a constant source of discussion with Ringo too. Instead of supporting me with my dietary restrictions, he'd always accused me of just trying to draw attention to myself whenever I stood at the store and scrutinized the nutritional info of just about everything there. But a lot of foods unsuspectingly contained gluten, not just bread and the like, so I had to be careful. "She can't have any gluten. She gets really sick if she does," Caro defended me for the first time, and I was truly grateful. Maybe the two morons would let it go now. But no, they just exchanged a curious look, and I had the feeling this could mean trouble. Finally, Ben got up, went to the fridge, and picked out a bottle of orange soda. "You can drink this, right?"

I nodded reluctantly. I still didn't trust him. He opened the fridge again while Toby stood up and made a beeline for the kitchen cupboard.

"How about this?" Ben held up a bottle of vodka.

"Yes, but I don't really feel like…"

"I won't take no for an answer." He cut me off. "Just a little welcome drink. What about you guys?" He nodded at the other girls.

"Count me in," Martha said, and Caro seemed interested, too.

Meanwhile, Toby had returned to the table with a handful of glasses.

"Have you guys had submarines before?" he asked.

We said that we hadn't. I started to get a bad feeling as I watched him pour the glasses half-full with the soda and fill the shot glasses to the rim with vodka. Then, he pushed the glasses towards us, and took his glass of soda in one hand with the shot glass in the other. Ben copied him, of course, and then both of them lowered the shot glass into the larger glass and held them there between their thumbs and forefingers so that the shot glasses hovered over the soda. Reluctantly, we did the same.

"After we say cheers, drop the vodka into the soda, then drink it all in one go."

"Oh!" Caro was grinning. She actually seemed to enjoy the stupid game. "A submarine!"

Toby nodded. "A submarine."

I decided to join in, but only to avoid any more dumb commentaries about my negative attitude. After dropping the shot into the orange soda, I knocked back the concoction. I wouldn't let it be said that I was a spoilsport. From the corner of my eye, I could see that Ben was amused by my shudder.

"Not bad." Martha pushed her empty glass in Toby's direction, and he happily poured again.

"I hope you can hold your liquor," Ben whispered in my ear.

"I can drink you under the table any day," I boasted, immediately regretting my cockiness. I was staring into his stupid eyes again. I'd never seen eyes that color before. Detecting an amused twinkle, I swallowed, slightly intimidated. He looked happy to accept my ridiculous challenge.

"C'mon, Luca, you show 'em!" Caro egged me on. I could've strangled her. Glancing around at the amused faces,

I was seriously cursing my big mouth. How I already hated this place!

"Shut up and pour," I ordered, in spite of myself. Of course, Ben didn't need to be told twice.

"Why don't we skip the soda—wouldn't want you to get sick."

"That's so kind of you," I replied in a saccharine voice as Toby pushed two full shot glasses towards us.

"You can do it!" Martha and Caro cheered for me. At least they were on my side. I glared at Ben as angrily as I could.

"On three!" he said dryly.

I nodded and felt as if I'd been challenged to a duel.

"Wait," Toby said. "Shouldn't the loser have to do something?"

The two of them grinned at each other. Was this a conspiracy? When had they had time for that? Were they communicating telepathically?

"What did you have in mind?" Ben asked, and I felt myself shrinking in my chair. They wouldn't dare suggest anything kinky.

"The loser gets to clean the bathroom for a month," Toby suggested.

"Perfect," Ben agreed without missing a beat, which I found a little strange. I shrugged. Okay. Those were acceptable terms.

"We'd actually prefer not to do the cooking, either," Ben declared magnanimously, then he turned to me.

"Are you sure?" I said, still overly friendly. "I could've made you such a nice mushroom stew!"

Laughing, he picked up his shot glass, saluting me mid-air. "You're a dangerous lady." He swallowed it down in one swig.

I reluctantly followed his example. I gasped for air as the fiery liquid burned my throat going down.

7

When I woke up, it felt like a sledgehammer was pounding on my head. In slow motion, I gently draped a hand over my throbbing skull and didn't dare move a muscle. Just the thought of moving made me want to vomit. What in the world had happened? Gradually, my surroundings came into focus—I was lying on a bed, a naked light bulb dangling above me. I flinched. Was I in jail? For as hard as I tried, I couldn't remember a thing.

With great effort, I turned my head and squinted. Painfully brilliant sunlight illuminated the room like a giant neon floodlight. Where the hell was I? Nothing looked familiar. I could feel my heartbeat pounding in my throat. A pale wooden desk and matching wardrobe faced each other against the cold white walls. Next, I discovered my suitcases sitting beside my books and a pile of my things. Blurry images suddenly flashed through my mind: a box falling, Martha and Caro, orange soda and vodka. Nothing made sense. Two vaguely suspicious male faces appeared and disappeared again in a haze. Who were they? Shit! Like a barrage of firebombs, flashes of memories exploded in my mind, and I leapt out of bed with adrenaline shooting through my veins. I slipped on my jeans, which were hanging on the back of a chair, and a gray t-shirt I found lying on the floor, and froze. Who had undressed me? The room was spinning, and I needed to lean against the wall for support. My mouth felt as dry as the Sahara. Then a name shot like an arrow through my brain, and my stomach heaved. Ben. The nausea became unbearable, and I ran out of the bedroom with my hand pressed to my mouth. Where the hell was the bathroom? Next to the front door was another door that I threw open, hoping for the best. After turning on the light, my stomach heaved again, but for an entirely different reason. I was met with unbearable chaos; towels were haphazardly hung up to dry, and a gray film encircled the bathroom sink. Something vaguely resembling a faucet was covered in a rock-hard white crust. I chanced a look at the shower and discovered the most disgusting shower curtain ever known to man. This must be a nightmare. In my mind, I faintly heard a man's voice say, "The loser gets to clean the bathroom for a month."

Those jerks!

But hold on. Who said that I had lost? I felt a faint glimmer of hope rise up inside me. Maybe fate had taken pity on me, and Ben was now laid up somewhere in the ICU after having to have his stomach pumped. I took a few steps into the bathroom. My bare feet stuck to the filthy floor and made a revolting sucking sound as I walked, as if someone had dumped a bottle of glue on the ground. After a brief glance in the mirror, any hopes of having won the battle were dashed— Quasimodo was staring back at me. My brown eyes were bloodshot and had dark bags under them, as if I'd transformed overnight. My light-brown hair stood up in every direction. Oh my God. I looked exactly the way I felt. At least, my nausea was slowly subsiding as long as I didn't move. But then, I saw a yellow stain on the toilet seat and was again seized with anger. That was the last straw. I shivered with disgust. Bet or no bet, there was no way I was going to clean this pigsty! That simply wasn't fair of them. I never would've agreed to the terms had I dared a single look inside this hellhole. I turned around to get out of the bathroom of horrors as quickly as possible. What I needed was a glass of water, hopefully without running into my new roommates. I didn't want those two pretty boys to see me at my worst.

I tiptoed towards the kitchen. Nobody was there, but I thought I heard a faint noise coming from somewhere in the apartment. Out of the corner of my eye, I saw an open door, but continued to the kitchen. I also needed to find my toiletry bag right away. That was where my painkillers were, and, boy, did I need them! I took a glass out of the cupboard— oddly enough, everything looked spotless here. While I ran the tap, I noticed the cheap Coca-Cola clock on the wall. Oh no, 11 o'clock already. I'd missed my favorite lecture: molecular genetics. What was happening to me? In the space of only one day, everything was turned upside down. I drained the glass in large gulps, refilled it, and gulped it down again like a dried-out, old sponge.

"Well, well. Look who's risen from the dead," a mocking voice commented from behind me.

As I turned around, Ben stood before me, not a hair out of place and looking no worse for wear. His white t-shirt hugged his body like a second skin. Was I mistaken, or was that a six pack? His tanned arms, contrasting with the white fabric, were firm and muscular, like an athlete's. Was there nowhere safe from this guy? To my utter dismay, he didn't seem hungover at all. He even looked well-rested, as if he'd gotten a good night's sleep.

"I guess we partied a bit hard yesterday," I mumbled. Next to him, I felt like an earthworm that had been pulled up out of the soil.

"You could say that. Who knew…"

"What?" I snapped.

"Nothing." He shrugged, and I suddenly felt my knees starting to buckle. I needed to sit down.

Ben walked to the sink, refilled my glass, and put it in

front of me. He also set a bottle of painkillers beside it, then sat down next to me. Who had invited him to join me?

"You didn't stop drinking until you literally fell off your chair," he said, staring at me expectantly. His words didn't really make sense.

"You don't remember?" he asked when I didn't react.

"No," I said, after opening and closing my mouth a couple of times, probably looking like a carp. What a nightmare! Why had the girls let it go so far? He dumped two pills into my palm before explaining more as I dutifully swallowed them. "I actually wanted to stop drinking and forget about the deal with the bathroom, but you wouldn't hear of it. You called me a mama's boy." He rubbed his chin, and made it sound as if I'd cast a curse on him.

No, no, no. My brain refused to process this information, but he relentlessly went on.

"You said I was all talk and no action, and that the stupid little dimple at the corner of my mouth wasn't going to get me out of this either."

Embarrassment shot through me like a lightning bolt. There was no way I had said that out loud. And if I did, I would never drink again. "I'm sure I didn't say anything about dimples."

While I shook my head, Ben nodded.

"You even said that my impossible good looks weren't going to help me at all. You were like Darth Vader! Ice cold and unscrupulous."

I covered my ears and shrank into myself. "No, no, no." Make him stop, this was pure torture. Don't tell me I had actually fed this jerk's already inflated ego! What had that vodka made me do?

Unperturbed, Ben continued. "Then you made a claw-like gesture with your hand and said you were going to choke me with the power of the Force." He imitated the gesture, shaking with laughter.

I stared at him, my eyes as big as saucers. Fright must

have been chiseled onto my face like the Ten Commandments on the stone tablets.

"And then you fell off your chair," Ben concluded, standing up to make coffee. He looked over his shoulder. "Would you like some?"

I nodded, speechless. "Where..." I croaked, cleared my throat, then repeated. "Where's Toby?" Suddenly, I didn't feel like being alone with Ben anymore.

"He's out. Had a class."

My head was spinning. If he was busy long enough with the coffee, maybe I could grab my stuff and run away from this horrible place. Maybe I could possibly skip town while I was at it to make sure that Ben and I never crossed paths again. He seemed to sense my panic and turned around.

"It was good fun. Really. No reason to feel embarrassed. We've all been there."

"Now that's a relief," I spit out and was overcome by the next scary thought. "How—how did I even get to my room?" What I actually meant was: Who had taken my clothes off?

Ben returned to the table carrying two steaming mugs. "I guess you don't remember anything, do you."

I just shook my head in silence.

"I was good enough to..."

"Oh, no," I groaned miserably.

He made a calming gesture. "We played strip poker later on, actually. It was your idea," he added quickly when he saw my hands ball into fists. "Just kidding." He ruffled my hair.

"No worries. Martha carried you to your room. That girl's strong. I wanted to help, but she said you'd kill me if you found out I'd touched you."

"She was right." I nodded emphatically. Where was that famous hole in the ground that opens up and swallows you whole when you needed it?

Ben laughed. "Come on. I'm not that bad, honestly."

Ignoring my snort, he went on. "Caro made your bed, and the girls undressed you and tucked you in. Toby and I looked in later to make sure you were alright. By the way, do you know that you snore?"

Come on, he was deliberately making it worse than it was. "Only when I've had too much to drink." I felt the need to defend myself. But hold on, the two guys looked in me? Why? They weren't exactly Mother Theresas. Maybe Toby was nicer than I thought, but I had no illusions about Ben. Toby had probably made him. Ben pointed to a bag on the kitchen counter.

"That's your food. Caro said you only eat special stuff."

Great. Now it sounded like I was a spoiled, picky eater.

"What are you studying? What's your major?" I asked, quickly changing the subject.

He took a sip from his mug, and I took the opportunity to study his face. Objectively speaking, I could admit that he was extremely handsome. I had to give him that. However, he seemed distant. Something about him made all of my alarm bells go off. I didn't trust him.

"Computer science," he answered readily.

It sounded so normal that I was beginning to ask myself what my problem really was. To take my mind off of things, I started sipping my coffee. It tasted surprisingly good, considering who had made it.

"What about Toby?" I asked.

"Math."

Oh no. Not only were the two of them gorgeous, they were also extremely smart.

"What's yours?"

"Biology." That was enough small talk for me. "By the way, your bathroom is gross." I got up to get a slice of my gluten-free bread, and to put some distance between us.

"Not for long." He grinned.

"Forget it. I'm not cleaning up your mess."

"Fair enough. I'll admit we haven't been that great about keeping the bathroom clean." He waved dismissively. "But it's not a big deal."

Did I hear him right? Not a big deal? How could a person who obviously put a lot of effort into looking good care so little about the state of his bathroom? I was going to have to teach him a lesson, I decided, biting back a smirk.

He got up and sauntered to the door, simply leaving his cup on the table. Who did he think was going to clean up after him? It certainly wasn't going to be me.

"Gotta run. I'm supposed to be at the Ark," he tossed back over his shoulder.

I had just taken a bite of dry rice bread. "The what?" I asked with my mouth full.

"I volunteer as a basketball coach for the kids there, three times a week."

Oh. He was talking about the youth daycare center. Who would've thought he actually had a social conscience? As far as I knew, he wasn't being paid for this.

"You play basketball?" Dumb question. He'd just said he did. It seemed only logical, him being like six foot five and all.

"Used to, not anymore. I tore my ACL. Now I'm just working with the kids. It's a good cause."

He was right. I was beginning to feel bad for treating him the way I had. He invested a good part of his free time for the greater good, after all. Not a lot of people did that, including myself.

"You could come with me if you want. We could use your help," he invited me, to my surprise.

"That's okay," I declined. I wasn't going to be of use to anybody in my current state. Nodding at my chest, he remarked: "We'd never run out of balls if you were there."

The nerve! My shoulders tensed up. How could I have actually thought for one minute that this jerk could be nice? Before I could think of an appropriately biting retort, he walked out, laughing.

8

Before leaving, I'd ended up scrubbing down the bathroom after all. I needed to shower, and I was afraid I might catch something in that cesspool. Just to be sure, I wore two pairs of rubber gloves. Better safe than sorry! When I had the time, I'd do a deeper clean and disinfect things like the grout and drain. I also drew up a cleaning plan— wouldn't want the guys to think today's cleaning spree absolved them from doing their part in the future. In addition, I cleaned and reorganized the fridge, particularly the beer. Because it took up half the space in the fridge, I banished the lion's share of the beer to the cupboard, and assigned each of us one of the three shelves in the fridge. My food went on the top shelf, and I labeled each item with my name to prevent the guys from taking my food. The meager rest I scattered among the two lower shelves. Let them worry about whose food was whose. That was none of my business.

On the way to campus, I called Caro. "Why did you guys abandon me?" I accused her.

"Excuse me? You live there now, remember?" she replied calmly.

"I was passed out. Those guys could've raped me."

Caro giggled. "You were really out of it. I swear, you were

talking big until your eyes closed and you literally fell onto Ben's lap. If he hadn't caught you at the last second, you'd have landed spread eagle on the floor."

That was definitely too much information.

"I thought you were my friend. How could you just leave me with them like that in my condition?" I insisted.

"Oh, come on. You're lucky. They're really sweet, and they promised to keep an eye on you. Besides, Martha and I wanted to go clubbing at Desi's."

Fuming, I clutched my iPhone so hard that my knuckles hurt. Sweet? Those assholes got me drunk and humiliated me. Sometimes Caro had a very twisted way of seeing things.

"I have to go." Her voice cut through my chaotic thoughts. "I have a job interview at the gym around the corner from your new place."

"Since when do you go to the gym?" I asked, perplexed. Caro was at least as un-athletic as I was.

"I'm not going there to work out. They're looking for someone to help out on Saturday mornings. Hand out locker keys, sell energy bars; stuff like that. Martha knows the owner and got me the interview. I could definitely use the extra cash."

"Fingers crossed. Want to stop by afterward? I'll be back around 5:30."

"Sorry, can't. Martha's coming over around six."

Right. And when Martha showed up, nothing else mattered. I felt a little pang of jealousy. Caro was *my* best friend, but since Martha had entered the picture, everything else came second. I didn't remember ever ditching Caro like that because of Ringo. Not after the first six months anyway.

"How's your dad doing in Atlanta?" she asked, a little breathlessly. Either she was running or... I stopped that thought in its tracks. I didn't want to think about it.

"He's fine. He wants to Skype later tonight. Says he has news."

"Okay, I gotta run..."

"Yeah, me too. Later." I hung up and hastily crossed the street. I was running late for my afternoon lecture. A white Mercedes sped past me, missing me by an inch. Wasn't the driver watching where he was going?

As one of the last students to arrive, I slipped into the lecture hall and grabbed one of the worn wooden chairs. I was hit by a lingering odor of salami in the air. The professor didn't appreciate students being late, and he took his revenge by making the stragglers answer the most complicated questions. So far, I'd been spared this humiliating fate. Breathing heavily, I fished my pen and notebook out of my bag.

"Just in time," Rhashmi grinned at me. I was a little envious of the exotic almond-shaped eyes she'd inherited from her mother. In comparison, I was quite ordinary. She and I were in the same study group which met once a week. As I watched the professor take his place at the podium, I leafed through my lecture notes. I could remember quite clearly how proud I'd been when I attended my first lecture with him and had taken a seat in the front row, with Professor Naumann right in front of me. Instead of welcoming us, he'd said, "Take a good look at the people sitting to your left and right, because only one of you will end up getting your degree."

I joined a newly formed study group right away after that, and in the face of the rapidly dwindling number of members, I couldn't help but admit that the professor was right. Three rows behind me, Martin waved at me wildly. I gave him a brief nod, then turned back to listen to the lecture. Good old Martin was also part of our study group. He'd skipped two grades in high school, so he fit right into our circle of over-achievers. He was interested in biology and, strangely enough, fiscal policy. Getting him to talk about any other topic was practically impossible. Professor Naumann began his lecture on protein and sugar molecules, and I took copious notes, yawning repeatedly behind the back of my hand. The professor droned on and on. Today, he wore a forest-green sweater vest, which combined with his darting movements, reminded me of a gecko. He scribbled formula after formula on the board at lightning speed. From a distance, his shirt had a slightly gray tinge to it, which made me wonder how old his clothes were. As I pondered this, his collar slipped slightly to the side, exposing a ragged-edged birthmark on his neck. I was instantly taken aback, tightened my fingers around my pen, and struggled to concentrate on the lecture, which proved nearly impossible. Why should a birthmark be so distracting? Suddenly, a dark memory threatened to resurface, making it hard for me to breathe. I mentally wrestled it back down and continued taking notes. I pressed my pen to my notebook so hard you could see the indentations on the next three pages.

"Did you know that semen also contains sugar?" the Professor asked. His question made me flinch.

"Then why doesn't it taste sweet?" called out someone behind me.

I whipped around. A pretty girl with blonde curls and big blue eyes stared at the professor expectantly. Was she really the one who'd asked that question?

There was snickering all over the auditorium. The blonde girl looked confused, and I turned around, interested as to what the answer would be.

The professor's deadpan reply was, "Because the taste receptors for sugars are located on the tip of the tongue and not at the back of our throats."

Everybody burst out laughing. Rhashmi and I exchanged incredulous glances, and then turned around at the same time. Blondie's face was as red as a tomato. She silently packed up her things and dashed out of the lecture hall as if she were being chased by wolves, while the professor continued like nothing had happened.

"Think she'll be back?" Rhashmi smirked at me.

I shook my head, feeling bad for the girl. It was no fun to be humiliated in public. And who knew that better than me?

9

Martin followed us out into the hallway. He was barely taller than me. "Let's get a cup of tea," he suggested, bouncing after us like the Energizer bunny.

I shrugged. "Sure."

"I'll come too." Rhashmi took my arm. Her bag banged me in the back with every step. We stopped in front of the cafeteria, which buzzed with activity. Rhashmi peered inside.

"Oh no, Anoob is standing at the coffee bar. Can you get me a café au lait, and I'll find us a spot?"

I giggled. Anoob was from India, and he kept trying to talk to Rhashmi in his native tongue. But poor Rhashmi, despite being half-Indian, didn't speak a word of Hindi, and was too embarrassed to admit it. As she repeatedly told us, her mother had had her hands full with getting her to learn German. She seemed to think she needed to apologize for not having grown up bilingual.

A few minutes later, I found our spot. She had actually managed to snag us an empty table at the busiest time of the day. As I passed Rhashmi her coffee, Martin sat down next to me.

"Isn't that the girl from the lecture?" he asked. Following

his pointing finger, I saw the blonde student drop her gaze when she realized we were talking about her.

"Why doesn't semen taste sweet?" he repeated as he opened a packet of sugar, pouring the contents into his steaming cup. "Why would she ask such a dumb question?"

"No idea." Rhashmi hid her face behind her large café au lait cup. Apparently, she wasn't interested in discussing this topic any further with Martin. And neither was I. Every time I had even a slightly longer conversation with him, I always felt a strong urge to take a nap right afterwards. Watching him stir his cup reminded me of those bobblehead dachshunds in the back window of an old lady's car. His blond hair was carefully parted on the side, and a few whitish zits dotted his cheeks. Suddenly, I heard a cheerful voice.

"Hey, Luca, is this seat taken?" It was Toby, arm slung around an absolutely stunning brunette. Her hair was pulled back into a tight braid. It was a look few people could've pulled off, but she definitely rocked it. I quickly turned back to face Toby, who was beaming at me. Unlike Ben, he was very approachable and had that nice smile. A guy you wanted to be friends with.

"Oh, hi. Sure." I pointed to the two empty seats. "This is Rhashmi and Martin."

"I'm Ellen." Toby's companion introduced herself. Her voice was just as perfect as the rest of her, with a smoky twang that gave me goosebumps. They sat down.

"Are you doing okay now?" Toby pointed his chin at me.

"Yeah, I'm fine." I replied hastily and swallowed. Hopefully, he wasn't going to share the story of last night. I shot him a desperate look.

"What happened?" Rhashmi asked curiously, sipping her coffee. Martin was still blowing on his tea.

"Oh, she moved in yesterday. That's all. I just wanted to see that she's settling in okay." Toby winked at me, and I silently thanked him for sparing me further embarrassment.

"You guys live together?" Rhashmi gestured at the two of us. "I thought you'd moved into a dorm."

"Long story," I brushed her off. I had no desire to explain my current living arrangements. I turned to Ellen and asked, "Are you studying here too?"

"No, I'm a model, actually."

Of course, she was. Why did I even ask? Her dark brown hair shone under the neon lights like polished china. How did she do that? None of the conditioners I used ever had that effect.

"She just got back from Paris," Toby said with a loving glance.

"Where did you two meet?" Rhashmi asked. She could be really nosy sometimes, but for that matter, I wanted to know too. Where did super-beautiful people meet each other? Probably not at the supermarket checkout like Ringo and me.

"I model part-time for the same agency as Ellen. We met there."

Naturally, where else? Why would I even ask? He was a part-time model—it seemed obvious now that I thought about it.

"And Ben works there, too?" I concluded, because it only seemed logical.

"No?" Toby shook his head, surprised.

"Why would you think that?" Ellen asked. She seemed truly astonished that I would suggest that, and I felt trapped.

"No idea. I thought maybe he—I don't know—might make copies for the agency or something. Dunno." I broke into a sweat.

"You mean because Ben's such a womanizer," Ellen commented, eyeing me coolly.

"Ben who?" Rhashmi butted in.

"My other roommate," I muttered.

"I'll get us something to drink." Toby said. "Water?" he asked Ellen, who nodded.

Guiltily, I looked down at the gluten-free chocolate muffin I'd brought from home. I suddenly wasn't hungry anymore.

"What do you mean, he's a womanizer?" I asked cautiously.

Ellen crossed her legs and sat sideways on her chair, as if striking a pose for a magazine cover. From the corner of my eye, I saw the boys at the next table put their heads together and casually point our way. It certainly wasn't because of my strikingly good looks.

"Let's just say Ben isn't relationship material. He's more into casual hook-ups."

"Oh," was all I could say.

She smiled. "You'll see. Women come and go with him. You'll never see the same one twice."

"He doesn't really seem the type," I lied, and to my dismay, I felt myself blushing.

"He can have anybody he wants. Night after night. And so far, he hasn't been rejected even once."

Ha, so my first impression was right!

"What does he do with all the women?" Martin piped up.

Ellen shot him a look that clearly indicated he was a moron. "He screws them," she said placidly. Shocked, Martin put down his tea cup.

"But when does he find time to study?"

Jeez, what was with this guy?

"In between."

It was obvious that Ellen didn't want to keep talking to Martin, which I could totally relate to. But what did she mean, *in between*? For God's sake, how many notches did he have on his bedpost?

Toby came back with a muscular, olive-skinned guy in tow. His spiky hair reminded me of Sonic the Hedgehog.

"Hey, Ellen," the guy said. He walked up behind her and started to massage her shoulders.

"Cut it out, Erdie," she hissed, whipping around.

With a laugh, he threw up his hands. "Oh, relax. Maybe if

you ate something, you wouldn't be so hangry." Uninvited, he set down his tray and grabbed a chair from the table next to ours. His plate was piled high with cake.

"This is Luca, our new roommate," Toby introduced me and sat down again.

Erdie turned to me with a grin. "Oh, Ben already told me about last night..."

"Uh, this is Martin and Rhashmi," I cut him off hastily. I didn't want him to spread the story. Ben. What a snitch. With amusement, I saw Erdie's eyes brighten as he stared at Rashmi. She reached her hand out to him gracefully like a Bollywood star while absently rubbing her neck with the other.

"Hi," she said breathlessly.

Since when was Rhashmi into Popeye types? Had I missed something?

"Hey, princess."

Oh no, he was just as much a sweet talker, as Ben was— what a pair! Rhashmi seemed flattered nevertheless.

Next to me, Martin got up and looked at me.

"Gotta go. Luca, did you still want to read my old *Financial Times* issues?"

I wasn't interested in the slightest, but pretended to be, in order not to seem rude.

"I can lend you some copies, if you'd like. They're always fun to read."

"Um, sure. Thanks." What else was I supposed to say?

"Awesome. Sayonara!" He beamed and waved to the group without noticing the stares.

Sayonara? Who even talked like that? We watched him skip away.

"He likes you," Rhashmi noted with a grin.

"Does not," I protested, crumbling up my muffin.

"Yes, he does. He's had a crush on you since freshman year."

Why did I always attract guys like him? The world was so unfair. Ellen's pitying stare made it even worse.

"It's obvious that guy likes you," Erdie added. "Like, so obvious."

"You're all crazy. Just leave me alone." I folded my arms.

"Hey, Erdie, how's your brother's store coming along?" Toby brought an end to my misery. He was the best.

Erdie waved him off. "Oh, he's still got a ton of work to do until he can open."

I watched Toby rub Ellen's neck the entire time. He obviously couldn't keep his hands off of her.

"Do you come here often in the afternoons?" Erdie asked Rhashmi, his eyes glittering. Looked like someone else was in love.

"Tuesdays and Thursdays," she shot back without missing a beat. She ran her fingers through her jet-black hair. "Why?"

"Because that's when I'll be here too. From now on."

Oh my God, he was laying it on thick, but Rhashmi didn't seem to mind one bit. Erdie checked his phone and said, "Crap, I'm late. I promised Phyllis I'd take her out for ice cream. She's going to kill me." He jumped up and waved. "Ciao."

Rhashmi, the corners of her mouth now drooping, followed him with her eyes as he disappeared through the door. This Erdie guy seemed to be playing the field too. Hardly surprising if he was friends with Ben.

10

———

L ater that evening, I prepared myself for our first official apartment meeting—the one the two lucky guys didn't know about yet. I was counting on the element of surprise to help me in my ambush on them, which would hopefully force them to go along with all the improvements I had planned without any discussion. Armed with three copies of my agenda, I knocked on Ben's door. After his muffled "Yeah." I opened it a crack. Ben was on his bed and—I couldn't believe my eyes—was reading a book. A vintage *Point Blank* movie poster hung over his bed, where I'd have actually expected pictures of naked girls to be instead. He was certainly an expert in the art of subterfuge.

"Do you have a minute?" I asked, peering at the cover. *The Shadow Prowler*. I didn't get fantasy at all—yet another thing we didn't have in common. His eyes, that peculiar, hypnotic blue, sparkled in amusement.

"Why? You need someone to cuddle with?" He propped himself up on one elbow and patted the bed next to him. "Climb right in!"

I growled at him like a watchdog. "I'd just like to discuss a few things with you and Toby. So, would you mind coming to the kitchen?" I saw a bag of chips next to him; the exact same brand I'd just bought. Maybe we did have some things in common after all.

He seemed taken aback but got up without protest, which was my cue to leave the room. My knock on Toby's door was answered a lot friendlier. Toby was sitting at his desk, working on math homework, and Ellen was sitting cross-legged on his bed with her laptop on her knees.

"Could you come to the kitchen for a minute? I'd like to discuss some things with you and Ben."

He smiled. "Sure." Turning to Ellen, he asked, "Wanna join us?"

Without looking up, she declined. "No, I need to email my agent. There's been a mix-up with Milan."

In the kitchen, I pointed to the list I'd hung next to the refrigerator.

"You've probably seen this and are wondering what it's about," I started mildly. After all, I didn't want to scare them right away.

"Oh, was that there earlier?" Ben asked with a nod to the neon red sheet of paper before going to the refrigerator and taking out a yogurt. My yogurt! One that I'd personally marked with my name in thick black marker.

I grabbed his wrist. "Hey! What do you think you're doing with that yogurt?"

"Gonna eat it?"

"But it's mine. Are you blind?" I pointed at the lid. "It has my name on it."

"I'd wondered why you'd scribbled on all the food."

He'd wondered? I opened the fridge on a hunch and couldn't believe what I saw. All the beer bottles were back in place, and the rest of the food was haphazardly thrown in between them—

except for the yogurt. Of the five I'd just bought, the rest of them were gone. I gritted my teeth so loudly, I was sure even Ben could hear it. What a jerk!

I turned to face him.

"You." My voice took on a menacing tone. "You ate them all!"

"Those were only for you? All of them?" Ben seemed bewildered. I'd expected remorse, at least, or maybe the shadow of an apologetic smile; but there was nothing. He was already rummaging in the drawer for a spoon. "We always share our food around here," he defended himself.

"You don't even have any food here!" I yelled. "All you have is crap!"

"We have beer."

"Like I said. Crap!"

I snatched the yogurt from his hand. "This is mine, and you don't get to eat it, you greedy, conniving thief!"

"Alright, alright." He tossed the spoon back into the drawer.

Then, I opened the top cupboard, and gazed into a cavern as big as a black hole.

"You stole my chips, too? Do I have to lock up all my food to keep it safe from your piehole?" I hissed.

"I thought you were on a diet," he replied. "Why would you be eating chips? They've got at least ten thousand calories."

"I!" I yelled, took a deep breath, and then went on more quietly. "I am not on a diet. I have a food intolerance, but explaining the difference to you is obviously a waste of time. Your mental intolerance seems a lot worse."

Ben waved me off, completely unimpressed by my outburst.

"I'll buy you a new bag tomorrow, okay? Don't worry." He sat down at the table and studied the list I'd made. A thin smile played on his lips, showcasing his dimples. For the millionth time, I had to ask myself why women liked this guy. Though the answer seemed clear enough. None of them had to live with him—they all left the next morning without ever having to see him again.

"And now that that's out of the way," Toby interjected,

who had silently followed our debate thus far. "Was there anything else?"

My cue. I slapped the plan on the wall with my open palm. "As a matter of fact, there is. This is the new cleaning schedule. It says here who will do what every week. And when you're done, you just check off the list. Easy as that."

"Easy as that," Ben repeated and got to his feet. He slowly sauntered over to the list and studied it.

"What's BR mean"?

I'd used abbreviations, for practical purposes.

"Bathroom."

"I see. And BR+G&D?"

"Bathroom plus grout and drain. As you can see, it's only required every other week."

He burst out laughing. "You can't be serious."

Excuse me?

Without warning, he ripped my list off the wall. I couldn't believe my eyes.

"I think we'll just leave everything the way it is. Whoever has the time does the cleaning. It's worked fine for us till now." He gestured broadly at the room

Worked fine?

"Hey, Luca," Toby now chimed in. "I think you're being a little uptight about this whole cleaning business."

I was being uptight?

"We can vote on it if you like," Ben suggested. "Be like all democratic about it."

"Yeah, right." I could already see what would happen. It'd be me cleaning the bathroom every week all on my own.

"Also, I'd like for you guys to sit down. You know, like, when you pee."

Their heads shot up, and they gaped at me, stock-still.

"You don't think that's over the top?" Toby inquired carefully, and Ben added, "How will you know? You gonna stand right there and watch us?"

"The seat is absolutely filthy. No woman would ever sit on it."

"I thought women squatted," Ben retorted with a deadpan expression and then insisted on giving a demonstration.

"In public bathrooms," I hissed. "Not at home."

Toby patted his friend's shoulder. "Come on, we can do that much." They grinned at each other, probably thinking they were off the hook that easily. They obviously hadn't read the list all the way through. Reluctantly, Ben nodded. "Alright." He made it sound like he was making a huge sacrifice.

"Will that be all?" he asked on his way out.

"Nope!" I said sharply. "Come back here, old pal."

With a heavy sigh, he turned around.

"Now what?"

"I've got another list."

"Ugh," Toby said in a grief-stricken voice, picking up his copy.

"You know what?" Ben said, annoyed. "This is a waste of time. Everything has worked out just fine before now, *without* lists and schedules."

"Yeah, I can see that." I held up the yogurt as proof. "I was thinking about a garbage list," I said with a hint of nervousness, as my initial confidence was quickly shrinking like a deflating balloon. "We can take turns taking out the garbage, and whoever takes out the trash marks their name on the list." These arrangements had worked just fine when I lived with Ringo. Why were the guys so dead against it? This was a matter of fairness.

As anticipated, both guys shook their heads. Ellen came sauntering into the kitchen, crunching into a crispy red apple.

"Hey, Luca," she said derisively. "You're wasting your time with the garbage list. Ben will never agree—he's into single-use products." She sat down in Toby's lap.

Ben frowned at that, and a deep line appeared between his eyebrows. Yes! It looked like somebody else didn't get along with Ben, not that that was surprising. After all, he wasn't exactly a popular guy. Why couldn't she live here instead of him?

"I'm leaving," Ben said abruptly, disappearing into the hallway. The front door slammed shut.

Totally baffled, I turned to face the other two, who were now snuggling close together and sharing her apple.

"That was out of line," Toby reprimanded Ellen softly. "Ben's a good guy."

"Someone needed to take him down a peg or two," Ellen retorted, unimpressed, and took another bite of her apple.

I, on the other hand, felt guilty that the meeting had gone so badly that one of my roommates had even stormed out of the apartment.

"Where's he going?" I asked.

Ellen looked up, her eyes narrowing. "Out hunting."

11

Ellen and I were standing in the hallway, chatting. Toby had escaped to the living room to watch some random soccer game on the oversized flat screen TV that was mounted there on the wall. I'd quickly vacuumed the room earlier that afternoon and gotten rid of the empty pizza boxes; to my surprise, they actually owned a vacuum cleaner.

"And tomorrow you're off to Milan?"

"Yeah. My agent managed to get me another flight, only now I have to get up at five." She sighed and seemed exhausted.

"Didn't you just get back from Paris today?"

Ellen nodded. "And next week I'm off to Berlin and London."

"Wow, it must be so exciting to be a model." I couldn't help but envy her life. I mean, who could say, today New York, tomorrow Paris, the whole world the day after tomorrow? I'm sure she even knew a few stars or famous athletes. Suddenly, I felt even shorter next to her than I already was, and not only physically-speaking. I had grown up in a village near Munich, and the only places I'd ever been to were Mallorca (once) and Austria, but this girl had the whole world in the palm of her hand.

She laughed. "It's not all that exciting, really. All I see is airports, photo studios and my hotel room. If it didn't pay so well, I'd have given this all up a long time ago."

"Oh."

"My mom lives on a tiny pension," she continued. "My job allows me to support her a little, so she can make ends meet." She stared at the wall. "I come from a small town on Lake Brombach, and I still have my old room there, but I spend most of my time here at Toby's when I'm in town anyway. I don't need anything of my own."

"I think it's great that you're helping your mom out."

"My sister's a lawyer in Berlin, and she only graces us with her presence twice a year when she takes our mom on a spa vacation and leaves again."

I swallowed. "That's a shame. My mom died when I was little. I really wish I could still spend time with her."

"I'm sorry to hear that." She patted my arm sympathetically. "My dad left us when I was fourteen."

"Shit."

She nodded and gave a lopsided smile.

"I'm looking forward to Toby finishing his degree in August. Then we can finally get a place of our own, maybe even somewhere abroad. Our own apartment, with no Ben in it."

"You don't like Ben?" I looked at her closely. "Why?"

Ellen snorted contemptuously. "He's just so distant and aloof. For him, girls are just disposable objects, to use once and throw away when he's done with them. Like an empty yogurt cup."

I stared at her in surprise. Ben was a bit full of himself and a little macho, but I never would have thought he was that bad.

She leaned over. "He never sees the same girl twice, you know. He never gives a woman his number or asks for hers. And there's one other thing he never does." She paused to fix her hair, while I waited for the bomb to drop. "He never kisses a woman on the mouth."

For real? I'd never heard anything like that before. He never kissed a woman on the mouth? "Why not?"

Ellen shrugged. "No idea. Probably to let them know how little they mean to him. To Ben, all women are completely interchangeable."

"You shouldn't judge him so harshly," Toby said from behind us in the doorframe. "He must have his reasons. Ben's a good guy, I've lived with him for three years, and I should know. The women know what they're getting into with him. He never makes a secret of it. No one's forcing them."

"Yeah, right," Ellen sneered. "What a woman says and what she really feels are two very different things, but you guys just don't understand the difference."

Toby spread his hands. "What do you care anyway?"

In a split second, Ellen's face changed, becoming soft and sensual. With swaying hips, she walked towards Toby and put her arms around his neck. "I don't care," she said, kissing him like that blonde Bond bombshell in *Goldfinger*.

I went back to my room. Ben's love life was certainly none of my business, and I felt no desire to invade his privacy. I also thought that Ellen had acted a bit odd. Looking at the time, I was startled. Ten already. My father would soon be logging onto Skype in Atlanta. I wondered what he had to tell me.

I pulled up Skype, and my father was already online. I shook my head as I looked at his tousled gray hair, which stood out on all sides and was starting to thin in the front.

"Hey, bro, what's up?" I teased him, knowing he still wasn't fluent in American slang.

"What?" he asked, leaning closer to the screen. "There's something wrong with the line, all I hear is gibberish."

"I asked how you were, Dad."

"I'm fine. And you, darling? How's Ringo?"

"Ringo and I aren't together anymore," I declared curtly, "but tell me, what's new with you?" I was hoping he'd fall for my little diversion. Sometimes he could ask very nosy questions.

"What happened? Where are you living now that you're not with Ringo?"

I sighed. "We just grew apart. Irreconcilable differences, you know." If celebrities got away with that excuse for a breakup, so could I. "I moved into the dorms."

"That's too bad. Do you need money, dear?" He tried to calm his messy hair, using his screen as a mirror.

"Dad, I can see you," I reminded him. "No, I'm good." He already sent me 600 euros a month, and along with the money I earned as a student assistant, I was making ends meet. Besides, I was determined to pay him back every cent after graduation. "So, what's your news?"

"Oh, right." He fussed with the monitor. "Georgia State extended my contract for another two years."

"What?" I pursed my lips. "But I thought you were moving back to Munich so we could see each other more often."

"I know, sweetheart, but they offered me this wonderful job, and the two years will just fly by. I don't want to let my colleague down. She's counting on me. She's a really nice woman, and I owe her a lot."

Was this woman more important to him than me? His own daughter? I was living here all alone, but he didn't seem to care one bit. But now wasn't the time for this discussion. It could wait until the summer. "Let's talk about it when I get to Atlanta. It sucks to do this over Skype."

"You're right. Just wanted to give you a heads up."

I looked at the time. "Hey, I need to study. Can we Skype again next week?"

"Sure, honey. I'll let you go. Oh, Aunt Hertha called. She broke her leg and can't go visit your mother's grave for the next few weeks. Would you mind going there and taking some flowers?"

I gulped. I hadn't been back home since moving to Erlangen, which also meant I hadn't been to visit my mother's grave all that time. Even though I felt bad about it, I couldn't take the risk of running into the person I wanted to avoid. Just the thought of seeing him made my stomach churn. I quickly shook off the feeling.

"I'll see what I can do," I said weakly, knowing there was no way I could do him this favor.

"Thanks. Bye!" He blew me a kiss through the screen.

"Bye, Dad," I replied and closed the browser window. It felt like I'd just lost another parent.

12

The next morning, I was standing in the kitchen, washing my breakfast dishes and thinking nothing evil when Ben's door opened with a soft jingling sound, as if he had Santa's sleigh in there. The *hunter* then appeared in the hallway with his prey, an admittedly very attractive girl with short dark hair. Ellen was right. I paused in the middle of what I was doing to watch them until Ben glanced in my direction and caught me in the act.

I hastily scrubbed the crumbs from my plate, but kept glancing in their direction. The high-pitched ringing sounded every time his overnight guest moved. What the hell was that?

The two stood facing each other. The doe gazed longingly at her huntsman. Apparently, she was quite content with what had transpired between them, which, frankly, was a mystery to me. Men like Ben were usually more concerned with their own gratification in bed than with their partner's. My hands suddenly came to a stop as I was too busy observing how this scene was playing itself out. How would Ben get rid of his one-night stand? Would he just kick her out the door with some lame excuse? That possibility seemed the most obvious to me.

He stood close to her and put both hands on her upper arms, as she looked up at him, smiling. A tender gesture, I had to give him that, even from my distance. The pretty girl was totally into him, I could even see that from where I was standing. Slowly, he bent forward and—I held my breath—kissed her on the forehead.

"I enjoyed that. Are you sure you don't want me to drive you home?"

She slipped her arms around his waist.

"Me, too. No, that's alright, I'll walk. I don't live far." She lowered her eyes, and his hands slipped down her arms. He rubbed the back of his neck. "Okay, then…"

The doe looked back up. "Will I see you again? I mean, we could talk on the phone or something."

Grabbing a dish towel to cover up my eavesdropping, I was waiting almost as eagerly for his answer as she was. Only, Ellen had given me background information that the poor girl didn't know about.

"Listen…" he began, then broke off. To my surprise, he seemed thoughtful. Shouldn't he be a pro by now, armed with a number of ready-made excuses for any given situation?

"Like I told you yesterday, this was just a one-time thing."

Wow. He really had been honest and upfront? I had to admit that he was showing more spine than I'd given him credit for.

"I know, I know. I just thought that since we both had such a good time and all," the doe persisted.

Now what was he going to do? Suddenly, Ben glanced to the side and caught me drinking in the scene. And yes, his eye-rolling was meant for me, but I was immune to this by now. I gave him a broad smile, and he turned back to the girl.

"I enjoyed myself, too, but I want to be honest with you. I'm not the relationship type."

She sighed. "That's too bad. Well, take care."

"You, too."

Ben had a hand on the doorknob when Bambi rose up on

her tiptoes, trying to kiss him goodbye on the mouth. At the last moment, Ben turned away, and her lips merely brushed against his cheek.

Wow!

So, it was true. Ben didn't kiss women on the mouth. Mine, on the other hand, hung open. The woman paused before disappearing through the open door, accompanied by that strange tiny jingling. All of a sudden, I was extremely busy drying and polishing my coffee cup. Despite my busyness, I noticed Ben coming closer. When I dared to look to the side, he was leaning in the door frame, watching me expressionlessly. I faked a pleased smile. "Good morning. Sleep well?" I chirped, as if we were the best of friends.

"Very well indeed." He bent one arm behind his head, tightening his muscles. He was such a poser! "You could've been a little less obvious."

I looked at him in mock confusion. "What are you talking about?" I couldn't bite back a grin though. Was he actually embarrassed by this heart-touching goodbye scene? I couldn't be that lucky.

"Forget it." He stepped out of the doorframe and walked over to the refrigerator while I pretended to clean the sink. After pulling something out of it and grabbing Toby's bread bag, he sat down at the table with a cup of coffee. I heard him slice open a roll, probably scattering a million crumbs all over the place. I sighed—he was such an ignorant jerk. When I turned around, I caught Ben generously spreading *my* butter on *his* fucking wheat roll.

"What are you doing?" I yelled, snatching up my butter. "This is my butter!"

He put the knife down.

"Jeez. You really are a Scrooge."

"That's not what I meant."

"What is it then?" He didn't seem to have a clue what I was talking about.

"Are you really so dense?" I slammed the butter on the

table. "I've explained this to you guys over and over again. You contaminated the whole thing with your stupid bread crumbs!" I gestured at the crumb-encrusted knife marks in the golden yellow mass.

"Just scrape it off!" He took a sip of coffee and clearly didn't get what I was talking about.

"I can't scrape it off because I might miss some, and even the slightest bit could make me sick."

He looked up. "You wanna know what I think?"

"What?" I replied, eyes narrowing.

"I think you have ADD."

Unrestrained laughter gushed across my lips as I pointed at the front door where I had just been entertained by that romantic farewell scene. "And you don't?"

While Ben ignored me and generously smeared chocolate hazelnut spread on his roll instead, my lips moved on their own. "She jingled like the closing bell at the New York Stock Exchange!"

To my dismay, an amused laugh burst out of him. "She's wearing love balls. Never heard of them? I inserted them earlier." He stared at me intently as I felt my cheeks start to flush.

"You're a real pervert," I threw at him after laboriously pulling myself together again.

He shrugged. "What's so perverted about that? It's a toy, that's all. A little something different in bed. You're uptight, that's all."

"It's sad that you need sex so badly and have to take stupid toys to bed to get it." I shook my head. I didn't really want to have this conversation.

He leaned back. "Says the girl who buys handcuffs at a sex shop." His smile turned malicious.

Fuck! I had forgotten he had witnessed my story in the housing office. "That was different," I snarled. What was I supposed to say? He'd never believe that every word I had said back there was made up.

"Sure." He took a bite of his roll. "I bet you've never had an orgasm in your life."

I gasped. "I don't think my sex life is any of your business."

He raised an eyebrow. "Oh, you have one! I thought..."

"Shut. The hell. Up," I growled with clenched teeth. "You really think you're so irresistible, don't you?"

"I can bring any woman to orgasm. So, if you ever want to have one, you can always come to me. A little friendly service between roommates."

I wanted to punch that smug grin off his face. How could a single person be so full of themselves? His confidence was enough for ten average people.

"You'd do better worrying about your jingle bell girls." I couldn't believe this woman had let him... I didn't want to pursue that thought, but the image appeared before me like on a movie screen. Oh, my God. If he had really done that, he had seen all of her... All the way in. I swallowed. Ringo and I had never had our heads any further than our belly buttons, and quite apart from that, we'd never really examined each other below the waist either.

Ben suddenly got up and stepped close to me. I swallowed again. What was going on now?

"You're imagining it now, aren't you?" he whispered hoarsely as he moved closer. His warm breath grazed my cheek and sent a shiver down my spine. I shook my head hastily.

"Yes, you are. You're imagining yourself lying naked on my bed, me spreading your legs and kneeling between them, and slowly pushing these two balls inside, one by one. Do you want to try it? I have some more in my room."

Startled, I took a step back, my breath quickening, unable to hold his gaze. But Ben just sat back down on his chair. He took a hearty bite of his roll and chuckled softly. "She didn't have any love balls. It was just her jingly New Age ankle bracelet."

"You're such an asshole!" I slapped him on the shoulder, and his evil laugh grew louder.

"But you imagined it, admit it."

"No, I didn't." The dish towel fell out of my hands, I leaned over to pick it up, and tied my shoe at the same time. When I straightened up, I caught Ben staring at me with a smile. At the same moment, I realized I was wearing my black shirt with the cowl neckline today, which revealed more of my ample bust than usual, and in a flash, it was clear—

Ben Nowak had been staring down my shirt.

"You miserable creep!" I snapped at him, but he only raised his hands.

"I didn't mean to, but you just presented yourself to me. What was I supposed to do?"

At least I was wearing a bra, so luckily, he hadn't seen everything.

"I must say, they are really beautiful," he commented, as if I valued his opinion. I could totally do without that kind of compliment. Especially if it came out of his mouth.

"Just shut up, okay."

"Are those real, or did you have some help?"

"Do you really think I'd go through surgery for these?" Sometimes, men just sucked.

"So, they're real, that's good. I don't like those silicone ones. They look nice, but feel like hard balloons. I like them soft."

"You'll certainly never touch mine," I forewarned him, before making a theatrical exit. Ben really was the worst. The absolute worst!

His amused shout followed me, "Loosen up a little, will ya?"

13

Two weeks later, I met up with Caro. Martha wasn't around as much anymore, and Caro was feeling desperate. None of the discussions, threats, or tears were having any effect. Martha wanted more space, and Caro reluctantly agreed to take things slowly, so as not to lose her completely. Which was why I was with her now. I had spent the night, comforting and cheering her up. We were now strolling across Nuremberg's main market square, up towards the shopping mile to numb her sorrow a little with some retail therapy.

"I really don't know what's going on with Martha," Caro said for what felt like the two hundred and ninety-ninth time. I then realized what I had done to Caro when I had vented so much about Ringo. Still, I felt sorry for her. I knew from my own experience how horrible it was when your feelings were no longer reciprocated.

"She'll probably come around soon," I repeated, also for the two hundred and ninety-ninth time. "She won't find anyone better than you anyway."

"You're the best." Caro smiled with effort. "I just don't get it. She keeps coming up with stupid excuses. She needs to work out for her dumb bodybuilding competition, or help out at Anita's new bar. It's always something, she's always busy… or maybe she's secretly seeing Sarah again behind my back."

"Things'll smooth out, you'll see," I tried again. "Sarah is ancient history. But you know what? You should go out by yourself and have some fun – without Martha. Maybe she'll hear about it and be super jealous."

Caro stopped and lifted her foot. Disgusted, she looked at a piece of gum stuck to the sole of her shoe. "Yuck!" She scraped her foot across the cobblestones. "It's not even that, really."

I stopped, too. "Then, what is it?"

"I went to my parents' place on Sunday and didn't take Martha with me. She took it hard and thinks I'm ashamed of her."

"Oh, shoot."

She nodded. Caro hadn't yet dared to tell her parents that she was gay. They were both devout Catholics. And I knew she hated to keep secrets from them. She had only dared to come out in Nuremberg – in the anonymous big city.

"Why don't you talk to them?" I began cautiously. "Maybe your parents would be more understanding than you think. After all, you're twenty-four years old and not a little kid anymore. They should accept that you're allowed to live your life the way you want to."

"I know." She sighed heavily. "But every time I'm home, my mother looks at me wistfully and asks if I've finally found a boyfriend yet. You know what she said to me on Sunday? *Child,*" she imitated her mother in a high voice, "*if you don't make up your mind soon, the best ones will be taken. Then you'll have no choice but to become a lesbian.*"

I giggled. "For real?"

Caro nodded, unamused.

"Maybe that would've been the opportunity …"

"Sure," she cut me off. "Mom, Dad, all the men in Nuremberg are taken, so I'm now officially introducing you to Martha." She rolled her eyes as we started moving again. I put my arm around hers.

"Not all of them... you could take Ben home with you, and then they'd be thrilled with Martha, I guarantee it."

We both burst out laughing.

"Oh, come on, he can't be that bad," Caro replied plaintively as we rounded the corner onto Breite Gasse with its throngs of people.

"Or don't say anything and just wear this t-shirt the next time you visit." I pointed to the bold black print on her white top: *Nobody knows I'm a lesbian!*

Caro waved dismissively. "They wouldn't get it anyway." She headed for a clothes rack and pushed the hangers apart. The smell of roasted potatoes wafted out of a Dutch potato stall, while I checked out a gray shirt that Caro was holding up.

"Hate the neckline," I decided.

"I agree." She hung it back up. "How are things going with your roommates, anyway? You haven't said a word about them."

"I get along great with Toby now, but Ben's pretty much the same idiot he was when I moved in."

She laughed. "You need to give that poor guy a break. He isn't as bad as you say."

"He's a pain in the ass." We walked on. "His body count is through the roof. I swear he's with someone new every night, either at the apartment or at their place. I mean, who even needs that much sex? It's a mystery to me." Ringo and I had done it maybe once a week, and always quickly without much fuss.

"Maybe he's compensating for something?" Caro rummaged through a mound of scarves.

"What do you mean?"

She turned to face me. "I read somewhere, for example, that people who had thrifty parents as children can sometimes grow up to become compulsive shoppers. Or adults who were never allowed to eat chocolate when they were little, will later gorge themselves on nothing else."

I scratched the back of my head. "What on earth does this have to do with Ben? He's neither fat nor does he come home with piles of groceries." *Just the opposite*, I thought grimly, angrily remembering my grilled chicken he'd gotten his teeth into last week when I was in the shower. He had told me in all seriousness that he had merely sacrificed himself so that it wouldn't go bad.

"Maybe he didn't get enough love as a child." Caro shrugged as she held up a bright yellow scarf.

Not enough love? It seemed much more likely he'd been spoiled excessively as a child, considering how selfishly he always behaved. He had probably had helicopter parents who kept telling him how great he was and how special he was just because he managed to stack three wooden blocks on top of each other when he was seven. Well, that was what happened in the end. After raising an arrogant monster, they were now forcing the rest of us to suffer the negative consequences of their poor child rearing skills.

I waved her off. "Enough about him. Let's go get some coffee somewhere."

"Okay," she said, tossing the yellow atrocity back in the box and taking my arm. Suddenly a man in his fifties stopped next to us, arms akimbo, staring at Caro.

"Do you know this guy?" I asked under my breath
She shook her head.
"Do the two of you have no shame?" he yelled.
"Excuse me?" I looked at him, bewildered.
"Doing your filthy crap is one thing. But do you also need to advertise it on your shirt? There are children running around here. What if they turn out like you two? Have you ever thought about that?"
Caro stared back. "For real?"
"And disrespectful on top. Well, that's just like you riffraff. You're sick, all of you."

"With men like you around, being a lesbian is the only option," Caro commented coolly.

He came a step closer, his eyes flashing. "You better watch your mouth, or you'll have an even bigger mess to deal with."

"Hey, hey, now, take it easy." I stepped in front of Caro protectively. Unfortunately, it wasn't the first time she'd heard this sort of garbage. And just when she was starting to feel better too. I was so sick of this intolerance. Why didn't they mind their own business? What was this dude's problem anyway? I decided a counterstrike was the best course of action. "You would dare to hit a pregnant woman, shame on you!"

He flinched, staring at Caro, who was standing there with drooping shoulders. Her face lit up. We exchanged a mischievous grin before she rubbed her belly, sticking it out a little.

"How'd that happen?" he asked.

"With me," I told him with a big smile. "In vitro. Two eggs are fused together. Anything is possible nowadays. And the good news is, it'll always be a girl."

"You two've got a screw loose. No wonder no man would ever want to touch you."

Behind me, Caro giggled, and I replied: "You should be more considerate. My sweetie is in a really vulnerable phase right now." I pulled Caro into my arms with a flourish. "Oh, baby." I pretended to kiss her deeply and only stopped when the guy hurried away through the crowd, cursing. We burst into laughter, but then I noticed someone out of the corner of my eye who had been watching us with interest.

14

Erdie, the guy from the cafeteria, was standing only a little way off and watching us. He had his arm around a very pretty woman with strawberry blond curls. Rhashmi instantly popped into my mind. She had been babbling on and on about him since that day they'd met. Despite his big proclamation, he hadn't shown up at the cafeteria again. And I now knew the reason.

"Let's go," I said to Caro as Erdie started moving in our direction. Was that really necessary? The guy was just as idiotic as his stupid friend. He kept showing up at our apartment all the time to visit Ben; the two of them seemed inseparable. Whenever he dropped by, I hid in my room, but I could still hear the two of them talking and laughing at full volume in the kitchen, with the clink of beer bottles in between. Thoughtfulness was a foreign concept for the both of them.

"What's up, Shorty?" he asked, smiling.

Why did he always have to call me Shorty? Practically everyone was shorter than him.

"Not much." I turned away to imply that this inspiring conversation was over for me, but he stopped me in my tracks.

"If that asshole had touched either of you, I would have made him regret it."

"Well, nothing happened, so..." One of those protective types. Usually I didn't mind, but strangely enough, I always felt like someone needed to protect me from Ben and Erdie.

"I think a kick in the ass would have served him right," said Caro, which made Erdie laugh. He looked at me like he was waiting for me to introduce my friend. I remained silent.

"Erdie," he finally said, holding out his hand. She shook it.

"Caro. You know each other?" Her index finger passed between us.

"I'm an old friend of Ben's, and dear Luca here is my new friend." Erdie put an arm around my shoulders and squeezed me against himself. He was clearly trying to provoke me, but I didn't give in; just peeled myself from his massive arms.

"This is Hanna." He introduced his companion.

Wait a minute. Hadn't he mentioned a girl named Phyllis at the cafeteria? No wonder he and Ben got along so well.

"Hi," said Hanna.

Her pretty smile made her seem really nice. I secretly wondered why she would get involved with a guy like this.

"That weirdo really did look threatening from a distance," she went on, but Caro waved it off.

"Just your regular intolerant asshole. You can't let guys like him bother you too much."

"True," Erdie agreed. "You have to be above it, idiots are everywhere. Still, I don't like it when they think they need to assault women."

"I feel much better now." Theatrically, I put a hand over my heart, but he didn't seem to mind my irony. Instead, he made a fist and playfully punched my chin. That was sort of his thing; he did that to people all the time.

"Wow, I love your earrings," Caro said, admiring Hanna's silver hoop earrings. "Where did you get them?"

"From that little jewelry shop over there. They always have great stuff." She pointed vaguely straight ahead.

"Don't I have great taste?" Erdie proudly tapped his chest. "I picked them out."

"What a stroke of luck!" Hanna stuck out her tongue, which made him mock-punch her chin too.

They seemed very comfortable with each other—poor Rhashmi. While Caro and Hanna exchanged details about the store's jewelry inventory, Erdie bent down to me.

"How's Rhashmi?"

I couldn't believe it. Did he honestly think he could ask me about her in front of his new flame?

"She's doing great," I replied euphorically. "She's always busy, goes out a lot." I leaned forward and whispered as if I wanted to tell him something in confidence. "You really have to try hard to get with her."

"I thought so." He sighed, suddenly seeming unusually shy. His eyes lost their sparkle. "Tell her I said hi."

I gave a thin-lipped smile. "Sure."

"We need to go to that store, like now," ordered Caro.

I was all for it, even though I wasn't much into jewelry. I enthusiastically hooked my arm through Caro's and waved to the others.

"Take care of yourselves, okay? Two beautiful girls all alone..." Erdie had mastered the art of slime to perfection. In my generous moments, I'd call myself pretty, but I was definitely no great beauty. A melody suddenly sounded from our midst, some kind of rap song, not all that bad really.

"Whose phone is that?" Erdie looked around confused, then he seemed to recognize the melody. "Oh, that's me." He fumbled around in the pocket of his light blue denim jacket. "New ringtone, still getting used to it."

I didn't tell him the correct expression would have been: "That's mine." The other day, I had kindly pointed out to Ben that he shouldn't say *because of those low temperatures* but *because of the low temperatures*. And he had called me a smartass. Me? He was! It was just ridiculous. My mind snapped back when I heard Erdie cheerfully say, "Hey, Ben."

That was the sign for me to clear out. Was there no escaping from that guy?

"Guess who's standing next to me right now." I heard Erdie say loudly into the phone. "Luca... Yes, some guy was harassing her downtown while she was making out with her girlfriend. You never told me she was a lesbian." He winked at me. "Oh, she's not?" Now he looked at me in confusion.

"Are you sure? The two of them looked hot... Oh, really. Bondage with her ex-boyfriend, that sounds..."

It was too much for me. While Caro silently shook with laughter, I ripped Erdie's phone out of his hand and shouted, "It wasn't bondage, and your pal here shouldn't believe everything that comes out of your mouth, tell him that instead!" I shoved the tall guy's cell phone back into his hand before my roommate could respond. Erdie's jaw dropped.

"Gotta go," I said, feeling red throbbing blotches starting to appear on my cheeks as I pulled Caro away with me. Maybe I had overreacted, but it had had a liberating effect on my mental health. Caro looked at me sideways.

"They're all really nice."

"They're all really crummy," I grumbled.

"You're not even giving them a chance."

"They don't deserve one."

Caro giggled. "You're impossible. Even though you may seem cold-hearted sometimes, I know you better."

Cold-hearted. So that was how I came across. It hurt me a little that my best friend of all people thought of me that way. But by not opening up, you couldn't get hurt. It was that simple. I knew what I was talking about, and Caro knew it too. After all, she was the only one who knew the story I would never talk about again for as long as I lived.

15

Later that night, I returned home, heavily loaded down with shopping bags. Today's run-in downtown had indeed resulted in a little retail therapy. In my opinion, a shopping spree was better than any orgasm could be.

Toby was talking in his room, probably on the phone with Ellen, who was once again off jet-setting. He had told me that these long separations from her made him anxious, and he hoped that things would be different once they started a family. Apparently, he was in it for the long haul. I was happy for them. Toby was such a nice guy and only had eyes for her.

Soft music came from Ben's room, the melodious voice of some female blues singer. I headed to my own four walls to finally get rid of my bags. Heavy raindrops splattered against the window. Sighing, I looked at the cloudy night sky. What should I do now? After a longer visit with Caro, I always felt a little lonely afterwards. Sighing again, I relocated to the living room to watch a little TV, which I could do if neither of the guys were in here watching a boring sports show. Luckily for me, an old episode of *Grey's Anatomy* was on. Staring at the screen, I sat down on the couch. McDreamy was preparing for surgery, looking all sexy in his light blue scrubs with that adorable, bright smile. I sank into the pillows, weak in the knees. Why did men like him only exist in Hollywood?

I ran my hand across the sofa cushion, imagining myself holding Patrick Dempsey in my arms, while I watched the show, transfixed. All of the sudden, my fingers touched something soft and sticky, almost like a balloon. I bolted upright, and holding my breath, I pulled out a used condom from under the pillow. It was knotted and full. My stomach turned. Disgusted, I threw the thing onto the dark green carpet and jumped up, furious. *Ben,* the spawn of sex hell! Couldn't he do that dirty stuff with his bed buddies in his own room? And why did he have to leave his disgusting evidence lying around?

"Ben!" I screamed shrilly, tapping my foot impatiently.

No reaction. Typical.

"Beeennnn!"

Nothing happened for a long time. As usual, he was making me wait so it didn't look as if he were immediately giving in to my request. I knew that tactic so well because I did the same to him.

I was about to shout for him again when he appeared in the doorway.

"What is it?" He couldn't have sounded more bored.

"There." I pointed to the floor.

Ben followed my gesture, but he seemed unfazed. Unbelievable.

"A water balloon?" He grinned. "Did you hook up with a guy and do it on the couch? Congrats. You're not as uptight as I thought."

"You really shouldn't project your own failings onto others." I stamped my foot. "That is so gross, it's borderline sexual harassment. And just for your information. I have never had and never will have a one-night stand. Not everybody is into cheap, meaningless sex, you know. I really don't give a crap how many women you have to lay to stroke your fragile ego, but it's unbelievable that you'd leave your trophies out for public display." I glared at him.

Leaning against the doorframe, Ben listened to my outburst. He didn't seem to give a damn about his outrageous behavior. It was so like him.

"Don't you have anything to say in your defense?" I snapped, because he still wasn't making the slightest attempt to talk his way out of it. What a jerk! He could at least apologize. I felt like I was a dragon breathing fire, and it wouldn't have surprised me if steam was pouring out of my nostrils.

"What are you watching?" He stared at the TV in fascination. A surgeon was making a thin incision with a scalpel across a naked torso.

"Are you even listening to me?"

"Yes, I did. You made a big fuss about a tiny condom. Just throw it in the garbage."

"That's right; a tiny one," I agreed, stressing every word.

"Smartass," he muttered.

Toby appeared. "What's going on over here? Luca, the entire building can hear you."

"Your pal here leaves his used cock socks lying around..."

Ben snorted, and I took a deep breath.

"He left one in our living room. It's disgusting."

Toby stared motionlessly at the condom, which looked like a slug crawling across the carpet. Finally, someone seemed to share my outrage, and to my relief, he seemed just as disgusted. Someone was finally coming over to my side, while Ben kept watching my show as if none of this was his business.

"Um... Luca." Toby rubbed his legs awkwardly. "Sorry, that's mine..."

I exhaled sharply. "What?"

"You were both out yesterday, and well, Ellen and I had the place to ourselves. We got bored, so we decided to have a little fun. I'm really sorry. I completely forgot about it."

I stared at the wall, studying a tiny black spot that I had just discovered. Damn it. I had just wrongly accused Ben... So now what? I would have to apologize to him. This was a disaster, a worst-case scenario, the absolute worst thing imaginable.

"It's okay," I said to Toby, before I turned to Ben as slowly as possible to postpone the moment of my humiliation. Of course, he was watching me expectantly, with a hang-dog expression as if he were deeply hurt.

"I'm sorry," I pressed out between clenched teeth, my neck muscles tightening. I felt on the verge of choking. The bastard clasped his hands behind his head, savoring the moment of my humiliation while Toby grabbed the used condom and disappeared.

"Sorry, what was that?" Ben put one hand behind his ear. "I didn't understand you, your voice was too soft."

For a moment, I wondered how many years I would go to jail for if I killed Ben right now. Surely, some smart lawyer would be able to plead my case as a crime of passion and cite mitigating circumstances to have the charges reduced. "I'm sorry, okay?" I snarled at him. Ben stepped closer. His devilish grin made me suspicious, and even the blue of his eyes seemed to darken a bit.

"Never mind. But I know how you can make up for all those unfounded accusations."

"I won't sleep with you, forget it."

"Who's talking about sex?" Ben honestly sounded surprised. Goddamn it, did the humiliation need to go on forever?

"You could clean the bathroom for me, and we'd be even."

"Fine," I mumbled, while *Grey's Anatomy* captured Ben's attention again. He grimaced as a surgeon reached into a patient's open abdominal cavity and held up a dripping kidney, which he gently slid into a stainless-steel bowl. Then the camera zoomed in on his bloody hands.

"And you choose to watch this stuff?" Ben shook his head. "No wonder you're always on edge." He sauntered back to his room while I needed to sit down for a minute, staring at the screen. What was so bad about this? It was just abdominal surgery, not half as gross as touching a used condom.

16

After a restless night, during which my masochistic brain kept replaying the events of the evening, forcing me to relive every embarrassing detail in high definition and slow motion, I finally woke up around six o'clock, soaked in sweat. Ben could have cleared up this little mix-up right away and saved us both a lot of embarrassment. But no, out of pure spitefulness—as I strongly suspected—he had played this comedy to the end. Actually, it was all Ben's fault, as I now clearly realized.

After a short shower, I tiptoed out of the apartment to go to the lab.

In the two hours I was there, I evaluated lists for my professor, corrected a handful of freshman papers, and did several other odd jobs. Now, I was standing in the lab cleaning test tubes, flasks and petri dishes, wiping down the work surfaces, and sweeping the floor at the end. This was also part of my job, despite the fact there was no mention of having to clean the lab in my job description. But I was glad to have found a job at all, and I could also use it for a reference on future applications after graduation. I had just finished when Rhashmi walked in. She had texted me earlier that she was going to come by and pick me up for our lecture.

"Hi, I just finished," I said. "Just have to put my tools away." I held up the broom and dustpan.

Rhashmi giggled. "They're using you as a cheap cleaner."

"I know." I gazed at Rhashmi, astonished. Her kohl-lined eyes sparkled, and her lips shimmered with gloss as she incessantly twirled a strand of hair around her thumb and fingers.

"Is there something new about you?"

She nodded immediately. "I've applied for the environmental project in Mumbai. If they accept me, I'll be in India next year for six months. Isn't that awesome?"

"It sounds terrific, but..."

"But what?" she interrupted me, her voice rising an octave.

"They speak Hindi there."

"I know that," she snapped as she jumped up and sat on the lab table.

"If Anoob makes you sweat, what are you going to do in Mumbai?"

"The people there speak English too." She swung her legs.

"Okay." I could vividly imagine the Indian students trying to chat with my pretty friend while she stood there red-faced, only managing to stutter out a few chunks of English.

"Just stop, I know what you're getting at. My mom even told me I should take language classes at the community college to at least learn the basics. Can you imagine that?" She snorted. "I, Rhashmi Reinhardt from New Delhi, taking a Hindi 101 class."

"I always thought you were from Dortmund."

"My roots are in Delhi." She jumped off the table, flipping back her hair. "Imagine me sitting in a class with a Claudia and a Jens, and not understanding a word the teacher's trying to teach us. And then the two of them being able to speak my ancestral tongue fluently while I can hardly put together even one decent sentence."

I sighed. Sometimes I really envied Rhashmi's problems.

"I'm sure you'll do fine without going to language lessons. A semester abroad is a great opportunity and a unique experience. Why don't you just see what happens?" I loved the idea of studying abroad, but hadn't worked up the nerve to apply yet. Especially since I didn't know it would work out being gluten-free somewhere else in the world. Even as a child, I'd been unable to go to summer camp because they couldn't ensure gluten-free meals there. So, I spent my summers by the lake with my dad, while my friends enjoyed themselves at various camps.

"True." Rhashmi waited at the door as I got my backpack out of my locker and headed her way.

"Say." Rhashmi lowered her eyes, a slight blush rising on her cheeks. "Have you seen Erdie around lately? After all, he is your roommate's friend."

Oh, no. Now I got why she was all dressed up—it was Thursday. Apparently, she hadn't given up hope that this womanizer would still show up at the cafeteria one day. I didn't want to be the one to break the bad news to her.

"Um... Yes... In town, just for a moment," I stammered, searching my backpack for a non-existent tissue. When I looked up quickly to check the situation, I stepped right into the Rhashmi Trap. Her almond eyes were as big as saucers, glimmering with hope.

She looked at me so imploringly that there was no way I could tell her the truth, even if it was the only right thing to do to save her from that self-absorbed bad boy.

Thinking hard, I broke out in a sweat.

"You know, uh... I ran into him downtown the other day, we talked a bit... Uh... Then his phone rang and... Uh... I went on." Phew. That wasn't a total lie. I wondered how Ben managed to come up with cheap excuses all the time to keep his floozies satisfied. Continuously lying like this would be way too stressful for me. Rhashmi raised an eyebrow. Rats, I was acting way too suspiciously, as my cheeks blushed telltale red.

"That's all you talked about?"

I cleared my throat. "No," I answered a little too quickly and waved her off. "You know how it is. He was in a hurry, and I was in a hurry... Speaking of hurries, we'll be late for class." I grabbed Rhashmi by the sleeve of her sweater to drag her out of the lab before I locked up.

"Men are bastards," she suddenly said, to which I nodded.

"Especially the good-looking ones," I couldn't help it. "Actually, it's women's own fault if they allow themselves to get so wrapped up in a nicely-sculpted bicep and attractive face that they mutate into insecure rodents, basing their self-esteem on the patronizing whims of some self-indulgent guy."

Rhashmi's face darkened. I could see in her eyes that she took my words personally. "Who are you talking about?"

I gave her a quick sideways glance as I walked on. "The modern, self-confident woman of today should reflect more on a man's inner values and not fall for good-looking jerks just because they buy them a few drinks at the bar. It's unacceptable that sensitive, good-hearted guys are left behind just because they don't meet the stereotype of an attractive man, while well-built ego maniacs unscrupulously jump from bed to bed and leave countless broken hearts in their wake. And to top it off, they won't even kiss their conquests on the mouth." I was on a roll and panting for breath as we climbed the stairs to the lecture halls. I could have easily omitted the last sentence, since this attribute probably only applied to one person.

"Everything okay with you?" Rhashmi asked carefully. "You almost sound like a man-hater."

"I don't hate men, but I'm keeping my eye on the future," I announced cockily. "From now on, I won't judge men purely by their looks, and will only be with someone who is sensitive and caring. A man of character."

"You'll still have to kiss him though" Rhashmi replied, deadpan.

"What do you mean?" I stopped in my tracks.

"In a way, you're right. I also want a boyfriend with good qualities. But what can I do? If I don't like a guy's looks, he won't do it for me in the bedroom, no matter how nice he is."

"Beauty is in the eye of the beholder." I raised my chin. "I'd give any man a chance, no matter what he looks like."

Rhashmi shook her head. Strangely enough she didn't seem to share my opinion. Yet she was a woman and apparently one of those who always fell for the heartbreakers and learned nothing. Someone squeaked behind us: "Hey! Wait up."

We turned around and found Martin hopping towards us, the sides of his black and white diamond-patterned cardigan sweater flapping around his slim torso. He was holding a thick stack of magazines, which was threatening to slip out of his hands.

"I brought you something." He beamed at me, making me feel uneasy.

I faked a cheerful smile. "Really? That's nice of you." A quick glance at his magazines, and I moaned silently. Rhashmi giggled quietly.

"*Financial Times Magazine* issues from January 2017 to today." He held them out expectantly. His nasally voice always reminded me somehow of a toad with a bad cold.

"Oh, thanks." Crap, what was I supposed to do with this useless pile of paper? "You know what? I think one magazine will do for now. I'm an absolute beginner when it comes to the stock exchange."

He pouted like a toddler whose mommy had just refused to get him a sweet.

"What would you even do with just one issue? You have to go through them one by one. I always read a few pages before going to sleep. Right now, I'm browsing through the latest issues of *The Stockbroker*. It's fascinating. If you like…" He smiled at me shyly, "You could have them next."

I took a deep breath. "Great." I accepted the heavy pile

reluctantly, and the weight almost brought me to my knees. How was I supposed to get these to the apartment unharmed? I needed a forklift.

"Well, aren't you a real sweetheart," I heard Rhashmi say brightly, enunciating every word.

"Yeah? You think so?" Martin's face lit up like a Christmas tree as she nodded.

"Sure," Rhashmi continued. "You're caring and sensitive. You seem to know the way to a girl's heart." With her chin, she pointed to the wastepaper in my arms, which was slowly dragging me down. "Luca's really into men like that."

Oh no, she didn't just say that! She had just stabbed me in the back!

"You do?" Martin blushed up to the roots of his hair. "You like me?"

The shock ran through me like touching a 10,000-volt line.

"That's not what Rhashmi meant," I said hastily, trying to salvage what I could. I pictured myself gagging her and tying her up for her duplicity, like Hannibal Lecter in *Silence of the Lambs*. "She means guys in general, no one in particular."

"Weeell..." Rhashmi started, but shut up again when I rammed my elbow into her side, making her double over for a second. Served her right.

"Would you like to go out with me sometime?" Martin ambushed me from behind, his face turning as red as a tomato.

Shit, what should I do now? I needed an escape.

"What happened to you giving every man a chance?" whispered my former friend in a voice distorted by pain.

Defiance rose up inside me. Why was she making fun of Martin's invitation? He wasn't a bad guy. He was smart and helpful and... I was running out of attributes for him. Surely, one could talk to him about other things than the current price of gold. "Sure, why not?"

"Really?" they both asked at the same time, looking at me with open mouths.

My daring worried me, but at least I wouldn't end up the one lonely and miserable because of a rotten old Erdie or Ben. I imagined Rhashmi's dark future at the side of a callous pretty boy. Martin seemed elated. He was jumping up and down, arms aloft and cheering. The people passing by stared at him as if he were bonkers. I felt a twinge of regret.

"So, dinner tomorrow night?" he asked shyly.

Dinner? I liked the idea of dinner. We'd go to a nice restaurant, which of course I would choose to make sure they offered gluten-free entrees. Then we would say goodbye again before I went home, by myself, with a clean conscience. "Okay." I heard myself agreeing.

Next to me, Rhashmi was gasping for breath.

"I'll pick you up tomorrow night around seven."

Pick me up?!

"No need," I declined hastily. "I'll meet you on campus. That'll be easier for both of us."

"Cool. See you tomorrow." Martin dashed off. I wouldn't have been surprised if he had clicked his heels in delight.

"You sure made someone very happy," Rhashmi remarked. She couldn't take her eyes off the animated Martin any more than the rest of the people around us could. Without a doubt, he attracted the attention of others in his own special way.

"It'll be great," I said to encourage myself.

We started walking again.

"Well then, I hope you'll have fun tomorrow."

"I will," I replied, clutching the heavy stack of magazines to my chest; my arms were aching. I couldn't shake the feeling that I had just outsmarted myself, though.

Gasping for breath, I arrived home that evening with those dumb magazines, and leaned with my forehead against the door of my room. With my last ounce of energy, I stumbled in and dropped them on the floor, where they would probably gather dust. I had just come from my study group, the one Martin also belonged to. In all seriousness, he informed me that he had just come from his apartment. I wanted to strangle him. Then why had I been dragging a ton of wastepaper around with me all day? He could have easily brought the magazines with him in the evening. Sometimes I really didn't know what was going on inside that guy. A cramp in my left calf forced me onto my desk chair. To distract myself from the dull pain, I checked my text messages. There was one from Caro asking if I would like to go to the LGBTQ gala next month. She wanted to secure some Early Bird tickets. Why not? I had gone with her the last two years as well, and the live bands were always awesome. I texted back to say she could get me a ticket.

Three people had liked a picture of me and Caro that I had posted on Facebook yesterday. One of them was Martha, which I took as a good sign that the two were getting closer again. Also, Toby had left a nice *"Hot!!!"* with a winking smiley, which he honestly could have skipped. By pure chance, I had spotted Ben on his friends list. Not that I was snooping around or anything. I had just checked to see who Toby was friends with. Of course, *the copulator* had jumped out at me immediately. Neither Ben nor I had sent each other friend requests, and I wanted to keep it that way.

I got up and strolled into the kitchen to drink a glass of orange juice and eat some cheese puffs. After a long search, I had found some in an organic food store labelled as gluten-free, and yesterday I had drawn a huge black skull and crossbones on the bag, just to give my personal burglar a little warning. Full of anticipation, I opened the cupboard door and found it empty again. My pulse started racing frighteningly fast. Ben. The most selfish bastard in the whole world! I would get him back for this unforgivable outrage. That guy had to stop stealing my food for God's sake.

Listening down the hallway, I couldn't hear any sounds coming from either of the other rooms. Apparently, everyone was gone, and I was home alone—perfect. First, I needed to gather evidence. The empty bag wasn't in the kitchen trash, so the corpus delicti, or what was left of it, must have been stashed somewhere in Ben's room. I planned to grab it and present it to him at his later trial. Tiptoeing down the dark hallway, I stopped in front of Ben's door. For some reason, I didn't want to turn on the light. My pulse was throbbing in my throat. I felt like a burglar, but I calmed myself down again. After all, I was defending my right to my cheese puffs. I hated Ben for the hundred thousandth time since we'd met.

To be on the safe side, I first pressed an ear to his door, but didn't hear any suspicious noises, so I turned the knob and opened the door a crack. Just as I was about to sneak in, I froze.

17

I held my breath and should have backed out immediately, but I couldn't move a muscle. Instead, I stared at the scene before my eyes, while a strange warm feeling spread through my stomach. A naked blonde woman was keeling on all fours on Ben's bed, and he was right behind her, rocking his pelvis back and forth in a gentle rhythm. His eyes were closed, and his head was thrown back, a few strands of hair plastered onto his forehead. The blonde woman moaned softly. Ben's breathing was shallow. He thrust himself into her quicker and quicker, taking her faster without getting rough. With one hand, he gently ran his fingers up to her neck and wrapped her hair around them. Then he pulled her head backward—it seemed dominant, but not brutal. He never stopped moving back and forth in this controlled rhythm, circling inside of her, while his bed bunny moaned with delight. As hard as I tried, I simply couldn't leave the room. Almost mesmerized, I watched their lovemaking and felt myself start to throb between my legs. Damn it, watching Ben have sex was turning me on.

The shock of this realization finally broke the spell. My gaze glided from Ben's waist to his chest. His flat stomach was toned with well-defined muscles, his chest looked smooth and firm, athletic and yet as soft as velvet. Then I paused. A tattoo was emblazoned on his left pec, intricate lettering which I couldn't decipher from where I stood with barbed wire coiled around it, seemingly encircling the words. Ben's face contorted slightly. He looked wild and ecstatic, as his eyes turned completely black. Passion flashed within me like lightning and pounded through my body with growing intensity. Suddenly, I wanted to be the one on all fours on his bed while he took me just as tantalizingly as this unknown woman. It was hard for me to breathe suddenly, and I realized I needed to disappear before they discovered me. But I couldn't. I wanted to follow this spectacle to the end. So, I stood there as if rooted to the ground, watching with a beating heart as he bent over her, slowly sank down onto her back, and nipped her neck.

Moaning loudly and achingly, the girl pressed herself over and over against him while Ben gave her what she was hungering for. All of a sudden, I felt as if I had accidentally stumbled across a late-night program on the porn channel, and I knew that I needed to change channels as soon as possible. Yet, I couldn't move.

And then Ben looked up, directly into my eyes, while I stood transfixed and stared. His eyes bored into mine as he moved faster inside the woman, and a predatory expression spread across his face. In his eyes flashed greed; hunger. It was then obvious to me that Ben Nowak had known the entire time that I was standing in the doorway. Flooded by hot embarrassment, I bit my lip as I turned around and fled to my room. I paced that space like a panther in a cage, desperately trying to calm down a bit. What was I thinking, walking into his room without permission? I had violated his privacy—all because of a stupid bag of snacks.

There was no way I was ever going to be able to look him in the eye again. In a flash, I darted through my room and turned the key, leaning my hot cheek against the cool wood. Why on earth hadn't he locked his door? And why had he looked at me so strangely? Like a lion on the prowl, devouring his prey yet still unsatisfied. Ben was dangerous, and his body was so incredibly perfect. Never before had I seen such a beautiful man. I wondered if they were still going, making love all night long, lusty and passionate until dawn. Or was he as embarrassed as I was? My sense of shame just wouldn't let go. It stuck to me like superglue, as hot waves of embarrassment surged through my body.

18

ours later, the shame still blazed in me like a wildfire. Compared to my disgraceful behavior from last night, the incident with the condom seemed like a joke. Around midnight, I heard the apartment door click. Either Toby had come home, or Ben had lost the desire for further interaction with the blond. I decided to never leave my room again and to stay in my bed until the blackness of death graciously enveloped me. Death seemed to me the best and only way to get out of this situation. Unfortunately, I couldn't even blame Ben for this little indiscretion. After all, I had entered his private room. I had watched him having sex. I was sure he could even get a restraining order against me for that. I would have a criminal record and be right there in the sex offender files. Branded forever.

When I noticed where my thoughts were getting to me, I swung my legs out of bed and paced again restlessly.

Then I stopped in my tracks.

Or I could deny everything. Claim that he had only imagined my presence in the heat of passion. I was sure I could convince Caro to give me an alibi. Angry at myself, I kicked my bed frame, and a sharp pain immediately shot from my big toe up to my ankle. I gritted my teeth and threw myself on the bed. Make up for it, I had to make up for it. Hadn't I promised Ben to clean the bathroom for him?

I'll do that!

Yes, I would go out there right now, scrub every stupid joint, and spray the tiles with window spray until everything was shiny and sparkly like at Tiffany's.

Yeah, that was a good plan.

In a flash, I was at my bedroom door. I turned the key in slow motion and opened it a crack. Cautiously, I peeked outside, where I found everything empty to my relief. Either they were still sleeping, or both of them were out. Or Ben was going at it again with Blondie, which I was really hoping for right now. Hurrying into the kitchen, I grabbed a bucket, cleaning materials and rags, before I headed for the bathroom. Two more steps, and I would be safe again for now. I glanced over my shoulder. Thank God everything was quiet in Ben's bedroom. Jerking open the bathroom door, I jumped inside and pulled it shut behind me. Done! I hurriedly turned the key in the lock, turned around and froze. The bucket clattered out of my hand. I wanted to escape, but had just locked myself in. Panic flooded through me, while I hoped for the Grim Reaper to get me on the spot, to spare me this humiliation. There was Ben, wearing nothing but black boxers. He stared at me in astonishment. His hair was all messy, as if he had just toweled it dry, and it looked so, so hot.

"You locked the door? Do you have something special in mind?" His sneaky grin showed off the cute dimple at the corner of his mouth.

I deflated. This must be a bad dream. "No, no, no, no, no. That was an accident. I was just going to clean the bathroom. How was I supposed to know that you're in here? Why don't you ever lock the door?" As my voice turned a little hysterical, my last question gave me away, as I now realized. It must have been the shock, but I had a lump in my throat. As Ben stepped closer, I pressed myself against the wall.

"Ten seconds earlier, and you'd have caught me naked." He wasn't the least bit embarrassed.

"I would have closed my eyes," I hastily reassured him while groping for the key behind my back. His muscles bulged a little on his chest, but not too big. He just seemed really fit and well-defined. And now I could decipher his tattoo. It said *Guilt and Atonement* in intricate lettering with the barbed wire coiling around it, right over his heart. I swallowed. His scent reached my nose. He smelled freshly showered, like a sporty shower gel, and to my dismay my body responded very powerfully. It took all my willpower not to run my fingers down his athletic arms. If he had ripped off my clothes right then, I wouldn't have resisted.

"Did you enjoy the little show last night?" he asked in a dark voice.

Unfortunately, my treacherous cheeks blushed. "I... I'm really sorry about that. I just wanted to ask you something, and didn't mean to…"

"It's okay. I don't mind an audience." He shrugged and laughed. "But I bet you were too embarrassed to sleep a wink."

I was done feeling guilty. He obviously thought I was uptight. "Just for your information, I've seen two people having sex before. You're not the first, and let me tell you something else; your performance wasn't that impressive anyway." That was clearly a lie, both of them, and I prayed that he wouldn't be able to read it on my face.

Ben seemed amused. "Oh, that's right. I forgot all about the porn movie."

Crap. I hadn't even been thinking about that. The guy had the memory of an elephant.

"So what? I watched a porn film once, big deal. Why don't you call your pal and tell him that too, you snitch?"

Of course, he laughed. No surprise there.

"Why don't you ever have one?" he suddenly asked.

"One what?"

"A one-night stand. An orgasm every now and then would do you good. Why are you so uptight about sex? Or rather, why do you deny yourself the pleasure?"

"I don't deny myself anything." I was gasping for breath. "I just prefer to make love with someone I care about. Besides, I have no need to be used as a punching bag for some guy's urges."

Ben snorted. "Is that really how you see it?"

"Yes, or are you trying to tell me that you care about any of your playmates? That you're not just using them to get your kicks?"

"Trust me, they have a good time too. Believe it or not, there are women who enjoy sex." He leaned over and propped one arm against the wall. "I agree with you on one thing though. I don't care about the women I meet, but I respect them, as women and as people."

As I gazed into his beautiful, black-blue eyes, which conveyed something special to his face. I could easily imagine how women sank into this dark ocean when they met him. His aura, his dominant yet gentle charisma, his mixture of wickedness and passion, all made him fatally irresistible to me. This could only be a moment of weakness. "And that's enough for you?" I asked in a low voice, secretly hoping he would pull me into his arms like Rhett Butler did Scarlett O'Hara, but instead he straightened up again.

"What do you mean?"

"A different one every night, constantly on the prowl, random acquaintances, never really being with anyone." I was trembling. Right now, the wolf in him made my knees weak.

Ben stared at the wall behind me, my words seemed to hit him hard. Why though? Then he focused on me again. "What about you? You let your old boyfriend screw you over from top to bottom, and the guy didn't respect you for a single moment. He cheated on you and treated you really badly. But I bet that was entirely different, right? Because you were in a relationship and all that, somehow that's okay. I'm so sick of this hypocrisy." He reached behind me, and I flinched as his hand brushed my waist. I heard him unlock the door, and felt a pang of disappointment when he made no further move to touch me. Yet his reproachful words cut into my chest like a scalpel.

"I didn't… I didn't mean to judge you, I really didn't," I stammered and honestly meant what I said.

Suddenly, he looked straight into my eyes, and I had a hard time holding his intense gaze.

"Don't let someone like me talk you into anything. You're doing the right thing. May I get dressed now? I'm late for my shift."

"Sure." I squeezed out the door he held open for me.

19

———

The time for my date was inevitably approaching. What was I getting myself into? I truly hoped I hadn't raised any expectations with Martin. After all, he was a grown man, even if that was sometimes hard to believe. He had to know that an innocent date meant nothing. Despite my big mouth in front of Rhashmi, Martin was just not my type. What could I do? To make matters worse, Rhashmi had sent a text wishing us *lovebirds* an unforgettable evening. She totally deserved Erdie, and I thought about writing back just to let her know that he had asked about her. Let the chips fall where they may.

Feeling thirsty, I got up from my desk to fetch a can of prosecco from the kitchen. Ben wasn't home. I had scouted that out when I came in, so I could move freely around the apartment.

My favorite roommate was in the kitchen, reading a book and sipping a beer. He smiled when I came in, which was a nice change. Ben never bothered to smile when we bumped into each other.

"Hey, Luca. What's up?"

"Not much." I took a can of prosecco from the fridge that hissed when I opened it, and popped in a straw.

Toby shot me a questioning look. "What's wrong with you? Wine in the afternoon?"

I waved him off. "I have a thing tonight."

"A thing?"

I sat down next to him. After a few sips from the can, the bubbles went straight to my nose and made it tingle, like I was about to sneeze. I twitched my nose to get rid of the unpleasant feeling.

"A date. A guy asked me out to dinner."

He clinked his bottle to my can. "And you don't really want to, right?"

I looked him in the eye. "No. I mean, he's a nice guy, but he's absolutely not my type at all, and now I feel bad that I accepted his invitation."

"Why did you accept it?"

"He blindsided me."

Toby shook his head. "Oh, Luca."

"What?" I crossed my arms. "It happens."

"It's never happened to me before." He seemed amused. Great.

"What do I do now?"

"Tell him the truth," he suggested, which I dismissed immediately.

"Maybe he's not even interested, and I'm reading too much into it?"

"Any guy who asks a girl out is interested in her. If he just wanted to chat, he could always go out with his buddies."

"Hey, I'm great to hang out with." How could Toby be so cruel? Lost in thought, I sucked at my straw. "Maybe I'm a buddy for him."

Instead of answering, he laughed and ran his fingers through his dark blond hair. Whenever he smiled boyishly like that, I always wanted to pull him towards me and cuddle him like a teddy bear. Ellen was such a lucky girl.

"Just be real with him, and let him down easy. It's important not to send out any mixed signals, or he'll get his hopes up. Afterwards, though, you might want to put some distance between the two of you."

Distance?! Why? How could I possibly put some distance between Martin and myself when we had so many classes together and were in the same study group?

"We could just pretend nothing ever happened," I said, but he shook his head.

"Turning a guy down can get really ugly. It's better to stay out of each other's way for a while."

Was he speaking from experience? Crap, I'd hoped it would be easier to pull out of a date. Why did men have to make everything so complicated? "Where's Ellen?" I asked, moving on from the awkward subject.

"In New York."

My poor roommate seemed depressed. I felt bad for him.

"I thought you were a model too. Why don't you ever travel?"

"I only do local shootings or get booked during the holidays. I'd rather focus on finishing my degree."

That was smart. But something seemed to be bothering him, worry lines marked his normally smooth forehead. "Are you all right?" I asked carefully.

He snorted. "It's Ellen."

"What's the matter with her?" I held my breath. They weren't going to...

"My parents are celebrating their twenty-fifth wedding anniversary on Sunday and they invited her. But instead she had to take this stupid, last-minute catwalk job in New York and won't be back until Wednesday. I really wanted her to go with me, but she just took off."

"Oh, that's unfortunate." Why hadn't Ellen done him this little favor?

"I think she has a problem with my parents being happily married while her alcoholic dad left years ago."

"But that's not your fault."

"Still, she keeps blaming me, saying I don't understand

her problems. Just because my parents aren't divorced doesn't mean I can't put myself in her shoes." He got up, went to the fridge, and came back with another beer and can of prosecco.

"Thanks." I opened the can, spraying liquid across the table. "My mother died when I was six. I was jealous of my friends and angry that it was my mom who was gone. I was so frustrated that I stopped playing with my friends, just to punish them." I swallowed. I usually didn't speak about my mother dying since I didn't want to make people feel uncomfortable. The only one I talked to about her was Caro. "It was only much later that I realized those people weren't to blame for my mother getting sick. I had punished them for something that wasn't their fault. However, it took a long time for me to get to that point."

Toby considered my words for a moment. "You mean she blames herself that he ran away?"

"I have no idea. There are many reasons why people bury themselves in their work or only hurt the ones they love. Even still today, it hurts when I see my friends with their mothers. It always reminds me that my mom will never know who I've become."

Toby patted my arm. "I'm sure she looks down on you from up there and sees exactly what you're up to."

Almost choking on my prosecco, I squawked, "Oh God, no. That would be terrible."

We both burst out laughing. It felt nice to laugh, it was good for both of us.

"All right. I won't blame Ellen on Wednesday," he promised generously. "Instead, I'll talk to her and see if I can support my girl in any way."

I emptied the rest of my can in one gulp. "You do that. I'm sure that'll make her happy." I got up slowly and hesitated for a second, my head was spinning from the bubbly. "I'll jump in the shower and get ready for my date."

"Good luck," Toby laughed "Luca?"

I turned around. "Yes?"

"You're a good buddy."

"You too," I replied, delighted with his compliment. I wanted someone just like him, a Toby who cared about me and made my every wish come true. Why were the best ones always taken?

20

At six-thirty sharp, I found myself back at the kitchen table drinking more prosecco. I was wearing jeans and a baggy black sweater that hid all my curves. The walk to campus took less than fifteen minutes, so I had some time for more liquid courage, which would also hopefully flush away my frustration.

But no such luck—the front door opened, and Ben walked in. He was wearing light gray workout gear, and had dark sweat stains across his chest and under his armpits. His hair was fuzzy and damp, a few strands stuck to his forehead, yet he showed no signs of exhaustion whatsoever; as I would have. Refreshed and in high spirits, he headed straight for the kitchen. He faltered for the blink of an eye when he spotted me, and a broad smile spread across his lips. I immediately became suspicious. What did that mean?

"Solo drinking?" He poured water into a glass before he sat down beside me without being invited.

Normally, my flight instinct would have kicked in by now, but tonight I found his proximity somehow pleasant. What was wrong with me? Probably I was just too bummed out about my imminent date to let him upset me.

"Just a little sip. I'm going out."

"You're pregaming? Looks like you've got a lot going on tonight."

"Nothing special," I quickly tried to brush him off. Ben was not to know about this disastrous date—under no circumstances! He smelled of fresh sweat mixed with a whiff of laundry detergent. I took a deep breath as inconspicuously as possible. Heaven forbid he noticed me sniffing at him. My body soaked up his scent, whereupon my heart fell into a restless rhythm. Reluctantly, I had to admit to myself that I liked the way he smelled. My gaze fell on his neck. His Adam's apple moved as he swallowed, and the skin there seemed delicate.

"Girls' night out, or you going out hunting?" He tipped backwards in his chair. I was tempted to give him a little push.

"You got it all figured out, Mr. Know-It-All. Your little performance last night got me all hot and bothered." I smirked and saw him biting his lip.

"You don't have to go out to take care of that."

I slapped my forehead. "Stupid me. I have the ultimate women's pleasuring device right under my roof, and I'm not taking advantage of it."

"Better late than never." He leaned his elbow on the tabletop, resting his head in his hand. And now I noticed his long eyelashes. This guy just drove me crazy. "Come on," he said softly and hoarsely. "Are you telling me you never imagine what it would be like with you and me?"

"Oh, God. Do you ever think about anything else? You're a walking sex machine."

"Why are you getting all upset? Letting loose can be really liberating."

I yanked the straw out of my can to chug the rest of my prosecco, feeling like I was about to burst. "You're so full of yourself, it's unbelievable." I snorted. "Why don't you just cut it short and tell me to go lie down so we can *talk*."

He laughed. "Nice comeback. But that doesn't answer my

question."

Toby sailed into the kitchen and saved me from this ridiculous conversation. He stopped in his tracks. "You're still there? Isn't your date like at seven?"

I looked at the Coca-Cola clock. Dammit, it was ten to seven. I jumped up.

"You've got a date?" Ben asked, sounding surprised. "Who's the lucky guy, if you don't mind me asking?" He was pretending to be interested. Like he cared about my life.

"Just for your information, Mr. Nowak. The man I'm going out with tonight embodies everything you're not. He's sensitive, entertaining, and intelligent. I can talk to him for hours. He worships women and also has a great sense of humor." I ignored Toby's bewildered look and hoped he would keep his mouth shut.

Ben snorted. "If after all that talking and deep conversations you feel like making out a little, come knock on my door. It's always open for you," he added superfluously.

I put both hands on my hips. "You know what, save your breath for a woman you might actually end up with." He winced. Bullseye. In my mind, I patted myself on the back for my unusually good repartee.

Ben waved dismissively. "Calm down. Go out and have fun. Let your hair down."

That guy was really asking for it.

"I'm certainly not going to do that," I replied, just to be argumentative, but I immediately beat a hasty retreat to the hallway.

"Why don't you enjoy your single life a bit more? Find yourself some men and eat them up. Tomorrow it might all be over. You can do it," he called after me, as if we were in a motivational seminar.

I turned around, giving him two thumbs up while I shouted: "Yes, I can!"

His stupid laugh echoed down the hallway. Typical. Ben Nowak had ruined my evening before it had even started.

21

With my gray tray in my hand, I stood next to Martin. In front of us in the line were about twenty people, all waiting for their food, while women in plastic caps filled the divided plates. My date had insisted on going to the cafeteria because they were serving his absolute favorite dish tonight.

"You have got to try the lasagna. It's really good." Martin peered over the other students to make sure there was enough left for him.

"I can't eat that. The pasta's not gluten-free."

"Oh." He pushed out his lower lip, as if I'd mentioned my condition just to spite him. "Can't you make an exception? For me." He cocked his head and winked at me, probably to give me some kind of *seductive look.*

I looked around discreetly to see whether people were watching. Yeah. A lot of them were shooting us amused glazes.

"No, I can't." I was fed up with having to explain again and again to everyone around me that certain foods were taboo for me.

"But lasagna isn't made with bread." Martin flipped his tray back and forth, just missing the man in front of him.

"But pasta is made from wheat."

"I see." He stopped fidgeting. "Then you can just have a taste of mine."

I decided to let that slide and to change the subject once we reached the table. Finally, we were next. Luckily, we were served by Svetlana, a robust sweetheart from Russia in her late fifties. She didn't have the slightest idea what my celiac disease was, either, but at least she took my dietary wishes seriously and always tried her best to put together something for me when there was nothing on the normal menu that suited my needs. If it weren't for her, I'd be forced to live on salads and rice bread from home several times a week.

"Ah, Luca." she greeted me with a smile. She truly was a good soul. "Not much luck with menu today?" She looked at me with pity. I could see she was considering what to offer me instead.

"Never mind," I said. In cases of emergencies like this, I always kept a small gluten-free snack in my bag.

Svetlana's face lit up. "There are leftover potatoes from lunch. I can heat them up for you."

I watched wistfully as she scooped up a large piece of steaming lasagna, slicing the cheese strings that stretched from Martin's plate to the edge of her serving tray. It smelled divine, and my mouth watered. I was sorely tempted to just devour the pasta on the spot, but I knew that I'd suffer the consequences.

"Potatoes sound great," I forced out, watching enviously as Martin accepted the full plate, tore off a piece of the cheese crust, and stuffed it in his mouth right in front of me. Could he be any more insensitive?

"Mmm, it's delicious."

"Good for you," I grumbled. Svetlana returned quickly with a plate of steaming, plain potatoes straight from the microwave.

"Here, sweetheart. No need to go home hungry. At least, this will fill you up."

"Thanks, Svetlana."

"Poor girl," I heard her say. "In Russia, we don't have this disease. I've never heard of it before. I think it's only you."

I had to laugh against my will. Svetlana was really kind, a real Babushka. A disease all my own.

After I got a Coke and paid for my own food, we carried our trays to a free table. There was such a crowd in here that my companion didn't attract too much attention. We sat down across from each other, and I picked up my silverware to savor my epicurean delights while Martin shoveled his lasagna into his mouth with loud enthusiasm. He didn't feel bad at all for enjoying his meal in front of me. He couldn't have been happier if Wolfgang Puck had personally prepared it for him.

Resigned, I speared a piece of potato and put it in my mouth. Lasagna was nothing more than a nasty cholesterol trap anyway. At least, I wasn't going to die of blocked arteries, I reminded myself. A stale earthy taste spread over my tongue while the spicy aroma of Martin's lasagna blocked my airways.

"Have a bite." Martin held his fork out across the table, tomato sauce dripping onto my tray. I jerked my plate aside in panic.

"What are you doing? Are you crazy?" I exclaimed. "You almost contaminated my potatoes."

"Huh?" He didn't move as a piece of melted cheese dripped down from one of his fork's prongs, dragging a yellow strand across the table. "It was just cheese and sauce, I swear. I didn't even give you any of the noodles."

He stuck out his lower lip again, and I felt a tiny pang of remorse. I shouldn't have yelled at him like that.

"Sorry about that," I said, putting my tray back on the table. "But if noodles are swimming in the sauce, I really can't have it. The entire dish is affected." At least, he was trying to be friendly. Why didn't I just give him a chance? Maybe I should try a little harder. Martin wasn't all that bad. He'd sped through college in half the time it was taking the rest of us, and a few professors had already approached him with offers to mentor his doctoral thesis. None of them had ever asked me, even though I had been scrubbing their lab floor for two years.

I was sure Martin was going to earn a lot of money one day. We could live in a mansion, travel, surround ourselves with smart friends, and have brilliant kids. Have kids?! I hastily wiped away that scary thought. Even Martin would inevitably demand his marital rights, and what would I do then? Maybe I could stall him until the wedding, but after that, I wouldn't be able to put things off any longer. I discreetly examined Martin's pale, bony hand, as it guided his fork to his mouth; in addition, his fingernails were chewed down to the quick. A cheese string stuck to his chin. I imagined him touching me—touching me everywhere, throwing himself on me like a rabbit while moaning in my ear. Beads of sweat formed on my forehead, and panic spread throughout my body. What would I do if he tried to kiss me after we ate?

"Did you know the DAX was up 0.1 percent today?" He looked at me expectantly.

"No, I haven't had time to follow the stock market news today." I barely suppressed an eye roll.

"Oh, but you missed out." He was drawing zigzags in the air with his fork. "That's the way the market went today."

"That's great." I took a sip of my Coke, hoping the caffeine in it would be enough to keep me awake.

"What do you think?" he asked excitedly.

I sat up straight and suppressed a touch of panic; he wouldn't want to start a relationship conversation now, would he?

"Yes?" I held my breath, trembling inside.

"Do you think the DAX will crash by the end of the year?"

"What?" I didn't understand a word he'd said. What did he want to know?

"Well, whether…," he intoned dramatically, but I interrupted him quickly.

"What do you like to do for fun?" I'd be damned if we couldn't have a conversation like normal people. I looked at him more closely. His eyes were bright blue, a really nice color I had never noticed before. There you go.

"For fun?" he asked incredulously, as if I wanted to know if he was going on the next expedition to Mars.

"Yes." I nodded encouragingly at him, which made him beam.

"I play backgammon, do you?"

"No."

"Oh, too bad. We could've played together." He stuffed a large forkful of lasagna into his mouth. The string of cheese was still stuck to his chin, and it was hypnotizing.

"I play the accordion in a music club," he said with his mouth full.

"That's great," was all I could think of. I had no problem with people playing an instrument, but the accordion wasn't exactly among my top favorite instruments. In my mind, I pictured us sitting in front of a fireplace, Martin belting out polka music.

"I can play for you some day. I never realized we had so much in common." Martin seemed happy, apparently considering the date to be a great success. He went on, "If you like…" Suddenly, a high-pitched voice interrupted him.

"Martin!" She sounded truly pleased to see him. Glancing up in surprise, a girl with short brown hair appeared in my field of vision. She wore a colorfully striped sweater, and looked back and forth between us as she gripped her tray tightly. Her face gave nothing away, but my female intuition instantly picked up her rigid posture.

"Jo…hanna." Martin almost choked on her name. "What are you doing here?"

"Eating!" she snapped back. "I called you earlier, but you didn't pick up."

I couldn't believe it. There were actually women in Martin's life, women who spent time with him willingly. To top it off, women who seemed to enjoy his company. Besides, she wasn't even bad-looking. I shouldn't jump to conclusions.

"Luca asked me out," he twisted the facts without blushing.

I stared at him with my mouth open, but he didn't notice me. Instead, Johanna examined me intently.

"And you guys know each other, how?" she asked pointedly, while Martin seemed close to hyperventilating.

"From our study group," I helped him out, noticing he'd begun scratching his neck as if he was about to break out in hives.

"Yes," he agreed, his voice rising a few octaves. "By the way, Johanna knitted this sweater herself," he told me before taking a big sip of his apple juice spritzer.

"That's great." I smiled at Johanna. "It looks fantastic." People still knitted these days? I didn't know that.

"Thanks."

I could hear her silent *screw you* loud and clear.

"Want to join us?" I asked kindly, pointing to the empty seat next to my date.

"I don't want to disturb you," she replied.

I was just about to assure her that she wasn't disturbing us, which was even the truth, when Martin butted in.

"Then you'd best sit somewhere else." He swept his arm out wide. "There's plenty of room."

I could hardly believe it. Martin had flat out rejected Johanna.

"I'll call you tomorrow." Johanna left to sit five tables away.

"Um," I started carefully. "Is she your girlfriend or something?"

After draining his glass, Martin swallowed audibly. "We used to be together, but it's coming to an end. She's so boring." He sighed. "All she talks about is knitting or her environmental group. She makes a fuss because I don't wear fake leather shoes..." he paused and graced me with his *seductive smile* again. "I like you better."

I forced myself to smile back.

This evening had brought me another critical insight. Men were all the same, even the ones with nothing to show in the looks department. I caught Johanna's eyes on us several times. Turning my attention back to my now cold potatoes, I wondered whether I should fake an illness to get out of there gracefully, but then I heard a voice beside me.

"Luca, you're here?"

22

Ben. Of all people. Couldn't he have eaten at home? My fruit yogurt was in the fridge. Why hadn't he just helped himself to it like always?

"Go away," I hissed and threw him a warning glance, which he deliberately ignored and instead gave my date a thorough once-over. His conjoined twin stood beside him, and they both carried trays laden with a mountain of food.

"Hey, Luca, are these seats taken?" Without waiting for an answer, Erdie was about to push himself past Martin's chair towards the free seat, but Ben held him back.

"We shouldn't crash Luca's date."

Erdie stopped and threw me a look, clearly doubting my sanity.

"Like right now?" Behind Martin's back, he pointed at him questioningly.

Now I hated them both. I was just about to make an excuse that hopefully wouldn't hurt Martin too much when my eager companion butted in saying proudly, "Yeah, Luca asked me out to dinner."

Now I was the one who ignored Ben, while he watched me like a hawk. I played with my fork, turning it over in my hands and reading with interest the engraving on the back.

Stolen from the University of Erlangen Cafeteria. Well, that was foresighted. My thoughts went back to Martin. Where had he gotten the stupid idea that I was the one who had done the asking? In a quiet minute, I'd have to take Rhashmi aside so we could reconstruct this whole mess, piece by piece. Maybe I'd been sending ambiguous signals after all?

"Great location for a date." Ben looked around the crowded room, taking in the cacophony of voices and the harsh neon lighting.

"Huh, why?" Martin looked at him in confusion, his mouth a little open.

"I would take the woman of my dreams out to a nice quiet restaurant and have drinks afterwards. It would have never occurred to me to choose the cafeteria."

How was my date any of Ben's business? When had Mr. One-Night-Stand started giving dating advice? Why were these two even still here, staring?

"Your food is getting cold," I hissed at him, waving them away like pesky flies. But no, Ben was oblivious to my well-meant warning. He just shrugged.

"But it's lasagna night. With double cheese for three fifty," Martin replied, cluelessly.

Ben glanced at my cold potatoes. "Clearly."

"Come on, bro." Erdie jerked his head to the side. At least he seemed to have a little decency. "I'm sure the two of them want to enjoy their romantic evening undisturbed," he added unnecessarily. That was the last straw.

"Exactly. So, why don't you two get lost, and prepare for your bar-hopping, or whatever it is you do after nightfall." I'd raised my voice, causing some people nearby to turn around and looked in our direction.

"Hey, Luca, calm down. No hard feelings." Was I wrong or did Erdie seem guilty? "We're only messing with you, don't take it personally." He nudged Ben in the ribs, who now stared at me with a serious expression. What was wrong with him? Was he offended? Who was it that had shown up at our table uninvited? Typical. First, he attacked me and then he snuck off when I shot back. This was just so like him.

"No offense." Erdie put his big paw on Martin's shoulder. It almost sounded like an apology. What the hell was wrong with him?

"For what?" Martin asked, staring up at them.

"Let's go." Ben started walking, and Erdie followed him. But then Ben stopped abruptly next to Martin, so that his buddy almost rammed him in the back with his tray.

"You've got cheese on your chin," he said quietly, and kept walking. I saw the two of them whisper as they walked away. They were probably having a good laugh at me and my cheese-smeared date's expense.

23

I stood up. "I have to go to the bathroom. I'll be right back."

"Okey dokey." Martin fidgeted in his chair like he was sitting on a pincushion, while I made sure I got away.

In the restroom, I was washing my hands when the door swung open, and Johanna swept in. She stood beside me, watching my every move in the mirror. A few freckles were sprinkled across on her perky nose.

"May I ask you something?"

"Sure," I answered with a sinking feeling.

"Is there something going on between you and Martin?" She lowered her gaze to the floor as if she had dropped something.

"Well... Uh..." I tore a paper towel from the dispenser. "We're just classmates, nothing more. I guess Martin must have gotten the wrong idea or something."

She looked up. "It doesn't look like that to me. I've known Martin for a while, you know?"

"Really, you have nothing to worry about," I reassured her and wanted to pat her shoulder, because I detected a hint of despair in her eyes—all because of Martin. Wow.

She dodged my hand and continued staring.

"You really can have him." I couldn't believe I was having this conversation about Martin.

"I don't get what he sees in you," she finally said, and despite the insult, I secretly couldn't have agreed more. Now Martin just needed to understand how much better he was off with Johanna.

"I better get going." I squeezed past her and escaped through the door.

As I reached the table, I grabbed my red cardigan from the back of the chair and slipped it on. "Sorry, but I really have to go. Thanks, this was fun."

Martin seemed disappointed. "Already? I thought we were going back to my place."

What? I was so glad I couldn't read minds. I seriously needed to get out of here.

When I got back to my apartment, I felt like I had aged twenty years and would have given anything for a hot bath. Unfortunately, we only had a shower. I would definitely put some distance between me and Martin, as Toby—my wise and knowledgeable roommate—had advised. How could I have been so wrong about Martin? In my naiveté, I'd actually pitied him as a poor nerd who couldn't get any dates.

As if the evening hadn't been bad enough, the door to Ben's room opened. I spun around, hastily pretending to hang my jacket on the hook. Instead of disappearing into one of the rooms, Ben stopped behind me. After a moment of hesitation, I turned around and found him staring.

"Why did you go out with that guy?"

Excuse me? I felt like I was being summoned to an audience with the Pope. "What business is it of yours?" Right now, I had no desire to explain myself to him.

"I just want to know if you went out with him because of me."

"Because of you?" Sometimes male logic was beyond me.

What in the world did this disastrous date have to do with him? "If you only went on this date because I always tease you about being uptight and stuff." He seemed contrite. "I just want to make sure you didn't do it to prove anything to yourself."

"Well, I didn't." Ben could be so complicated sometimes.

"Then why did you go out with him?"

"I don't know. *He* asked me." I could finally make it clear that I hadn't asked Martin out. "I wanted to give him a chance. Not everything is always about looks."

"It's not," he agreed. "That's what you think of me, isn't it? That I'm a superficial jerk who thinks only of himself and takes advantage of all women." His eyes darkened to tourmalines, black as night. He stood so close to me that his body warmth enveloped me like an embrace. I had to lean against the wall to stop myself from touching his chest, which rose and fell slightly as he breathed. As tense as he was, I didn't have the heart to tell him that this was exactly what I thought of him.

"Your life is none of my business," I declared instead. "You're your own person, and you can do whatever you like. Same as me." Why did I get the feeling he didn't like my answer?

"He's not your type," he said bluntly.

"You don't even know him." I tried to breathe evenly, because his irresistible scent wafted up my nose and made me all shaky.

"He will never be able to satisfy you."

In one fell swoop, I was back to earth and standing in our hallway.

"Do you ever think of anything else?" I shook my head. I was on the verge of seeing him in a different light, and now I had to admit, I was wrong yet again. My instincts had been way off.

"I don't just mean that kind of satisfaction," Ben whispered. He gently touched my temple with two fingers.

"But here too." His fingertips lingered on my skin, sending a tingling sensation down my back. His warm breath touched my cheek. I audibly gasped, at a loss of words. "And here," he whispered as his hand wandered down to my chest. He gently tapped my chest with a finger, right where my heart was beating like crazy. My stomach began to flutter, and my body craved his touch. I stood before him with trembling breath.

"That is why he will never be able to satisfy you," he repeated, unusually hoarse. With that, he turned away abruptly and disappeared into his room, while I remained standing rigidly in the same place.

Why did he tell me all these things? And why had he appeared so unexpectedly, only to leave again just as suddenly? What was wrong with him? I just couldn't figure him out.

24

I had managed to avoid Martin for a whole week. However, in order to do that, I'd had to skip the two classes we attended together, which didn't count as a long-term solution. Luckily, Rhashmi took the same classes, so I could borrow her notes. I was a pathetic coward. Toby had said something about *staying out of his way for a while*. That was a flexible concept, so I decided to stop hiding from Martin starting Monday. Ten days seemed like plenty of time to get over me. Just like yesterday, I waited for Rhashmi at the back entrance to snap pictures of her notes. When the door swung open, Rhashmi came out. She was wearing a super short denim miniskirt, which made her petite frame look amazing. I hurried over to her and waited while she rummaged through her bag.

"Don't you think your behavior's getting to be a bit much?" she chided as she handed over her notebook. "All this hide-and-seek just because of Martin. The guy took you out to the cafeteria, for God's sake. He should be ashamed and hiding, not you."

"He's hurt," I defended my date while I snapped pictures of Rhashmi's notes.

"He's a moron."

"Rhashmi," I rebuked her in shock.

"What?" She flipped her hair back. "He came over today after class complaining that you were just using him to get his *Financial Times* magazines."

My jaw dropped. "He actually said that? What a moron."

"See?"

"But I guess that means he's still mad."

"Why did you go out with him in the first place?" Rhashmi eyed me reproachfully. "I'd never go out with someone I wasn't serious about. What were you thinking?"

I saved myself the trouble of snidely pointing out to her that a certain Rhashmi Reinhardt had played a huge part in that. Granted, I'd agreed to go out with Martin in a moment of weakness, but she was the one who had set the ball rolling. On the other hand, I didn't know when I would be able to attend another lecture, so I didn't want to mess with her. I waved her off. "It's the weekend. I've had a terrible week. I'm going clubbing in Nuremberg with Caro tonight, and we're gonna party till the sun comes up."

Rhashmi stuffed her pad back in her bag. "You do that, have fun. He'll calm down sooner or later, and if not, I'll have a few words with him." Waving, she walked away, leaving me alone in my misery.

Maybe it would be best to stay at Caro's until Sunday night. She was still in the middle of her relationship crisis with Martha. Although Martha wanted to go out with us tonight, she had called for a *relationship break* for Saturday and Sunday, whatever that meant.

Exhausted, I returned to the apartment. I wanted to take a quick nap, since Caro had suggested going to *Mach 1* for dancing tonight, and we didn't need to bother showing up there before midnight. Luckily, Martha knew the bouncers, so we also wouldn't have to stand in line. Martha knew everyone who was anyone in this town. She had over two thousand Facebook friends and just as many followers on Instagram. I had just seventy-six, all of them locals, since I had broken off contact with my school friends. There was no way I was going to chance anyone from my past finding me.

I had just snuggled into bed and plugged in my earphones when the doorbell rang. I ignored the obnoxious ringing, because I'd heard noises coming from both Toby's and Ben's rooms. Let them get the door. After the sixth ring, one of them finally answered it. The next thing I heard was a squawky voice that I knew all too well.

"Is Luca home?"

"No idea." That was Toby. He knocked on my door. "Luca, are you in there?"

I pulled the blanket over my head. What now? Martin was here and wanted to talk to me. Couldn't the guy read any signals at all?

"Luca?" The knocking grew louder and more insistent, then the door opened. Why? If a person didn't react when you called their name, it usually happened for two reasons: either the person wasn't there, or didn't want to be disturbed.

"Luca, is that you under the blanket?"

Great! Could he have been any louder? Traitor. I threw the sheets off and sat up.

"Thanks a lot," I hissed, catching a confused look from Toby.

Toby jerked his thumb over his shoulder. "Oh, you didn't want to..."

"Never mind." Sighing, I got out of bed. Thanks to my tactless roommate, I had no other choice. He shrugged apologetically, as if mouthing *sorry* did any good now. I decided to play dumb. Martin was waiting for me in the hallway, both hands buried deep in his pockets. He was bouncing with his knees.

"Hi, Martin, what's up?"

"Like you need to ask." He pointed at me accusingly. "You stole my *Financial Times* magazines."

I stared. "Are you out of your mind? You forced them on me. I didn't even ask for them."

"Oh, yeah?" His left eyelid twitched.

"You know what? Just take your magazines, I'm not going to read them anyway."

Toby stood behind me "You mean the dusty pile in the corner?"

When I nodded, he disappeared into my room to get the magazines. To make matters worse, Ben's door opened. He stared at Martin in bewilderment as he was bounced on the balls of his feet.

Then he stopped in his tracks to say: "You led me on, you bitch."

"Excuse me?" I was speechless and felt blindsided.

"Sooner or later, you'll have to come back to class. Wait until I tell everyone what a teasing slut you are," he sneered, and I felt a tightness in my throat.

My hand weakly tugged at the neckline of my shirt so I could breathe more freely, as a fear I hadn't felt in a long time shook my whole body. Was everything starting over again? Hadn't I learned anything? Ben grabbed Martin by his collar and slammed him hard against the wall, before Toby soared past me into position next to Ben. They both towered over Martin by more than a full head. Ben didn't put much pressure on his neck, just held him in place and leaned in.

"Are you threatening our friend Luca?" he asked, while Toby braced one arm against the wall. His voice now took on a sharp edge. "We don't like that."

"She... She's a real bitch," Martin insisted.

"You won't be saying that again," Ben said with an edge to his voice that scared even me. "Did I hear you right? She's too scared to go to class because of you, asshole?"

"I never said she couldn't come to class," Martin defended himself like a petulant child.

"Stop your whining," Toby snapped. "You weren't crying a minute ago when you gave Luca a hard time."

Martin looked from one to the other, trembling.

"Let's get one thing clear, if you cause Luca problems on campus and we find out about it, we'll pay you a little visit, got it?" Ben tightened his fingers slightly around Martin's throat, who gasped. "I won't, I swear I won't. I promise."

Lightning fast, Ben changed his grip. One hand released Martin's neck, while the other moved to the back of his neck. Toby pressed the stack of magazines against his chest and opened the door as Ben pushed my fellow student out the door by the neck.

"Ouch, you're hurting me," Martin whined.

"You won't really get hurt unless you forget our warning. Now fuck off."

The door slammed shut with a bang, and I could breathe again.

My two roommates high-fived each other, then came towards me, grinning.

"How about a submarine?" Ben nodded to me.

"Okay, but just one." I smiled at them. For the first time, I could see the benefits of having male roommates. "Thanks, guys."

Toby put an arm around my shoulder as we strolled to the kitchen. Ben set the glasses on the table, and Toby poured. We sat down.

"Gosh, Luca, we can't leave you alone for a minute," Toby said. "That guy is a total psycho."

"Stop, just stop. I'd rather forget the whole thing, if you don't mind. File it under *lessons learned*."

We toasted each other and let our submarines sink, then chugged the orangey mixture.

"How about a little drinking contest?" Ben asked me with a wink. I grinned back and shook my head while the warmth of the alcohol spread through my abdomen.

"Never again." All of a sudden, everything felt different. I was comfortable with them, and for the very first time, I was glad the confused secretary had assigned me to this apartment suite. My boys were just fine.

"For Luca's own safety, we should insist that she bring all potential lovers home for us to approve before they're allowed to take her out," Toby suggested.

"That way, we can prevent the worst," agreed Ben. "Once they pass our test, then they can take Luca out."

"And only if she's home by midnight." Toby added, raising a finger.

"And no sleepovers," Ben concluded. "Everyone sleeps in their own beds," he added while Toby nodded affirmatively.

I snorted.

"I think the guys should also have to bring gifts when they pick Luca up, not just for her but for all of us roommates," Toby went on.

Ben walked over to the fridge and took out my fruit yogurt. "Do you plan on eating this?" He looked at me questioningly.

"No, take it," I replied generously, while Toby continued to think up further methods of torture for my future dates.

"It's probably for the best to give them a little scare right up front. Drop a few hints about our last stay in the nuthouse," Toby continued.

Ben came back with two bottles of beer and the fruit yogurt. "The proseccos are all gone," he told me.

"I know." I reached for the soda bottle. When I looked up, I noticed two faces staring at me and waved them off. "No vodka. Forget it, I have plans tonight."

"What are you up to?" Toby asked. "Another date?"

"Hell no." I shook my head vehemently. "And if I did, there's no way I would tell you two about my plans, after all the fun things you just dreamed up for my future dates. I pity your poor unborn daughters already. Somehow, I can't shake the feeling that the two of you are a little crazy, and that the joke's on me."

That made both of them crack up.

"No, really, what are you up to tonight?" Toby insisted.

"I'm taking the train to Caro's later, and we're going clubbing."

Ben shoved a spoonful of yogurt in his mouth and swallowed. "We're also going to Nuremberg tonight. If you want, we can give you a lift so you won't have to take the train all alone."

"That would be great." Happily, I accepted his offer because I honestly didn't like taking the train late at night by myself. "When are you leaving?

"Around seven-thirty. We're going to a party. And before that, we're meeting Erdie and Ellen for dinner."

"Oh." I shook my head. "That's too early for me. We're not going out until after ten. I'll take the train."

Ben scraped the rest out of the yogurt cup. It was unbelievable how quickly he could scarf down food.

"Well, come for a bite, and we'll drop you off at Caro's afterwards."

"Yeah," Toby agreed. "We don't plan to go to the party before ten anyway."

"You could ask Caro if she wants to join us for dinner," Ben suggested.

I thought about it. The timing sounded good. I could get to Caro's place more easily, and having dinner before was always good.

"Okay, I'll come along. Just let me jump in the shower." I looked at the red-and-white wall clock. "It's six o'clock already, I have to hurry. The bathroom is now mine for a while."

The two sighed.

"Just do it," Toby said stoically and clinked bottles with Ben.

After a slightly lengthy shower, I hastily threw together an outfit. Dressing up was usually not my thing, but Caro would kill me if I showed up for clubbing in my everyday clothes. More importantly, I was going to dinner with the guys—some very good-looking guys, and didn't feel like being a wallflower tonight. So, I searched in my closet for a suitable outfit, pushing my hangers apart, before I realized that I only owned comfortable clothes. Crap. What was I supposed to do now? I rummaged through my pile of laundry one more time and located my black skin-tight jeans. Although my bust was annoyingly large, my legs were nice and slim. Hopefully the pants would distract a little from my cleavage. I finally decided on a thin black wrap-around shirt that elongated my upper body optically, with a white lacey top peeking out from underneath.

I checked myself out from all angles in the wardrobe mirror. Well, still no Ellen, but I looked okay. My phone buzzed. A message from Caro that she was too broke to go out for dinner, but suggested I should just drop by her place afterwards. I told her I'd be there around ten and grabbed my few pieces of makeup. Most days, I didn't bother and was careful not to overdo it, but tonight, I wanted to look good.

25

Shortly before seven-thirty, I finally stepped out into the hallway. I had left the two boys a mere thirty minutes for the bathroom and felt a little guilty, which wasn't necessary since they were freshly showered and chatting in the kitchen by the time I emerged from my room. How did they do that in such a short time? As I approached, they looked up. Ben was wearing a black dress shirt, sleeves rolled up to his elbows. It emphasized his athletic upper body, and I knew right away that he could easily take home any woman tonight, which gave me a brief pang. His hair was tousled, but parted to one side and so effortlessly styled that it looked natural. Toby wore a tight gray v-neck and a stylish black leather jacket. They definitely knew how to dress fashionably.

"All done." I stopped in the doorway.

Toby gave a little wolf whistle. "Why don't you always dress like this? You look hot." He nodded appreciatively.

Ben, on the other hand, remained silent, but his gaze wandered from my face downward, before slowly working its way back up. When his eyes stopped on my bust, I suddenly felt naked, like a pin-up girl, because of where he was so obviously staring. If Ben dared to laugh at me or even made one little remark, I would turn on my heel and lock myself in

127

my room for the night. I nervously crossed an arm over my chest, casually grasping my shoulder. He really needed to stop ogling me.

"Shall we go?" I urged them.

We got into Ben's ancient metallic blue Audi. Of course, he had been granted the spot right next to the entrance of our building. I sat in the back and enjoyed letting myself be chauffeured. Trees and houses rushed past the side window, while the guys in the front talked, as so often, about some dull soccer game.

After a very fast trip, we arrived in downtown Nuremberg, lucky to have avoided getting a speeding ticket on the way. I pulled myself out of the low back seat while Toby pushed the passenger seat forward to let me out.

"The restaurant's about two blocks away," Ben remarked as he locked the car. "Getting a parking spot in Nuremberg is harder than picking up a woman."

I rolled my eyes. Sometimes he should really keep his mouth shut.

Toby fished his buzzing cell out of his jacket pocket. "Ellen and Erdie are already at La Gondola."

La Gondola?! Had I heard that correctly? We were going to an Italian restaurant? What was I supposed to order at a pizza place? There was nothing for me to eat there except salad.

"Can't we go somewhere else?" I asked cautiously.

"Why?" Ben buttoned up his gray corduroy jacket.

"Because I can't eat anything at a pizza place."

To my dismay, I saw the two exchange glances. The vibe of *Why did we bring her again?* was very easy to read.

"Come on, just make an exception for once. You won't gain weight right away." Ben measured me with what I thought was a dismissive look. "You're really not that fat, anyway."

Whoa. I couldn't believe it. "If you're going to spread that much charm around tonight, better strap on your walking shoes," I snapped.

With an eye roll, he replied. "There you go, putting every word in the wrong light. What mean thing did I say this time? Why are you always so touchy?"

"You're. Not. That. Fat," I repeated back to him slowly. He was really getting on my nerves tonight. I was this close to taking off.

"You can see for yourself that you're not fat. That's just your stupid insecurity talking, again."

I gasped. "Insecurity? Just because I don't have an ego that's completely blown out of proportion, like yours?"

Ben snorted. "As if you'd know the first thing about blowing…"

"You sexist assh…"

"Luca, since when do you even listen to Ben's bullshit?" Toby slipped an arm around my shoulders. "I'm sure we'll find something for you to eat." He tried cheering me up, so I decided to stop talking about it. After all, salad was great for your figure. I could always eat a chocolate bar at Caro's, or maybe not.

The restaurant was packed, and the guests were chatting over their pizzas or pasta. I ogled the towering plates longingly. Ellen and Erdie were sitting at a table in the back, and they waved as we approached. Thank God, Ben had stopped to say hi to some guys he knew.

"Hey, Shorty. How's it going?" Erdie beamed at me as if he were actually glad to see me.

"Hi," I answered curtly before greeting Ellen.

She looked gorgeous as always in a red mini dress and perfect makeup. We hugged for a moment before I sat down across from her. Toby kissed her tenderly on the lips, everything seemed fine between them again.

"I heard you had a bit of boy trouble." Ellen remarked, sympathy in her voice.

"I did, but the guys took care of it for me." I picked up the brown menu. "They have to be good for something if I feed them," I teased Toby, who playfully shook his fist at me.

"Don't look at me. I never touched your stuff."

"That's true, we have another specialist for that." I let my gaze wander through the restaurant. Ben was still engaged in an animated conversation.

"Are you coming to the party?" Ellen sipped her water.

"No, I have other plans."

"Too bad. I'm stuck with the boys all by myself again."

"Oh, don't worry, we won't be in your hair all night." Erdie replied, taking a big swig of his beer.

"I'm not worried," she declared. "Especially not about that one." She nodded vaguely in Ben's direction. "I'm surprised he still finds fresh meat. You'd think he'd have sampled everything out there by now."

"Cut it out, Ellen." Toby sounded annoyed.

"Actually, you should thank Ben for getting you two together." Erdie flexed his middle and ring fingers when he pointed at them. Probably some cool sprayer pose or something like that. How old was he? Thirteen? "I really don't get what your problem is with Ben. He only came tonight because you promised to let up on him."

Ellen leaned back. "I'm not doing wrong, or do you see him sitting here?"

I followed the conversation with growing surprise. Why *did* she badmouth Ben all the time?

"He's coming," Toby hissed.

Taking the seat next to me, Ben ignored Ellen as best he could, and addressed Erdie. "Hey, man, did you bring the CD?"

Erdie slapped his forehead. "Damn it, I forgot."

"Never mind." Ben reached for a menu and studied it.

A plump Italian waitress came to our table to take our order. "Buona sera. Are you ready to order?"

Ben closed the menu. "A large Coke and a ham and mushroom pizza, please."

The woman wrote everything down. While the others ordered, I scoured the menu, hunting for something gluten-free.

"Why don't you get the Vienna Schnitzel and fries?" Ben suddenly suggested.

"I can't eat the breading."

"How about just fries, then?" He sounded annoyed, so I decided to ignore him. Why didn't he just mind his own business? Sometimes he could be such a jerk.

"Is the deep fryer used for anything besides fries?" I asked the waitress who, to my dismay, nodded.

"For the potato croquettes."

"Then fries won't work."

"Why?" Ben butted in again. "They don't fry them at the same time."

"No, but they use the same oil," I said slowly, as if speaking to a toddler.

"Oh, boy," he said, exchanging another annoyed look with Toby.

"I'll have a large garden salad and a glass of Lambrusco," I said, closing the menu resolutely, hoping to escape Ben's company as quickly as possible.

"I'll have that too." Ellen smiled at me. "But a small one. I have a lingerie shoot on Monday."

Ellen told me more about her job while the guys talked loudly between themselves over our heads. Three waiters returned with our food. Ben's pizza smelled tempting, and I was sure he was going to make a big deal about it just to spite me. I was amazed at how well I knew him by now, but decided not to give him a platform to annoy me. Instead, I smiled at one of the waiters who had winked at me earlier. Of course, Ben didn't even notice me flirting with the nice Italian guy. Typical, he was so blind. When the waitress put my salad down in front of me, I groaned inwardly. This was unbelievable. I couldn't even eat my salad. Three home-made breadsticks were arranged appetizingly across my salad bowl, effectively contaminating all the leaves they touched. If only I had opened my mouth earlier! I usually asked if restaurants sprinkled croutons or something like that over their salads. But Ben had made me so insecure with his bad mood that I hadn't had the courage to ask. And now I wouldn't even get to enjoy my salad, while he happily munched away on his stupid pizza. I wanted to scream.

"What is it now?" he griped. "Is something wrong again? They didn't decorate it nicely enough?"

"There's bread on top." I sighted, wistfully looking at my bowl while the other two guys dug into their pasta dishes. Even Ellen had a bite of Toby's spaghetti carbonara.

"Just take them off," Ben replied, as if I were dense.

"I still can't eat it."

He put his silverware aside. "How long have you been on this diet?"

"Seventeen years."

Ben shook his head. "And in all that time, you've never had a slice of pizza or a roll?"

"None that contained gluten."

"Leave her alone, if she doesn't want it," Toby interjected. "Why do you two always have to fight about everything?"

Ben ignored him and turned to me instead. I wanted to crawl under the table.

"So, how do you even know you can't eat normal things? Maybe you're depriving yourself for nothing." He took a slice of pizza and held it up to my face. The aroma of melted cheese reached my nose, and I wondered what a real Italian pizza would taste like. I'd never eaten one before.

"Why don't you at least try it?" Ben held it closer to my lips.

The others looked at me expectantly. What should I do now?

"Why not?" Toby shrugged his shoulders. "Ben is right. Maybe it's just in your mind."

The stupid pizza slice had me under its spell. I couldn't

take my eyes off the melted cheese. I sat there like a hypnotized rabbit in front of a snake.

"The pizza's really good here." Ellen pointed at Ben's plate and continued eating her salad.

Maybe I should give it a try to see if I was really as sick as I thought I was. Maybe I was lucky and had recovered from my celiac disease by now, but I would never find out if I didn't even try something containing gluten. But a little voice of reason whispered in my head, warning me that I shouldn't take the chance. I listened to it and obeyed the words of warning. I pushed Ben's arm aside. "Just drop it, will you?" Couldn't this guy just shut up for once?

"Yeah, leave her alone, man," Erdie said, smiling at me encouragingly. At least one of them seemed to have some brain cells left.

"Then don't." Ben took a big bite of his pizza and made delighted sounds while chewing. "This is so good. Sure, you don't want some?" He held the slice in front of me again. "You don't even know what you're missing. We can work off those calories later tonight, don't worry. I'd be glad to help you with that." He grinned before shoving the rest of the pizza slice in his mouth. He could choke on it for all I cared.

"Don't spoil my appetite," I snapped. All eyes were on me. I was the center of their annoyed attention. Somehow, I felt like Forrest Gump sitting on that bench, spouting what his bench mates perceived as slow-witted nonsense. I decided to ignore my companions and finish the meagre rest of my meal as quickly as possible, only to sneak away later with some excuse like, *Screw you, Ben.*

Ben flicked a breadstick off my bowl, making it touch a whole row of lettuce leaves. Was he nuts? Everybody laughed; they all seemed to be on Ben's side now.

"Stop that crap. Don't touch my food. What's wrong with you?" I elbowed him, hoping I'd given him a bruise.

"This is beyond ridiculous," he declared, as he kept eating his pizza. "You're such a princess."

"And now I remember why I can't stand you." With the tips of my fingers, I gathered the rest of the breadsticks off my bowl. Dammit! Dammit! Dammit! Dammit! Dammit! What should I do now? The others had turned back to their food. They continued to exchange glances with Ben. Why with him?

"Luca, aren't you taking this a bit far?" Toby asked cautiously.

I decided to ignore everyone and not take the bait. Instead, I peeled off the top layer of lettuce. The rest should be edible. I'd be on my way, as soon as I finished. Ben was dead to me. I speared some arugula with my fork and ate everything that seemed safe.

"I like you much better like this," I heard Ben mock. "Almost normal," he added unnecessarily.

"Shut up, Nowak." I took a large sip of my wine and leaned back.

The others were chatting about the party they were going to later, thankfully without me, when my stomach started to rumble. With a twinge of nausea, I tried hard to concentrate on the fake bouquet of flowers on the table. But then the first wave of nausea hit, and my intestines cramped up with a jerk. I groped for my wallet and put it on the table to pay my bill as quickly as possible, because I had to get out of here. The nausea intensified, and sweat was beading on my forehead. I desperately tried to keep the contents of my stomach in place.

Ellen looked at me intently. "Are you okay?"

I nodded. "I need to go to the bathroom, be right back." Jumping up, I dumped over my wine glass. While the Lambrusco spread a dark purple over the white tablecloth, I hurried through the restaurant with one hand in front of my mouth. I wouldn't be able to hold it in much longer. In panic, I looked around for the restrooms, but couldn't see a sign anywhere, so I raced out the front door.

26

The first gush of vomit hit the ground right outside the pizzeria. Retching and choking, I stumbled around the corner to get away from there. My stomach contracted rhythmically, my eyes were blurred with tears, and my airway was blocked. I gasped furiously for air, while the bile burned its way up my esophagus. The cramps became more severe, and I had to walk bent over, supporting myself on walls, street lamps, and parked cars. Again, I threw up. With one hand clasped around a street sign, my body threatened to collapse. My stomach alternated between stinging pain and violent tearing sensations. I knew there was a taxi stand somewhere close by, all I wanted was to go home and lie down in bed. Doubled over, I staggered on until a vicious cramp forced me to my knees. The convulsion sensation worsened, as if fiery tongs were reaching down my throat to rip my guts out. Eventually, I fell over forwards and panted, trying to breathe through the pain, but it wouldn't ease up. My arms and legs were numb, unable to carry me any longer. Slowly, I sank to the ground, scraping the asphalt with my fingernails, searching for support, while the pain literally crushed me. As if through fog, I heard a woman's voice.

"Can we help you?"

I struggled to open my eyes. A lady was crouching next to me, looking at me with a worried expression. Next to her stood a man, but I only saw his shoes and pants. The wind seemed to call my name from afar.

"A cab," I gasped with my last ounce of strength, as I pressed my fist against my burning chest. "Please call me a cab."

"I think we'd better call an ambulance." I heard the man say.

I raised one arm. "No, a cab." A little bile dribbled from the corner of my mouth, and the woman stood up. They were debating what to do.

"She needs to see a doctor," the man said under his breath.

"You're right," she agreed, then someone shouted, "Luca!" through the streets, but I couldn't move. My intestines were knotting up, as if someone were tearing me to pieces. The cramps intensified, radiating into my thighs.

Someone touched my shoulder, shook me gently, and I gasped for breath.

"Luca, what's wrong with you?" It was Ben, his voice was shaky.

"Diet mistake," I groaned, "nothing to worry about."

"Should we call an ambulance?" I heard the man ask again; the couple was still standing next to me.

"That would probably be best." Ben sounded terrified.

"No," I gasped. "They can't do anything." I paused and tried to breathe through another seizure. "It'll go away on its own. Will... Will you take me home?"

"You guys live together?" the lady asked.

"Yes." Ben knelt down and stroked the sweat-soaked hair from my face. "I'll take care of her. Thank you."

"Okay." The couple walked away, calling "Get well soon" in our direction.

"Luca, God, I'm so sorry. Can you stand up?"

I shivered on the cold pavement, while flashes of heat burned my body on the inside.

"Yes, I want to go home." I tried to lift my head up but felt too weak. Ben pulled me gently to my feet and held me up. However, the sudden change in position caused my stomach to contract in another jolt. I retched and retched while Ben supported me. Eventually, he reached under my knees and picked me up. Exhausted, I laid my head against his shoulder, my heart pounding irregularly against my ribs. I felt like I was going to faint. Over and over again, I writhed in pain.

After a while, Ben said softly: "Luca, we're at the car. Can you stand here for a moment so I can unlock it?"

With my eyes closed, I nodded even though I wasn't sure if my legs could hold me. My knees shook, and agonizing pain burned my esophagus. Ben set me carefully down on my feet, still supporting me, while he fumbled in his pocket for the keys. He opened the door, eased me into the seat, and then strapped me in.

"Are you alright?"

I nodded, my eyes still closed, then I heard him start the engine and felt the car move slowly. The motion only made the nausea worse, and I kept dry-heaving. I pulled up my knees. When my cell phone rang, I fished it out of my jacket pocket but felt too weak to answer and let it ring in my hand until Ben took it.

"It's Caro," he said, taking the call. "Hey Caro, it's Ben. Luca isn't doing so well; I'm just giving her a ride home... She's caught something... Yeah, caught something," he repeated more decisively. "No, you don't have to come, I'll stay with her tonight... Okay, I'll let her know. Bye."

He put my phone in his pocket and then pulled out his own.

"Erdie, Luca's not well. I'm taking her home. You guys go on without me, okay? No, there's nothing you can do, I've got it... Yeah, sure, because of that. Shit... I'll let her know. Bye. Caro and Erdie hope you get to feeling better soon."

"Thanks," I gasped through the unrelenting pain. I

wanted to die, to jump out of the moving car just to end my agony, but I couldn't move.

Ben stopped right outside the door of our building and helped me get out of the car.

"You'll get towed if you park here," I gasped, holding onto his shoulders so I wouldn't keel over.

"Fuck that." He picked me up again and carried me the entire three flights upstairs. I never would have made it up the steps on my own. In the apartment, he laid me down on my bed, where I desperately tried to ease my cramps by curling up into the fetal position.

Ben sat down beside me and stroked my back. Eventually, I let my neck relax, unable to hold back the tears anymore. The pain just wouldn't let up, I felt like I was being ripped apart. With one finger, Ben wiped the tears from my wet cheeks.

"I'm so sorry, Luca. Please forgive me. I'm the biggest idiot in the whole world. Shit."

I could hear by the sound of his voice how much he blamed himself.

"I shouldn't have eaten it," I gasped, as Ben took off my shoes.

"I'm gonna take your jeans off now, alright? So you'll be more comfortable. I won't look, I promise." He carefully unbuttoned my pants and pulled down the zipper, then he peeled my jeans off and pulled the covers over me. I shivered and felt dizzy, but without the pressure around my waist, I actually felt a little better.

"Be right back." Ben disappeared while I continued to suffer. I sat up, since laying down made my pain worse, and leaned against the cool wall. My left arm, with which I supported myself on the mattress, began to tremble from the strain. The hard wall hurt my temple and sent a sharp pain into my eye, but I couldn't move. Then Ben came back.

"Why aren't you lying down?" Gently, he put something

warm on my stomach. A hot water bottle, and it helped ease the cramps a little.

"I can't lie down," I gasped. "It only hurts more."

He slid his hand between my face and the wallpaper, reducing the pressure on my temple. Then he sat down behind me and lifted my wobbly arm off the mattress.

"Lean against me, I'll support you."

With my knees pulled up, I leaned my head against his chest. Ben wrapped his arms around me and rested his hands on the hot water bottle.

"I don't even know where to start to tell you how sorry I am," he whispered in my ear. "I didn't mean for this to happen."

His body warmth felt good, but I wasn't able to talk. Luckily, the chills slowly subsided, and the stomach cramps gradually eased up a little, though I still felt as nauseous as before. I clung to Ben like a little baby sloth and closed my eyes. I felt safe in his arms, and it was nice not to be alone. Carefully, Ben reached under my shirt and rubbed my battered stomach in a circular motion while I cuddled up to him. His soothing touch soon made me slip into a dreamless sleep.

27

When I opened my eyes, the sun was shining into my room, spreading a bright beam of light across the blue-gray carpet. I was alone in my bed. Ben was gone. I cautiously groped down to my stomach where the hot-water bottle was sitting. It was still warm; Ben must have refilled it recently. To my relief, I wasn't in pain anymore, only a lingering sense of nausea remained. However, I felt exhausted, as if I had partied all week long. Slowly, I sat up. My blood pressure was still low, and every move I made was met with dizziness. After waiting a bit, I felt strong enough to get up. I was still wearing the thin cardigan and the wrap-around shirt from the night before, as well as my lilac-colored cotton underwear. Ben had undressed me, as I now became embarrassingly aware. He must have seen my not-entirely-attractive granny panties. With a sigh, I went to the wardrobe before Ben could swoop in again, grabbed a purple sweatshirt and my cream-colored sweatpants. I had to sit back down to dress myself, because suddenly white dots were dancing before my eyes.

Finally, I made my shaky way to the kitchen for a glass of water. My throat felt dry and sore. To my surprise, Ben was standing at the kitchen counter scrubbing the worktop, the fridge was gaping wide open. He had taken out all shelves and set them upright in the sink.

"What are you doing?" I leaned against the door frame.

He paused, his eyes resting on me. For a moment, he looked at me silently, the hint of a smile appeared on his face.

"Good morning. You're upright again. That's good." He walked over to me. "You'd better sit down, you're still very pale."

I did him the favor. Judging by his words, I must have looked terrible. I didn't even want to know what my blood levels were, and I had better not mention that to Ben. He seemed remorseful enough as it was.

"I'm much better. Today, I feel like I was dragged by a car for only two miles."

"Jeez, what was it like yesterday?"

"You don't wanna know." I struggled to smile. "I survived it, that's enough for me."

He showed me a yellow and green box. "Chamomile tea. I bought it for you this morning."

"Thanks, that's exactly what I need right now." I could tell he wanted to make up for last night. "What are you doing?" I pointed at the empty fridge.

"Cleaning so that no crumbs or anything with gluten in it will be flying around. I really don't want you to get you sick again."

I was touched by his concern. Who would have thought he could be this considerate? I almost didn't recognize him. He set a steaming cup on the table in front of me. The subtle aroma of chamomile rose up to my nose.

"Thank you. Where did you get that hot water bottle yesterday? It really helped me a lot."

He smiled a little bashfully. "I often feel cold in bed in the winter, so I like to put it under my covers. But don't ever tell anyone!" he threatened jokingly.

I giggled. How cute. The cool womanizer felt chilly in his

bed at night. "I won't tell anyone if you let me borrow it sometimes in the winter."

"Hey, that's blackmail," he protested while I blew on my steaming tea. His tousled hair fell across his forehead, giving him the daring look of an adventurer.

"Exactly."

He patted my shoulder. "You can have it whenever you like. I'll even warm it up for you. You can't imagine how happy I am to see you sitting in front of me. I was this close to calling an ambulance yesterday." His voice echoed last night's scare.

"A mistake on a gluten-free diet looks worse than it actually is. It causes a lot of pain and nausea, but you don't usually need to go to the hospital."

His fingers were digging into my shoulder. "I'm such an ignorant prick. God, I'm the worst."

"Come on now." I reached for his hand, but he flinched. "After all, I'm to blame as well. Ultimately, I ate that salad, even though I should've known it was probably contaminated."

"But only because I pushed you to."

I was startled that it wasn't just remorse and pity coming from his mouth, it was self-loathing.

"I wasn't taking care of myself," I said decisively. "Things went sideways yesterday, but it was what it was. We screwed up. So what? Happens to me all the time."

Ben stared at me with his black-blue eyes, as a fever glowed in them that I'd never seen before. He looked at me intensely, as if trying to read my mind. But I wasn't the one keeping him out. He had his guard up. Something inside of Ben kept him from showing me what he was feeling. His eyes displayed the tortured expression that I'd seen flash once before when he'd let his guard down for a moment. I didn't look away, but tried to make a connection. Finally, I got up and reached out to touch the dimple next to the corner of his mouth; lightly stroking it with my finger. It was soft, a tiny little dent. Ben stood still and breathed shallowly.

"My stupid dimple won't help me get out of this either," he whispered, and I chuckled. How things had changed since the day I moved in, and yet there was still this invisible wall between us. Right now, he was building it higher to keep me out. I had to accept that. Probably I just wasn't his type. In fact, I was sure of it.

"What about your car?" I asked, to break the tension.

"It was still outside the building. After you fell asleep, I went out and moved it. I figured you probably wouldn't want to see my face first thing when you woke up anyway."

Why did he keep doing that the whole time? Why was he beating himself up? Granted, the night could have gone better, but he acted as if I were on his conscience.

"I've seen worse things you know," I said, attempting to be funny.

"You were in terrible pain because I'm a stupid selfish jerk who can't put himself into other people's shoes," he snapped. "So, stop acting like it was nothing."

"Wow, you really belong under lock and key," I replied in mock outrage. "Listening to you talk, you must be more terrible than all the dictators of world history put together. May I have another cup of tea, Comrade Stalin?"

Ben paused, shaking his head. A tiny smile stole across his face.

"Hang on." He walked out and came back with my wallet and my phone. "You left your money at the pizza place. That was pretty careless of you."

"I had other things on my mind, but thanks."

"Toby also called this morning to ask how you're doing. They stayed with friends in Nuremberg because they couldn't get a ride home without me."

"Oh." I covered my mouth with one hand. "I'm sorry about that."

Ben rolled his eyes, rustled a tea bag out of its paper

packaging, and sank it into my cup, which he refilled with hot water.

"Here you go." With a flourish, he placed the beverage on the table.

Then he turned back to the fridge again and slid the clean shelves back in place. His shoulder blades bulged sexily under his tight-fitting white t-shirt. The hem of his shirt slipped, exposing a part of his tanned back above the waistband of his jeans. A tiny birthmark adorned his spine, and it took all my strength not to slide my hands under his shirt to explore this small, dark elevation with my fingers. Yesterday, he had held me in his arms, but I had been too sick to enjoy it. I wondered if he would ever hug me again. I strolled towards the door, because Ben had just closed the fridge and thus finished his implied little strip show.

"Hey, wait a second." I heard him behind me. "You dropped something."

I turned around as he leaned down to pick something up.

My ID!

It must have slipped out of my wallet.

My ID!!!

The shock almost knocked me off my feet.

"No!" In panic, I rushed up to him to rip the plastic card out of his hand, but Ben was faster and held up his arm. And there, the old look of mischief was back on his face.

"What's the matter? Why are you making such a fuss?"

"Give it back. Right now." My voice rose higher. Under no circumstances could I let him look at it—that would be the end of me. Wringing my hands, I begged, "Please give it back." My voice squeaked like a rusty hinge.

He looked at me quizzically. "Why are you freaking out?"

"Give. It. Back!" I hissed and jumped up his arm like a kangaroo, but with no luck. He stretched his arm up even higher. Finally, he turned halfway around to examine my ID in peace. Ben Nowak was still a jerk. My lower lip quivered as he turned to me, trying hard not to burst out laughing.

"You lied to us," he exclaimed in amusement when he gave me my ID back. I snatched it out of his hand.

"I'll kill you if you tell anyone. I mean it. I'm not kidding, you hear me?"

"You'd go to jail for that." He grinned when I nodded furiously.

"Lucrezia Vogt." My full name literally melted in his mouth. "What were your parents thinking?"

Groaning, I closed my eyes, letting my head fall back.

"My father is a history professor," I reluctantly explained. "He named me after Lucrezia Borgia, the daughter of Pope Alexander VI. He wrote his dissertation about him." Why in the world did I talk Ben out of his guilty conscience earlier? I couldn't think of one good reason. Why hadn't I encouraged him instead? To jump off a bridge or something? Now it was all too late.

"Promise me you won't tell anyone my real name." I clung to his arm. "Promise me!"

His gaze wandered to my hands clawing at him. "It's all right, I won't tell. And now we're gonna get you back to the asylum, okay?" He laughed.

I let go of him and tried to look a bit less like a crazy person. Maybe I could somehow secretly get rid of Ben before he opened his big mouth and told anyone about his hot discovery. Perhaps I could get my hands on some hydrochloric acid or something similarly effective. In desperation, I went through all kinds of murder scenarios.

"You're thinking about how you could get rid of me now, aren't you?"

I nodded to intimidate him.

"How would you do it?"

"There's an old, half-buried sewage pipe by the railroad tracks. You'd fit perfectly in it. It would take a long time for someone to find you there," I threatened him, which unfortunately seemed to have no effect at all.

He just sat down again and leaned back. "And how are you going to get me there?"

"I'd roll you up in a rug or something."

He rubbed his chin. "I'm way too heavy, you'd never be able to carry me by yourself. But you could saw me into pieces to get me out of here," he suggested, and I thought this was a pretty good idea.

"All I'd need is a chainsaw. I can get one of those at any hardware store."

"But it would be a huge mess, I can tell you that much. Toby would be so mad if you got our bathroom all full of blood."

With a heavy heart, I ditched my murderous plot. Unfortunately, Ben was right.

I sat down next to him and took a sip of my now lukewarm tea.

He leaned in. "I won't tell anyone, I promise." He held up three fingers. "After all, I owe you one. Besides, you're totally exaggerating. Lucrezia actually sounds kinda cool."

"Yeah, very cool." Dammit. It wasn't just the stupid name that bothered me, but the reason why I'd chosen to shorten it.

28

W e sat in silence for a while. Ben had poured himself a glass of water while I sipped my tea.

"Shall I make you something to eat?" he asked eventually, but I shook my head.

"No thanks, I don't really feel up to eating."

But Ben wouldn't let up. Sometimes he could be really persistent. "You should eat something. It's almost lunchtime, and you're still so pale that you're starting to scare me."

Subtlety was certainly not one of Ben's strengths.

"Alright, I'll have a rice cake. They're up there on the shelf."

He got up and rummaged around in the cupboard until he pulled out a white roll. "You eat these? They look like Styrofoam."

"I'll have to be on a bland diet for a few days to ease my stomach into digesting normal food, or else I'll get cramps all over again."

His guilty countenance hit me on the spot. He handed me the rice cakes.

"It's not a big deal." I broke off a piece, put it in my mouth, and chewed.

Ben looked at me expectantly. "How is it?"

I broke off another bit. "It's fine, tastes good with the tea. I don't feel queasy anymore."

"See? You just needed something in your stomach. Told you." He sat back down.

"You took good care of me." I sipped my tea. "You put me into bed, you even took my pants off." I faltered.

"What—do you mean?" Rigidly, Ben waited for an answer. My stomach started to go queasy again, but not from the rice cakes.

"Nothing," I brushed it off. "Nothing, really. It's just…" I searched for the right words. "It just doesn't feel so great knowing you undressed me when I was in such bad shape."

His larynx bobbed as he swallowed. Oh, no, that had come out all wrong.

"Are you asking if I felt you up? Why don't you ask me directly if the lecher took advantage of your situation?" He jumped up and seemed deeply hurt. "Let me reassure you. I certainly didn't feel any urge to get into your pants last night."

"That's not what I meant at all."

"What did you mean then?"

"You…" I lowered my eyelids. This was hard. "You've seen so many beautiful girls, and then there I was yesterday, the mess I must have looked like… And then… That."

"That's a load of garbage." He finished the sentence for me. Before I could say anything back, he grabbed me by the wrist and pulled me to the hallway. He stopped in front of the mirror. He made me stand right in front of it, while he stood behind me and held me tightly by my upper arms.

"What do you see?" he asked, looking at my reflection in the mirror.

Shocked, I held my breath. I looked terrible. My skin was ghostly pale, and I had dark circles under my eyes.

"Oh my God," I gasped. "I look like a drowned corpse."

"Nonsense." Ben sounded annoyed. "So, you're a little pale. But take a closer look." He ran his knuckles across my cheek. "Your skin is velvety soft, and usually you have a bit of color here. Every time you smile, your eyes sparkle. When you lower your eyelids and slowly look up again, it goes right through me—like a jolt of electricity."

Staring at my own face, I felt he must have been talking about someone else. His chest pressed gently against my back; I couldn't help it and leaned into him.

"And I really don't get why you always wear these baggy clothes either," he whispered into my ear, his lips touching my earlobe as if by chance.

A tingling sensation spread throughout me. "Because... Because..." I couldn't tell him the real reason. His arms moved around my waist, inch by inch, while he watched every move I made in the mirror. I let him do it and leaned my head against his neck, with a wildly pounding heart.

He caressed me gently beneath my breasts, brushing them as if unintentionally with his thumbs. "You're so sexy," he murmured hoarsely. "When you showed up in the kitchen last night it almost blew me away."

"My breasts are way too big!" burst out of me.

Ben held me tighter and continued to caress me in this amazingly tender way. "They're beautiful. There's absolutely no need to hide them. Your breasts suit you; you are curvy and exciting. But that's not all. You're funny and pretty. You're easy to talk to and joke around with. When you're angry, your eyes sparkle like diamonds. It's all part of who you are. All of it makes you attractive." He had lowered his head while talking, now he was watching me over my shoulder while he kept stroking me gently.

I closed my eyes, wanting him to never stop. My breath quickened as he leaned his cheek against my head—then a key turned in the lock, and we separated hastily. The door opened. Toby and Ellen appeared in the hallway, observing us with interest. I was sure they had noticed how we jumped apart.

"Hey, what are you doing in the hallway?" Toby pulled

his key out of the lock, while Ellen stared at us with a stony expression.

"We were just talking." Ben shrugged

I brushed back a strand of hair and threw Ben a glance. His face didn't reveal what was going on inside him, but he looked past me to Ellen.

"Are you feeling better?" Ellen asked.

"Yes, everything's okay now. I just felt a little sick yesterday," I hastened to explain.

"I'm sure Ben nursed you back to health quickly." Ellen sounded snide.

I nodded. "Yes, he did."

Toby tapped me on the shoulder. "So, your cee-le whatchamacallit wasn't your imagination after all."

"Nope." I winked at Ben as discreetly as possible, but he wasn't paying any attention to me, instead he stared at the floor.

"Well, guys?" Toby nodded towards the kitchen. "Anyone up for a late breakfast?" He held up a bakery bag.

"I don't feel like eating today. I'm going back to bed to try and sleep this off," I declined.

"What about you?" Toby addressed Ben.

"I already ate."

With a shrug, Toby pointed Ellen, who had been leaning against the wall with her arms crossed, towards the kitchen.

Ben ran his fingers through his hair before he finally looked at me. "I should get some sleep too, didn't get much last night." He went to his door and put one hand on the doorknob.

Reluctantly, I also started to move. Even though I didn't want him to disappear into his room, and if he did, I wanted him with me. Why had he said all those things earlier if he was acting so nonchalant now? I didn't dare ask him though. I was just about to turn into my room, when I heard a quiet "Luca," coming from his direction.

"Yes?" My heart jumped.

"About just now."

"Yes." I held my breath.

"I just wanted to show you how men see you—in general. Okay?"

"Okay," was all I could think to say. What a bastard! Anger rose up in me, anger and humiliation at such a cocky statement. How right he was earlier! He wasn't able to put himself in other people's shoes; he was much too preoccupied with himself. Of course, he assumed I'd taken his words to heart. Because no girl could resist him. So, that's how it worked when he was on the prowl. He charmed women, made them feel special, and when he was done with them, he showed his conquests the cold shoulder afterwards. Grudgingly, I had to admit his act had worked on me too. This guy was definitely out of my league. Ben had mastered this art to perfection, and the most amazing thing was that I hadn't even realized for a moment that he was just stringing me along.

few days later, Caro and I met at Starbucks to pick up coffee to go. She'd just come from a job interview at an art gallery, and we used the opportunity to catch up before her shift at the fitness club started. I ordered a caramel macchiato to test whether my digestive system was fully operational again. Caro had a caffè mocha. With our cups in our hands, we strolled along the pedestrian zone towards the city square. There was a light breeze, and cotton-ball clouds frolicked in the sky above us.

"What happened at the gallery? Did you get the job?" I sucked at my straw, carefully tracking my internal state.

"Not really yet." Sighing, she headed for a park bench. "It seems there are several applicants, and now the boss has given each of us an assignment. We have two weeks to put together a portfolio, and she wants to make a decision based on that."

I sat down next to her on one of the benches. "You'll nail it, no question. You're such a good artist. She'd be stupid not to hire you."

Caro crossed her legs. "She doesn't just want the portfolio. In two weeks, she wants to test us all at the same time on a Saturday to see how we work under pressure." She snorted.

"As if I were applying to MoMA in New York and not some crummy little gallery in downtown Erlangen."

"Why do you let her walk all over you like that?" I took a deep sip of my macchiato, and to my delight, my stomach seemed to be behaving today.

"Because Nuremberg and everything around is like a developing country when it comes to art. I'll be lucky enough to find a job in this field at all."

"That sucks."

She nodded.

"How are things with Martha?" I asked cautiously. Although Caro's relationship status on Facebook still showed *in a relationship*, she was being very quiet about it, which was never a good sign.

"Martha." She groaned as if in pain. "Martha says she's getting tired of our incessant relationship discussions. Can you believe that?" She propped her heel on the bench. "We're only arguing because she won't commit to this relationship 100%."

"Have you told your parents about her, yet?" I threw my empty cup into a trash can next to the bench.

"No."

"I see."

She lightly punched me on the arm. "What do you mean, *I see*?"

"That you're not 100% committed to her either."

"But I totally am. At least, here in Nuremberg. Besides, it's complicated. My father had a bypass a few years ago. What do I do if I spill the beans, and he has a heart attack? I couldn't handle having him on my conscience."

I burst out laughing. It was amazing how Caro always turned everything around. "Take a defibrillator with you, just in case."

Caro crossed her arms. "I'm so sick of fighting with Martha. Sometimes I think I'd be better off straight."

Giggling, I leaned my head against her shoulder. "Oh, that's not easier at all, believe me."

"What's going on with Ben? Has he seriously not tried to hit on you again?"

"Definitely not." I shook my head. "I think he's even been avoiding me."

"What's with that guy?" Caro smacked her forehead theatrically. "At first, he almost jumps on you..."

"He didn't jump on me, he hugged me."

"Okay." Caro rolled her eyes; it was obvious she thought they were the same thing. "So, first he hugs you and whispers sweet nothings in your ear, and the next thing you know, he pretends nothing happened?"

"That's exactly how it was," I grimly agreed. "You should've seen him. He almost had me buying the stuff he spouted. It was so electric between us, and the next moment... Boom! Sorry, Luca, I didn't mean me, but some random guys who might be into you." I snorted. "He's still nice and polite and everything. When I run into him in the kitchen he always asks if I want a drink and stuff. But..." I sat up.

Caro hung on my every word. "Here it comes," she whispered.

"He makes sure we're never alone in a room. If Toby disappears, he also leaves immediately. He's acting so immature."

"Makes me glad I am a lesbian," sighed Caro with relief. Her own drama obviously didn't seem so bad to her anymore.

"You can be," I mumbled, pushing all thoughts of Ben aside for now. He wasn't worth the headache. That particular evening, after he had dragged me in front of the mirror, he had gone out and brought back a pretty redhead to the apartment. We ran into each other in the hallway when I came out of the bathroom. Without a word, he had propelled his new bed bunny into his room. That was all it took for him to put me in my place. But damn, that had hurt. Why was it suddenly so painful to see him with other women? His bedmates had never bothered me before now.

"Hey, I have to get to the gym. My shift starts in half an hour."

"That's okay. I have to go to class too."

"What about that weirdo who was harassing you?"

I got up. "Martin?"

"Yes." Caro took my arm as we walked.

"Thank God he's ignoring me. It seems like the boys' threats worked. He even dropped out of our study group. Rhashmi told me everyone was sick of his stupid babbling anyway; they just didn't say anything because I was being so nice to him."

"Be happy he's leaving you alone."

"Oh, I definitely am."

"Just imagine if it had gotten out of hand the way it did when…"

The hair stood up on the back of my neck. "I don't want to talk about it, okay? Never again."

"Course not." She stroked my arm.

At the crosswalk, we parted ways, since the campus was in the other direction.

"Bye, I'll call you." I hugged Caro.

"And don't forget the LGBTQ gala in two weeks."

"I'm looking forward to it." I marched off to get to my class on time, which unfortunately Martin attended as well. Although he stayed out of my way, I felt him staring at me the entire hour and regretted going out with him for the hundredth time.

30

Around three in the afternoon I was sitting at my desk studying. Toby had been picked up by some friends to go play soccer, and Ben was off at the Ark. Apparently, the kids there had a basketball tournament today, which he and a couple of coaches had organized. Those two were way too athletic for my taste.

Over and over again, I caught myself logging into Facebook to check out Ben's profile picture. Unfortunately, I couldn't see any more than that, because he had made his personal info private. His profile picture was a snapshot of him sitting on a rock, his legs bent and arms resting on his knees. Smiling, looking relaxed and happy. In fact, I'd never seen him this relaxed at home. With one finger I traced the contours of the tiny picture - that was totally juvenile, but nobody would ever know. His lips were beautiful and sensually shaped, and I asked myself once again why he never kissed a woman on the mouth.

The doorbell cut into my thoughts; I flinched and paused for a moment.

I wonder who that could be. Perhaps one of the boys had forgotten his keys and locked himself out. Maybe even Ben. I briefly considered making him wait by ignoring the bell until it rang continuously, just to offer the excuse that I had been talking to a guy from my genetics class on the phone and hadn't heard him ring. Of course, I'd be all contrite about it.

Finally, I went to check. After all, he would only congratulate me for taking his stupid advice to hit on guys and enjoy my single life. I could do without that. But it wasn't Ben. To my surprise, it was Erdie holding hands with a little dark-haired girl, who couldn't be older than five years.

"Hey, Luca," he greeted. "Is Ben home by any chance? I can't reach him on his phone."

I shook my head. "As far as I know, he's at the Ark for a basketball tournament."

"That's right." He smacked his forehead and turned to the little girl. "What are we going to do, now?"

She just shrugged.

I took a closer look at Erdie's little friend. She was super cute with long, dark-brown hair and light-blue eyes. What a combination! Glittery clips held her hair to one side, and she wore a pink dress that made her look like a doll.

"What's the problem?" I asked.

"It's my day with Phyllis," he explained. "But I really need to go with my brother to pick some things up for his wholesale market opening tomorrow. But I can't take my little girl with me, it's too chaotic inside. I'd have to leave her in the car for two hours, and I can't do that either." He rubbed his neck. "Well, I guess I'll just have to cancel on my brother if I can't reach Ben."

Was this the Phyllis he'd mentioned at the cafeteria? Obviously, I'd misjudged him completely. But how in the world did Erdie have a five-year-old?

Phyllis tugged on his sleeve. "Who is that lady, Daddy?"

"She lives with Ben."

"Oh, are they married?" She stared at me as critically as Vada checking out her father's new girlfriend in *My Girl*, and I had the distinct feeling of not passing muster.

"No, she's just Ben's roommate." He pointed with his

thumb over his shoulder. "Let's go. We need to tell Uncle Yasir he'll have to go by himself."

"I could watch her."

"You?"

"Why not? I'm home anyway. So if you want, you can leave her with me."

Erdie was still considering my offer, when Phyllis wrapped her arms to his leg. "I don't want to stay with a strange lady, Daddy."

I figured that might be the case, so I stepped aside. "Why don't you two come in for a bit, have a drink, and we'll take it from there?" I winked at Erdie, who gently freed himself from the girl's clutches.

"Now that you mention it. I'm actually really thirsty. What about you, Phyllis?"

Phyllis frowned. "Only if you stay too."

"Of course, I'll stay." He led her to the kitchen by the hand, and I followed.

Phyllis took off her unicorn backpack before she sat down at the table. Meanwhile, I got some orange juice from the fridge and some glasses.

"What do you have in your backpack?" I asked.

"My drawing things and a couple of games."

"What kind of games?"

Phyllis went through her backpack, and I smiled at Erdie, who was pouring juice into the glasses.

"Memory, Uno," Phyllis told me as she put a pack of cards on the table. "Do you know how to play?"

"Of course." I nodded. "I'm actually the best Uno player in Erlangen."

"Really?" Phyllis' face lit up. "Ben is the worst Uno player in the whole world," she went on. "He always loses."

"You better watch out, Phyllis cheats," Erdie warned me, gently stroking his little daughter's head. "Besides, she's always inventing new rules."

"Not true at all," protested Phyllis and pouted.

I already liked her; her face really was too sweet. I grabbed the cards and shuffled them. "Will you join us for a game?" I asked Erdie.

He looked at the clock and moaned, "If I have to…"

While I dealt, I said, "Does Ben watch Phyllis a lot?"

"He used to, but since she started kindergarten, it's easier."

I picked up my cards and was pleased to discover that I had gotten both a Wild Draw 4 and a Draw 2 card. Poor Erdie, his turn was after mine.

"How do you know Ben anyway?" I decided on the spot to seize this opportunity and get some information out of Ben's best friend.

"From school," he willingly told me. "We were in the same class."

"Oh, you've been friends for that long? I'm sure you drove all the girls in your class crazy back then," I teased him a little and laid down a card.

He laughed. "I did, Ben not so much."

"Why not Ben?"

Phyllis played a red six, the same color as my red Draw 2 card, which I now played.

"Dang," mumbled Erdie, and picked two cards.

"Ben was fat as a kid."

My jaw dropped.

"Really?" Phyllis giggled. "As fat as Adrian from kindergarten?"

"Much fatter." He played a card. "The first time I ran into Ben on the schoolyard, I beat him up. That's how we met."

I had a sip of orange juice. "Why did you beat him up?"

Erdie shrugged. "Because he was fat."

"That's it?"

"You were a bad boy, Daddy," Phyllis scolded him.

"Well, I was a stupid brat," he defended himself. "When my mom found out, she made my life a living hell. She invited Ben to our house and forced me to play with him after that. At first, I didn't want to." He turned to Phyllis, who was listening with her mouth hanging open. "But your grandma threatened me that if I didn't improve my attitude, I'd have to clean everybody's shoes in the family for the rest of my life. So, I played with him, and to my surprise, he was a lot of fun. That's how we became friends."

"But Ben's not fat," Phyllis objected.

"Not anymore. He grew up and started playing basketball; Ben got thinner and thinner. And that's why," he poked her nose, "you should never judge anyone just because they're different. Get to know them first. So, you won't be as dumb as your daddy was."

The little girl chuckled. She couldn't be older than five, and Erdie was about my age. So, he had become a father really young.

"Uno!" Phyllis yelled, and slammed her last card on the table.

"Oh no," Erdie whined in mock outrage while his daughter did a little victory dance around the table. He shot a glance at the clock on the wall.

"I really should get going." Erdie turned to Phyllis. "What do you say? Think you can hang with Luca for a while if I promise to hurry? Uncle Yasir could really use my help."

"What else do you have in there?" I poked a finger in the open little backpack, and Phyllis sat down next to me again.

"You can go, Daddy," she graciously dismissed him. "I'm going to show Luca my unicorn sticker book now."

Erdie got up and blew her an air kiss through his puckered lips while pulling his cell phone out of his pocket. "Can I get your number, in case of emergency?"

"Sure." I rattled off the numbers. Immediately, my cell phone rang in my room as he test-called me.

"Now you also have mine, just in case. Thank you so much, Luca." He waved in my direction before he headed for the floor, but then stopped again. "By the way…" He looked down and suddenly seemed nervous. "I wanted to stop by the cafeteria to see Rhashmi, but I forgot what days she's there. Do you think I could give her a call sometime?"

You'd make a certain Miss Rhashmi very happy, I thought. I was sure Rhashmi wouldn't mind me giving out her number without her permission, considering how often she had asked me about him.

31

Two hours later, I was coloring unicorns with Phyllis when my phone rang. An unknown number appeared on the display, probably Erdie calling to check in.

"Hello?"

"Luca, is that you?" I heard a familiar voice ask, the purring sound of an engine in the background. "It's me, Ben. Erdie told me Phyllis is with you. How's it going?"

At the sound of his voice, my heart beat faster. He talked as if nothing had ever happened between us. Suddenly, I felt like a radio host had put me on his live show.

"Um, yeah, everything's fine. We were playing, and now we're coloring. She's fine."

"Great, thanks for watching her. I'll be home in a bit to take over."

A little dazed by the brief conversation, I returned to the kitchen table where Phyllis had just finished applying pink glitter on her unicorn.

"Ben will be home any minute."

"Okay." She answered without looking up.

I stared at the display for a couple of minutes before I finally tapped on the *recent calls* icon. What had Ellen once said? Ben never gave a woman his number. But wasn't it different for me? After all, I wasn't one of his one-night stands. Mechanically, I typed in his name and saved it in my contact list. I officially had Ben's number—a happy shiver trickled down my spine, but I tried not to think about it too much.

Soon after, the door opened, and Ben came in. He gave Phyllis a kiss on the head. "Hi, Munchkin, are you good?" he asked in a soft voice and sank next to her into a chair.

"Ben!" she shrieked and jumped onto his lap.

"Hi," he greeted me, friendly, but clearly reserved.

Phyllis knelt on his lap and took his face in her little hands. "Luca played with me a lot. She's so nice."

"Yes, she is," he agreed. He glanced at me but quickly looked away. His hair was messy and wet, as if he'd come straight out of the shower.

"Where is Daddy?"

Ben rubbed her back. "He's still stuck at Yasir's shop. I'm supposed to drop you off. Your grandparents are there too, and they'll take you over to your mom's."

"Ben." Phyllis sat on his lap and pulled her coloring book across the table. "What's an IQ?"

He paused in wonder. "An IQ? Where'd you hear that?"

She looked at him, blinking. "Mommy told Daddy that today he has the IQ of fried chicken."

That made Ben snort. "Mommy didn't mean that. I bet she was just mad at your dad."

"But what is an IQ?"

"An IQ is a number that tells you how smart you are. The higher the number, the smarter you are," he explained in a calm voice.

Phyllis beamed. "Then I'm a Z."

I covered my mouth with one hand to hide my quiet laughter. Ben smiled too. She was adorable.

"Something like that," he finally agreed.

I watched the two of them. Phyllis clearly loved Ben, and he adored her too. They seemed very comfortable with each other.

"So," he lifted her off his lap, "I'm gonna take you over to the store now to get you out of Luca's hair."

"Oh, that's okay," I reassured him. "I had fun with Phyllis. I even beat her twice at Uno."

"Impossible," he put both hands on his hips. "Nobody ever beats Phyllis at Uno."

"It's true, she did." The girl nodded.

"It seems you, on the other hand, are the worst Uno player in the world; or so I've heard."

"You told Luca that?" he asked Phyllis and put one hand on his chest.

"Yes." She nodded again dead serious. "Don't be sad, though. Daddy plays just as bad as you do."

"That's a relief," he muttered and stood. Taking Phyllis' hand, they walked out of the kitchen, so I stood up, took her backpack and put her things in it, before I followed them to the door. All of the sudden, I felt nervous being this close to Ben. His self-confident charisma inhibited me; his mere presence filled the entire hallway. Next to him, I felt like a plump little hamster.

"Your backpack, sweetie."

Phyllis looked up at me. "Can we play again sometime?"

"Sure, we can." I gave her a hug. "Bye."

Ben put one hand on the doorknob. "Would you... Would you like to join us?" He turned to me. "It's not far. Just a few blocks away. A little evening stroll."

Our eyes melted together, and a swarm of butterflies fluttered in my stomach. Though I would have loved to say yes, I remained silent. Going with him would mean being alone with Ben on our way back, if he didn't simply ditch me on the way, which was entirely possible. He didn't want to be alone with me, as he had made clear to me all week. So why had he just invited me?

"Yay!" Phyllis cheered, grabbing my hand. "You have to come too!"

32

We strolled leisurely down the street. It was still light outside, and the sun shone warmly on us. Phyllis was between us, each of us holding one hand. Lost in thought, I stared straight ahead, while Phyllis did all the talking.

"Is Luca your wife?" she suddenly asked. Immediately, Ben's back tense up suspiciously. Obviously, he didn't consider me a candidate for that position.

"No," he replied curtly, shooting me a sideways glance which I deliberately ignored. Let him explain that one to her on his own.

"Then why are you living together?"

"Because we live in a dorm. That means the university decides who gets to share the apartment. It's not up to us." He stroked her hair. "Besides, you already promised to marry me when you grow up."

She hopped on one foot. "Yeah. But Timo from my kindergarten said that when I'm a grown-up, you'll be really old and die soon, and then I won't have a husband anymore if I marry you."

I burst out laughing at Ben's alarmed look. Served him

right. Mr. Nowak obviously got rejected every once in a while. My pity was limited.

"Timo really said that? Looks like he and I need to talk. I won't be all that old when you're a grown-up."

"In their eyes, you will," I declared, opening my mouth for the first time since we had left the house.

Ben sighed. "There goes my fiancée."

"You poor thing. I'm sure you'll meet Miss Right one day," I soothed him. What would she look like, the right girl?

"I highly doubt it," he replied softly. Suddenly, Ben seemed so closed off that I didn't dare ask any more questions. What was on his mind? A strange awkwardness seemed to drape over us like a heavy coat, and we remained silent for the rest of the way until we reached a brightly lit storefront.

"This is Yasir's new grocery store," Ben said. "Tomorrow is the grand opening, and the way Erdie sounded, they'll have to pull an all-nighter to get everything ready. If you hadn't helped with Phyllis, it would've been even worse."

"It was fun. I loved spending time with her."

We entered the store, and indeed, the place still resembled a construction site. I had my doubts about the opening tomorrow. Empty white shelves lined the walls. Two men were drilling holes to mount more of them, and there was a cloud of dust in the air. Towers of boxes and crates were piled everywhere. I discovered Erdie in the back of the store, inserting boards into the shelf brackets. When he spotted us, he came over. His black hair was coated in a layer of gray dust.

"Hey. I hope Phyllis wasn't too much trouble."

"No, she was a good girl," I assured him, when I was interrupted by a deafening noise. The two men were drilling into the wall with a high-pitched grinding screech.

Phyllis covered her ears and yelled, "Too loud!"

When the noise finally stopped, Erdie turned around. "Cengiz, Yasir, come here a minute. I want you to meet Luca."

The two came over. They looked just like Erdie; three huge bears.

"Hey, sweetie." They greeted Phyllis, who was hopping towards them, then said hi to me and patted Ben on the shoulder.

"You've got a lot to do before tomorrow," Ben said to Yasir, who crossed his arms, his muscles bulging like a bodybuilder's.

"We're behind schedule, but we'll get it done."

"Are you sure you don't need another hand?"

Cengiz shook his head. "No, it's alright. With your bad knee, this isn't for you." Then he turned to me and remarked, "But Phyllis found herself a really pretty babysitter." He winked. "Makes you want to be a kid again."

"And color unicorns with me?" I said, laughing.

"That too." He raised his left hand and pointed to a golden wedding band. "Unfortunately, I'm already taken." Then he elbowed Ben in the ribs. "She'd be a great match for you, though," he said, as if I wasn't even there.

Ben's jaw tensed, and he ran his hand through his hair uncomfortably. I'd never seen him like that. This family was truly merciless.

"Stop trying to hook me up all the time," he snapped at them.

"Calm down," Cengiz replied, unfazed.

"If you just stand around chatting, you'll never get finished." Erdie reminded his brothers, waving his hands as if he were shaking out a dust rag, whereupon the two of them went back to their work.

"Bye, Luca." They waved.

"Your brothers talk way too much." Ben frowned.

"You'd better get a move on, or you'll be single forever," Erdie replied drily. He opened his mouth to say something else, but Ben inconspicuously shook his head.

Ridiculous. He could keep his secret stuff to himself. I

wasn't even remotely interested, no, really not. Not one single bit.

"You know the crossword clue for *life sentence*, right? 8 letters?" Ben went on.

Erdie grinned broadly. "Marriage."

Oh, God. I rolled my eyes. Some men were certainly better off staying single, really.

"Phyllis," I heard someone call from behind us as an elderly couple entered the room.

"Babaanne." Cheered the little girl as she jumped into the lady's arms.

"How are you, sweetie?" she asked.

"Luca's been playing with me all afternoon."

The woman gave me a warm glance.

"Luca, meet Nursel and Cemal Dirim, Erdie's parents," Ben introduced them. "This is Luca; my roommate," he quickly added, as if he were afraid they'd make the ridiculous mistake of thinking I was his new flavor of the month. He was really starting to annoy me. By now, even I had gotten the message that I was not girlfriend material. For my sake, he didn't have to explain it to everyone around him all the time.

"We get it," I said under my breath. "Even I got it, don't worry. Relax."

His eyes narrowed, but he didn't say anything back.

"Hello, Luca." Erdie's parents shook my hand, then Erdie's father yelled something and rushed towards his sons. He pointed at the wall, gesticulating with both hands in the air, while he gave them a lengthy speech in Turkish.

"They screwed up," Erdie said, matter-of-factly.

"Ben." Mrs. Dirim took his hands and inspected him. "It's so good to see you. You haven't been around much, lately."

He kissed her on the cheek. "Hi, Nursel, I'm very busy right now, sorry."

"Erdal," Mrs. Dirim went on sternly, "Why haven't you offered our guests anything? Don't you have mocha in the back? What is Luca going to think of us? Why does Allah punish me with such a bunch of impolite sons?"

Erdie rubbed the dust from his hair, releasing a gray cloud. "We're working."

His mom didn't accept that. "Go on, go." She shooed him towards the back while I watched in amusement as this six-foot-tall guy obeyed the petite woman.

"I'm going, I'm going." Grumbling, he disappeared behind a curtain, and the next thing I knew, Yasir was shouting: "Ben, can you hold this for a second?"

Ben went over to help. Their every hand movement was being critically watched by Phyllis, who offered them non-stop advice. They endured her commentary without a flinch.

Mrs. Dirim winked at me, little wrinkles materializing around her dark brown eyes. "We're a bit chaotic, but when needed, we help each other and always get things done."

I smiled. "I love big families. I don't have siblings, but I always wished I did."

"Siblings are for life." She nodded, righting her pale blue hijab. "It's sad to think you're by yourself. Ben doesn't have any siblings either." She looked at him wistfully. He was still standing at the wall, helping Yasir. "He is like a son to me, and my sons are like his brothers. He's family."

I swallowed. "That sounds nice."

"Ben's very dear to me," she said thoughtfully. "He's a good boy, but he just can't love himself." There was concern in her voice. "He's a tormented soul."

"Why?" I had always assumed that Ben loved only one person: himself.

"Oh, *güzelim*," she sighed, patting me on the cheek. "He'll have to tell you himself."

Erdie came back bearing a tray of small, steaming gold-rimmed cups.

"Hurry up," his mother urged him.

"She's like a general." He handed me a cup. "Caution, hot."

"Somebody's got to teach you manners," his mother replied unimpressed and claimed a cup for herself. "I don't want to get in trouble with my daughters-in-law." She gave him a scowl. "One has already left."

"Would you please cut it out, mom?" Erdie seemed annoyed and rubbed his forehead.

Ben returned and helped himself to a cup. "You don't dare mess with Nursel."

"That's right." She pinched him in the side. "It's obvious I didn't raise you."

We all laughed. I'd never had much of a family life, but this was exactly like I'd imagined it.

Ben turned to me. "Don't drink all of it. The last sip is only coffee grounds. You don't want to drink that."

"Okay." I carefully tried the hot, sweet drink. The mocha tasted wonderful; strong, with a fine coffee aroma. As Ben had recommended, I left the dregs in the cup, but, I still felt a little powder on my tongue that left an earthy taste in my mouth.

"I got some." I rubbed the tip of my tongue against the roof of my mouth.

"You've got a little coffee..." Ben wiped my upper lip with his thumb, and I felt myself blush. The sensation of his touch still lingered, and my upper lip burned a little. This time he didn't avoid my gaze but looked me straight in the eyes. The moment lasted for an eternity.

"Oh," I finally said and turned, when he made no effort to look away. Mrs. Dirim was watching us.

"We should go, we're keeping everyone here from working." Ben pointed his chin at the door and gave Erdie's mother a kiss on the cheek. She whispered something in his ear that made him shake his head vigorously. But Mrs. Dirim grabbed him by his jacket and pulled him closer. "You'll see," she said insistently.

I would have given anything to know what she had said to him, but Ben was suddenly in a hurry to get out of here.

33

Silently, we walked back through the now dark streets, the soft halo of the street lamps lit our way.

"Do you really think they'll have everything ready by tomorrow?" I asked to start a conversation, because Ben seemed absent.

"Sure. They've got a few more people coming over later on. They'll get it done."

We strolled so close together that our arms almost touched, which made me tingly and nervous.

"Phyllis is so cute. You're really good with kids." I wonder what was on Ben's mind.

"Phyllis has us all wrapped around her little finger." He smiled. "I've known her since she was born. I've looked after her since she was a baby, changed her diapers, and warmed up her bottles."

"You really did all of that?"

He nodded. "Of course."

"Erdie must have been really young when he became a dad." I looked at him from the side. He seemed relaxed now.

"He was seventeen when Hanna became pregnant. They'd been together for six months." Ben ran his fingers through his unruly hair. "She was desperate and about to get an abortion.

But Erdie convinced her not to do it, promised he'd support her and that she wouldn't be alone. I told them they could count on me if they needed me. They were in a very difficult situation, but in the end, she had the baby. When I saw Phyllis for the first time in the hospital though, I almost ran."

I stopped in my tracks. "Why?"

"She was so tiny." He used both hands to indicate how small she'd been. "I was really scared I'd break her or drop her. So, Erdie dragged me off to one of those baby care classes where they taught us everything we needed to know."

"You guys went to a baby care class?" I grinned broadly.

"Yes, what else were we supposed to do? We'd promised Hanna. She had to drop out of school. And six months after Phyllis was born, they broke up, on top of everything else. They constantly butt heads and argue with each other, even in front of Phyllis." He shook his head. "I've told Erdie many times not to do that in front of her. She always asks questions, like earlier about the IQ."

We went on. I remembered Hanna, the pretty woman I'd seen with Erdie that day Caro and I had gone frustration shopping. Once again, I'd been completely wrong.

"I'm sure you'll make a good dad one day." I subtly rubbed my cold arms.

"I don't think I'll ever have kids of my own," Ben murmured, staring off into space. "Are you cold?" Without waiting for my answer, he took off his corduroy jacket and put it over my shoulders.

"Thanks." I slipped into the long sleeves, which were still warm from his body. It almost felt like Ben was hugging me. Happily, I snuggled into the jacket and inhaled his pleasant scent on the fabric, which penetrated my nose.

"Where are you from originally?" I asked.

"From Nuremberg."

"You haven't gotten very far, have you?"

He laughed softly. "No, not really. Actually, I was planning to move to a much cooler city, Berlin or something.

But the computer science department at Erlangen University is among the best there is. I'd have been stupid not to take advantage of it. Anyway, the place has sort of grown on me."

"I always imagined computer science to be really boring," I blurted out undiplomatically.

"Hey." He nudged me with his elbow. "I like it. Computer science follows a certain logic. When I'm coding, I know exactly what comes next. There are no surprises if you do it right. I find that very satisfying. What made you choose biology?"

"I want to work in molecular biotechnology," I explained and noticed his questioning glance. "I want to help heal genetic disorders, such as my own."

"That's very laudable," he sounded honest. "How were you actually diagnosed with celiac disease in the first place?"

I wrapped his jacket up a bit tighter around me. That was a delicate question for me, and at first, I wasn't quite sure if I was ready to tell him about it. On the other hand, our conversation was flowing so easily now, in fact, more easily than ever before. "My mom was diagnosed with end-stage colorectal cancer when I was six years old."

"I'm sorry about that," he said softly.

I smiled sadly. "Yes, it was a difficult time. During her treatment, they also diagnosed her with celiac disease. She'd had symptoms for years, but no doctor had managed to figure out the cause. Since it was left undetected for so long, the celiac disease had developed into cancer. Therefore, they also tested me. I had this big inflated belly, but skinny arms and legs. Also, I hadn't grown for at least one year and always had stomach aches."

"Oh no, now I feel even worse for the pizza incident," he groaned.

"About the incident," I corrected him.

"You're such a know-it-all," he said. "But then what happened?"

"My mother died shortly thereafter, but I got better

quickly on a gluten-free diet. It also decreased my risk of cancer." I shortened the story.

"I'm really sorry about your mom."

"It was a long time ago. But it showed me how fast everything can be over. One day she was baking cookies in the kitchen, and shortly after that, we buried her." I raised my head. The old wound in my heart that had never really healed gave me a painful stab. "I remember one thing she said to me, not long before she died."

"And what did she say?" He smiled pitifully.

It felt oddly normal to walk through the darkened streets with him, talking about my dead mother. "She told me I needed to have at least one big dream in life and to try to make it come true. Do you have a dream?"

Ben thought for a bit. "Not sure," he finally said. "I never really thought about it. So, what is yours?"

"To take the Trans-Siberian Railroad all the way to China."

"For real?" He looked at me sideways.

"Yes," I confirmed.

"That's cool. I'm impressed."

We arrived at our building, and Ben unlocked the door. We climbed up the stairs side-by-side, and I wondered if I should ask Ben if he wanted to hang out in the kitchen for a while. I'd really enjoyed our conversation. Even more, I almost had to pinch myself, because I could hardly believe how close I suddenly felt to him. Besides, he had looked at me so strangely earlier. Outside, we had somehow been so very far away from it all, as if we were somewhere else altogether and two completely different people.

I handed him back his jacket. "Thanks."

He gave me a warm smile before disappearing into the bathroom, while I lingered undecidedly in the hallway. I would simply ask him. What was the worst thing that could possibly happen? The bathroom door opened, and Ben came out. To my surprise, he was wearing his jacket and strode towards the front door.

"Where are you going?"

"Out," he replied curtly without even looking at me, before he pushed the front door open and disappeared.

I stood in the hallway and felt as if someone had hit me in the head with a brick. *Ben's out hunting*. It sunk into my consciousness while I walked numbly into the kitchen and sat down. Earlier on the street, I could've sworn that something had really sparked between us, an invisible connection, something special that went deeper than our usual small talk. How many times was I going to misread this guy and not learn anything?

I must have been sitting there thinking for quite some time. The kitchen clock already showed eleven when my phone, which was sitting on the kitchen table, vibrated with an incoming message. When I looked at the display, my hand began to tremble. Ben had texted me.

Ben: Climbing the K2.

I read, puzzled.

Me: What r u talking about?

I texted back. It buzzed again.

Ben: My big dream in life.

My lips curled into a broad grin. Ben Nowak had confided his great dream to me. I felt like a teenager with a huge crush. Hastily, I typed an answer.

Me: Count me out, way too high for me.

The answer came promptly.

Ben: If you climb the mountain with me, I'll take the train with you.

My hand was shaking. He wanted to go with me to China.

Me: You can come along, but I won't climb that mountain.

Ben: *lol* lazy bum

My cell announced another text.

Ben: What are you up to?

Me: Hanging out in the kitchen. You?

For a while I waited for an answer, but it never came. He didn't have to reply anyway because I knew exactly what he was doing. With a heavy heart, I got up to go to bed. I took my phone with me, although it was unlikely that he would text again tonight. Why had he texted me in the first place, though? For no real reason, just for fun? Was it suddenly now boring out there? What did I even want with this guy? Ben, of all people. My heart rate accelerated as I imagined his face. Had I fallen for him already?

34

Over the last few days, I had been so incredibly busy. So busy, that I hurried to the university in the early morning, holed myself up in the library in the afternoon, and only left when the staff turned the lights off on me.

Now I was the one who was avoiding Ben; we hadn't seen each other since our evening stroll. The next day, Erdie texted to thank me for sharing Rhashmi's number. At the same time, he invited me to the grand opening of his brother's store, but I made up a few excuses. Ben was going to be there for sure, and I wanted to postpone seeing him again for as long as possible. As a matter of fact, until I had grown out of my childish crush and was able to finally face him again in my old, cherished dislike. Somehow everything had been so much easier, clearer, when I couldn't stand him. Rhashmi, on the other hand, was bubbling over with happiness, because Erdie—unlike his friend—was not a complicated person. On the contrary. He had promptly invited Rhashmi out for a coffee. Since then, they had been inseparable, and Rhashmi was floating on cloud nine. So, it could be as simple as that. I, on the other hand, had fallen back into my old aversion to men in general. Why had I decided to stay single for the next few years? Right, it saved on a lot of frustration.

Unfortunately, today was a Saturday, so escaping to campus was not an option. I heard Toby and Ellen rattling around out in the kitchen, but nothing from Ben. However, as I had already painfully learned in the past, that didn't mean anything. Luckily, Caro had invited me to a trial Zumba class at the gym where she worked. Under normal circumstances, it wasn't something I would volunteer to do, but it was a good way to kill a few hours, check out other trial classes, and pretend to be interested in exercise. That would take care of half of the day. I wouldn't have to hang around in the park or loiter in front of the dorm until sundown, waiting for Ben to go out hunting again, so that I could finally sneak into my room. I knew I was behaving a little like a psychopath, but justified this to myself as pure self-protection. To make matters worse, I made the big mistake of stepping onto the scale yesterday when I went to the pharmacy for painkillers. In horror, I saw that I'd gained two pounds. Probably because of the binge-eating I'd been doing for the last few days to distract myself. But now, my dissolute lifestyle was coming to an end, right this minute. I wasn't going to gain any more weight because of Ben. Especially not because of him!

Without further ado, I pulled the first pair of leggings out of my closet that I could get my hands on. They were bright yellow. When did I buy these? Anyway, I stuffed them into my bag, along with a black t-shirt with a white *Snipes* logo on it. I packed a bottle of shower gel and a small towel as well. Then I picked up my phone to log onto Facebook and stare at Ben's photo for the millionth time today. I was so pathetic. After I had entered my password, I paused, because the number "1" was highlighted in red in the upper right corner. When I clicked on it, I almost fell off my chair. I stared at the display in awe and couldn't believe it; Ben had sent me a friend request. My heart leapt in my chest like a bouncy ball. What should I do now? I could hardly think straight with all my gasping. Ben Nowak had friended me! I clicked *accept* and then yanked back my hand as if my display was a hot stovetop. I studied his page and read all the posts. He didn't seem to post much; there wasn't a lot on his Facebook page to see, and he also hadn't uploaded any other pictures of himself apart from his profile picture.

But the things he had posted were funny or just nice; he seemed likeable and friendly. A whole bunch of people had left birthday wishes on his page. Apparently, Ben had turned twenty-four the day before yesterday. I had no idea it was his birthday. I hadn't even wished him a happy day. Guilt spread through me—I didn't even know my roommates' birthdays. I wondered what he had done for his birthday. Had he celebrated with his friends or his family? I realized I knew next to nothing about him. Just a few things that other people had told me. That night, as we wandered through the chilly streets together, he had opened up a little for the first time since I'd met him. Only to immediately restore his distance.

I had to admit to myself that I missed Ben, so I got up, hurried down the hallway to his room and knocked. No answer. Once again, I banged on his door, but nothing happened. Instead, Ellen stepped out of the kitchen.

"Ben left about ten minutes ago."

"Oh." I dropped my hand. A feeling of disappointment pervaded me. "Too bad."

"What did you want with him anyway?" She came closer.

"To wish him a happy belated birthday. I just found out by accident. Did you know?"

She shrugged as if bored. "Yeah, we wanted to have drinks with him, but he didn't feel like celebrating."

"Why not?"

"Maybe he's getting old and frustrated. Toby said he hasn't even been out the last few days to pick up any girls. He's probably gone through them all by now." Ellen sounded bitter. Her cheeks were tense, which made her look haggard and thin.

"I need to get going. I'm meeting a friend." I rushed back to my room and grabbed my bag. *Ben sent me a friend request, I* thought, smiling to myself. Ellen wasn't on his friends list, but I was now. I left the apartment with a spring in my step.

I entered the modern building made of concrete, steel and glass. A mixture of disinfectant and sweat hit my nostrils. Caro was leaning against a chrome counter talking to a muscular man whose bald head was colorfully tattooed.

"Hi," I greeted her, and Caro jumped up.

"Oh great, you're here, the class starts in ten minutes. Axel is covering for me."

The muscleman raised his hand briefly, without paying any attention to me. He restocked the glass shelf on the counter with energy bars. My first doubts now started to creep in. I was not exactly a paragon of physical finesse; my dancing skills were limited to the usual hopping around at the club and only after a few glasses of bubbly. Unlike Caro, who could move like Beyoncé.

"Are you sure we should try this?" I asked again, just to be on the safe side.

Caro immediately pursed her lips. "Zumba is great for your figure, and fun to boot."

"I thought you hadn't tried it yet."

"I haven't, but everyone raves about it. Plus, we'll look sexy doing it." She wiggled her hips, spinning in circles, attentively observed by her co-worker.

Maybe you will, I thought grimly. Unfortunately, Latin dance and my humble self didn't agree with each other, which Caro knew all too well. But, so what? I was here now.

Axel paused in his work and tilted his bald head to the side. "My spin class starts right after Zumba, it's great for endurance. Thirty minutes non-stop power cycling followed by circuit training. Come check it out."

Truthfully, I hated bike riding, and certainly wouldn't be tackling power-cycling with Superman here.

"I think Zumba's enough for now. Maybe I'll go back to

the machines afterwards," I said smugly, although I knew I would never do that. Caro came around the counter and put her arm around me, spinning a keyring around her finger. Her fitness outfit flattered her slim silhouette.

"Come on, let's go to the locker room. We'll show your love handles who's boss," she said to motivate me.

"Love handles?" someone repeated behind my back with amusement, and we both turned around.

My heart almost stopped beating; Ben and Erdie were standing next to the counter. What the hell were they doing here? Was Ben stalking me now? I wanted to flee on the spot, but Caro seemed to read my mind. She held me in a vice grip.

Axel gave both of them keys without even blinking, and I realized the guys weren't here for the first time. I was going to strangle Caro later, whether she was my best friend or not. Why hadn't she ever told me that Ben worked out here?

"Oh," Caro shrugged, "I was obviously joking. Of course, Luca doesn't have love handles. See for yourself." She pinched my side only to grab a big chunk of *me* between her thumb and the other fingers.

Heat shot up to my cheeks. She was definitely in trouble. I knocked her hand away. "Stop that, are you crazy?"

"But..." Caro seemed at a loss.

Ben and Erdie laughed with restraint, whereupon I was tempted to mention that I knew about Ben's childhood obesity.

"Luca is perfect just the way she is." Ben looked me in the eyes. In my eyes—not at my breasts, and I felt like he was trying to understand me. My blood surged through my veins. Then Erdie patted my shoulder, tearing me out of my brief, but beautiful, trance.

"Of course, she is!" Erdie announced. "What man would ever go for a skeleton. An extra pound or two is fine with me!"

He could have spared his pep talk, especially since

Rhashmi probably weighed no more than 110 pounds soaking wet.

"I would love to stay and chat," I replied as regretfully as possible, "but unfortunately, I have to go change." I pushed Caro along with both hands, throwing a quick glance back at the guys. They seemed to be waiting for something. What was wrong with them again?

"What are you doing?" Caro leaned against me.

"Getting out of here, you traitor," I hissed, shooing her along.

"Stop!" She tried to slip out of my grip.

"Not until the locker room."

"But they're over there." She pointed in the other direction. "This is the men's side!"

I stopped in my tracks. Ben and Erdie hadn't moved. Damn it. With my head held high, I turned around and walked past them.

"Are you lost?" Ben asked, but I ignored him. Why had I accepted his friend request earlier?

In the locker room, I launched into my interrogation. "Why didn't you ever tell me they work out here? Have you gone crazy?"

"I never mentioned it?" Caro seemed tense.

"No!"

"It must have slipped my mind." She smiled and shrugged again. "It doesn't matter. They are always over there on the machines. Now hurry, the class starts in two minutes."

After I'd changed, Caro shook her head at me. "You can't be serious?"

"What?"

"Your legs look like a pair of bananas. Where did you buy those? At Bad Taste 'R' Us?"

"No," I retorted, "They're from a store called 'Strangled My Best Friend with a Pair of Leggings!'"

She held up her hands. "Alright, alright. Come on."

35

I stood with a group of energetic women in a pastel-pink room, one wall was entirely made of glass so that every passer-by could watch what we were doing in here. That didn't help calm my nerves, because some of the ladies were already warming up with fancy hip moves even without music. Undoubtedly, this was not their first class. I gave Caro a pleading glance, which she pretended not to notice. Today was the last time I'd do her any more favors, I swore to myself.

An animated blonde woman in her mid-thirties swept in. Her skin was deeply tanned, which made her teeth glow like snow drifts in the sun when she opened her mouth.

"Let's get to it!" she called out, clapping her hands before skipping over to the CD player. "You girls ready for some Zumba?!"

"Yeah!" cheered everyone, even Caro. I remained silent; I had never been a fan of over-motivated super-women. We had literally nothing in common. Fast Salsa rhythms roared from the sound system, and in a flash, the instructor got into position. She marched in place, circling her hips and waving her hands in the air—all at the same time. I knew right away I was not cut out for this type of exercise. Nevertheless, I gritted my teeth and danced along. I even tried to keep to the beat, but the steps were too fast for me, and I repeatedly danced in the wrong direction, while my hips made more angular movements. Sweat dripped down my temples and cheeks. I huffed and puffed, but didn't give up, I kept up the good fight. Zumba was not going to beat me, even though I would certainly feel every single muscle tomorrow. I shot Caro an envious glance. She performed every move with a playful ease, as if she had done nothing else her entire life. I knew it! She had been secretly practicing.

To make matters worse, I stumbled, but caught myself again. When I happened to look out of the glass, I froze with rattling breath. Ben and Erdie stood outside, watching us as if the class were a peep show. The instructor must have noticed my distress because she followed my gaze. She also stopped dancing before resolutely marching outside. The guys' amused expressions morphed into alarm while the blond woman obviously chided them. They kept shaking their heads and holding up their hands in defense, trying to appease her, but our instructor shook her head mercilessly. Finally, she grabbed them by the arms and dragged them into the studio.

"Two new participants have just joined us," she announced. "The guys here didn't know about my rule: You stare, you dance."

The women clapped and cheered. Ben, on the other hand, seemed shocked, which filled me with gloating satisfaction. Yep, what goes around comes around. The Empire was striking back.

"We only stopped to look for a second. Come on, Jenny, you can't be serious," Ben pleaded.

"Give it a try," the teacher encouraged him in a sugary sweet voice. "You're going to have a blast."

"I'm sure, but still..."

Erdie patted Ben's shoulder, interrupting his pitiful tirade. "We might as well join in. Just suck it up."

"Dude, you can't be serious." My roommate sounded horrified.

"Enough chit-chat. Get into position," the instructor told him, before she cranked up the volume. The guys, their heads hanging, looked for a spot between the participants. Caro nudged me and grinned. In response, I clenched my fist and pumped my arm. Strike! Ben had noticed my gesture. Wonderful.

Jenny now put on some faster music. With wide, alternating strides, the women also raised their fists rhythmically into the air. Ben looked like a gorilla—his sense of rhythm seemed to be about as lousy as my own. Elated, I spun around and circled my hips, all of the sudden feeling light and carefree—compared to Ben. Erdie did better, I had to admit. The hip swinging seemed to come more naturally to him. As the women giggled louder and louder, Ben realized he was the center of attention, but he continued to give it his best. I had to give him that. For Zumba, however, he was clearly too tall. He couldn't manage any of the finer movements.

Finally, the instructor had mercy and wrapped up the class. Ben, bathed in sweat, leaned on his thighs and gasped for breath. A few strands of hair were plastered to his forehead.

"Damn, that's exhausting," he swore breathlessly, but I was right there with him.

My knees were weak; with every step, I felt like I was walking on pudding.

"Good job, boys!" the instructor called after them. "You're welcome to join the class any time!"

"You'll never see me again," murmured Ben.

I patted his shoulder. "What's the matter? Did that little lady's gymnastics class wear you out?"

"I'm into a different kind of gymnastics," he grinned.

Apparently, he wasn't the least bit embarrassed by his pitiful performance.

"Show-off," I muttered, making him laugh. "Happy belated birthday, by the way."

"Thanks." Ben's eyes began shimmering. His black T-shirt was plastered to his chest, clinging to the contours of his well-toned torso. My gaze froze at his muscular biceps. I wondered what they felt like. And then I became embarrassingly aware that my own shirt was probably clinging to my chest as well. On top of it, I was wearing those ridiculous banana leggings. I looked down and saw that my top was stretched tightly over my breasts, just as I had feared. Embarrassment burned hot in my cheeks.

"You don't have any love handles," Ben whispered. "You're finally not wearing something baggy. See how good you look?"

He couldn't be serious. I didn't know what to say.

Caro squealed next to me. "Shit, the locksmith is finally here. I need to show him the two lockers that are stuck." She put one hand on my arm. "Be right back."

"Okay."

Meanwhile, Erdie came over, having wrapped up his chat with the instructor. "Jenny sees potential in me," he announced with amusement. "But it looks bleak for you, my friend."

Ben snorted. "That *really* hurts."

"Want to hit the sauna?" Erdie asked. "What about you, Shorty? Want to join us?"

I tapped my forehead. "Keep dreaming. I'm definitely not going to sit around naked in the sauna with you guys."

"Oh, come on, Luca," Ben piped up in an amused voice. "It's way too hot in there to even sneak a peek, honestly." He winked at me.

"Forget about it," I started, when I was interrupted by a dark voice.

"Lu-ca." Someone stressed every letter of my name. I

turned around, and my heart stopped for a beat. First, I saw his cold gray eyes, then his curly brown hair. A star-shaped birthmark decorated his cheek. I felt nauseous, while he grinned at me with narrow lips. I was so horrified that I couldn't move, at the same time I just wanted to get away. To flee to the end of the world, to hide from him.

He had found me!

"How've you been, Luca?" he asked in a friendly voice. "Nice to see you again."

I shook my head and took a step backwards. Tears welled up my eyes, fear raged in me. "No," I said, feeling suffocated.

"Luca, are you all right?" Ben inquired before turning to the guy. "Hey, Konstantin. You guys know each other?"

I put my hands over my mouth to suppress a scream. They knew each other. Ben knew him! What should I do now?

"Ben. What's up, man?" Konstantin asked.

Turning on my heel, I stumbled towards the locker rooms to grab my stuff. I needed to get out of here, away from Konstantin. He had found me. The most terrible nightmare of my life had come true! What was I supposed to do now? I wiped the tears from my face and hectically threw my clothes in my bag. Sweaty as I was, I rushed out of the locker room and to the exit. I had to get away—far away from there. My hands were shaking. When I pushed the glass door open, someone grabbed me by the arm. My heart stopped and a frightened scream escaped from my lips.

"Leave me alone," I yelled and broke free. Was he after me already?

"Luca, it's me, Ben." Again, he grabbed my arm and stopped me. "What's the matter, Luca? You looked like someone was trying to kill you."

My voice shook when I said. "I have to go. Let me go."

With a strong grip, Ben pulled the door shut again, I pressed myself against it, but he held it closed.

"Not until you tell me what's wrong." He lifted my chin with one hand and forced me to look him in the eyes. "How do you know Konstantin? And what's the deal with you two?"

"That's none of your business." My lower lip was trembling. I couldn't tell Ben the truth, ever.

"It is my business if you're afraid of someone," he strongly objected.

"I'm not afraid of Konstantin," I hastily affirmed, but kept looking over my shoulder to check if he was coming after me already. "How do you know each other?" I asked, hoping they weren't friends, otherwise I would have to move out immediately and probably leave Erlangen too, if he lived nearby.

"He works at the locksmith place, next door to the copy shop."

"Is he a friend of yours?"

"No."

I closed my eyes in relief. Now Ben just needed to let me go so I could hide somewhere.

"Let me go," I begged him.

"Only if you tell me what's wrong."

"Dammit!" I banged the glass door with my fist. "I knew him a while back, and I had a crush on him. There. Happy now? Just get out of my way and leave me alone."

He stepped away from the door, so I could open it. And yet I hesitated and turned around once again. Ben was watching me, serious and worried, and it pained me more than anything to look in his eyes. I didn't deserve his concern.

"Ben," I whispered without looking up. "Does he know where we live?"

"No," I heard him say in a low voice.

"Please don't tell him," I pleaded, struggling to hold back my tears.

"I won't."

I rushed outside into the light drizzle, which had started in the meantime, and ran through the streets with my heart pounding. My pulse was throbbing in my temples, and an intense pain shot through my side, but I ignored the sting. I needed to get home, hide, call Caro, and make a plan. Fear of Konstantin expanded in my chest. Why had I gone to that damn gym today?

I would never be able to use the copy shop on campus again either. Could I trust Ben not to tell him where I lived? Maybe I should move out right away, leave town, go to my father's place in America; I would be safe there for a while. But what about my degree? I was in my final year and couldn't just drop out now. With long strides, I hurried up the stairs to our apartment and rushed into my room. My body was trembling, and I was overcome by a feeling of powerlessness. Konstantin wasn't like Martin—the boys couldn't help me with him. He was on an entirely different scale. With shaking hands, I fished my phone out of my pocket and called Caro.

"Caro," I wailed.

"What's wrong? Why did you take off?"

"That guy, the locksmith…" My voice broke.

"What about him?"

"That was Konstantin!"

I heard Caro breathe into the silence. Finally, she asked: "That Konstantin?"

"Yes… What am I going to do now? Ben knows him."

"Holy shit. But listen, I don't think he's going to come after you anymore, stay calm. Wait. And if he does show up, you can always still go to the police."

I thought hard. "You're right. Ben promised not to tell him where I live."

"I'm sure he won't. And now calm down. Want me to come over later?"

"No, it's okay. I'm just overreacting. I'm being hysterical." I buried my hand in my hair and clawed all five fingers into my scalp.

"Call me if you need anything, okay?"

"I will." As I hung up, a horrible thought flashed through my mind. Ben could never ask Konstantin about me. Never!

The door clicked; someone entered the apartment. Cautiously, I peeked through my cracked door and spotted Ben in the kitchen. He was filling a glass of water from the faucet. As I slowly came closer, he turned around and looked at me with a serious expression on his face.

"Can I ask you a favor?" I asked quietly.

Ben sat down on a chair. "Have a seat." He pointed to the place next to him, but I remained standing. I couldn't talk to him; I couldn't tell him about Konstantin... He just had to promise me one thing.

"Please promise you won't talk to Konstantin about me."

He took a sip of water. "I already asked him about you."

My stomach knotted. It couldn't be true. How much did Ben know? "What... What did you ask him?

His eyes bore into mine, as if he were trying to x-ray me. "I asked him what went down between you two."

I held my breath, but he didn't continue, so I went on. "What did he say?"

"He said you had a crush on him."

"Then he told you the exact same thing I did. So, can we please forget about him now?" I was about to walk away, but he grabbed my wrist.

"Luca," he said softly.

"Yes?"

"I don't believe him—and I don't believe you either."

"Ben, please," I begged. "Let it go. I don't want to talk about it."

"Alright. But in case you ever do want to talk—I'm always here for you, and willing to listen, okay?"

"Okay." I looked past Ben and stared at the wall, because I knew, in my heart of hearts, I could never talk to him about my past. I realized my nightmare was never going to end, and that my past was going to chase me like a three-headed monster for the rest of my life. No matter where I went, Konstantin's shadow hovered over me, visible to everyone like a lighthouse in the darkness.

When Ben finally let go of me, I stumbled back to my room where I sank onto the bed. I could no longer hold back my tears. Why had I been so stupid?

36

I holed myself up in my room for the rest of the weekend and talked to Caro on the phone for hours. She had managed to build me up enough that I could go to class today. Still, I found myself stalling over breakfast. Everything inside me screamed that I shouldn't leave the safe haven of our apartment and brave the streets by myself, even though it was broad daylight. On the other hand, I knew that I couldn't give Konstantin so much power over my life that I no longer dared to leave the house by myself. I had already spent too much time worrying about that bastard. With a heavy sigh, I bit off a piece of my gluten-free toast and jam, watching the hands of the clock on the wall mercilessly jump forward. I needed to leave in fifteen minutes if I didn't want to miss my lecture, but my legs wouldn't move. I felt paralyzed. Then Toby walked in.

"Good morning," he said, interrupting my thoughts.

"Morning," I replied curtly, licking some jam off my thumb.

He grabbed a mug from the cupboard, poured himself some coffee, and sat down next to me with his iPad to read the news. I gave him a closer look. If I was lucky, he had to go to class too, so we could walk part of the way together. In his company, I could discreetly scout out the situation outside, test out how it felt to be in the city.

"Do you have class now?" I asked carefully.

Toby blinked up. "Not until eleven."

Shit. That was too late, I had to get going. Today's class was important.

"We could walk together," I suggested anyway, which made him look at me quizzically.

"Why do you want to take a walk with me?"

"I don't want to take a walk with you." Why did he have to make everything so complicated? "I just thought it might be nice to walk together and chat a little bit."

Toby swiped across his iPad. "When's your class?"

"In a few minutes. Want to come?" I wasn't giving up hope yet.

"Luca, if I leave now, I'll have to hang around for two hours until my class starts." He seemed a bit annoyed. Toby wanted to read his iPad in peace and clearly didn't want to talk to me, but I kept going.

"You could have coffee," I suggested.

He held up his mug "What am I doing right now? Luca, I appreciate that you want to walk to class with me, but it's really too early. Sorry!"

I sighed. What now? It looked like I had to walk alone. Maybe I should call a cab. My fingers felt cold.

"I'll walk with you." I heard Ben say next to me. He put a hand on my shoulder. "If you want, we can go together. I need to get going myself."

"But you don't even have class on Mondays," Toby said in surprise.

"I have things to do," he replied curtly, and Toby turned his attention back to his iPad.

I sat for another moment. Ben had seen through me. He knew that I just didn't want to go out by myself. On the one hand, I was grateful that he wanted to accompany me, but I feared that he would use the opportunity to ask more questions about Konstantin. Ben had already taken his jacket off the hook and stood waiting by the door.

"Shall we go?"

I nodded. "Yes, let me just get my bag." My fear evaporated somewhat as I rushed to my room. At least today, I didn't have to walk alone, and I simply wouldn't answer any of Ben's questions.

Just like the other night, we strolled side by side through the streets, but today felt completely different. I was nervous and tense, glancing over my shoulder or looking left and right down narrow side streets, but luckily nothing seemed suspicious. I was grateful to have Ben by my side. We walked in silence for a while, but suddenly he started talking.

"Phyllis has been asking about you. She drew a picture for you and gave it to me. It's back home."

I had to smile as I pictured the little girl's face in my mind. "She's the cutest."

"Yes, she is. Actually, she drew it for me, but changed her mind at the last minute and told me she'd rather give it to you."

"Oh!" I put my fingertips to my mouth. "I'm sorry about that."

He seemed to take Phyllis' rejection in stride. "That's how women are, all alike. Even the very small ones."

"What did you do on your birthday? I didn't even know about it, sorry."

"I'm not that much into birthdays anyway. Erdie's mother made me come for cake. She even put twenty-four candles on it." He rolled his eyes. "I had to blow them out like when I was a kid."

"I think that's really sweet."

"Nursel is a very sweet person, but I guess we'll always be little boys to her."

"What about your parents? You didn't celebrate with them?"

Barely noticable, Ben's body tensed. He clenched his fingers on one hand before finally answering. "Yes, I saw them." He looked down.

"What do your parents do?"

"Look," Ben pointed ahead. "Isn't that Rhashmi?"

"You've met her already?" I waved, when Rhashmi turned towards us.

Ben sighed deeply and tormented. "For weeks now, I've heard about nothing else but her from Erdie: Rhashmi is so great, so pretty, so funny, and he's convinced he has no chance with her. And if I thought I could ask you for her number and so on and so forth."

I giggled. "Same here." I glimpsed in Rhashmi's direction. "How come you never asked me for her number? He asked me for it himself."

"Come on," he snorted, "as if you'd have given it to me. What did you have against me anyway? I never understood your problem with me."

I couldn't answer that question offhand. What had I actually had against him? "Let's put it this way. You didn't really make a great first impression, and I had a hard time letting that go."

"What?" he said perplexed. "I helped you get your coffee."

"And made fun of me."

"Just a little." He indicated a tiny gap between his thumb and forefinger. "But somehow I had to get you to talk to me."

"So, you were hitting on me?" I nudged him with my elbow, like I was joking. *Say yes, say yes, say yes…*

He smiled. "Of course."

"To get me into bed," I assumed on the spot, and he rolled his eyes at me.

"You always think the worst of me. Of course, I wouldn't say no if something happens." He shrugged his shoulders.

"But flirting doesn't necessarily have to end between the sheets. And I haven't been out a lot lately anyway."

"And why not?" Curiosity literally dripped from my voice like water from a wet sponge.

Ben looked at me for a long time, the blue in his eyes prevailed in the bright sunshine, making his face glow noticeably. His dimple was even showing, and I felt like he was showing it only to me.

"I'm getting older," he finally said. Unfortunately, I couldn't press any further, because we had reached Rhashmi, who'd been waiting for us. She was talking and laughing into her phone. Still, I couldn't shake the feeling that Ben had been about to say something else entirely.

"Yes, they're here right in front of me," she said into the phone and held up a hand in greeting.

"Erdie," Ben whispered, and I nodded.

Rhashmi's face glowed; she was head over heels in love.

They're really into each other," I whispered.

"Erdie can't stop smiling either, it's so annoying. But I'm happy for them, even if he has been making himself scarce lately."

"You poor thing," I consoled him, patting his cheek. A smart move, I thought, so I could touch him without being too obvious. He grabbed my hand and pressed it against his face.

"You could comfort me." His gaze wandered boldly along my body, sending sparks down right into my panties. I felt all tingly. I'd been wearing tighter shirts lately and had banned all the baggy ones to the back of my closet.

Why did I have the feeling that he was looking for a very special kind of solace? I liked that idea.

I liked it a lot!

"And what do you have in mind?" I was breathing shallowly, his gaze never wavering from mine.

"I'll think of something." The expression in his eyes became more intense; feverish.

"You know, I'm not that easy," I countered, laughing to mask my nervousness. He bent down to my ear.

"Still as uptight as when we met?" he whispered. I knew he was testing me as his warm breath brushed my cheek, sending a pleasurable shiver through me.

"With me, it goes step by step. In the beginning, the most you'd get is a kiss, then I'd have to see."

Immediately, he stepped aside, the passionate flicker in his eyes fading. "Can you walk the rest of the way with Rhashmi, or should I take you to your class building?" he asked suddenly matter-of-factly.

I swallowed. "Yes, go ahead, it's all right."

Running a hand through his hair, he said: "I'm gonna take off then. If you need anything, give me a call, okay?"

"Alright," I croaked. What had I done wrong now? From one second to the next, his mood had changed, and he'd become a completely different person.

"One more thing," he said softly. "Konstantin doesn't live in Erlangen, but somewhere outside of town. He said he doesn't know his way around because he hates it here. It's highly unlikely you'll run into him again."

"Thanks for the info," I replied curtly while my chest constricted once again. Did he have to remind me of that bastard now of all times? I'd just managed to forget about him.

Ben waved goodbye to Rhashmi, who was still on the phone, and hurried past me. Confused, I watched him go. Would I ever understand this guy?

37

"Hey, I gotta go," Rhashmi said. "Luca's rolling her eyes at me."

I was doing what? She couldn't have seen it; I had turned away.

"I can tell by your back," she hissed and then purred into the phone: "Yes, see you later… Can't wait." She put her phone away.

"So, you and Erdie have really hit it off."

Rhashmi's eyes sparkled. "He's so awesome. We get along so well, and he's an incredible kisser." She ran the tip of her tongue along her upper lip.

Definitely too much superfluous information for my taste, especially since Ben had just run away from me when I had mentioned the word kissing. *Do I have bad breath?* ran through my mind. Discreetly, I sniffed my breath behind my palm. No, thank God. Then I had probably just triggered his kissing phobia with my babbling. Maybe he was afraid of contracting herpes, or he was some sort of oral hypochondriac. How could he get intimate with a woman without kissing her? How did he do that? It was completely beyond me. Maybe Rhashmi could do some digging on Ben through Erdie. I dismissed the idea right away. Rhashmi and I weren't so close that I could trust her with my biggest secret weaknesses.

"Erdie asked me to go to the festival the week after next," she announced, beaming as if he'd asked for her hand in marriage.

"You guys are sure planning far ahead," I joked. "Is it getting serious between you two lovebirds?"

"Very serious. He wants me to meet his daughter."

"Phyllis?" I asked, even though I knew Erdie only had one kid.

"You've met her before?" Rhashmi sounded hurt.

"Ben watches her sometimes. She's been to our place," I explained to calm her down. "She's the cutest. I'm sure you'll love her."

"I'm not very good with little kids," she confessed in a whisper, as if Erdie were nearby. "I get rashes every time I have to pass the kindergarten on my street and the rug rats are outside playing. The noise they make!"

"Phyllis is really sweet, don't worry," I encouraged her. "She loves unicorns and playing Uno," I added as a little tip.

The two of them were really making progress in their relationship from zero to sixty in five seconds flat. Why was it so easy for some people? They met, were immediately aware of their feelings for each other, and could easily reveal them to each other. There were no concerns or fears of commitment in their love for one another. Everything ran perfectly smooth in a straight line to seventh heaven. Why had I never had that? Why did I always end up with the relationship misfits? The world wasn't fair.

We entered the university building through the large glass door. As usual, there was a buzz of people, a din of voices and laughter filling the air. We squeezed past a group of students wildly debating amongst themselves and climbed up the wide staircase. Martin was standing by the door to the lecture hall—he seemed to be waiting for someone. Oh no! Of all things. Just what I needed today.

I nudged Rhashmi in the side. "Hey, there's Martin."

"Ignore him," she sing-songed, taking my arm.

I decided to take her advice on the spot. He probably didn't want anything from me anyway, but was waiting for one of his nerd buddies.

Just as I was about to enter the lecture hall, I heard his mewling voice.

"Hi, Luca. Do you have a minute?"

"No, she doesn't," Rhashmi answered for me.

"May I?" A blond man bumped into me, since I was blocking the door, and pressed me against Martin. I hastily jumped aside.

"What do you want?" I snapped.

"I'm sorry about our fight," he said. "Are we good again?"

Are we good again? Where had he learned that? I hadn't heard that expression since elementary school. Rhashmi rubbed her forehead and took a deep breath.

"Uh, yeah… I guess… No problem." What kind of bullshit was coming out of my mouth? Was I out of my mind? Obviously, yes. Rhashmi was gesturing wildly at me.

Martin beamed.

"Yay! Maybe we can have a cup of tea sometime?"

Was he asking me out? Again! After everything that had happened? I couldn't believe it. "How's Johanna?" I asked instead of an answer.

"Johanna." He scratched his head. "Well, she's fine. We're still together, but that doesn't mean much. I still like you better."

I was speechless.

"You have a girlfriend?" Rhashmi sounded flabbergasted.

"Yes," he replied reluctantly. "But it's just temporary." He stared at me, his head wobbling. "What about us then?"

"This is a bad time. I really have a lot of studying to do. Maybe some other day," I stammered.

Rhashmi pulled me into the hall. "He really has a

girlfriend? That nutcase is just full of it, right?" she whispered excitedly.

"No, no, he really does. I met her."

Her mouth stood open. "Oh my God. She must be crazy to hook up with that weirdo!"

"I even think she's madly in love with him. She was really pissed off when she saw us together."

Rhashmi stared at me, her eyes huge. "You're kidding?"

I nodded. "It's true, I'm serious."

"There are more and more crazy people in this world. I swear it's because of all the plasticizers in packaging," she said in a fury. "That stuff dissolves and is absorbed by our DNA, and before you know it, we have a bunch of Martins and Johannas running all over the place..."

"A bold theory," I said dryly, and sat down in a free spot.

Rhashmi dropped onto the seat next to me. "I'm telling you, stay away from that Martin. The guy's definitely got a screw loose."

I peered behind me as unobtrusively as possible. Martin was sitting a few rows up from us, where he could keep tabs on me. When our eyes met, he waved with both hands. I turned forward hastily. I seemed to be a magnet for all sorts of nutcakes, as I was shocked to discover. How could Martin be back in the picture, again? I was really beyond help.

38

Ben grabbed me from behind in the hallway and pressed himself against my back, his breath hot on my neck. I closed my eyes in pleasure.

"Come with me," he whispered huskily, pushing open his room door and guiding me to his bed. I let myself be taken there; he was still behind me. I stroked his thighs, felt his muscular firm legs and much more... Moaning softly in my ear, he pushed me onto the mattress before covering my body with his. His eyes glittered with lust, and his gaze wandered greedily across my upper body, which made me quiver with excited anticipation.

"Take off your clothes," he commanded, stroking my breasts with one hand. My nipples stood up under the thin fabric of my shirt, and I tugged at the hem to finally get rid of it. Barely daring to breath, I watched him slowly bend over me. His tongue glided sensually and pleasurably over my breast, leaving a cold, wet trail on my skin. The pulsing between my legs increased, and I grabbed his hair and pulled his face down to my breasts, I needed to feel more of him. So much more... His hands brushed along my sides, approaching my thighs. I raised my hips and pushed against his touch while my body throbbed wildly. The stubble on his chin scratched across my neck and set off fireworks inside me. I gasped. His hand caressed my thigh, drew closer to my center; my skin was on fire.

"Kiss me," I rasped and put my hands around his neck, eagerly awaiting his sensual lips. I wanted him more than I'd ever wanted any other man in my life, longed to kiss him so badly, desired to play with his tongue, to surrender to him. Slowly, he approached my mouth, but stopped shortly before reaching it.

"You don't really think I'm going to kiss you, do you?" Ben threw his head back and laughed while I watched him in shock. Suddenly, Erdie, Toby, and Ellen were standing in front of my bed and joining in the laughter. Martin appeared too, giggling madly. Where had they all come from? And even worse, they were seeing me naked!

I woke up panting and looked around, confused. To my relief, I was alone in my room, and everything was quiet. Oh, my God. I just had a sex dream about Ben. So, that's what it had come to. Morning was just beginning to dawn, sending rays of sunshine into my room.

Slowly, I sat up, listening to my racing heartbeat. Desire for Ben was still pulsing between my thighs, spread warmly in my body, and it wouldn't stop. Only this wall separated us. He was asleep next door, by himself like the nights before. Longing overcame me; the need to go and lay down next to him, cuddle into his arms and breathe in his velvety scent, a mixture of sandalwood and a pleasant-smelling laundry soap.

I wanted to run my hands over his firm stomach and touch the dimple at the corner of his mouth again. I just wanted to be close to him. And I really wanted to kiss him, nibble on his lower lip and play with his tongue. Sighing, I got up to distract myself a little with studying to keep from rushing into his room like a sex-starved maniac. I had to be at the lab in two hours anyway. The last couple of days had passed uneventfully. Just as Ben had predicted, I hadn't run into Konstantin again all week. Six years had now passed, and there was a good chance that Konstantin had lost interest in me. I decided to simply continue with my life as if nothing ever happened. Although, I now made sure not to be alone outside after dark, just to be safe. My relationship with Ben was still friendly, but quite distant. More and more often, I got the impression that even the slightest trigger was enough to catapult our fragile friendship back into oblivion. He was back to only saying the barest minimum to me, while Martin, on the other hand, was becoming seriously annoying. He kept appearing on campus wherever I was, trying to talk to me. I had no idea how to get rid of him. The guy was a leech.

I wiped away the miserable thoughts of Martin and decided to take a long shower, since I was up this early anyway. The noise from the drain pipes would probably wake up my neighbors on the lower floors, but that wasn't my problem. Just as I stepped into the hallway, the door to Ben's room opened, and he came out dressed only in white boxers and a white t-shirt. It took great effort to keep my eyes off his shapely legs. A long scar ran across his left knee, and his hair stood out wildly to all sides.

Ben looked sleepy still, and in that moment, I wished with all my heart he could wake up next to me looking exactly like that every day. My stomach tingled and buzzed. He smiled when he saw me.

"You're up early," he remarked, yawning into his hand.

"Got tons of stuff to do in the lab. I wanted to get an early start," I lied hastily. After all, I could hardly tell him that I had woken up from a wet dream only a bit ago in which he played the leading role.

"I see." He walked past me towards the kitchen and lightly brushed against me with his arm. The brief touch tingled down my back like prosecco bubbles. Ben stopped in his tracks.

"You've got something in your hair." He plucked a piece of fuzz out and then stroked my hair. Next thing I knew, he was taking my face in both hands. I stopped breathing when I felt his fingers against my ears while his thumbs brushed across my cheeks. My blood surged through my veins; he must have felt it pulsating at his fingertips. We were standing close together. Ben's breathing quickened, stirring up an unbelievable nervousness in me. What did he have in mind? This man was the most unpredictable person I had ever met. What should I do? Nestle up to him, put my arms around his waist? None of my limbs were working, so I stood there and waited with bated breath for Ben's next move. For a few moments, we watched each other in silence. His dimple was right in front of me, and his black-blue eyes stared at me intently. Then I studied the arch of his eyebrows, memorizing every hair, every tiny bump. All of it formed a perfect image that I would carry with me in my heart. I had only ever been this close to him one other time, also here in this hallway and the very thought of it made me shiver with pleasure. He leaned towards me, and I hoped so badly that he would kiss me. Longingly, I closed my eyes and immediately felt his lips on my forehead before he broke away and released my face. Puzzled, I opened my eyes. In a strange way, Ben seemed to be dissatisfied, as if he had actually had something else in mind, but changed his plan at the last moment.

"Why did you kiss me?" I asked, barely audible, and looked at that handsome face that captivated me. I wanted to pull him into my arms, kiss him for real, and melt under his touch. It was hard to fight the impulse, hoping he didn't notice my desire, although everything inside of me screamed for him. Ben had to be blind.

"No reason." He gently tucked a strand of hair behind my ear while I was struggling to catch my breath. "You… You're just so pure and untainted. So innocent." There was a wistfulness in his voice.

My trembling stopped abruptly. What was he talking about? It was almost as if he imagined me as an immaculate virgin. He sounded distantly sentimental, which did not match his chosen lifestyle at all. His behavior made him seem older than he was—almost as if he was looking back on a long lifetime of debauchery and immorality.

"I'll be pure once I've taken a shower," I quipped to break the weird mood, whereupon Ben almost laughed in relief.

"Don't let me stop you." He gestured towards the bathroom then walked on to the kitchen. Why did he actively seek me out only to brush me off again? I'd been asking myself the same question for weeks and simply couldn't come up with an answer.

39

That afternoon, I returned to the apartment, exhausted. My early start was slowly taking its toll on me, and my body craved a nap. Then I spotted Ben and burst out laughing. He was sitting in the kitchen flicking through a sports magazine while Phyllis stood next to him on a chair, styling his hair. Thin strands of hair stuck up in all directions, held together by bright pink hair bands. When I came closer to check out her work, Ben noticed me and looked up. The front of his hair was parted to the side and held in place with two unicorn hair clips.

"You should wear pink more often." I chuckled as I sat down. "That color really suits you."

"Luca," cheered Phyllis. "Do you like Ben's hair?"

"It looks terrific." I gave her two thumbs up. "Ben should always wear his hair like that."

"Go ahead and make fun," he said. "She wanted to give me a haircut at first. I opted for the lesser of the two evils."

"Ben won't let me." Phyllis pouted. "I've watched Mommy cut hair. I know how to do it."

"Oh," I pretended to sympathize. "And he still won't let you?"

"No," Ben insisted. "I still won't let her."

"But why not?" Phyllis stomped her little foot, at which Ben reached to the chair next to him and pulled out a Barbie doll with chopped off hair. "That's why. I don't want to end up like her."

Phyllis tilted her head and stuck out her bottom lip. "Please?"

"Phyllis." He measured her with a stern look. "Forget about it."

Grumbling, she fixed another pink hair clip behind his ear. An oversized purple stuffed unicorn with a glittery mane took up the entire middle of the table. I picked it up to admire it from all sides. "This is beautiful. Is it new?"

"Rhashmi gave it to me," Phyllis explained. "She came to see Daddy yesterday and told me she likes unicorns just as much as I do."

I smiled to myself. "What do you think of Rhashmi?"

"She's nice." She vigorously combed out Ben's hair while he quietly groaned. "But not as nice as you are."

"Thanks, sweetie," I replied, touched.

"Alright, that's enough for now." Ben pulled a band out of his hair, but Phyllis clung to his hand.

"What are you doing? Stop it, you'll wreck your hairstyle."

"I have to take you to Grandma's in a few minutes, and I'm certainly not going out looking like this."

"But then it was all for nothing," Phyllis whined and frowned again.

"I'm not going out in public with my hair like this. The deal was just for inside."

"But your hair is so beautiful now." With her little hand, she stroked his head in admiration.

"I can imagine," he grumbled.

"You know what, Phyllis?" I pulled my phone out of my pocket. "I'll snap a picture of Ben, and he can print it out for you."

"Yay," the little girl cheered, while Ben glared at me murderously. Unfazed, I held up my phone.

"Smile, for the camera. Say *Ouistiti*."

Ben laughed "*Ouis...* What?"

And there I made a shot. "*Ouistiti*. That's French for 'tiny monkey.' It makes the greatest photo smiles," I explained, looking at the snapshot of Ben. Without a doubt, he looked funny, but he was still really attractive—nothing could make him look bad.

"Tiny monkey, huh," Ben repeated, tickling Phyllis until she giggled. "That suits you!"

I showed him my phone, and his smile froze.

"Phyllis," he gasped in horror. "What have you done to my hair? I look like your unicorn."

"I think you look cute," I said, while Phyllis gurgled at the picture.

"I'm going to take this to kindergarten and show it to all my friends."

"Don't you dare," Ben warned her. "Delete it." He tried to snatch my phone, but I was faster.

"No way."

"You guys are ganging up against me." Ben started to pull out the bands, while Phyllis screeched in protest. Then he got up. "I'm taking you home now before you cook up any more nonsense."

Phyllis packed up her things and grabbed the unicorn. "I tried so hard."

Meanwhile, I laid with my head on the table and laughed.

"You know what?" Ben suddenly said to his little visitor. "Next time, you can make up Luca. You've got a little makeup kit at home, bring it along."

"Oh, yeah!" Phyllis agreed. "I'll draw a unicorn on Luca's face."

My laughter died. "You'll regret that." I hoped Ben would miss the one band that was still stuck in the side of his hair.

He grinned. "She draws great unicorns."

Phyllis hugged me. "See you soon," she said, but it sounded like a threat. I could see Ben smirking next to me. He would definitely pay for this viciousness.

Ben went to the mirror in the hallway to check on his hair. Unfortunately, he found the band he had missed and pulled it out. He held it up between his thumb and forefinger. "Not so fast, I noticed you staring at it. You really would have let me go out like that?"

I nodded.

Phyllis had already opened the door and skipped outside. "Wait up," Ben called after her.

Still giggling, I went back to the kitchen counter where a pile of letters was stacked and flipped through them to see if there was anything for me. One of the boys must have brought the mail up earlier. But before that, I took one last look at the snapshot of Ben on my phone. At his aquiline nose and strong jaw, and I found his very tiny dimple.

I blew a stolen kiss onto the screen, then lost in thought, turned back to the envelopes. There was a loyalty voucher from a clothing store I'd last shopped at two years ago, a letter from my dentist, which looked a lot like the bill for my last cleaning, and then there was a letter simply addressed to *Luca Vogt* in blue ink. No stamp, so it must have been delivered in person. What was that all about? I stuck a finger in the side flap and ripped the envelope open. My hands started shaking, and I stared at the message as if petrified. I sank into a chair and repeatedly skimmed the one sentence.

Watch out, you stupid, horny slut!

Suddenly, I was chilled to the bone. I pressed my hand over my mouth, unable to take my eyes off the sheet of paper shaking in the other. Konstantin. Who else would write me such a horrible thing? So, he had merely kept his distance over the past few days, but he hadn't forgotten about me. Somehow, he had figured out where I lived. What was I supposed to do now?

I grabbed my phone and called Caro, but only got her

voicemail. Dammit. Abruptly, I jumped up and took a look out of the window, suddenly paranoid that I was being watched, even though I didn't spot anything suspicious anywhere. My eyes welled up with tears. I needed to calm down—breathe in and out. What could he possibly do to me? Konstantin couldn't do anything worse to me than what he had already done. Again, I realized that nothing had ended or been forgotten just because I had run away from it and tried to erase it from my mind. This nightmare would haunt me for the rest of my life. Konstantin had sworn something to me, and he was not a man who broke his promise. He was making me pay for one single, drunken mistake.

40

Caro, Martha, and I strolled through the dark streets of Nuremberg to attend the LGBTQ gala. At first sight, things seemed to be okay again between the two of them; they even held hands, although Caro still hadn't worked up the courage to introduce Martha to her parents yet. I had asked Ben for a lift to Nuremberg—and he did me the favor. Not only without asking questions, but he had even offered to pick me up again. I didn't tell him about the anonymous letter. It probably would've only led to an awkward conversation and wouldn't have done any good. If Konstantin denied having sent the letter, there was nothing Ben could do about it; assuming he'd have actually wanted to deal with my mess. I didn't want to bother him.

"Konstantin came by the gym again this week." Caro interrupted my thoughts, and I stopped in my tracks.

"Why?" My guts twisted up.

"He had to fix something." She turned around, only now realizing I'd stopped walking. "He says hi."

"You spoke to him?" My voice broke. What was that slimeball up to?

"I told him I didn't know you," she reassured me. "You

were taking a trial class, and I haven't seen you since. That's all he knows."

"I'm pretty sure he wrote that letter."

"Luca, go to the police." Caro let go of Martha to give me a hug.

Suddenly, I was freezing.

"Why don't you kick him in the balls?" Martha suggested pragmatically, stuffing both fists into the pockets of her baggy cargo jeans. "If I were you, I'd grab him and slam him up against a wall…"

"Great idea," Caro interrupted in an annoyed voice. "Luca can't just slam this guy against a wall, he's bigger and much stronger than her."

"I can't go to the police," I whispered. "If he found out…"

"They'd lock him up." Caro grabbed me by the arms, but I pulled free.

"They won't, though. I have no evidence against him. At most, they'd question him and let him go again. And that would only piss him off even more." I crossed my arms and started walking. "Let's not talk about that creep anymore. I'm just gonna ignore him and do nothing until he gets bored with his lousy game. I won't let him ruin my life all over again."

The two of them caught up to me, and Caro put an arm around my shoulders. "Let's start now and just forget about that creep. We won't let him spoil our evening."

"Exactly," I agreed, absolutely determined to have a good time at the gala. Martha slapped Caro's butt with her flat hand.

"I hope that goes for both of us too."

"What do you mean?" Caro asked.

"No drama tonight just because I'm talking to another woman."

"Why do you always make me look like a jealous cow?" Caro put her hands on her hips. "It's not that you can't talk to other people. How many times do I have to tell you that? It's about flirting, and there's a big difference."

"You always get the wrong idea right away."

"Yeah, right," Caro snorted. "Then why did you post on Sarah's Facebook how much you were looking forward to seeing her tonight?"

"What, are you spying on me or something?"

"No, it showed up on my feed. In case you forgot, I'm also Facebook friends with Sarah." Caro marched off. "Those days might be numbered, though," she threw back over her shoulder.

Martha and I followed her. You could have cut the tension with a knife. Well, this was gonna be a fun night. Fortunately, we could already hear voices and laughter, mixed with booming music ahead of us.

The place was packed. People were dancing. Extremely stylish boys rubbed up against their male dance partners, and the women were also dancing together with the beat; there was a great vibe. And mixed in between were heavily made-up transvestites in big wigs and fancy costumes like vibrant birds of paradise. Many of them had some very enviable bodies. Many of the women had short haircuts and wore baggy jeans with button-down shirts like Martha, and then there were women with long hair and sexy clothes like Caro. It was a colorful mixture of all types of people, all celebrating and having a good time.

"Let's get a drink" Martha yelled in my ear, leaving behind a high-pitched ringing noise. Then she repeated it to Caro, who just shrugged, but eventually started to move. I followed them to the densely-crowded bar. Martha bulldozed her way through the masses and set her arms on the marble slab surface. A red-haired woman sitting close by raised her glass in a toast at Martha, clearly trying to catch her eye. That was cheeky. Martha casually put one arm around Caro while she whispered something into the other woman's ear. My poor friend seemed like nothing more than an accessory.

"Luca," a high-pitched voice screeched, and I turned around. Michelle, formerly Michael, stood behind me in an absolutely breathtaking red dress. Her blonde hair flowed in corkscrew curls down to her waist, and her makeup surpassed anything I had ever seen before, even Ellen's. Michelle had the sexiest smoky eyes I'd ever seen. I knew Michelle through Caro; they were really good friends.

"You look amazing!" I yelled through the noise as I wrapped my arms around her. Squealing, we danced around in a circle. Martha tapped her finger against her temple.

"Sweetie!" Michelle held me at arm's length. "You need a makeover! Pronto! Look at you!" She put a hand to her cheek. "No, that doesn't work at all."

"Thanks," I said with an eye roll, which made her realize how unflattering she just had been.

"But I looove your green top." She pinched my left boob and made a honking sound. "Oh, what I'd give to have real ones like yours. You're one lucky girl."

I didn't think so, but I took it as a compliment. As it was, I hadn't heard too much flattery lately. Except for a couple of times when Ben said something equally stupid about my bustline. I wondered what he was doing tonight. I forgot to ask earlier. Was he on the prowl again? Scanning women like a piece of meat at the supermarket? What were his criteria? Breasts, vagina, and noticeable breathing? I hadn't been able to figure out a consistent pattern between his previous bed bunnies. They were all across the spectrum: redheads, blondes, brunettes. A drop of jealousy landed on my burning heart like gasoline and made it flare up. He hadn't brought home any coitus consorts for a while now, and it seemed like he wasn't interested in resuming the hunt for the foreseeable future. Had he sworn off women for a while? I found that hard to imagine. Maybe he was just taking a creative break. Hopefully, he wasn't nursing an STD! I wouldn't put anything past him. Perhaps I shouldn't think about him so much tonight.

Caro and Martha joined us. Martha handed me a glass of bubbly, while Michelle greeted Caro much the same way as she had me. They hopped together like mad in one place. The foxy redhead from the bar joined us too, which seemed to piss off Caro. She whispered something to Michelle before they both turned toward the redhead and shot her nasty looks.

"What does Caro even want with this ugly butch dyke?" Michelle murmured in my ear, not exactly flattering. "Why don't you two get together? You'd make such a cute couple."

"Because I'm not a lesbian."

"Have you ever tried it?" She played with her fake breasts.

"No, and I have no desire to either."

She waved this off. "Oh, you straight people are always so uptight."

In the meantime, Caro had grabbed Martha and hugged her so tightly the poor thing could barely breathe. Without a doubt, Caro was marking her territory.

Michelle smacked a handsome blond guy's butt. He turned around, annoyed.

"Hands off!" he snapped and hurried away.

"What's the rush?" Michelle shouted after him. "I won't bite! Only if you want me to!"

The blond disappeared into the crowd without giving Michelle a second glance.

"He's into me," she announced with conviction. "He's just playing hard to get. I'm gonna go test it out." Swinging her hips, she swept through the crowd. Her heels were at least six inches high, which made her tower over almost everyone else. I couldn't have taken even one step in such shoes, but she had mastered the hip swing as perfectly as a Victoria's Secret model. Somehow, I envied Michelle for her unwavering self-confidence. One-tenth of that would have made me happy.

The music picked up speed. Up on the stage, a group of well-built guys dressed in black leather were stripping along to the cheering enthusiasm of the crowd, which fortunately, distracted me from Ben. I enjoyed the show; these guys were definitely eye candy. I was completely immersed in the performance when, with a sexy move, one of the guys ripped his pants off and stood there only in a tiny thong. The audience shrieked, and the redhead spoke to me.

"Hi, I'm Jessica." She smiled. Her face was dappled with countless freckles, wild curls framed her face.

"Luca."

"Enjoying the view?" She pointed towards the stage.

"Yeah, they're really good."

"Oh." She seemed to understand. "Then you're just here to support the cause."

"Actually, to have fun and enjoy myself." I emptied my prosecco glass in one go. It was hot as hell in here.

"Would you like another one?" Jessica took my glass and hurried off to the bar, before I could answer. I looked around for Martha and Caro, but couldn't find them anywhere. I could only hope that Martha wasn't going to break Caro's heart again. Shortly afterwards, Jessica returned with a fresh glass of bubbly for me.

"Thanks."

We toasted each other.

"I'm only in Nuremberg for the weekend," said Jessica, close to my ear. "I'm from Hamburg."

"You came just for the gala?"

She nodded. "The most beautiful women are said to be here." She gave me a meaningful look, which made me all nervous. I hadn't really intended to flirt tonight, let alone at the gala. I quickly took a big sip.

"It's really good, not too dry." I gave an enthusiastic thumbs-up.

She came closer. "Would you like to dance?"

The show had ended in the meantime, and the DJ was playing house music again.

I hesitated for a moment considering whether I should actually bother getting to know Jessica. "I don't really feel like dancing tonight," I said lamely, which she acknowledged with a grin. "Then I'll dance, just hold on to me."

I involuntarily snorted and finally shrugged. "Why not?"

Jessica took my hand and led me onto the dance floor. On the way, I emptied my second glass of prosecco, before circling my hips like I'd learned at the Zumba class. My moves didn't really match the beat of the house music, but they seemed to be the easiest thing to do. Jessica, on the other hand, was a great dancer. She was limber and reminded me of that Indian goddess with the eight arms.

"Do you do Zumba?" she suddenly asked, without missing a beat.

"I had a trial lesson. Can you tell?"

She laughed and nodded. "Yes, but it looks good. Keep going."

Gradually, I loosened up. Jessica was actually a lot of fun. We joked about other dancers who were even clumsier than us, and just chatted nonsense. Eventually, I was ready for a break. "I'm exhausted," I gasped running my hands through my sweaty hair. I didn't even want to know what I looked like right now. "I need a break."

"Me, too," Jessica agreed, even though she still looked fresh and energetic, although her red curls clung around her damp hairline. We wriggled our way through the people, and this time, I bought the next round.

"Want to get some fresh air?" she asked, and I nodded. It was incredibly stuffy in the ballroom.

41

We walked out side-by-side. The crisp night air soothed my warm skin like a caress and gradually cooled my body. Still holding my glass, I toasted with Jessica, before we strolled to a nearby park bench and sat down. Countless stars glittered on the black canopy of the night sky above us, as a blinking dot slowly moved across the firmament.

"That was fun." Jessica tipped back her glass.

"Yeah, that was awesome." I also took a sip. "What made you decide to come all the way here just for the gala?"

Jessica looked down at the ground, lost in what seemed like a painful memory. "I was invited. I met a woman on a dating platform, and we really hit it off. Unfortunately, I realized that I didn't like her in real life as much as I did online."

"Did she look that bad?"

"Let's just say she didn't look like her pictures at all, and she was twenty years older."

"Ouch!" I clapped my hand over my mouth.

She shrugged her shoulders.

We sat for a while, cooling down.

"I'm going back inside. It's getting chilly." Jessica rubbed her arms.

"I'd like to stay for a bit." I was enjoying the quiet and wanted to rest for another few minutes before I threw myself back into the mayhem.

"See you later." Jessica went back inside, while I got up to walk a bit. Unexpectedly, Ben once again popped into my mind. I had to admit to myself that I missed him; he lingered in my thoughts longer than I wanted. Suddenly, I felt lonely—as if I were stuck in place watching time fade away. Ben didn't want me, but I, on the other hand, couldn't seem to move on and finally put him behind. Tomorrow I would go back home, tell Ben that everything was fine, and pretend I was not even remotely interested in him. Deciding to go back inside, I spotted two women a few feet in front of me standing close together in the shadows of a chestnut tree. Their voices sounded familiar, and I hesitated. One of them was definitely Martha.

"I really don't know what to do anymore. Caro is always mad at me," she said in a frustrated voice. I stopped in my tracks, which was a bad idea because there was nowhere for me to hide. If they turned their heads, I was screwed.

"Since when do you get so involved in relationships?" the other asked. Now, I recognized the platinum-blonde pixie cut —it was Sarah, Martha's ex.

"Caro is special. Somehow, she makes me really happy. Then again, she can get so annoying with her constant distrust."

As if in slow motion, Sarah extended a hand to stroke Martha's cheek, before she pulled her close. "Forget about Caro for a minute—since you've been with her, all you talk about is that chick. I swear, I hardly recognize you. Relax." Her hands slid down Martha's back, as her lips searched for Martha's. "Why don't you let me distract you for a bit?"

"Cut it out, Sarah," Martha gasped, pulling back abruptly. "I love Caro."

"What's the big deal?" Her hand wandered inside Martha's shirt, and both of them moaned before they kissed passionately, and Martha pulled Sarah's shirt up. Wow! What a cheat Martha was!

At this point, I could finally move again, so I cleared my throat loudly. They turned in my direction. Martha's jaw dropped, and hastily she pushed Sarah away, looking as if she were waking up from a trance.

"The two of you are the worst," I said disgusted. I really wanted to slap Martha right then and there; it felt as if she'd cheated on me along with Caro.

Sarah on the other hand just shrugged; she obviously didn't give a crap. "We were only making out a little." Her indifference made my blood boil.

"You guys are unbelievable." I turned away to look for Caro and tell her what I'd seen.

"Luca, wait," I heard Martha call.

I sped up, but she caught up with me and blocked my way.

"I didn't plan for that to happen. Please don't tell Caro."

"You gotta be kidding me!" I volleyed back at her like a tennis ball.

"Nothing really happened."

"Because I interrupted you." I shook my head at their brazenness.

"I love Caro, honestly. It was a slip-up."

I couldn't believe it. "Martha, there's no way I'm going to just sit here and watch you hurt my best friend, who happens to love you more than anything else."

"At least, let me tell her myself," Martha rubbed her hands. "But not today, next week."

"You're out of your mind."

"Luca. Caro's test at the gallery is next Monday. They really liked her portfolio. If I tell her tonight, she'll be a mess and ruin everything on Monday. We can't do that to her. She's worked too hard for this opportunity."

Grinding my teeth, I had to admit that Martha was right. Caro would certainly not get one straight brush stroke on the canvas on Monday if they broke up tonight. But the thought of having to pretend to my best friend for the next few days that everything was okay, even though I knew her partner was cheating on her, was unbearable for me. What was I supposed to do?

"C'mon Luca. Just for a couple of days. I won't tell her that you knew, either. Let me confess to her myself. I owe it to Caro."

"Alright," I finally agreed with a heavy heart, but this was an awful predicament because I really struggled with this decision. "But if you haven't come clean by next weekend, I'll tell her."

Martha patted my shoulder. "I owe you one."

"You don't owe me a thing," I replied coldly, meaning what I said. "And now, just go away."

Martha walked past me towards the ballroom, and I followed her at a distance. Inside, I looked for Caro and found her standing next to Michelle—they were laughing and giggling at something. Caro looked so happy that my heart ached. Martha walked up to them and slipped an arm around her waist as if everything was just fine. Caro immediately snuggled up to her.

Suddenly, I felt like I was the one ruining my friend's happiness, even though upon closer inspection, that was completely irrational. Sighing, I headed for the bar.

42

A few days later, I was watching *Sex and the City* reruns with Toby and Ellen in the living room. Actually, Toby had wanted to watch something else, but we'd overruled him. He gave in with a sigh and could only shake his head every once in a while.

"You girls are actually worse than us guys, you know?" he finally remarked, as Carrie gave her friends a detailed description of her sexual exploits from the night before.

Ellen sat up. "Why?"

"Men just do it, we don't carry on afterwards for hours about our conquests with our buddies."

"As if you guys never boast to your friends," I pointed out coolly. He couldn't tell me that.

"We might talk about it, you're right, but not in full detail like that. All we might ask is: Did you hook up with her? Yes. Did she let you? Yes. How was it? Awesome. End of conversation." He looked at me over Ellen's head. "But you women tell each other everything. Every little detail, starting with the size of his penis up to his bedroom skills. You zoom right in, that's just too much."

When Ellen nodded, which made Toby throw her a

shocked glance. "You do that too? Does Selina know stuff like that about me?"

"Course not." She winked at me. "Just that you're a crazy good lover."

Toby leaned back, a flattered grin on his face. "Am I?"

"You're the best," she assured him, patting his chest.

"Now that I know that, I can die happy," I remarked dryly, and they both laughed.

Ben appeared in the doorway. "What are you guys watching?"

"Certainly not soccer," I quipped.

"They won't let me," Toby complained. "Instead, I'm being tortured by having to listen to stupid conversations about female sex fantasies. The women there," he pointed to the TV screen, "are doing it all over the place. Imagine if we did that, put our sex lives on public display like them, we'd be called macho and chauvinist. But when they do that, it's something totally different, of course."

Ben sat down on the armrest next to me, just as Samantha, naked, enjoyed a romp in a love swing with some guy. He nudged me in the side. "Are you into that?"

"No," I replied curtly.

"Too bad, I haven't tried that yet."

"You should watch more *Sex and the City*, maybe you'd learn a new thing or two."

"I prefer to practice in real life."

"Not lately, though." I couldn't help myself, but whispered it so the other two wouldn't hear. Ben looked deep into my eyes.

"No, not lately," he confirmed just as quietly.

A tiny shiver of happiness went through my chest and flashed right into my heart. When I looked to the side, I caught a cold stare from Ellen, which she aimed at Ben next.

"Why shouldn't women be open about their sexuality?" Ellen suddenly asked. "We have as much right to indulge our sexual needs as guys, if we feel like it."

"That sounds a bit clinical," Ben observed.

"When I was single, I had one-night stands every now and then." She shrugged while Toby sat up to look her in the eyes.

"Good to know."

"What's the big deal?" She sat up too. "Don't pretend that you didn't have a sex life before you met me."

"Well, I did." Toby scratched his chin "But it's different with men. We need sex for stress relief."

I burst out laughing. Stress relief!!! Who was he kidding?

"Dude, we don't need sex for stress relief," Ben stabbed him in the back. "We do it because it's fun, because it's satisfying, and because we're happy afterward."

"It's exactly the same for us," Ellen agreed. "It's the world's favorite pastime."

"But not with a complete stranger." I was appalled.

"Why not?" Ellen seemed surprised.

They all looked at me skeptically, and I got the feeling I'd just said something phenomenally stupid.

"I mean, one-night stands are so impersonal," I defended myself.

I couldn't help but throw Ben a sidelong glance.

"What's a one-night stand like for guys, Ben?" Ellen addressed him. "What do you think about during sex?"

"I don't think about anything. Men can't fuck and think at the same time." He put one foot on the seat and propped his forearms on his thighs. "But I honestly think if Luca doesn't want to be with a guy for one night only, that's absolutely fine."

Did I hear him right? When had this change of heart occurred? I could distinctly remember him expressing very different opinions on this matter in the past.

"But she doesn't even know what she's missing," Ellen pointed out. "For me, Luca's just holding onto some very old-fashioned morals." Now, she looked at me as if I were nuts. "How can you even exist without having sex at all? That's just too weird."

"Yeah, Luca, how do you do that? How can you stand it?" Toby asked now as well. "Do you masturbate?"

"Course she does," Ben replied in my place, while I looked back and forth in bewilderment. "We all do it."

I felt myself turn bright red, while I hoped from the bottom of my heart that I hadn't moaned out loud during my dream the other night. If Ben brought it up now, I'd throw myself straight out the window. Right now!

"Um... Shall we switch to soccer?" I suggested cautiously and reached for the remote.

"Don't tell me we're making you feel uncomfortable." Ellen grabbed the remote out of my hand. "Girl, you definitely need a one-night stand. You just can't die without having that experience."

"I'm not suffering from a terminal illness. I've got a couple more years ahead of me, there's no need to rush into anything." I was starting to feel a bit nauseous now.

"Come on, you're twenty-three and you've never had a single one-night stand. That's so sad. We gotta get you one."

"Cut the crap. Are you out of your fucking mind?" Ben sounded angry.

"You stay out of this," she hissed.

"C'mon, Luca." She took my hands. "We'll find you a hot guy. Next week, at the festival. Why don't you come with us and see what happens? I know some very handsome men who could give you a run for your money."

"I... I don't know," I stammered. Dammit, I didn't want to have sex with a stranger. That just wasn't me.

"Are you insane?" Ben backed me up. "You're talking her into something she doesn't even want. Leave her the fuck alone. Some people are a little more inhibited in that regard, so what? You need to back off."

Inhibited? He still thought I was inhibited? Wow, that one hurt. Ben thought I was frigid.

"Why do you always keep butting in?" Ellen hissed. "Are

you really worried about her, or does it just bug you that Luca hasn't slept with you yet?"

"I haven't even tried," he replied, getting up. "Otherwise she'd have had one long ago."

What was that supposed to mean?

Ben turned and stomped out, slamming the door to his room with a loud bang.

"Did you have to do that again?" Toby sounded upset.

Ellen sank against the backrest. "He comes across as if he's this man of principles, but he really only uses other people." She turned to me again. "What about next Saturday? Are you coming to the festival?"

"I'll think about it." I took a look at my phone. "So late already." I got up hastily. "I really need to study for my exam tomorrow." After a quick wave, I hurried to my room. Honestly, a one-night stand was the absolute last thing on my mind right now. I certainly wasn't going to have a roll in the hay with some random wild stallion.

43

Isat at my desk, staring at my notes and trying to concentrate, while the previous conversation kept playing in an endless loop in my head. Those three had talked about sex the same way other people talked about the weather, and I felt completely left out. Did I seem so desperate to others that even Ellen wanted to set me up? Was Ben secretly making fun of me? *If he'd really wanted to, she would have had one long ago.* What did he mean by that? Was he that sure of himself, or was he just messing with me, and I didn't get it? Sighing, I flipped back a page, realizing with alarm that I hadn't retained one single thing. Tomorrow's test would end in a fiasco. The night was going to be a long one; I needed something to keep me awake. Why did I always wait until the last minute to study? After a thorough stretching, I got up to brew a pot of strong coffee and was startled when Ben entered my room without knocking. He closed the door behind him and walked up to me, seeming strangely agitated.

"Don't do it," he said, almost imploringly.

"What are you talking about?"

He put one hand on his forehead and ran it slowly through his brown hair. "Don't sleep with some random guy."

"Why do you even care?"

"You're not like that." He paused and took a deep breath. "You have principles. Values. Sex means something to you. Please don't do it."

I couldn't believe it. Ben was worried about my morals?

"I find it odd that you, of all people, a guy who has women lining up left and right, are advising me against a little casual fun."

Ben stared right through me. "Yes, me of all people. But this is different."

"Why is it different? Because you're a man?"

"No, goddammit!" he snapped at me, his eyes blazing. "Of course, that's not why. I... Because... Because..." He pressed both palms against his eyes and stood still, then he let his arms sink. "I can't tell you why, just please don't do it."

He was hiding something, and I decided to find out what it was. "Why shouldn't I have a one-night stand? Have some fun, no strings attached." He looked at me more appalled with every word that came out of my mouth, I saw the consternation literally grow inside him.

Slowly, he came up to me and took my face in both hands. His fingers were warm and pressed into my skin as if he were afraid I might break free.

"Don't do it," he implored me.

It took me a moment to sort out the chaos in my head and think clearly again. My heart started pounding restlessly in my chest as I realized why Ben had come to me. He wanted me—and I wanted him. I wanted to have the most wonderful and passionate sex with him I could imagine, then fall asleep by his side and nestle into the crook of his arm. And I wanted that every day. Cautiously, I put my hands on his hips. I felt his hip bones and stroked his back. Ben took a deep breath.

"Then at least have it with me, Luca. I'll make it a night to remember. I promise."

My chest constricted so violently that it almost hurt, only to erupt in an explosion of happiness. Ben's hand was on my neck, pulling me against him. Trembling inside, I closed my eyes, exploring the muscles on his ribs with my fingers. Ben's lips gently met my cheek, he blew a kiss on it before slowly moving his mouth to my ear. When he kissed me there, butterflies fluttered in my stomach, and I lost my breath for a moment. I gasped involuntarily as Ben breathed quickly and heatedly close to my ear. When he nibbled my earlobe, I clawed into his t-shirt, all dizzy. The feelings he evoked in me far surpassed those from my dream. Burning desire blazed from my stomach, over my chest, and seared down my back. I pressed myself against him, running my hands along his sides until they reached the waistband of his jeans and slipped under his shirt. Gently, I caressed his bare, soft skin. Ben moaned quietly.

"I know all about you," he whispered, short-winded. "I know your humor, your moods, your big heart, I even know your cycle, but I don't know what you look like."

I circled his belly button with my fingertips and stroked his stomach up to his chest. If he ripped my clothes off now, I'd help him. His lips touched my neck, and a pleasant shiver ran down my spine. I raised my head, felt his body heat, and nearly passed out from desire. He reached for my breast, tenderly and carefully caressing it. My most sensitive parts were throbbing. Oh, heavens, I wanted Ben so much. Finally, I took his face in both hands and stretched up to kiss him. I had risen to my tiptoes and leaned in, when he turned his head. I ended up brushing his chin with my lips while he slid his hands down to my waist. I froze. My body was white hot. Ben Nowak would not kiss me on the mouth. He wouldn't kiss me on the mouth! My heart broke as I realized I was just another one of his momentary conquests, nothing more. Of course, he had no deeper feelings for me. Abruptly, I pulled free and stepped back.

"Get out."

He looked at me confused. "What's wrong? Did I do something? Was I moving too fast?"

"Just get out." I swallowed back my tears. There was no way I was going to cry in front of him. Ben had screwed me over, just like Ellen had warned; he was only using me.

He stepped closer again, but I backed away.

"Find someone else, now go."

"Luca, can't we talk about this?"

"Talk about what?" I yelled, although Toby and Ellen could probably hear us. "About me being the next notch on your bedpost? About you using me like all the others?"

"It's not like that." He spread his hands. "Let me explain."

I laughed bitterly. "I get the picture."

"I'm not trying to use you."

"Then why don't you kiss me?"

"I did kiss you." He seemed confused.

"On the mouth."

We stared at each other in silence. Ben looked like a caged animal, his gaze darting in every direction as I waited for an answer with trembling breath.

"I can't kiss you," he finally said. It was the absolute worst rebuff anyone had ever given me.

"And why not?" My voice shook.

"I just can't, okay?" The tendons on his neck tightened, his arm muscles tensed.

"Then I can't sleep with you." He was crazy if he actually thought we could have sex under these circumstances. A quickie before we got back to business as usual. What he did to me hurt so, so bad.

"It's for the best," he finally said in a flat voice. "Better stay away from me, or you'll end up regretting it."

"I already do," I threw out, only to hurt him as much as he hurt me. Even though every single word was a lie. I didn't regret it; I was completely devastated.

Instead of giving me an answer, or finally an explanation, he turned around and stormed out of my room.

"Ben!" I yelled after him. "Wait!" But he'd already gone to his room, slammed the door, and turned the key in the lock, while I sat down on my bed and let my tears flow. For many minutes, I just sat there and watched my heart drown. The pain in my chest became overwhelming and threatened to break me into pieces. Ben would never kiss me. How could I have thought even for a second that a man like him would take a serious interest in me? I pressed both hands to my face and wept. More than anything in the world, I wanted to go after him now and throw all my bitter feelings right into his face. Ask him whether he even realized what he was doing to me when he trampled over my soul with his selfish manner. Tell him how shabby he had behaved by treating me as if I wasn't worth his love. I wanted to tell him all this so that he would finally understand; so that for once, he could feel what was going on inside of me. Instead, Ben was drowning in his own self-pity, pretending I could count myself lucky to be scorned by him. How abysmally stupid I'd been making myself believe things that had never been real. I let myself be blinded by his sweet talk until he had me right where he wanted me. I desired him, wanted him with every fiber in my body. Even worse, I loved him with all his flaws and weaknesses. Why did he do this to me? Once again, I had to admit that he was just out of my league. I had attributed even the slightest change in his character, in his behavior, to myself – that he had stopped hunting because of me. I'd misinterpreted his glances and words, and had hoped he felt something for me too. Now, I was sitting here and realizing the exact opposite was true. And yet, there was still the one thing he wanted so badly, but didn't get from me. Apparently, he didn't want anyone else to have me either; for whatever reason. So, I made a decision. I would go to the festival on Saturday, find myself a one-night stand, and bring him home with me to our apartment.

My phone rang in the middle of the night. *Dad* glowed on the display.

"Hello," I said sleepily.

"Hi, sweetheart," I heard my father's deep voice. "Did I wake you up?"

"No, what's up?"

"I have to tell you something."

Silence.

"What is it?" I finally dared to ask. An uneasy feeling joined my already desperate mood.

"You won't believe what's happened. I met somebody, and I like her a lot."

His words hit me like a ton of bricks. He hadn't had any relationships since my mother died. He couldn't just... I had no words. I just listened in silence, not knowing a single thing to say.

"Sweetheart, please. You have to understand. She makes me really happy. You'll meet her when you come over summer break. I'm sure you'll like her."

"And what about Munich? I was going to move there too, mainly because of you. What am I supposed to do there all by myself?"

"Can't you find a job in Erlangen for two years until..."

"Until you don't come back at all," I bitterly ended the sentence for him, although I knew that I was being unfair and possibly taking out my frustration with Ben on him.

Silence spread on the line.

"You're not a child anymore," he finally said. "I do want you close too. But sooner or later you'll get married and have a family of your own. Your old man will be nothing but a burden to you then."

"It's okay," I relented. A bittersweet feeling rose inside of me. On the one hand, with all my heart, I truly wished him a second chance at love with a woman who made him happy. On the other, however, a childish feeling of jealousy gnawed inside my chest. After wrestling with myself, I decided I would give his new lady love a chance. Who knew how things would turn out? Besides, I couldn't deal with my father right now. Ben's barging into my room earlier had devastated me. I still couldn't think clearly. Luckily, my father couldn't see that tears were streaming down my face.

"When we meet in August, we'll talk more, okay? I am happy for you." I wiped my cheeks. "Can we talk again this weekend? This is all a bit unexpected."

"Thanks for understanding. Of course, we can. You'll like her, I'm sure of it."

"I'll talk to you soon." I hung up and let my tears flow freely. Suddenly, I felt abandoned by everyone I loved.

44

"**Y**ou don't seriously want to go through with this?" Caro asked, aghast. We were at the Havana Bar for happy hour, enjoying melon daiquiris. Caro had made it to the final round at the gallery, even though she hadn't even known there was another evaluation round. The final decision would be made on Saturday.

"Why not?" I sipped on my straw, letting the melony goodness melt on my tongue.

"Because you can't sleep with a guy just to get back at Ben. Luca, that's sick."

Of course, my plan was sick, I knew that. After all, I had spent days trying to talk myself out of it. Until I realized it wasn't only about Ben. I didn't even know whether Ben would feel hurt. It was much more likely he'd find a bed bunny to bring home on Saturday night.

In fact, I couldn't shake the feeling that Ben had put the whole thing behind him, because he was behaving strangely indifferent towards me. Although he talked to me as if nothing had ever happened between us, our conversations never went beyond small talk. As if I were an acquaintance he'd run into sometimes in town. The gorge between us was as deep as the Mariana Trench.

"It's not just about Ben." I lifted my glass off the table and leaned back. "It's about me too. Why shouldn't I let loose a little? Obviously, everyone around me does. I'm the only dummy who's stupid enough to let outdated moral standards stop her from experiencing new things."

Caro leaned across the table. "Because you're doing your best to talk yourself into it, that's why. There is absolutely nothing wrong with having casual sex when you're single. But you have to actually be ready for it, and you're not. Not the way you're overthinking it. Either you do it and stand by it, or you don't. At least, that's what I think."

I slipped on my white cardigan; it was getting a bit chilly. "But maybe I just need to do it once. How else will I know whether I enjoy quick, uncomplicated sex if I don't give it a shot? And, who knows…" I twisted the black straw between my thumb and forefinger. "In the end, maybe I'll be a natural. Maybe a one-night stand is just what I need right now."

Caro blew a strand of hair from her face. "And what exactly do you plan on doing with your hookup? Lie down and say, 'Let's see what you've got, big guy'."

We giggled.

"Sounds about right, yeah."

"You're crazy."

"Why?" I put my now empty glass back down.

"Honest opinion?" She looked at me very piercingly.

"Don't hold back."

"Then you could've slept with Ben; who already promised to give you the night of your life."

My shoulders tensed. "Ben's a completely different story."

"Why, though? If all you care about is sex, then he's as good as anyone else."

"But it wouldn't be all about sex with him."

"I see."

"Nothing, *I see*," I hissed and waved the waitress over. "It's over with Ben."

"Talk to him," Caro said earnestly, "I find it hard to believe he's that much of a jerk. He's always so nice at the gym. I'm sure he is a good guy. Maybe there's a reason behind his strange behavior."

"No way," I snapped. "Ben is history. Saturday, I'm going to the festival, and if I like somebody there, I'm taking him home. This has nothing to do with Ben."

Caro snorted. She seemed upset, and I didn't quite get why. Why was she all up in my business? Even worse—why on earth was she defending Ben?

"Why would you take your conquest home with you? So Ben sees him?"

That's exactly why. "I'm not set on that," I said breezily. "There's a chance we might end up at his place. Now, let's not talk about this anymore, please."

The chubby waitress finally made it to our table. "What can I get you?"

"Two more, please," I ordered. "Are you going to the festival on Saturday?" I didn't feel comfortable going into this battle by myself. Actually, I felt like I was about to walk the plank.

"Of course, we'll be there. I'll have to check out the guy that you're planning to hook up with first," she threatened me.

"Who's we?"

"Me and Martha," she explained, as if I was a bit dimwitted.

Oh, apparently Martha didn't intend to fess up any time soon. What was I supposed to do now? If I told Caro about Martha's infidelity, I would have to admit that I'd known about it since last weekend. And she would never forgive me for that. Never ever, for sure. Caro's phone rang. She took the call, and chirped into the phone for a bit. "Martha's on her way," she announced after ending the call.

The waitress came back with full glasses and put them on the table.

I took the melon slice off the glass and bit into it. How

was I supposed to act around Martha? As angry as I was at her, Caro would immediately notice with her x-ray vision that something was off. I silently cursed Martha; the cheater.

"Something wrong?" Caro asked, but then a bright smile lit up her face. Immediately, I discovered the reason for her dazzling mood. Martha sauntered towards us and gave Caro a kiss on the lips without batting an eyelash before sitting down as if everything was just fine.

I hadn't seen such impertinence for a long time and glared at her.

"Hello," I growled as she blinked in my direction.

"Hi... How'd it go?" She turned hastily to Caro, and— completely ignored me. Unbelievable.

"Friday is the final round. Three candidates remain in the running. We have to create a painting, and they'll decide on Saturday."

"You'll get the job." Martha leaned an arm on the back of her chair at a slight angle away from me. That was the last straw. I drummed on the tabletop with my fingernails. How I would have loved to take out my frustration on Martha. At least she'd deserve it.

"I have to." She put a hand on Martha's thigh. "But I'm so nervous."

"Fingers crossed," I promised. "And Saturday, we'll celebrate at the festival."

"Which festival?" Martha raised an eyebrow when she noticed me shooting daggers at her with my eyes.

"Yeah, we're all going to the annual spring festival," I said sweetly. "Caro's final round will be over—something we can all look forward to."

A sudden coughing fit shook muscle-bound Martha.

"Are you alright?" I asked pointedly. Having to maintain this charade in front of Caro was really hard. What Martha did was inexcusable, but even worse, she'd made me her accomplice.

"It's okay," she gasped, but Caro quickly held the cocktail glass to her lips, and her *sweetheart* took a big sip.

"What the hell is this?" she asked, wiping her mouth in disgust.

"A melon Daiquiri."

"I'm gonna get a beer."

"I'll get you one." Caro stood up, but Martha held her by the wrist.

"I can go myself."

"I don't mind." Caro blew a kiss on her lips before she wriggled past the tables.

It hurt me to watch Caro being taken for a fool, especially since I knew exactly how that felt.

"Now that we're finally alone," I said in a saccharine-sweet tone. I was pleased to notice a single bead of sweat run down Martha's temple.

"Hey, Luca, you heard her. There's another round at the gallery on Friday. You've given me until the weekend."

"How can you sit here without a guilty conscience, have Caro bring you a beer, and pretend everything's fine?" I didn't understand Martha at all.

"I just want to enjoy our last days together." Martha took a coaster from the stack on the table and fiddled with it.

"You're really sick." Only she could make me as mad as Ben did.

"What?" Martha sounded upset. "You two are way too emotional. The one has nothing to do with the other."

"Don't give me that crap again."

"Just because I make out with someone else doesn't mean I don't love Caro anymore. Honestly, a little fling is no reason to throw it all away. So, I tripped up one time over one woman…"

"That's a nice way of putting it," I interrupted her furiously. "So, you tripped over Sarah and landed right in her blouse."

Martha folded the coaster in half as if it were my neck. I swallowed.

"I'm going to tell her everything, but you'll have to live with the consequences."

"So, you're going to tell her I caught you guys."

"No." She threw the broken coaster back on the table. "But you won't keep your mouth shut, I know you. You never can."

I gasped at the insult.

"Because, I still have a conscience," I snapped, but Martha was wrong. There was no way I was going to ever tell Caro about this. On the contrary! I intended to take this secret to my grave.

"You're arrogant, that's all." Martha gnashed her teeth. "What do you even know about Caro and me? Nothing. You've made up some shit about me in your head. You believe I'm cheating on my partner because all I care about is myself."

That was exactly what I thought of her. It was unbelievable how alike she and Ben were, in terms of selfishness—they definitely played in the same league. On top of that, she had cheated on my best friend, and now she was pretending to be the love of Caro's life.

"You're behaving just as badly as guys do," I yapped, thinking about Ben, that miserable narcissist.

"And you take a one size fits all approach! What does this have to do with guys? I know men who have been with their partners for years, and women who take what they need. You like to file people away according to their crimes."

I stared at her speechlessly. My motto had always been: "Live and let live," and "Everyone as they please." Still, Martha's accusations gave me pause for thought. Was I perhaps not as open-minded as I'd always believed?

"Maybe there is something to that," I admitted. "I have my own flaws, but Caro is my best friend, and I don't want her to get hurt. I am always there for her, and I've got her back."

"And that's awesome," Martha said softly as she grabbed Caro's cocktail. She took a big sip straight from the glass and grimaced again in disgust. "I grew up in an orphanage and in foster care; my childhood wasn't pretty," she went on. "I was always being moved around, got in trouble with my teachers and my foster parents. So, the best thing for me to do was not to allow myself to develop feelings for anybody, because I never knew how long I was going to stay in one place." She looked down, and my heart sank. "When I was sixteen, I had a counselor at the group home who really spent a lot of time with me. She took care of me and listened to my problems. She was my first love." Martha laughed softly and somewhat painfully. "It was unrequited. I never told her about my secret crush on her, but every time she hugged me, it was like the sun came up, and a warmth spread in my heart that I didn't know I had. For the first time in my life, someone gave me affection, and I clung to this woman, hoping she'd eventually love me back. One day, she came in with this huge smile on her face and told me she was going to have a baby and was getting married. And I completely lost it. I trashed her room and smashed everything into little pieces, before I slashed my wrist open." Martha pushed up her sleeve to show me a long scar that ran up her forearm. She blinked a couple of times. "Afterwards, I swore to myself I would never again allow anybody to do that to me. Do you understand? I'm doing great today. I've built a life for myself; I know hundreds of people, have business connections, and a good job. And I've achieved all of that by myself. I didn't have parents to give me a leg up, and I never ever want to go back to that point in my life, even if it means letting my emotions run low. But Caro really means a lot to me. I'm not lying."

My heart sank to my stomach. "I had no idea, Martha, I'm really sorry. I didn't know anything about you having a difficult childhood—it would have made me see things differently if I'd known." I clamped a hand to my mouth and felt as if I'd personally inflicted that deep cut on Martha's forearm.

"And there you go again with the emotional crap," she grumbled and was back to the tough old Martha. "Don't always pretend like you're responsible for all the injustices in the world. I will talk to Caro this weekend. In my own way. Can we leave it at that?"

I nodded. "Okay." I was at a loss of words. Me and my stupid big mouth. In order not to have to look Martha in the eyes any longer, I gazed past her. "Caro is coming back." To be honest, I'd never been so glad to see my best friend.

Caro hugged Martha from behind and held the brown beer bottle in front of her face. "Here you go, darling."

Martha turned to her, and her features softened and appeared almost wistful. For the very first time, I recognized deep emotions in Martha's eyes and felt torn. On the one hand, I didn't want my best friend to be betrayed; on the other, I truly hoped they would get their relationship back on track after this incredible confession.

45

I spun around in front of my mirror so that my skirt flared out. For the first time, I was wearing my green dirndl dress with the red checked apron. I had originally bought it for the festival last year, but then stuck it back in my closet and wore baggy jeans and a loose-fitting top instead, because the dirndl had emphasized my bust too much. Today, however, I felt comfortable in it, even though I rarely wore dresses. Over the past weeks, I had started wearing tighter clothes and, to my surprise, nobody had made fun of my breasts. Now and then, I registered a flattering look from a guy, but that was about it. And tonight, I wanted to look hot. Tonight, I was on the prowl.

I stepped out into the hallway where Toby and Ellen were already waiting for me. Toby was wearing a blue checkered shirt that really looked good on him. Ben also planned to join us.

Toby gave a whistle. "Wow, Luca. Now, that's what I call a rack!"

I rolled my eyes and stole a glance at Ellen's cleavage. She must have been wearing a padded push-up, because her breasts looked bigger than usual, though altogether she looked ravishing. Her dirndl wasn't a simple off-the-rack dress like mine—hers was black and red, with intricate orange-red flames embroidered on the apron. Her hemline ended a good bit above her knees, which accentuated her long, slender legs. Without a doubt, Ellen knew how to draw attention to herself.

She stepped towards me. "You look great. Ready for your big night?" she asked ambiguously.

"You know what?" I tried to brush it off. "I'll just let things run their course. If something happens, okay, if not, whatever."

At exactly that moment, Ben joined us. He wore a red plaid shirt with his jeans and had definitely heard what I said, though he ignored me. Instead, he turned to Toby without paying any attention to me or Ellen. Crap, he was obviously still mad.

"We can go. Erdie is already there."

"Let's roll." Toby opened the door and let us file out, before he locked up after us.

Toby and Ellen held hands as they strolled along the narrow sidewalk, so Ben and I had no choice but to follow behind them side-by-side. I racked my brain for a harmless topic to start a conversation.

"New shirt?" I smiled, but he remained impassive.

"Yes, even I buy new clothes from time to time."

Once again, he was showing his most amiable side. So typical. Idiot. "Do you have to be so snotty?"

He snorted. "Did you join the Wardrobe Monitoring Commission?"

"Did you join the I-Act-Like-An-Ass Commission?

"In your eyes, I always am."

"Right now, you are."

"So sorry, if I'm spoiling your *big night*."

"You're such a jerk."

"You're gonna meet even bigger ones tonight. Trust me."

"That's none of your business."

He waved me off. "I really don't give a shit."

Toby turned around. "Guys, be peaceful for once."

With my crossed arms, I kept on walking beside Ben in silence. And they say that we women are complicated…

Finally, we reached the fairgrounds, which were already overflowing with people. We pushed our way through the chattering masses while Ben talked to Erdie on the phone and got directions. I had no choice, but to follow Ben and had a hard time not losing him in the crowd, because he stubbornly hurried along without a thought for his companions. Ellen took my hand and pulled me behind her. At least I wasn't going to lose her. Finally, we found the new lovebirds at a bar table with a group of other people.

"Hey." I hugged Rhashmi, who was also wearing a traditional dirndl, which complimented her dark complexion.

"Hey, what a crowd," she said.

"It's crazy," I agreed, as a young guy bumped into me from behind, pressing me up against Rhashmi.

"Hey, Shorty, what's up?" Erdie greeted me with his signature fake punch.

"Nothing much."

"What did you do to Ben?" Rhashmi whispered in my ear.

"Nothing. Why?"

"He looks pissed."

"And how is that supposed to be my fault?" I defended myself. "Maybe he's got a beef with Erdie." But then I noticed the two of them talking to each other, laughing quietly. Well, I guess that excuse didn't work. To escape from the inquisition, I pretended to be thirsty. "Hey, I'm getting a drink. Be right back." I took off before she could ask any more uncomfortable questions. Why did Rhashmi immediately assume that I was responsible for Ben being grouchy?

After a half an hour, I finally had a glass of prosecco in my hand. At least, I had bumped into a couple fellow students in line and had someone to talk to, thankfully. But after looking everywhere, I couldn't find my friends. Crap. Wherever I turned, there were throngs of people. I didn't see any of them. Every other person was wearing either a checked shirt or a dirndl; obviously, searching for my friends by their clothing wasn't going to help. Sighing, I got out my cell phone and dialed Toby's number. I had briefly considered calling Ben, but quickly changed my mind. He'd probably ignore me when he saw my name show up on the display. The call connected, and at the same time, I heard the Darth Vader theme behind me, the one that always plays whenever he appeared in the movies. When I turned around, I spotted Toby and the others crack up laughing. Even Ben joined in!

"You gave me the Darth Vader ringtone?" I snapped at Toby, while the boys laughed some more.

"I still have it saved from the day we met," Toby affirmed, "Remember, how you wanted to strangle Ben with the power of the Force that night?" He mimicked Vader's stupid death grip with his hand.

If I'd only succeeded. "How funny."

Ellen came to stand beside me. She also had a glass of Prosecco in her hand. How did she get a drink so quickly?

"Forget those idiots. I'd like to introduce you to someone, if you want." She pointed to a slender man about my age, with wavy brown hair that reached the base of his neck. No doubt he was handsome, but his hairstyle made him look slightly too feminine in my eyes.

"Not now," I decided hastily, because the guy was openly ogling me. Ellen wouldn't have let him in on my plans, would she?

"This is Leon. He's cool."

"Later." To my delight, I discovered a few bottles of alcohol on the table next to Erdie. The boys had stocked up. He waved me over with an open prosecco bottle and, without asking, topped off my glass. Rhashmi was really lucky; the guy had good manners.

"Afterward, we'll go for a ride on The Twister," Rhashmi announced, pointing at the roller coaster.

"Don't count on me," I declined, finishing my second glass. I needed to slow down if I wanted to get through the evening—the alcohol was already going to my head and the sun beamed down on me mercilessly.

Erdie filled up my glass again. That was incredibly practical. In a second, I decided to stay with them so I wouldn't have to stand in line for drinks again.

"Where's the beer, bro?" I heard Ben ask next to me.

"Damn it, I forgot." Erdie scratched his neck. "Just went to the wine booth." It was unbelievable how forgetful that man was. "Want some of this?" He showed him the prosecco bottle.

Ben glanced at my full glass. "No, thanks."

"I didn't drink from the bottle, so you have nothing to worry about. My lips didn't even come near it," I blurted out. He was such an arrogant prick.

Ben looked at me like I was nuts. "What?"

"You're not having prosecco because I am?" I spelled it out for him.

"I'm not drinking prosecco because I don't like it. What's that got to do with you?"

What should I answer now? That my imagination had played a trick on me? I decided to go on the defensive. "Forget it," I replied haughtily and turned away, before I took a big sip from my glass to calm back down.

Ben walked away in a huff, leaving Rhashmi and Erdie to stare at me in confusion. Luckily, my phone rang. It was Caro calling, and I guided her towards us. A short time later, she appeared along with Martha. I ran towards them.

"Looks like you've had a few already," Caro remarked, when I gave her a really big hug, but I was just so happy to see her. "It's not even five yet. Slow down, or you won't live to see the night." She poured water from her bottle into my empty glass. "Have some water in between."

"Thanks. How did it go at the gallery?" I wavered a little. I really needed to slow down, otherwise the festival would end badly for me.

Caro beamed. "I got the job."

Cheering, we hugged each other. "We need to celebrate," I shouted exuberantly and gulped down the water to make room in the glass.

46

Three hours later, we were still partying at the same spot. In the meantime, I had eaten half a grilled chicken, one of the few things safe for me to have at festivals like this, and thankfully, the delicious bird soaked up some of the alcohol in my system. I felt good. A little tipsy maybe, but I wasn't falling-down drunk. Meanwhile, Caro drank with me, which increased the fun factor immensely. From the corner of my eye, I noticed that Ben and Martha were having a really good conversation. They stood close to each other, sipping beer out of their steins, and they didn't seem to be partying quite as hard as Caro and I were.

"What about your plan? Are you gonna go through with it?" Caro took a sip of her prosecco. She was wearing traditional Lederhosen and a red checkered blouse, which looked really cute on her.

"Nah," I declined. "I'd rather drink with you."

"An excellent plan." She patted my shoulder. "Martha's acting so weird tonight, like something's bothering her. You don't think she's gonna break up with me, do you?" she added with an anxious frown.

What was I supposed to say? Again, I silently cursed

Martha. "Forget about your worries for one night. Let's have a good time." I clinked my glass against hers. "Cheers."

"Luca, I'd like you to meet Leon." I suddenly heard Ellen beside me and turned around.

Caro raised an eyebrow.

"Hi there." Leon flashed me the whitest toothpaste model smile I'd ever seen.

"Um, hi," I stammered embarrassed while he unashamedly stared at my neckline.

"Can I get you another prosecco?" He reached for my glass.

"Um, sure," I agreed hesitantly, whereupon he went off to the bar.

"You haven't told him anything, have you?" I double checked with Ellen, who was nursing a glass of water.

She acted astonished. "Course not, what do you think of me? I just told him I had a cute friend he should meet." She put an arm around me. "Leon's a good guy. I've known him for a while. He's a DJ."

A DJ. DJs didn't usually take much interest in me; they seemed to prefer hanging out with blondes in hot pants. I couldn't shake the feeling that Ellen wasn't being straight with me, but then Leon came back balancing two full glasses. Obviously, I was the only one who had to stand in line to get a drink.

"Here we go." Leon handed me a full glass, before he took my other hand and pulled me over to the tall table where Erdie and Rhashmi had been standing earlier. They had moved on to a bench and were wrapped around each other, murmuring.

Leon and I clinked glasses.

"So, you live with Ellen's boyfriend?" he remarked, sipping his drink.

"Uh, yes. We share an apartment in the dorm." Suddenly, I felt unsettled. I actually wanted to party with Caro rather than talk to this hipster. Leon seemed way too cool for me.

His unbuttoned, gray Henley shirt showed off his hairless chest. Traditional Bavarian clothing didn't seem to be his thing.

"And you're a DJ?" I asked, trying to keep up my side of the sluggish conversation.

"Yes, I play house clubs all over the country."

"That's amazing."

Silence. My head was spinning, and I was sighing inside. If you had to go through all this build-up to get a one-night stand, I was just fine without it.

"I'll be at Mach 1 next Saturday. You should drop by."

I clung to my glass. "I'll think about it. So, I guess all this probably isn't your scene?" I pointed to one of the tents where oom pah-pah music was playing.

"I'm only here because Ellen asked me to come." He looked deep into my eyes, and I swallowed hard.

"Where did she go?" I turned around, but couldn't find her anywhere. Even Caro had left me to join Martha and Ben. Why wasn't she helping me out of my dilemma?

"I don't really care." He took my hand and stroked it.

"Umm... I'm not sure what Ellen told you about me, but..."

"Not much. She just mentioned you're looking for a one-night stand," he finally admitted, and my knees went weak.

"She really told you that?"

"Listen, I'm not here to hook up with you. I just wanted to talk to you. So, take it easy. If something comes up, I'm all for it. But I'm not gonna push you into anything you don't want to do. Relax," he said in a hoarse voice that gave me goosebumps.

At least he seemed honest. I should really loosen up if I didn't want to end up an old maid. Here was a good-looking guy in front of me, trying to get to know me, and I was acting all weird. Erdie strolled over to give Leon a thorough once-over.

"You okay, Luca?" Erdie put an arm around my shoulder. "You look like you've had a few too many."

"I'm doing great," I quickly assured him. "This is Ellen's friend."

Erdie raised to his impressive 6'3" next to me, all the muscles in his body tense. I didn't even have that many.

"If you need anything, we're sitting over there." He pointed to a row of picnic tables. Unimpressed by Erdie, Leon grabbed a pack of cigarettes from his pants pocket and lit one.

"Want one?" He held up the open pack, but I declined. Then he pointed to my empty glass.

"Let's move over to the bar so we can keep talking, and won't have to go back and forth for more drinks." Without waiting for my answer, he grabbed my hand and dragged me behind him before I had a chance to protest. At the bar, he ordered two more glasses of prosecco, and our conversation started flowing more smoothly. However, I had to prop myself up against the bar to keep from swaying.

"You look amazing in your dirndl," he said with an appreciative glance at my chest. "Are those real, or did you get help with a push-up?"

"No, they're all real," I casually replied. Right now, I cared more about my drink than his babbling.

"I wish I were your bra," he whispered in my ear hoarsely, leaning in. Without any warning, he planted a kiss on my lips.

I immediately backed away. "You're moving too quickly."

"Your lips were asking me to." He kissed me again before I could react, leaving behind a stale taste of ashtray on my lips.

"Not so fast," I scolded him with a heavy tongue, at which he held a fresh glass to my lips.

"Drink up, sweetie."

I chugged half of the drink, while he put an arm around my waist and pulled me closer. *No flirting,* I admonished myself. I would avoid anything that might remotely encourage him to misinterpret my signals. I hesitantly stroked his chest with one hand, but didn't like what I felt. He was very slim, if not to say bony, and didn't feel half as good as Ben did. Being this close to him started to make me feel uncomfortable. As I tried to break free from his grip, my glass slipped out of my hand and broke on the cobblestones. Prosecco sprayed on my bare legs.

"Ewww." I used the accident to peel away from him; he was like an octopus. My head was spinning.

"Don't worry about it." Leon signaled the bartender and ordered two Black Bettys.

"What's that?" I asked, as he handed me a glass full of a blackish liquid.

"A Black Betty. Sort of a cocktail." He toasted me, but I just stared thoughtfully at the strange concoction. Just as I was about to taste this unknown drink, I heard a familiar voice beside me.

"What are you drinking?"

Ben was next to me. Where'd he come from? "Ben!" I exclaimed ecstatically, trying to throw myself into his arms, but he stopped me.

"What are you drinking?" he snapped at me instead. Brushing me off like that made my anger flare up again.

"What's it to you?" I hissed, but he wouldn't budge.

"Why can't you answer one simple question? I want to know what you're drinking."

I held my glass up. "It's a Black Betty. Happy now?"

"You're not drinking that."

"Excuse me?" I must have misheard him. "Watch me." I brought the glass to my lips, when Ben knocked it out of my hand. The contents splattered all over the place, hitting other people who turned toward us furiously.

Ben ignored them; he seemed so mad. But so was I.

"Are you crazy?" I hissed unsteady on my feet, as I wiped the sticky liquid off my arm.

"That drink is made with dark beer, gluten, you know. It'll make you as sick as last time in that pizza place."

"Don't hit on my date," Leon interfered.

"Stay out of this," Ben snapped at Leon before he gave me a piercing look. "You're drunk. Why don't you go home?"

"Here." Leon pushed his Black Betty over the counter towards me. "Have mine, I'll order a new one. And you fuck off. It's her own business when she goes home, and if she does, it'll be with me."

"Aren't you listening, moron?" Ben grabbed Leon by the collar. His eyes sparkled menacingly, but Leon pulled away and shoved him back.

"Don't touch me, or are you tired of living?" Leon suddenly lunged at him, swinging his fist, but Ben ducked and shoved him against the bar. "Keep your dirty hands off her," growled Ben before he attacked him. They rammed into each other, and punches started flying.

"Ben," I screamed, when Erdie and Toby rushed over and threw themselves between the two.

"Ben, chill out." Erdie grabbed his friend from behind, under the arms, and pulled him away from his opponent, while Toby kept Leon at bay with both hands. "Stop it now," Toby talked him down.

Meanwhile Ben tried to break free from Erdie's grip. "Let go of me! I'll give that fucker…"

"Calm down, man. What's wrong with you?" Erdie held him in a vise grip.

Leon pointed at Ben over Toby's shoulder. "I'm gonna kick your ass."

Erdie pulled Ben, who was now flailing around wildly, aside while Toby tried to get Leon to calm down. I was standing in the middle of it all, my head was spinning, and I had no idea what had just happened.

"You need to give it a rest, Ben." I heard Erdie say in a warning voice. "Or do you want the cops to show up and take you in?"

Ben broke free. His gaze fell on me. There was more anger

in his eyes than I would have ever thought possible. Finally, he turned to walk away.

Erdie grabbed Ben's arm. "Where are you going?"

"I need a minute."

But Erdie didn't let go of Ben, instead the two exchanged a long look. Finally, Erdie raised both hands in surrender. "Okay, but I'll call you later, and when I do, you better answer your phone. Got it?"

"Yes, dammit. And now, let go of me."

"Ben!" I called out, wanting to run after him, but Erdie stopped me.

"You better leave him alone."

"Where's he going?"

He shrugged. "No idea. Someplace where he can cool off; just let him."

My eyes filled with tears. "This is all my fault."

"It's not your fault," Erdie reassured me. "He just lost it; he'll be fine. As for you, you should stop drinking right now."

I nodded meekly.

Leon came over. "Now that that wacko's gone, wanna have another drink?"

"No." I crossed my arms. All of a sudden, he reminded me of Jason in *Friday the 13th*.

"Come on now, just one more. Don't be such a lightweight."

"Didn't you hear what she said? Go the fuck away." As Erdie straightened up to his full height, Leon took a step back.

"Alright, alright. Fine." Leon strolled back to the bar to talk to a dark-haired woman who was standing there by herself, while I worried about Ben. If it hadn't been for him, I'd probably be as sick now as that night at the pizza place. I sat down on a bench, away from the hustle and bustle, to avoid Rhashmi's questions. She was already on her way over to me. Taking out my phone and staring at the dark screen, I debated in silence if I should call Ben. I dialed his number because I needed to know if he was okay. With trembling fingers, I listened to the tone, let it ring countless times, but Ben didn't pick up. He had even switched his voicemail. Finally, overwhelmed with remorse, I lowered my phone. This disaster had only happened because of my stupid and childish plan. Only because in my wounded vanity, I'd wanted to put one over on Ben instead of talking it out with him like an adult.

Caro sat down next to me, and I was surprised to see tears in her eyes.

"What's wrong?"

"I just broke up with Martha."

"You did?" I asked, perplexed.

"She cheated on me with Sarah," she sobbed, pressing her face into her hands.

I felt like crying right along with her and put my arms around her.

"I knew about it," I blurted out without thinking. "I'm so sorry."

She slowly sat up and looked at me dumbfounded. "What are you talking about?"

"I caught them together at the gala."

"And you didn't tell me?" She stood up and pressed both hands against her temples. My sweet Caro looked so hurt that shame burned through me to the bottom of my soul.

"Martha wanted to tell you herself, and you had your thing at the gallery. We didn't want to ruin that for you."

"Wow, aren't you two just so generous," Caro snapped. "I can't believe that you, of all people, kept this from me."

"Please don't be mad." It was obviously my day for pissing everybody off. "Of course, I would've told you everything if Martha hadn't come clean herself. But she owed you that confession, don't you think? Maybe you can forgive her, or at least talk with her tomorrow, when you've had a chance to cool down." I gave her a small apologetic smile, though I felt like a traitor.

"You're out of your mind. How am I supposed to forgive her?" She sank down on the bench again.

"At least try. Martha really does love you." I kissed her on the cheek. "Please give her one more chance."

Caro leaned her head on my shoulder. "Maybe I'll talk to her in a few days."

"You should do that," I whispered.

"What about Ben?" she asked.

"Ben will probably never speak to me again." I stared into the crowd and flinched. For a split second, I thought I had spotted Konstantin among all the people.

47

Tired and hungover, I sat at the kitchen table and stared into my cup, watching the whorls my spoon made in the hot dark liquid and feeling lonely. Caro had spent the night at my place, but had gone home earlier. We spent the night nestled in the pillows and consoling each other while we each complained about our lost loves. This, unfortunately, didn't help at all. Sometime early in the morning, I had heard the door click. Ben must have come home, because Ellen and Toby had gone to a club in Nuremberg intending to spend the night with friends. It was strange to think of him lying next door in his bed, while I was sitting here by myself, unable to think of anything else but him. I still couldn't get over the fact that I had entertained the stupidest, meanest, and most immoral idea I could think of just to get back at Ben. I'd wanted to make him suffer the way he'd made me suffer.

Ben's door opened, sending a lightning-fast jolt through my body. Hastily, I sat up, trying to appear as normal as possible. I heard his footsteps come closer down the hallway, and he entered the kitchen without acknowledging me. He fiddled with the coffee maker then walked back toward the door. My throat tightened, and tears welled up in my eyes. I needed to talk to someone. Now. Maybe I could make Ben understand me if I told him what was weighing heavily on my soul.

"Ben," I said slowly, and he stopped in his tracks but didn't turn around.

"What?"

It was obvious, he didn't want to talk to me.

"Remember when you said once that if I ever needed someone to talk to, you'd be here to listen?"

"I do." Ben finally turned around. His face remained so impassive that I couldn't read him at all.

"I could really use someone to talk to now." I held my breath.

He was reluctant to come back, but he finally sat down at the table and set down his coffee cup with a thud. Silence spread throughout the room, stretching on unbearably.

"When…" I cleared my throat and stared at the wall as if a thriller movie were being screened there. "When I told you guys I'd never had a one-night stand, I lied." I pulled a strand of hair behind my ear. "In fact, I did have one, six years ago when I was still in high school." My voice broke in the wrong place, and I felt like I was about to burst out in tears right then and there.

"Konstantin," Ben said softly.

I nodded. "Yes."

We sat still, neither of us moving, while I didn't know how to continue.

"What did he do to you?" Ben asked, which started me sobbing.

Tears flooded my eyes. Actually, I had intended to talk about this all cool and unemotionally, but the feelings overwhelmed me. I got up and went to the cupboard, took out a glass, and filled it with water from the tap. Breathing heavily, I pressed the cool glass against my burning cheeks before I made myself sit down again. Ben had waited for me silently, and he now looked at me intently. Something like concern glinted in his gaze, which touched me deeply. I had to gather all my courage to go on.

"I was seventeen," I whispered, "and still a virgin. The only virgin in my class, and it bothered me so much. One night, I was out at a club with two friends, and I met Konstantin. He approached me, and we danced. Konstantin was three years older than me, and all the girls in town had a crush on him. How proud I was that he'd noticed me that night." I propped one elbow on the tabletop, leaned my forehead into the palm of my hand so I wouldn't have to look at Ben. Shame burned in me like a blazing fire, nothing but shame. "He got a bottle of whiskey and apple juice. We mixed it and drank all night, partied till dawn. At some point, he asked me if I'd like to go to his place." I raised my head in slow motion. "Of course, I knew where that was going to lead to. I wasn't that naive, but I finally wanted to get my first time over with. To sleep with a guy so I could say it was done. Besides, by that time, I was so drunk I didn't care anymore."

Ben had his forearms crossed on the tabletop and was listening quietly. His expression didn't reveal what he was thinking, which made me even more tense. Yet, I kept talking. "We—we finally got to his place and had sex. It was terrible. He was rough and hurt me, and I just wanted it to be over so I could go home. After he'd finished, I got dressed and took off. As I left, he said, "Until next time," but I just thought, *we're not doing this again, never ever.* I spent two hours walking through the empty streets, blaming myself. How could I have been so stupid and have sex with Konstantin?" I drank some water. My mouth felt dry, and the tears I was swallowing burned in my throat. "The next day he called me and ordered me to his place. I told him to leave me alone and that the night with him had been a mistake. Shortly afterward, he texted me something. A photo, with a note that there was also a video. The picture showed us having sex. Konstantin had secretly set up a camera somewhere and positioned it in such a way that I was the only one in view. But his head was cut off by the camera, so I panicked. Later, he sent me another text demanding that I come over."

I wiped the tears that wouldn't stop from my cheeks. They were dripping onto the tabletop. "So, I went back to his place and told him to delete the footage. But he just laughed and threatened to post the video online and make sure everybody at my school saw it if I didn't do what he told me." I broke off to collect myself. My heartbeat pounded painfully all the way to my throat. "In my desperation, I slept with him again," I sobbed more than I talked and looked up at Ben. "You know, so he would delete the video." It sounded like I was defending myself. He must have thought the worst of me now. Even though I had addressed Ben directly, he remained silent, which was perhaps better, otherwise this conversation would probably have ended in even more crying on my part. I fought the impulse to downplay the situation and decided to remain honest, relentlessly honest. "In the end, I let him do anything he wanted to me. Anything. Just so that nobody would ever find out. Afterward, he laughed and said that in the future, we would have a lot of fun together. I totally panicked and took off, ran through the streets, trying to figure out what to do. I couldn't let him touch me again, and wished he'd just leave me alone. Then suddenly, I got so incredibly angry with Konstantin that I turned around and went back. I warned him that I'd go to the police if he didn't stop and destroy that shitty video."

Meanwhile, I was completely in tears and could hardly get the words out. The memories pelted down on me like a dark hailstorm, making me feel very small, destroying every warm feeling inside of me, and leaving behind only pain and emptiness. I searched for the right words, not wanting Ben's impression of me to grow even worse. What must he think of me now? I longed to bundle all these memories in a towel and throw it into the deepest spot of a lake, so they could never come back up to bother me again.

"And then he beat me up and threatened to kill me if I

turned him in." Suddenly, my voice was gone; I couldn't talk anymore. Instead, I grabbed for my glass with trembling fingers and knocked it over. The contents poured over the bare wooden table and collected in a shimmering trickle. Ben was still listening, so I went on despite my exhaustion. "I became so afraid of Konstantin that I did nothing except ignore his calls. A few days, later he posted the video online. He had even built a homepage for it, using my full name along with keywords like 'big boobs,' 'giant tits,' and other disgusting stuff. Everyone at school saw the website and watched me in action. My last years at school were hell. When I moved to Erlangen, I shortened my first name. I was so scared someone here might Google me. Like maybe one of the professors I wanted to work with. But I was lucky, and everything's gone smoothly. No one from my high school applied to go here, so nobody knew me. But now, Konstantin is here." I ended in a fragile voice. Even though I had gotten everything off my chest, I felt dead inside. It was humiliating and degrading to have confessed this ugly incident to Ben. I wondered what he thought of me now and dared a sideways glance.

Ben sat motionless in his chair, staring at the blank wall. His features looked frozen, only his jaw tightened and his eyes narrowed. Why didn't he say anything? He was condemning me. He had to be! Why had I told him everything? My heart thudded dully up to my temples, and my throat constricted, while I waited for Ben's reaction. Anything. Eventually, he got up and left the kitchen without saying a word. He just left me there, all alone with my pain and shame. Was he going to go watch the video on the internet now?

48

Caro had been behaving very oddly lately, if not to say paranoid, in fact. After a few discussions, she and Martha were slowly getting back together, but Caro still didn't fully trust her ex. At her insistence, I had let myself be talked into coming to Nuremberg to help her spy on Martha; which I found highly questionable and had told Caro so. Unfortunately, my appeals to her sense of decency hadn't made much of an impression on her. On the contrary, she took my well-intentioned objections as an opportunity to reproach me for not telling her about Martha's infidelity right away. Her accusations made me feel guilty again, and so I found myself sneaking through the streets of Nuremberg on a sunny, June day like a private eye, wearing a hat and sunglasses, to catch poor Martha in the act.

"Are you going to spy on Martha for the rest of your life?" I asked as we stood at the intersection where the pub where Martha worked on Thursdays was located.

"Yup." The subject seemed to be settled for Caro.

"You can't be serious." We ducked behind a protruding wall, when Martha stepped outside to settle the bill with some people sitting in the sunshine.

"I even considered creating a second Facebook page and writing to her."

"You need to see a therapist," I replied incredulously. "Besides, I don't think Martha is flirting on Facebook." I pointed over to where Caro's ex was engaged in a conversation with a slightly overweight woman.

"See, this is exactly why I need to keep an eye on her," whispered Caro excitedly, as if we were close enough for her to hear us.

"Talking to guests is literally her job." Suddenly, I felt the urge to defend our poor stalking victim.

Caro fished her phone out of her bag. "She gets off in five minutes, let's see where she goes next."

"How long do you want to keep this up?"

"Another two hours. I'm meeting her after that, and if she does anything before then, I'm gonna throw it up in her face."

"That sounds like a great way to start all over again." Oh, man, I would never tell anybody about this, not even my grandchildren.

When Martha's shift ended, she came out and turned right, heading toward the city wall. We followed her, hiding behind advertising pillars and billboards, squeezing along walls and ducking behind cars. If someone had put us in straitjackets and taken us to the asylum, I wouldn't have blamed them. Especially since Martha was doing absolutely nothing suspicious. She entered a cell phone store, came back out carrying a small box, and treated herself to a smoothie. Just as I was about to tell Caro that we HAD to stop this nonsense, she grabbed me by my shirt and dragged me behind a silver BMW.

"What are you doing? Let go," I hissed. "She's not even looking our way."

"Not Martha." She nudged me with her elbow. "Look."

My gaze wandered in the direction she was pointing, and my heart skipped a beat. Ben had just crossed the street right in front of us. Luckily, he hadn't noticed us.

"Where's he going?" I whispered. My heart started beating like crazy.

"Maybe Ben's incognito too." Caro pointed to the black baseball cap covering his head.

"Let's follow him."

"What?" Caro cocked her eyebrows. "Why should we do that? We're staking out Martha."

"It's not like she's doing anything exciting anyway; buying a phone and drinking some juice. Leave the woman in peace and come on." I dragged Caro behind me by the sleeve, since Ben had just turned into a narrow alley. "What's he doing in Nuremberg?" I wondered. "I bet Mr. Casanova has a date."

"Since when do you have a claim on him?" Caro followed me, sighing as I half-jogged in order not to lose sight of Ben.

"Well, we live together," I defended myself, because I couldn't think of anything better to say.

"That makes it completely different, of course," Caro said, slapping her forehead. "So, you can stalk your roommates, but if I spy on my ex, I'm a psycho."

"Something like that," I replied. "Come on."

I paused in mid-run when Ben stopped in front of a house with reddish lit windows.

"You know what alley we're in, right?" Caro put a hand on my shoulder.

I gave her a questioning look. "Is this a special neighborhood?"

"That's a brothel."

"No!" My heart almost stopped. "You're not seriously telling me that Ben just walked into a whorehouse?" I squeaked in horror.

"It certainly looks like it."

"But why?" I touched my hot cheeks, as blood rushed in my ears. "He could've had me… I mean anyone else."

"Maybe he has fetishes," Caro conjectured.

"Like what?"

"Well," she elaborated, gesturing wildly. "Bondage, SM, or something. Maybe he's in there having a hooker change his diapers."

"Change his diapers?" I repeated incredulously.

"Some guys are really into that. They secretly wear diapers and…"

"That's a load of crap," I interrupted her. "In fact, it's the biggest bunch of bullshit that ever came out of your mouth."

"You're right," Caro agreed after a moment. "I don't believe that either. He'd more likely play a little dom and get off on whipping escorts."

I leaned against the wall; my knees were shaking. "Maybe he just dropped something off, and he'll be right back out. Let's wait for a bit and see how long he's in there."

"Alright. But after this, I don't want to hear another word about my secret agent activities." Grumbling, Caro accepted her fate and leaned against the wall next to me.

"Maybe that's why he stopped hunting." It suddenly hit me.

"Huh?" Caro stuffed some gum into her mouth.

"He's gotten tired of picking up women at night, or he wants to make me believe that he's not sleeping around anymore. Instead, he pays for his pleasure with a hooker." The epiphany hit me like a ton of bricks. That's why Ben had seemed so chaste lately. He'd just been pretending to have sworn off his lifestyle, wanting us all to believe he'd changed. But why? It made no sense. At the beginning, he'd had no inhibitions about bringing a woman into the apartment. So, why was he seeing a prostitute now? I checked my phone—he had already been in this house of ill repute for thirty minutes, so the odds that he was only delivering a package didn't look so good anymore.

Caro put an arm around my shoulders. "Oh, sweetie. Don't take it so hard. Maybe it's a good thing that nothing happened between you two. In the end, you might have found yourself tied to a bed frame with him swinging a whip above you."

I just nodded. With the force of an avalanche, disappointment surged through my body. Had I really been so wrong about Ben? On the other hand, his private life was none of my business; if he wanted to spend time with a prostitute, he had every right to do so. There was nothing wrong with that. At least, that's how I'd always seen it. But why did it hurt so badly to find this out about Ben? It was my own fault—I was a despicable snoop, spying on other people. Ben had disguised himself for a reason. He hadn't wanted to be seen, and I had violated his privacy with my curiosity. An unforgivable breach of trust. With each minute that passed, I felt more and more miserable.

"Let's go," I said after an hour of pointless standing around in front of the brothel, when Caro hissed, "He's coming out." We hastily ducked behind a parked car and waited until Ben was out of sight.

My shock went deeper than I would have liked. Also, I had completely lost the desire to go on another foray. It was fundamentally wrong and reprehensible to dig into other people's business. Since my confession, we hadn't spoken a word to each other anyway. For Ben, I no longer existed. Maybe it was time for me to move out.

49

———

As night fell, I finally ventured home. To my relief, Ben seemed to be out. Ellen was watching TV, because Toby was still working on a paper with a fellow student in the library. Still feeling unsettled, I flopped down on the couch.

"Hey, what've you been up to?" Ellen gave me a puzzled look.

"I was in Nuremberg with Caro."

"I see." Ellen turned her attention back to the finale of *Germany's Next Top Model*. "If they only knew what they're getting into, they wouldn't try so hard." Bored, she pointed to the TV screen, where one of the hopefuls sashayed down the catwalk in a ridiculous outfit. "I just got in from Rome, and I'm beat." She yawned discreetly.

"Awesome," I murmured absently, pulling out a loose sofa thread.

"What's so awesome about that?"

I startled. "What?"

"You weren't even listening." Ellen sat up and pulled in her knees. "Something on your mind?"

"No, no," I hastily affirmed, suddenly fascinated by the razor blade commercial that had just come on.

"Leon says hi, by the way." She started playing with a

269

strand of my hair. "Sure, you don't want to meet him sometime?"

"You told him about the one-night stand." I turned on her. "That's not what we agreed to. Besides, I rather choose the guys I sleep with myself."

"Leon's a big deal in the club scene. I introduced you to a hot celebrity. What more could you want?" Ellen asked with a biting laugh.

"I—I might not be into casual sex, after all." I couldn't help feeling like Ellen expected a little more gratitude from me for her efforts. "Thanks for arranging this with Leon, but no more guys for me in the future, please. I'm comfortable with the way things are, really."

"Has Ben fed you this nonsense?"

The cold tone of her voice made me prick up my ears. "I have no idea what you're talking about."

"Not to sleep with a random guy."

"No, he hasn't. Can we please change the topic now, because I felt much more comfortable when all of you weren't so worried about my sexual well-being."

"Of course, Ben put you up to this." Apparently, Ellen couldn't be dissuaded from believing her absurd theory. "He picked a fight with Leon because he couldn't bear to watch him getting something he hasn't had himself. Ben will drag you into his man-cave sooner or later if you're not careful."

I noticed the simmering anger in Ellen's expression, and wondered, not for the first time, why she always got so mad whenever the conversation turned to Ben. "Ben doesn't want me, I'm 100% certain about that."

"He's just pretending not to," she spat.

Ellen really was a tough nut to crack. Again, I wondered what Ben had done to her to make her talk so badly of him. I was tempted to ask her about it, but my curiosity seemed inappropriate. After all she was involved with Toby, and I couldn't imagine Ben mistreating his friend's girlfriend on purpose.

"We're not even talking. At the festival, he just wanted to save me from drinking something with gluten in it, so I wouldn't get sick. Then Leon provoked him, and Ben freaked out. End of story."

"I don't believe a single word you say," Ellen insisted and shook her head. Why was she being so stubborn all of the sudden?

"I know for a fact that he doesn't want to sleep with me."

"I wouldn't be so sure about that."

"But I am. I'm not even his type, he's into something else."

"Don't give me that shit." Ellen sounded unusually irritable.

"I really shouldn't tell you this…"

"What's he into?" She cut me off. "What do you know about him?"

I squirmed like a snake on the ground. How was I supposed to get out of this mess?

"You've already banged him," she threw out, rather bluntly for my taste. "And you had the gall to get me to introduce you to a really great guy? I can't believe it."

"I didn't have sex with Ben," I stressed every single syllable. Ellen clung to her theory like a bull terrier. "He's not into me, okay, and he never was. We didn't sleep together nor will we ever, because Ben's seeing prostitutes. I saw him going into a brothel."

"What did you just say?" Ellen sounded stunned, her jaw dropping.

What had I, the idiot, just blurted out? I covered my mouth to stop myself from saying another word. My stomach contracted. I'd just done an abysmally stupid thing. *Damage control!* I needed damage control.

"That was a joke." I laughed shrilly, slapping Ellen's thigh. "Got you, didn't I, ha-ha."

"You're just joking?" She looked at me skeptically. "Didn't really sound like you were. At what point should I have laughed?"

A sudden desire to migrate to a faraway country hit me. Could I get an expedited visa for Chile by tomorrow? My blood was rushing in my ears. Why couldn't I ever keep my big mouth shut?

"Ellen, I'm begging you, please don't tell anyone what I said. Let's keep it between us. Promise me?" I drew a shuddering breath while praying for an affirmative answer. Dammit, I was such a huge idiot. Ellen, however, appeared strangely appeased.

"So, there's really nothing going on between you two?" she asked again, to my surprise.

"Nothing at all."

"Okay," she generously promised, "I'll keep it to myself. Ben's life is none of my business anyway."

"Thanks." I hugged her warmly, hoping she'd be true to her word, then I beat a hasty retreat to my room. I couldn't help the feeling that I'd done something really terrible to Ben. If Ellen opened her mouth, Ben would never forgive me for my indiscretion. Why had I even mentioned his brothel visit in the first place? Was I out of my mind? I couldn't even remember the words reaching my brain before they came out.

I lay on the bed and put my arms under my head. Never again would I speak another word about Ben to anyone, I promised myself.

50

The following days, I worried constantly about running into Ben. Besides that, I couldn't get the image out of my mind of Ben letting loose with a bullwhip on a paid sex worker. I'd never be able to look him in the eyes again, that much was certain. I'd been sitting in my room for a solid hour after sneaking into the apartment at six o'clock in the evening. And now, my bladder was about to burst, but I didn't dare to use the bathroom, because I could hear muffled voices from outside—one of them definitely belonged to Ben. Why did he have to be home tonight? He had made himself scarce the past few days as well. Frustrated, I sat down at my desk to log onto Facebook and check yet again to see if Ben had unfriended me.

The voices grew louder, as if they were right outside my room. I hastily clicked the browser window shut—the last thing I needed was for Ben to catch me staring at his Facebook page. I heard a "See you later." from Toby, and Ben replying "See ya." Then the front door shut, and I breathed a sigh of relief. Ben had left. I got up and tiptoed to my door. Better safe than sorry; I felt no desire to talk to Ellen anytime soon. She was staying with Toby for a few days. All clear, only the TV was on. I stole into the hallway, voices were coming from the living room, and I stopped in my tracks when I realized who was talking. Shit. Ben and Ellen, so Toby must have been the one who had left.

"Why are you always so hard on me?" Ellen asked in a low voice, then the sofa creaked.

My pulse was pounding. What should I do now? Under no circumstances did I want to run into either of them, let alone both of them at the same time.

"I'm not hard on you. I'm simply neutral. You just interpret it that way, then you get all worked up and think I don't like you and stuff."

"But you don't like me."

I heard Ben take a deep breath, and I scampered to the door frame for a peek inside. Even though I knew I shouldn't, I couldn't help myself.

Ben stood at the window with his back to me, looking outside, as Ellen moved to stand behind him.

"Ellen, what are you doing?" Ben asked without turning around.

"There was a time when you were totally into me," she said softly.

What?!

"Yes," he finally admitted. "But that was a long time ago, not anymore. You're with Toby, one of my best friends."

Ellen leaned against his back. "And if Toby didn't exist?"

"But he does."

"But if I were no longer with him, would you want me then?"

A heartbeat passed. Ben didn't move, not even when Ellen slid her arms around his waist and leaned her cheek against his shoulder.

"No," he finally said in a firm voice, "not even then."

Abruptly, Ellen let go of him and took a step back. "You arrogant prick. No girl is ever good enough for you, huh?"

Ben turned around, and I quickly pulled my head back.

"That's exactly why I could never get involved with you. You're manipulative and selfish."

She laughed shrilly. "You're the one who stomps on everybody's feelings. What type of woman do you prefer? Let me guess… Naïve girls like Luca? She's the one you want, at least admit it."

"What's this got to do with Luca?"

"You think we don't notice you staring at her secretly and undressing her in your thoughts?"

"You really have a screw loose. And yes, I'd choose Luca over you any day. At least she's not devious."

Ellen snorted. "But she's the one telling everybody behind your back that you're into whores, you pervert."

The shock went through me like a jolt of electricity.

"What?" Ben sounded dumbfounded. "Ellen, you're out of your mind."

"Fine, don't believe me," she hissed. "But your precious Luca saw you walking into a brothel, and she's blabbing it all over town." Ellen's voice was full of hatred. "Now everybody knows that you hang out in whorehouses and are into hookers these days. Could you sink any lower?"

I peered around the door frame.

"Shut the fuck up!" Ben yelled, grabbing Ellen by the collar. Then he pulled her in tight. "Don't you ever talk to me again, you understand? I swear, the next time you talk to me in this apartment, I'll throw you out, Toby or no Toby. I don't give a shit." He pushed her away, and I ran back to my room, leaning heavily against the door. My heart was thundering.

Just as I had made it to safety, footsteps sounded in the hallway, and the front door slammed shut. For several minutes, I just stood there, pressing a hand to my mouth. Ellen had told him everything! Not only had she tattled on me, she had told *Ben*—in the ugliest way imaginable. I regretted nothing more than having stalked him. He had every right to hate me. I would completely understand if he kicked me out of the apartment as well. But before that happened, I needed to apologize to him. It was the least I could do.

With shaking hands, I reached for my phone, but put it back down on the desk. Ben had been so angry when he stormed out, today wasn't a good time for remorseful repentance. Maybe I should leave him a message on Facebook? How I wished I could turn back time. I wanted to hide behind that car in Nuremberg again, see Ben passing by without giving it another thought, and continue following Martha. No! I should have never gone to Nuremberg in the first place. Instead, I should have talked Caro out of her stupid plan, and the world would still be in perfect order.

51

Time stretched on like sand on a dune. I sat on my bed and stared into nowhere. The sun had already set, and only the faint ray of light from my bedside lamp lit my room. The sudden ringing of my phone tore me out of my trance. Reluctantly, I got up to answer it. Caro's name lit up on the display. Sighing, I took the call.

"What's up?" I asked in a depressed voice, hoping that Caro would instantly know that something was wrong with me.

"Luca, where are you?"

"Home. Why?"

"I'm in Erlangen." She sounded excited.

"Then come over, I could really use someone to talk to right now. Something terrible…"

"Not now," she interrupted me harshly, and my heart fell as I realized that my best friend wasn't interested in my depression. "I'm following Martha. She texted me that she can't come over because she has something to do in Erlangen."

Of course, that was more important! I sniffed loudly before I weakly admonished, "You've got to stop these wild goose chases, nothing good will come of it. You'll never guess what happened…"

"I couldn't find Martha anywhere," she cut me off again. "I've checked all the bars, looked in every window, but she's nowhere to be found. Right now, I'm in front of the Havana Bar, and Luca, you won't believe…"

"That's why you called me? I'm definitely never gonna stalk anybody again, and neither should you. It is vile and despicable," I raged.

"Listen to me," she cut me off again. "Ben's in there," she said pointedly.

"So what?"

"He's with Erdie and two other guys just as muscle bound as Erdie, they look like triplets…"

"Those are Erdie's brothers. So what? Get out of there. I don't wanna know what Ben does in his free time, it's none of our business. And don't even think about spying on him, you hear me?"

"Konstantin's with them." I heard Caro say softly, and my hand clenched around my cell phone.

"What—what did you just say?" I could hardly breathe.

"They are sitting with Konstantin in the Havana Bar. What does that mean?" Caro asked.

Suddenly, I felt sick with fear. "I don't know," I pressed out. "Please go away, don't let them discover you."

"Oh, there's Martha," she said excitedly. "I've gotta follow her. I'll call you later. At least you've been warned."

I sank back down to the edge of the bed. Ben had joined forces with Konstantin? Surely to take revenge on me. Why, for goodness sake, had I told him that old story? I was the dumbest person in the world for handing him this trump card. What was I supposed to do now? It was a challenge just to breathe. The mere thought of those five broad-shouldered guys ambushing me in my room made me shiver and stirred up the worst fear I had experienced in years. Now, I knew for sure that Ben would never forgive me. Should I lock myself in my room and call the police? My fingers were shaking so pathetically that I couldn't even hit the numbers on the display. I went through all my options, but couldn't come up with any solutions. What would I even tell the cops? That I had stalked my roommate during a brothel visit? A loud sob escaped my lips. I had no proof; nothing. There was only one thing to do. I had to go to the Havana Bar myself and talk to Ben in person. At least in a public place I wouldn't be alone with them; they couldn't do anything to me in front of the other guests. Maybe I would be able to talk some sense into Ben. I would apologize to him and swear to move out right away if he promised to leave me alone.

The very next moment, I grabbed my phone and keys, and rushed out of the apartment. I almost flew down the stairs, left the dormitory, and ran through the dark empty streets while countless adrenaline rushes made my pulse race uncontrollably. My heart was beating wildly in my chest. I shivered in my denim miniskirt and short-sleeved, dark-red blouse. I hadn't even thought of a jacket, but I didn't want to turn back either. Panting, I finally arrived at the Havana Bar and held my stabbing side. I peered through the window, pressing both edges of my hands against the glass to block the light from the street lamps. Not much was going on inside. Only a few people were sitting at tables. Ben and the others were nowhere to be seen; they must have already left. Dammit!

Suddenly, I realized that I was standing all by myself on an empty street, and a cold shiver ran down my spine. I spun around, breathing shallowly. If they waylaid me, I wouldn't be able to defend myself. I quickly dialed Caro's number— she had to come immediately so that I wouldn't be alone, but she didn't answer. Now what? Cautiously, I peered in all directions, my pulse pounding in my throat. Up ahead, two women were standing and talking, and from the other side, a car approached and drove past me. My hands went numb, I decided to return home, pack my things, and leave before Ben came back. Caro's spare key, the one she had given me for emergencies, was in my desk drawer, so I definitely had a place to hide from him. I rushed back toward the dorm while I kept looking over my shoulder.

Fortunately, everything remained calm. Every now and then, some passers-by or small groups of people crossed my way, but Ben and his companions were nowhere to be seen. Just as I turned the last corner, my phone rang. It was Martha, as I recognized after a quick glance at the display, and my blood pressure slowed down somewhat. Oh, thank God. In the pitch darkness, I was thankful even for her, and took the call.

"Martha, what's up?" I asked breathlessly, as I stopped walking to lessen the stitch in my side.

"Is Caro with you?"

"No, I have no idea where she is."

Martha gave a laughing snort. "So, you haven't talked to her?"

"Earlier on the phone, but I really don't know where she is now. Maybe she's at home," I lied.

"She's not. Kira called me. She spotted Caro in Erlangen earlier. Apparently, she's sneaking up on me, and now she's not even answering her phone."

It was unbelievable how small the world really was. Caro had been busted. The poor thing didn't even know about the trouble she was in, but I couldn't deal with her problems right now. "Listen, this isn't a good time. I have to go." A church bell rang nearby, making me flinch. My eyes involuntarily flitted to all sides.

"Where are you?" Martha sounded suspiciously. "You're out somewhere, right?"

Perfect, now I had Martha on my heels. Just what I needed. "Yes, I'm out," I admitted. What else could I say?

"Where are you exactly?" she asked again.

Why were all the people around me so insistent all the time? "At the Neustädter church, waiting for a friend," I fibbed in the hopes that she'd accept my not very ingenious excuse. Could Martha please just leave me alone? Right now, I had more serious worries. I resumed walking to get away from this gloomy place as soon as possible. "Listen, my friend's here, okay? Gotta go."

"You're lying," Martha said calling my bluff. Then I heard someone say my name and turned around briskly.

"Hello, Luca, what a lovely surprise!"

52

I had to look twice before I realized who was standing in front of me. Johanna. Martin's girlfriend. Everybody seemed to be coming out of the woodwork tonight just to make my life more difficult. Unbelievable. Martha was still yakking in my ear.

"Gotta go, Martha." I ended the call and aimed for a polite facial expression. "Johanna, what a coincidence. What brings you here?"

"What a coincidence indeed," she replied in an icy voice.

It took me some effort not to roll my eyes. There was no way I was going to deal with this strange nerdy girl right now. I had more important things on my agenda, like packing my bags and leaving town.

"Listen, I have to go, I'm in a hurry. See you later." Without waiting for an answer, I turned to go, but she yanked me back by my hair.

"Ouch, are you crazy? Let go of me!"

Johanna pulled me closer. "Who are you waiting for?"

"Nobody, I'm on my way home." I cocked my head to relieve the painful pull on my scalp since Johanna wouldn't let go. With both hands, I tried to free myself, which only made her yank my hair even harder.

"You're waiting for Martin. Admit it, you stupid, horny slut!"

"You're insane—I don't want a single thing from Martin. Now, let me go." Johanna really belonged in a padded cell. But wait a minute, what had she just called me? Stupid, horny slut? Something about that combination sounded familiar. She still wouldn't let go of me.

"It just so happens that Martin is taking a pottery class over here right now." She pointed at an illuminated building behind us. "And you seriously expect me to believe that you just happened to be loitering outside this very building by pure coincidence?"

Again, she roughly tore at the strands of my hair while I tried to wrestle her fingers open.

"Ouch, let go! I had no idea Martin's into pottery."

"You're so going to get it, you filthy liar." She shoved me against the wall and pulled my head down.

"Since you don't pay attention to well-intentioned letters, I need to change my tactics."

Letters? I pulled at her arm to get rid of this lunatic, when I suddenly remembered where I knew the phrase *stupid, horny slut* from. "It was you! You sent me that anonymous letter," I cawed. "You're really psycho."

"I'm really pissed off." She pulled my hair even harder. I was going to end up bald.

"Martin told me that you wanted to go out with him again."

I couldn't believe it. That nutcase.

"No, I don't. You can have that dumb-ass all to yourself." I moaned in pain, because the crazy woman was now bending my head backward.

"You'll never ever come on to my boyfriend again, I can promise you that." Johanna took a swing. I ducked as well as I could, protecting my face with one arm, and squeezed my eyes shut in anticipation of the blow, when the pressure on my scalp suddenly vanished. I opened my eyes and saw that Martha had Johanna in a headlock.

"You're threatening my friend?" she asked in a deadly calm voice, adding a little more pressure to Johanna's neck. "I don't like that at all."

And with that, I could breathe a sigh of relief. That was a close call. Meanwhile, Johanna's face turned red, and she gasped.

"I was just kidding around," she croaked.

"So, you weren't threatening her?" Martha asked.

"No," Johanna rasped weakly.

"She sent me an anonymous letter," I blurted out, still having a hard time processing. Johanna definitely had what it took to be another Annie Wilkes from *Misery*. All this time, I had suspected Konstantin. I'd hardly been able to sleep for fear. What a bitch!

Martha let go of Johanna, and she gasped furiously for breath.

"Threatening people is a crime." Martha crossed her arms, her biceps bulging as she made fists, which made her arms look even more muscular. Her hands held out in front of her chest, Johanna took a step backwards.

"It was just a joke." She forced a laugh. "I wasn't really threatening Luca, I just wanted to give her a little scare. You guys don't really want to run to the police just because of this little slip of paper?"

"Maybe I will, though." Suddenly, I was furious, thinking of all the anxiety that letter had caused me. "That was a real threat, not just some little joke. Who knows who you're going to mess with next if anyone even dares to talk with Martin."

"I won't do it again," said Johanna, close to tears now. "I swear. I've never been in trouble with the law before. I'm begging you." She pleaded, wringing her hands.

"Alright," I finally agreed. "But on one condition: you and Martin both have to stay away from me. Consider this your restraining order. Keep at least a hundred yards distance from me. Be sure to tell Martin as well."

"Now get lost." Martha faked a lunge, and Johanna dashed away like a scared rabbit.

I turned to my savior, still trembling inside. "Thanks for coming to the rescue. That really could've turned out badly for me."

A smile blossomed on Martha's lips, and for the first time ever, I detected a hint of sympathy for me on her face. "You do like me," I accused her, tapping on her shoulder.

"Busted." With a grin, Martha held up her hands, as if surrendering. "Of course, I like you, you're just as crazy as Caro. Never a dull moment with you two around."

We hugged each other; I didn't want to ever let her go.

"Enough," Martha finally said.

"Enough what?" I snuggled up to her muscular chest and let all my gratitude flow into her.

"Let go, girl. I can't breathe."

"Oh." I instantly took my hands off her strong neck.

"Well, I'll go find Caro. Seems like she really isn't with you," she said with a searching look around.

"Nope." I shook my head. "What will you tell her when you find her?"

"That I love her and don't want to lose her again."

"I really hope you two will work things out," I replied as my phone started ringing. "Maybe it's her." I fished my phone out of my skirt pocket, looked at it, and flinched. *Ben.* The display lit up the dark like a white emergency light. He was calling me. Now what?

"Are you going to get that?" Martha asked after the third ring.

"Yeah." I swallowed thickly before I finally took the call. "Hello?" I asked timidly.

"Luca, it's me, Ben."

"I know." My temples were throbbing.

"I really need to talk to you, can we meet?"

"About—about what?" I closed my eyes involuntarily. Hearing his voice almost blew me away, but I didn't feel up to a serious heart-to-heart with him. Instead, I wanted to apologize for all I had done, but not even one word came out. Just the thought that he might hate me was unbearable.

"Not over the phone. Could you come by the copy shop?"

"Why not at home?"

"I'm working. I've a huge order to copy for the university, and I'll probably be here all night. Could you come over here? Please? Can you do that? It won't take long." He sounded perfectly normal, not like he was about to murder me or something.

"I don't know." My thoughts were running circles, but at the same time I felt a powerful longing to see him.

"I need you." I heard him say, and melted on the spot.

Should I really risk meeting him? But then again, Ben sounded like nothing was wrong, as if I hadn't destroyed his life. Maybe he hadn't taken my betrayal so badly after all, and this was about something completely different. Apparently, he needed my help. Maybe he didn't care if the whole world knew that he was into hookers. Back when I caught him having sex, my spying hadn't bothered him much then either. If I met with him now, it would be a good opportunity to explain everything that was bothering me. We could talk things through rationally and settle this once and for all. Who even knew what Caro had seen, if the guy in the Havana Bar really was Konstantin—or maybe they had run into him by accident. Despite everything, I longed to see Ben; I just wanted to be with him. "Okay, see you soon." I hung up and bit my lower lip.

"Where are you going?" Martha asked. She was still standing next to me, a quizzical look on her face.

"Ben says he needs to talk to me." I was in emotional turmoil. All I knew was that I wanted to be with Ben, ask his forgiveness, and for everything to go back to normal between us.

"Want me to come with you?" Martha offered, and I considered it for a minute. Actually, that wasn't a bad idea. My phone went off once more, it was Ben again. "What's up?"

"Um, Luca, please come alone." He hung up before I could ask why.

A weird feeling crept through my stomach—yet I decided to agree to Ben's request.

"I'm going alone, sounds like it's private."

"Alright." Martha put her thumb and little finger to her ear and mouth. "Call, if you need me."

"Okay, bye," I said and took off.

For twenty minutes now, I'd been standing on the street corner near Ben's copy shop, unable to make up my mind. It was directly across from the student services office, where we had met for the first time many weeks ago. The moon dimly lit up the gloomy street, contrasting sharply with the beam of light from Ben's shop that shone brightly on the black asphalt. The glass door of the shop next to it was adorned with an oversized red and white key; everything in there was dark. Konstantin's workplace; just thinking about that made me shudder. I looked at my phone again without a clue of what I was actually waiting for. By now, it was already midnight, and the campus was deserted. I tensed my back before I started walking over there, woodenly. Then I saw Ben inside the shop, leaning against a copy machine and staring at the floor.

My heart was pounding like crazy as I watched him. Dark brown strands of hair hung over his forehead, and he looked tense. What was he thinking about right now? About what Ellen had told him? I was going to go in there now and apologize, swear to him that I was infinitely sorry for my stupid indiscretion, and that I would bear the consequences for my big mouth. I would leave. Move out. Even if it could never make up for what I'd done, at least he would be rid of me and no longer have to deal with a traitor. Then, I'd clear out my room and leave our shared apartment for good, right away. I took a deep breath before I pushed the door open and entered. Ben looked up and studied me impassively, only a hint of emotion in his eyes.

"Hello." I stiffly walked up to him, "Here I am."

"I'm glad you came after all."

"Sorry it took so long." I stared into his eyes, sinking into that sea of deep blue, hoping our talk would clear away any bad blood between us. That he wouldn't hate me for the rest of his life.

"No problem." He looked over my shoulder. The bell chimed as it had when I opened the door. When I spun around, my heart skipped a beat

53

Erdie and Konstantin entered the copy shop and stopped right in front of the closed door. My heart plummeted, and an icy cold chill crept up my spine. "What…" I turned to Ben. "What is this? Why is Konstantin here?" My voice grew higher with each word.

"You wouldn't have come if you'd have seen him in here," Ben said with frightening calmness.

I had walked into a trap!

"No." I began shaking my head as if in slow motion. Mortal fear seized me, constricting my throat like a python. I walked slowly backwards until I felt one of the copy machines against my back and couldn't go any further. My pulse picked up. There was no way I could get out of here.

"Please, Ben," I sobbed in a desperate attempt to appeal to his empathy and could no longer hold back the tears. They ran down my cheeks, one after the other, and kept flowing. "Please let me go. Please…" My voice cracked as my chest slowly contracted, and I couldn't breathe; I was starting to hyperventilate. Gasping for breath, I stared at the three impassive faces. "I didn't mean to tell Ellen. It just slipped out. Really. I swear I wasn't gonna tell her anything. I won't tell anybody else, I promise. Never. But please, just let me go.

Please!" I gasped for breath as Ben started walking towards me slowly with an indecipherable expression on his face. What was he going to do?

"Luca," he said softly and came very close. "Don't tell me you're afraid of me."

I put a hand in front of my eyes because I didn't know what else to do. "Please don't hurt me. Please, Ben. Please let me go."

Ben took me in his arms and pulled me gently to his chest. "Nobody here's gonna hurt you."

"What did you do to her, you son of a bitch?" I heard Erdie's furious voice, but I couldn't move a muscle. With my eyes closed, I leaned against Ben, wanting to hide in his arms even though I had no idea what he was going to do next. But anything was better than having to look into Konstantin's ice-cold eyes.

"I didn't do anything at all to that stupid cunt," he said, his voice sounding as hard as always.

I shivered in Ben's arms. "Make him go away, please make him go away," I begged Ben as I clung to his shirt.

Ben stroked my back. "I'll send him away," he whispered to calm me down. "I promise. But first, Konstantin has something to tell you."

"I don't want to hear anything, just make him go away."

"Luca," Ben replied in a soft voice, holding me by the upper arms. "You have to hear this from him in person, so you can find closure to get on with your life." Gently, he pushed me away, although I was still clutching his shirt. With one hand, he wiped the tears from my cheeks before he turned me around to look directly into Konstantin's disgusting face. Ben held me tightly and supported me from behind. Ben's closeness helped me to face him, but I was still shaking all over. The star-shaped mole on Konstantin's cheek looked like the devil's mark.

Erdie grabbed Konstantin by the neck. "Say what you have to say and then fuck off."

Konstantin batted his hand away. "Don't touch me, man. Well, Luca, your little homepage is offline now, but I don't give a shit. I got sick of looking at your tits, anyway. But you could be a bit more grateful. After all, I made you an internet star." He flashed his oh-so-familiar mean grin, and I realized he was playing all of us. That guy would never stop. Why was Ben interfering in this?

"Watch your big mouth," Ben interjected. "Your ugly mug is just screaming to get smashed."

Erdie grabbed Konstantin by the neck and shoved him roughly face-first against the wall.

"Alright, alright," Konstantin grunted. "The video has been deleted from my hard drive, and this jerk-off has the USB flash drive backup." He pointed at Ben, who instead of answering, smiled menacingly.

Erdie pulled Konstantin off the wall, only to slam him against it one more time. "There's more to say." He reminded him. "And if you talk more shit, what I'm doing to you right now will feel like nothing."

My knees went wobbly, like softened butter, and nearly gave way a couple of times. I couldn't keep from slumping. Ben wrapped his arms around my waist and held me tighter.

"I'm leaving this shithole," Konstantin said with another groan. "I already had that in mind anyway. I'm moving back to Munich, so fuck you all." He turned to Erdie. "Get your dirty hands off me now."

Erdie let go, adding: "I'd really love to give you a…"

"Now, fuck off," Ben growled like a pit bull, full of hate. "Don't show your ugly face here ever again."

Konstantin swallowed before he reached for the doorknob.

"And don't forget," Erdie called after him. "I have tons of friends in Munich. If you pull any more crap with Luca, they'll pay you a visit. And they're not squeamish, I can promise you that much."

For the first time, something like fear flickered in

Konstantin's eyes. "The slut's all yours," he said, which earned him a painful kick in the backside from Erdie, and Konstantin hurried out of the shop.

"Are you alright?" Ben loosened his grip on me and stroked my cheek with his knuckles.

"Yes." I swallowed, propping myself against the copy machine. The room was spinning around me. "I guess, but…" I let my gaze wander between the two guys. "How did you get Konstantin here? Caro saw you talking to him earlier at the Havana Bar."

Ben shook his head in disbelief. "There's no hiding anything from you two, is there? Unbelievable."

"I'm really sorry," I said, while my pulse gradually slowed.

Erdie shrugged. "You'd better tell her the whole story. After all, she has a right to know."

"Okay." Ben ran both hands through his hair. "When you told me the story about Konstantin, I immediately wanted to find that asshole and beat him up. At the same time, I hated myself for not being able to talk to you about it. I knew you needed me that day, otherwise you wouldn't have confided in me. But I was afraid of getting too involved and making things worse—like I did at the festival," he added, shrugging his shoulders apologetically. "That's why I got up and went to my room instead." He looked at me piercingly, as if it was important to him that I understood his reaction. When I nodded, he went on.

"Then I sat down at my laptop and Googled your full name. That page came up as the first hit…"

"No," I interrupted him in horror. I didn't want to hear any more and covered my ears. "Please don't say you watched the video. I couldn't take that."

"Hey, Luca." Erdie patted my back. "You're not the bad guy here, that jerk is."

Meanwhile, Ben lifted my chin, so I'd to look him in the eyes. "I clicked on the page."

My heart almost stopped when he said that.

"Konstantin had even installed a hit counter. The page had been visited over seventy-five thousand times."

That horrible news took a moment to sink in. Tens of thousands of complete strangers had seen me naked and watched me have sex! I just wanted to die. "Did… Did you…" I couldn't finish the question for fear of Ben's answer.

"I didn't watch it," he reassured me. "Of course not. But I did hack the website. The security measures on it were extremely low, then I broke it down until there was nothing left of it."

"Really?" The immense pressure on my chest loosened.

"Yes." He rubbed my arm. "Would you believe it, only a few days later he'd built a new site? And I realized, he'd never stop if we didn't put some pressure on him, so I filled Erdie in on the situation." He nodded at him.

"When Ben told me about the crap that jackass pulled on you, I was right in. We wanted to get the bastard, but we needed reinforcements. So, I called in my brothers."

"They—they all know?" I started to feel queasy.

"No details," Ben reassured me. "I called Konstantin and asked him under false pretenses to meet me at the Havana Bar. Erdie and his brothers told him they'd be paying him a visit if he didn't do as we told him."

"My brothers would never even hurt a fly, but Cengiz' ghetto talk is really convincing." Erdie struck a cool pose and imitated his brother. "Here's the deal, you fuckin' piece of shit, you be comin' at that girl again, we be puttin' your dumb ass in the fuckin' hospital. You feel me? I ain't playin'."

Despite myself, I burst out laughing, while Ben slapped his friend on the shoulder. "Perfect, bro." Then he turned back to me.

"So, we all went over to his place earlier," Ben continued explaining. "We made him take the thing offline. I also deleted the video from his hard drive and made him hand over the backup."

"And you still have it?" I asked.

He fished an USB flash drive from his jeans pocket and handed it over to me. "You can do with it whatever you want."

I stared intently at the silver flash drive in Ben's hand, transfixed; it looked so harmless. Hard to imagine how much damage this tiny object could cause. Anger rose inside me, an overpowering rage at Konstantin's deviousness and at the crap on that drive. I grabbed the damn thing, threw it on the ground, and smashed it to smithereens with my heel. I exhaled loudly. That felt so, so good. My heart was beating rapidly in my chest.

The two guys had quietly watched me.

"It's all gone now." Ben looked at the pieces on the ground. "You have nothing to be afraid of anymore. It's all over."

"How can I ever thank you guys?"

"It's alright," Ben replied. "Anything for a friend." He elbowed me gently.

Erdie scratched the back of his head. "Maybe you could watch Phyllis again sometime." His grin got wider. "She keeps asking about you."

"Anytime, and not just because you guys saved my butt. I love that little girl."

We stood there smiling at each other. It was like a weight had been lifted off of me, and I felt like I could breathe freely for the first time in years. I could never ever repay the guys for what they had done for me, and yet I'd been so mean to Ben.

"I'm really sorry about that thing with Ellen," I said, hoping he would be able to forgive me.

"And that's my cue to go." Erdie turned toward the door. "I think you two have a lot more things to talk about."

"Thanks for everything." I hugged Erdie, who held me close for a second.

"You can stop with the thank yous now," he grumbled and opened the door to leave.

"Erdie." There was one more thing bothering me. "Now you know the whole story… But I wish you didn't."

"Oh, Shorty," he replied with his signature jab to my chin. "You know what a crappy memory I have." Erdie waved goodbye and pulled the door closed behind him.

54

I turned to face Ben.

"About Ellen," I began cautiously, but he interrupted me.

"I don't care about what Ellen says. I've known her for a while now, and I know how she thinks."

"What happened between you two? Why does she hate you so much?"

A tight smile emerged on his lips. "Why don't we go back to the office? We can sit down and talk there."

"Okay," I agreed. He locked the front door before he pointed to the back room. I followed him into the tiny office and looked around quickly. So, this was where Ben worked. A filing cabinet filled with binders leaned against one of the walls with a desk next to it, cluttered with pens and papers. Ben offered me the office chair, but instead, I perched on the desk so I could look into his face.

"You take the chair," I said, swinging my legs, but Ben remained standing in front of me.

"You wanted to know what's going on between me and Ellen."

I nodded.

"Okay." He took a deep breath. "I met Ellen a few years

ago in a bar and took her home to sleep with me." Ben faltered, and I felt my eyes grow large. "When we arrived, Toby was still up. It was obvious that he fell in love with Ellen right then and there, on the spot. So, we hung out for a little while in the kitchen, talking. When Ellen went to the bathroom, Toby asked me to back off and let him have a go at her." Ben took a bottle of water from the desk, unscrewed the cap, and offered it to me. When I declined, he took a big sip before he went on. "I didn't care about Ellen; I just wanted to spend the night with her. So, I took off and left the two of them to it, because Toby was really serious about her, and I wanted to give him a chance to try his luck." He grimaced. "From that point on, they were inseparable. But every time Ellen got the chance, she freaked out, accusing me of passing her on to my friend like an unwanted toy and all that nonsense. Nothing ever happened between us, but she never forgave me, despite the fact that Toby's the better catch by a long shot. I don't know any man who could put up with her moods as patiently as he does." He raised his hands and sighed. "That's the whole story with Ellen."

"I overheard you two," I blurted out and could have slapped myself for my stupidity. Could I use my brain just one single time? This delicate subject could have been addressed more tactfully.

Ben stared. "Luca, are you sure you're not working for the NSA?"

"It was by accident. I swear I was just going to use the bathroom, and the walls are really thin."

"Just talk your way out of this." He snorted. "Then you heard everything?"

I nodded guiltily. "Every single word."

"Then you also heard me say to Ellen that she had no chance with me, Toby or no Toby?"

"I heard that," I admitted.

"I said that because of you."

"What?" A hot jolt rushed down my spine.

He came closer. "I'd choose you over her any day." His voice was rough and quiet. "At that moment, I wished you were standing there instead of Ellen. My answer would have been quite different. But let's drop it. It's not going to work with us anyway."

"Why not?" I held my breath. *It wasn't going to work with us?* He had no feelings for me. My heart broke instantaneously, and it hurt so badly.

Ben gave a tortured laugh. "Luca, this is complicated."

"I am capable of grasping complicated matters, if they're explained properly." I needed to know what he thought of me, how he felt about me. I needed to understand, in order to be able to move on—one way or the other way.

"You are so persistent." He seemed torn up inside. "Okay, let's start at the beginning." Ben took an audible breath as if he had to force himself to continue. "Let's just say, you were a bit distant when we first met. You totally blew me off, and I had zero chance with you from the start." His grin went crooked. "But then you came to live with us, and I thought this must be fate. Let's see if she's really as tough as she pretends to be. Turned out, you were. No matter what I said, you blew me off. But when you got so drunk that first day, you were talking in your confused state about my good looks, my cute dimple, and God knows what else. Thus, I knew you actually liked the way I looked, and that there must have been something else to blame for your negative reaction towards me. So, I started teasing you, because every time I provoked you, you revealed something about yourself in your anger." He kneaded his shoulder. "I admit, I wanted you. For years, I've had my pick of women, and then one came along who didn't want me. I couldn't believe it, and I wanted to change that."

I looked past him and didn't know why he was telling me all this stuff in the first place. His confession was so unnecessary; it just hurt. My temples throbbed. What he was telling me was so incredibly painful. I'd been completely wrong about him. Or had I? Was my first impression of him right after all? Was he nothing but a reckless, selfish jerk? Suddenly I didn't know what to think of Ben anymore. He'd wanted to use me just to prove something to himself.

"Hey, wait a minute before you mentally tear me to pieces, I'm not done yet," he defended himself, and I looked up.

"You don't need to say anything else; I get it." I was doing my best to blink away my tears when I felt his hand on my shoulder.

"Please let me finish, okay?"

"Keep talking," I said after a pause, because his gaze became more and more pleading, even though he could have saved himself the rest.

"And then you stood in for me and watched Phyllis. That evening we had our first real conversation. I enjoyed talking to you and..."

"You enjoyed it so much that you basically ran away," I interrupted him icily.

He nodded. "I don't even know why I left. Suddenly, I felt so close to you, and I liked you so much that it scared me. It was overwhelming. I needed to get out of there, to get a grip on my emotions." Ben sounded bitter. "That same night I went out to a bar, and some random woman kept chatting me up about boring, inane stuff, and all I could think about the whole time was you. It made me realize that I couldn't go on like this anymore. At some point, I just stood up and slipped out of the bar. And I haven't met with another woman since that day."

"Because of me?" I gasped incredulously. Ben quit going out on the prowl because of me? But that meant... I didn't dare finish that thought because this would only reawaken my strong feelings for Ben, and that never ended well.

"Yes, partly because of you." He nodded and looked up at the ceiling. "When Ellen talked you into that one-night stand, I knew that I should literally be the last person on Earth giving advice against having casual sex; I, of all people. But I still had to try. Picturing you in bed with a strange guy right next door to me drove me crazy. When you were with that idiot at the festival, I was so jealous. I had to watch that dipshit Leon hit on you; the two of you had this intense eye contact and..." He broke off and leaned his head back. "Then he kissed you. And yes, I was planning to take him out. I deliberately provoked him. He should've kept his hands off you, but I had no right to get involved, and I'm sorry about that."

"Don't be sorry," I quickly assured him. "Leon was a first-class idiot. I was glad to be rid of him." I stared at my hands as I considered whether I should even ask him the next question. Ben was so far out of my league in the looks department that it seemed utopian to even plant a spark of hope in my heart at all, let alone allow the idea of an "us" to take root. But once again, my mouth was quicker than my brain. "Can I ask you something?"

"Sure." He seemed tense.

"I—I never thought you cared about me much, but from what you just told me, it actually sounds like you kind of like me."

"Of course, I like you." He put his cool palm against my flaming cheek. "Even more than that."

"So, what does that mean for us? I mean..."

I nearly died saying it out loud, but Ben didn't let me finish. He quickly lowered his hand hastily off my face. "I know what you mean."

We stared at each other. I gazed into his eyes, and they returned a sorrowful, wistful look. It was obvious Ben was about to give me some bad news.

55

"**I**'m sorry, Luca, but we can't be together."

My heart drowned in the flood of my disappointment. I'd fallen in love with Ben, deeply in love. But he didn't want me. Moments passed as I tried hard to stop myself from bursting into tears.

"Am I not pretty enough?" He owed me an explanation at least. After all, he had just ripped my heart out of my chest.

"Luca, please, let's not have this discussion. It's not possible, it's really not possible. You should consider yourself lucky."

"Why can't you talk straight for once so that people can follow what you say?" I snarled at him. "I just want to understand. After that, I'll never bother you again."

"It's not because of you."

This threadbare excuse really hurt. "That's the cheapest and oldest excuse in the world. I can't believe you're feeding me that garbage," I threw back in his face. Then I bit my lower lip in order not to say something I would regret later.

"It's not an excuse, dammit," he snapped back. "And yes, I do think you're pretty, very pretty in fact, and I don't think that you're not good enough for me. It's exactly the other way around."

"What is it then? Talk to me, Ben." I almost begged him.

He tapped his shoe against the desk. "I can't tell you that."

"Why not?"

Ben got louder. "I just can't, okay?"

"I told you about my past." I looked him straight in the eyes. "Please, Ben. At least let me understand."

"I can't," he whispered.

Don't do this to me, I thought. I bared my soul in front of him, and all he was giving me was a cheap *I can't*?

"You're into something else, that's it," I threw out to provoke him into answering.

"What?" He shook his head back.

"You'd rather go to a brothel, that's why you don't want a relationship. A girlfriend couldn't give you what you need, right?"

"Luca." He seemed visibly shocked. "You sound like Ellen right now, and I don't like it at all."

"But you went to a hooker."

Ben exhaled heavily. "I didn't have sex with a hooker, if that makes you feel any better."

"Ben—I saw you walk inside a brothel myself. Are you gonna deny it?"

"No," he replied, "you saw right. I went to that whorehouse, but not to sleep with a prostitute."

"Why then?"

"Because..." He took a deep breath, his shoulders tensed up. "I went there to see my mother. She owns that brothel." His gaze was glued to the floor so I couldn't look into his eyes, which was probably better because that way he didn't notice my mouth hanging open. "Excuse me? What?"

"My mother is a prostitute. I bet you're incredibly glad now that you and I didn't get together, huh?" Ben finally looked up, and his indifferent expression contradicted the pain in his eyes.

"What in the world are you talking about?" I didn't mean to sound so dramatic.

He wiped his mouth with the back of his hand. "My mother's walked the streets for years," he said monotonously, as if he were moderating the weather forecast. "Long before I was born. Then she got pregnant by some john, and the result's in front of you."

"Ben." I didn't know what else to say, but he kept talking with that strangely detached tone, as if he weren't talking about himself.

"Initially, she'd wanted to have an abortion, but changed her mind at the last minute. You see? I wasn't even supposed to be born. I shouldn't be alive."

"Please don't say that. It sounds horrible."

"Why does it sound horrible?" His voice swelled. "Just because it's the truth, and you're shocked? This is my life. You wanted to know every tiny detail about me."

"I'm sorry." That wasn't a good answer, I knew that much, but whatever I said wouldn't be enough to let him know what was going on inside me. Yes, I was shocked, but not by his life story, but because he took his background so hard. After all, it wasn't like he had had a choice in it.

"I'm being unfair." Ben finally went on after moments of silence that stretched on like hours. "My mom always took good care of me and made sure I had everything I needed. And I know she loves me. As a kid, I didn't even know what her *profession* was. That came later." He broke off and sat down next to me on the desk, slumping his shoulders.

Our arms touched. I felt the warmth of his skin seep into mine, like we were connecting. Despite everything, I relished being close to him. "What happened later?" I asked timidly, as he made no attempt to continue talking.

"When I was sixteen, I dated a girl from my class and fell in love with her. She was so pretty and had that special something. I even lost my virginity with her, and at that time I thought: *This is the love of my life.* My mom was still out on the streets, and even though she wore a wig, a few of my classmates recognized her when they went to spy on the 'half-

naked hookers'. The next day, they told everyone that my mom was a prostitute. Antonia immediately broke up with me. She was embarrassed to be associated with me and wanted nothing to do with me because she was afraid I'd eventually make her walk the streets too." His expression hardened. Other than that, he didn't show a lot of emotion, but it was clear that the events of his youth had affected him so much that he hadn't recovered yet.

"Oh, Ben, I'm so sorry," I reaffirmed, because his confession sounded so incomprehensible to me. It was the absolute last thing I'd have ever expected. I could only vaguely imagine what he must have gone through over the years.

He gave me a sidelong glance. "Do you even want to know what happened after that?"

When I nodded silently, he went on. "Antonia broke my heart, and deep down, I knew she was right. I'm not worth anything; I'm scum who's only here because some streetwalker's john used a faulty condom," he said with contempt for himself.

"Don't say that. That's not true." I took his hand, but he pulled away and stood up. Ben stuffed both hands into his jeans pockets and went on, even though I sensed that he didn't really want to talk about his life anymore.

"My life at school was hell after that. Everybody knew, even the teachers would drop stupid remarks. The only one who stood by me was Erdie. He didn't give a shit about what my mom did. His family was also there for me, and I could crash at the Dirims' when I went rounds with my mother. I blamed her personally for my misery. She couldn't get through me no matter how hard she tried. I hated her from the bottom of my heart for selling her body. Her life choices had made my life feel like hell on earth. Back then, the only ones I could talk to about this were Erdie's parents. They supported me whenever the bullying at school got out of hand."

I wanted to take Ben into my arms, but I couldn't move a muscle. His faint, irresistible scent reached my nose, reminding me of all the times we had been this close before. It was so overwhelming that I felt powerless to resist. It was incredible how certain smells could affect the human body. I placed my palm on his left pec. Ben's body warmth seeped into my hand; his heart beat strong and fast. "That's why you have that tattoo, right? Guilt and Atonement."

He nodded, and the unspoken truth sounded even more terrible.

"Ben, you're not to blame for anything. Your classmates were morons. They were teenagers; at that age, you see things differently. You break up with people for all sorts of reasons—because their clothes aren't cool enough, or the guy suddenly shows up at school with a huge zit on his chin... There are thousands of stupid reasons."

He gave me a penetrating look. "Were you one of those?"

"No," I quickly assured him, repressing the unpleasant memory of rejecting Matt in eighth grade because he'd had a festering zit. "That was just an example."

"I see." He didn't sound convinced.

"What I'm really trying to say is that teenagers are immature. They're going through puberty, and you can't take everything they say to heart. Not after so many years. On the contrary, look at what you've become. You're warm, and you help others without asking for anything in return. You're smart, you're majoring in computer science, and everybody likes you. Your mother can't have done that bad of a job. In fact, she brought you up to be a great guy. You can be proud of her."

"Luca." He sat back down next to me, "That's really very nice of you to say, but..."

This time I interrupted him. "Why don't you kiss women on the mouth, Ben?"

He flinched. "How the hell do you know about that?"

"Doesn't matter, just tell me."

"Because—because I can't really love anyone. After Antonia broke up with me, I decided I'd never let myself fall in love again. No woman should ever have to be ashamed of me. So, I made up my mind to act like my own kind, the person I really was. I was conceived in the gutter, and that's where I belong. Hookers will do anything for money, except for one thing. They never kiss a john on the mouth. So, that's how I operate, too. In my early days as a student, I used to go out to bars a lot, and I realized how easy it was for me to find a hook-up for a night. To have casual, no-strings-attached sex. I went out every night and had somebody new every time. For a long time, it was fun; changing sex partners as I pleased, but I never lost my heart to any of them. I always got out in time, never gave any of them my number, no repeats, ever. Until..." His voice broke. What had changed? I needed to know the reason, and no matter what it was, and whatever came of this, I could handle the truth. Even if we didn't end up together, we would always be close.

"Until what?" I asked breathlessly.

He buried one hand in his hair. "Until you moved in with us. I saw you every day; I couldn't shake you off like the others. You became more familiar, more important, and that wasn't good. I started to develop feelings for you. You took up more and more space in my thoughts, turned everything upside down, and I couldn't get rid of you."

Ben's words felt like a warm spring rain, purifying me, and opening my heart.

"Ben, kiss me," I said to him.

"Luca." He shook his head. "I can't."

"Why not?"

"Because I'm the son of a prostitute. I'd only bring you misery."

"I don't care what you are, and I don't need you to tell me what or who you are. I can make up my own mind, and I happen to see things differently. You're a wonderful man, and

I want you. And if you want me, too, then you kiss me right now. Otherwise leave it. It's as simple as that."

He cocked an eyebrow, opened his mouth but closed it again. Instead, he carefully took my face in both hands, his palms cooled my hot cheeks. I was shaking inside.

"Luca," he said, and I knew he could feel me tremble. He looked deep into my eyes, as though he were trying to read my soul. "With me, it's either all or nothing. If I ever decided to be with a woman for good, it would be with all the consequences. Are you ready for that?"

Every word sounded like a compliment, a long-desired gift he'd been hiding from me and now laid down at my feet. I was overwhelmed. "Kiss me."

His soft laughter sounded incredulous. "Don't be so impatient. I haven't done this in a long time." He caressed my bottom lip with his thumb as if to test my reaction. Heat rose inside of me and triggered a wonderful shiver within me, which trickled down my back and took my breath away. Ben slowly moved closer. His expression had changed; he seemed relaxed and liberated, as if he wanted to prolong this moment as long as possible to enjoy every second. I forced myself to remain calm and stay seated, and not jump him or impetuously press my lips to his first, even though it was all I wanted to. Ben needed to make the first move. If he kissed me, it had to happen of his own free will. The impulse had to come from him; otherwise, I didn't want his love. His mouth hovered over mine for a second, and I didn't dare breathe. Would he change his mind? My heartbeat accelerated as his warm breath touched my cheek, and the moment grew bigger and wider like the horizon over the ocean. I looked into his eyes, into the two black-speckled sapphires that shone right through me. The image of my own face was reflected in the dark pools. Then I felt his lips on mine, a jolt of electricity struck me. Although his touch was gentle, it was as if he first had to test what it would feel like to kiss me. He nibbled my lower lip.

"Would you mind participating a little?" he murmured against my mouth. "I feel like I'm making out with a statue."

Giggling, I put both arms around his neck and pulled him closer. "I'd love to, Mr. Nowak." We let ourselves melt into the passionate play of our tongues, warm, alluring, and simply divine. I caressed the back of his neck and snuggled closer to him. His kisses became hungrier and more ardent, igniting a blazing fire inside me that he'd have a hard time putting out again.

I stroked every single hard muscle from his chest down to his stomach, hell bent on touching his beautiful body again. My hands ventured under his dark gray t-shirt, stroking his bare skin. Ben gasped into my mouth, rose to his feet, and parted my legs. He stood between them and pressed his lips on my neck, biting gently. The sexy hint of pain aroused me, giving me goosebumps. Taking hold of one of my thighs, he pressed my leg against his hip. His tongue dipped into my mouth, demanding and hot, trying to lure me. Our kiss grew deeper, making my skin tingle. My short skirt slipped up to my hips, and I wanted to rip his t-shirt off of him. The feeling of his warm, sensual lips on mine swept over me and carried me away, as a whirlpool of desire tugged at my core.

"I still don't know what you look like," he whispered hoarsely without interrupting the kiss. His voice was throaty and seductive.

"Why don't you take a look?" I replied breathlessly.

His hands wandered to my neckline, slowly opening my blouse button by button, taking his time. Everywhere his fingertips touched my skin, it tingled like champagne bubbles bursting on my skin. Eventually, he slid my blouse from my shoulders, kissing me softly, playfully, all the while not taking his lips off of mine. Heat rose inside me, nearly setting me on fire. He slowly ran his fingers from my sides to my back, tortuously slowly unhooking my bra. I gasped at the sensation of the straps sliding down my arms, and he gently broke our kiss to look at me. To look at my breasts, the part of my body that I detested the most. Blood rushed to my cheeks as he let his gaze wander over my naked chest.

"You're so damn sexy," he growled. "Your breasts are so beautiful." He fondled them, one then the other, and I sighed in pleasure at his tender, yet seductively confident touch. My nipples hardened and stood firm, just screaming for more of him. Gone was my initial embarrassment. I didn't know how he accomplished that, but what he did felt absolutely wonderful. My skin was aflame, my heart pounding erratically. Pulling up my knees, I wrapped my thighs around Ben's waist, pulling him closer, my mouth finding his lips again. We sank into another fierce kiss that became deeper and more intoxicating, while we explored each other with our hands. My longing for him grew; my core was throbbing as he broke the kiss to start teasing my nipples with the tip of his tongue, letting his fiery breath heat up my skin in hot little gushes. Suddenly, Ben's hand was on my thigh, and I stopped breathing. His fingers wandered up the inside of my thigh and slid to my panties.

He caressed me through the fabric and intensified the searing sensation in my abdomen to almost unbearable, and I heard myself moan softly. I pulled Ben closer and kissed him, helplessly trying to keep myself under control and stop myself from pouncing on him like a starving lion. What he did felt so divine. God, he was so talented. At that moment, I wanted him so much that it hurt; his touch was frighteningly exhilarating. Ben set my body into unexpected vibrations as he pulled my underwear aside, found my most sensitive spot, and gently started rubbing it in a circular motion. I gasped out loud and clung to his shoulders. Tingly shivers rushed through to my pelvis, tormenting me sweetly. Moaning, my mouth glided from his lips down to his neck. A pleasurable tingling spread through me, and my breathing accelerated. I grabbed his shirt with both hands to keep myself from sliding off the desk, as all tension left my body. I concentrated only on myself, on this incredible feeling that gradually built up inside me and made my body tremble. Ben kept stroking me, flooding me with warm desire, making me feel like I was about to burst. Suddenly, my core contracted, I was throbbing wildly, while a hot flood of lust surged inside me. Never before had I experienced anything like this. I leaned with my forehead against Ben's chest, unable to move, giving myself over to my own pleasure, enjoying Ben's nimble fingers, which filled me with bliss and made my body sing.

He kept up his rhythm, somehow knowing exactly how to touch me, at just the right pace and intensity. Every nerve in my body cried out for release—and then I exploded with a force I would never have thought possible. I could hear myself moaning while hot waves whipped over me like a stormy ocean. Only slowly did I get a grip on myself again. I was still gasping into Ben's shirt, clinging to him tightly. Ben moved his hand away and stroked my back. His lips touched my hair, and I hugged his waist. We leaned into each other's arms for what felt like an eternity, while Ben helped me recover from my internal explosion. So that's what everyone was talking about. For the first time, I understood why people made such a fuss about having an orgasm. I couldn't imagine a sensation more intense than this. I looked up.

"That was incredible," I whispered, and he smiled. Ben started kissing me again, like he couldn't get enough of me. When I ran my hand inside his jeans, it was obvious that my sensual high hadn't left him unaffected either. I hastily opened his belt buckle, unbuttoned his jeans, and slid my hand further inside, massaging him with gentle pressure and stroking his tip with my thumb. Ben struggled for breath and leaned his forehead against mine. His eyes darkened and he half-closed them, again and again pressing his lips to mine in helpless surrender, until he finally grabbed my wrist and gently pulled my hand out.

"It'll be all over if you keep that up," he gasped.

I laid my cheek against his chest and just held him, listened to his thundering heartbeat for a while.

"What did Erdie's mother whisper to you that day in the shop?" I murmured through our haze of bliss.

"Don't tell me you haven't figured that out yet," he joked, still sounding short of breath.

"I'm just about to find out," I giggled. He stroked my shoulders.

"You'd really like to know, wouldn't you?"

"Tell me."

Ben kissed me again with a passion that electrified me, as if he had to make up for lost time. His warm lips caressed mine. He was the best kisser I'd ever known. Just as I was drifting into this wonderful pleasure, surrendering myself to him with all my senses, he muttered softly against my lips: "She said you're the woman I'm going to marry one day."

I stopped mid-kiss, but Ben just went on kissing me as if he'd counted on my reaction.

"And what do you think?" I asked, pressed against his lips, bracing myself for any possible answer.

"That you're the woman I'm going to marry one day." He repeated it like it was the most normal thing in the world, and pulled me closer.

I couldn't help smiling. Suddenly, I was the happiest person in the world—I was never going to let Ben go. As his lips moved down to my clavicle, tiny stubbles scratched my skin, ratcheting my pulse up another notch. I buried all ten fingers in his hair while he traced a line down to my breast with the tip of his tongue and caressed my hardened nipples.

"Sleep with me," I whispered into his hair, and he raised his head. I was flooded with the desire for us to become one.

"We have plenty of time," he said softly, placing both hands on my waist. "It's not my plan to get you into bed as quickly as possible."

"I know, but I want to feel you."

Ben kissed me again. His lips stroked my own, while he caressed me with both hands. The fine hairs on my thighs stood up when he reached under my skirt and pulled my panties off. I held onto the desk to help him. He slid the piece of lingerie down my legs and dropped it to the floor. Eagerly, I pulled him closer by his waistband while I ran my tongue up his neck.

"Hold on," he whispered, then straightened up.

I brushed the tangled strands of hair from my face. Had I come on too strong? With one hand, he wrestled his wallet out of his back jeans pocket and fished out a red foil-wrapped condom. "I'm always very careful, and you're not on the pill, are you?"

I shook my head. Now, how did he know that? I had stopped taking it after my break-up with Ringo.

He ripped the wrapper open, pulled down his boxers a bit, and slid the condom on. As if in slow motion, he bent over me and pressed his feverish lips onto my neck. Feeling the weight of his body on mine was just wonderful, and I leaned up closer to him. Everything inside me longed for Ben as he finally pushed into me and stretched me open. He paused for a moment as I got used to his size. Heaving a sigh, I closed my eyes while he began to move slowly.

"Open your eyes," he suddenly demanded, and I looked up. "I have waited so long for this moment, I want to see you come for me," he said gruffly. He moved his pelvis a little faster, gliding back and forth inside me, and the intense eye contact made me panic for a moment. Oh, God, I was actually having sex with Ben. The womanizer. The sexy demigod. Suddenly, I was afraid I'd disappoint him, unsure what he wanted from me. He seemed to read my thoughts.

"Relax, stop thinking for a minute, just look at me." He rubbed my nipples with his thumb until they stood stiff and erect, sending another shiver of pleasure through my abdomen.

His movements felt magnificent. Increasing in speed and intensity, they stoked my desire even more. I watched him as he looked at me. His face twisted slightly, his cheeks tightened, and the blue of his eyes turned completely black.

His arousal ignited my own. I found it new and exciting to watch a man become more and more ecstatic because of me. His t-shirt clung to his chest, which heaved with every breath. A pleasant pulling sensation made its way into my stomach, releasing a load of endorphins, and suddenly my lower abdomen contracted around him again, while Ben pounded into me. I moaned loudly and clawed at his back. At first, it felt like I was falling, and then I was floating somewhere in weightless space, while my climax kept building up. My body was not my own anymore, and I arched my back, enjoying this incredible feeling with all my senses, clinging to him haplessly. Ben, too, was now panting loudly. His eyes never left mine, his intense gaze enhanced the rush inside me even more. Like tiny bolts of lightning flashing between our pupils, our passion shot up to a higher level. Finally, breathing heavily, we sank against each other. Ben leaned his forehead against my shoulder and gasped for air as I tried to get my wildly raging heartbeat under control. Sex with Ben was absolutely the most breathtaking and best thing I had ever experienced. I was left feeling both elated and like I wanted more. I wanted much more of this. A lot more, every day if possible.

While still inside of me, Ben lifted his head. A euphoric smile appeared on his lips, then he kissed me and said softly: "That was definitely not a one-night stand."

EPILOGUE

I looked around in my now almost empty dorm room, which suddenly felt bare and not very inviting. All my stuff was packed in boxes and suitcases, and stacked against one wall. A wistfulness crept over me. It was my very last day as a student. Starting on Monday, I would be entering the real world—with a regular job. Touching every single piece of furniture in goodbye, I ran a finger over the notch I'd carved into the bedpost. That was for Ben, a little joke at his expense. He had moved out almost six months ago into a nice apartment in downtown Nuremberg.

"Looks like you haven't added any more trophies to your collection over the last six months."

"Nope. Had my hands full with the leader of the pack."

Ben was standing behind me; he'd come to pick me up. When I turned around, he was there, casually leaning against the doorframe, looking all hot in his black suit and white button-down, no tie.

He walked up to me and pulled me into his arms. "I hope so," he muttered at my neck. His hot breath hit my skin, making me dizzy. I would have loved to jump him right then and there, but my knee-length black dress and complicated hairstyle held me in check. It was the day of my graduation ceremony.

"Don't ruin my makeup. Michelle worked on me for almost an hour."

He studied my face. "Well, there is—um—a lot of it. Why did she paint your eyes with all that gray?"

I sighed. "It's called smoky eyes, Mr. Country Bumpkin. And it's not paint, it's makeup."

"You look really hot, but I prefer you natural." His hands wandered up my waist, but I grudgingly stopped his advances. My stomach was humming. "Just a preventive measure," I gasped and wriggled away from him.

He cocked an eyebrow.

The memory of Ben's graduation party six months back was still more vivid than I would have liked; a lot of alcohol had flowed that day. Unfortunately, I hadn't noticed the photographer taking pictures of everybody before putting the album online. I was in quite a few of them. It was a clearly documented account of my physical deterioration as the evening progressed. This was not going to happen to me twice, especially not at my own graduation party.

"I'm wearing camo makeup tonight," I explained with dignity. "Absolutely waterproof and alcohol-proof. It'll stay on all night. I'll look fresh as a spring morning if any photographers sneak up on me again."

He laughed. "You just need to be clever about avoiding them. Erdie and I weren't in any of the pictures."

I patted his shoulder. "That's because they were shooting above the tables, not under them."

He pinched me in the side. "We were still standing at the end, Darth Vader."

Before I could even think of a reply, he planted one of his scorching kisses on my mouth, one of those that made me melt every time and were absolutely addictive. Yeah, I admit it, I was addicted to Ben's lips, a kiss junkie.

"C'mon, let's go," he said against my lips. "We can take your stuff over to the apartment tomorrow."

I gave him a big smile, probably resembling a happy Buddha figurine, but I didn't care. As of tomorrow, we'd officially be living together.

Hand in hand, we entered the great lecture hall of the Department of Organic Chemistry, where the graduation ceremony was to take place. Ben's event had occurred at the Nuremberg Opera House. Obviously double standards were also prevalent at the university.

A jumble of people were already gathered; students standing with their families in small groups, chatting. A tinge of melancholy crept into my heart. Apart from Ben, nobody was here for me today. Toby and Ellen were going to join us later. Caro and Martha were on a weekend love trip to a spa. They were getting along great now, and I was happy for them.

My father hadn't been able to make it over the big pond to see his only daughter receive her average diploma. Was I allowed to feel bitter? I thought so. Granted, I'd failed to go to the States to see him in August. One reason was Ben, whom I'd helped redecorate his new apartment. But in exchange, we were flying to Atlanta next week for a visit.

The last six months with Ben had been incredible. Not only had he shown me a few tricks in bed that had lifted me straight up to heaven, but we also had so much fun together. Of course, he was still Ben, and often drove me crazy with his stupid jokes, but you can get used to everything, and, by now, I really enjoyed our little arguments.

I spotted Rhashmi and Erdie in a corner, surrounded by a group of about twenty Indian family members of all ages. Undoubtedly, her family placed value on sticking together and being there for each other at important events.

"Look who's here," Rhashmi whispered when we reached

her, pointing her chin to the side. I followed her gesture and discovered Psycho-Johanna among a crowd of people. Martin was standing next to her and, strangely enough, had only eyes for her.

Rhashmi giggled. "It looks like she's got her Martin back for good."

I hadn't spoken a word to that weirdo for all these months, and luckily, he'd made himself invisible in class. "He looks like he really worships her. Thank God."

Ben and Erdie were chatting about the soccer game they were missing, while Erdie kept discreetly checking the score on his phone. Toby came over, and looked at Erdie's phone before even saying hi to me. Where was Ellen? She'd been notably peaceful in Ben's and my presence over the past few months, so we'd decided not to make a big deal of it, for Toby's sake.

"Hey, Luca, life's about to get serious." We hugged. I was really happy to see him. Toby had also moved out of the dorm in August, and had found his own place in Nuremberg. Ellen was about to move in with him as well. I, on the other hand, had spent the last few months at the dorm in the company of a not very talkative exchange student from China and a theology student, who frighteningly reminded me of Johanna. I hadn't wanted to rush into things with Ben right away, preferring to take things slow. And also, because he had only asked me to move in with him three weeks ago.

"I am glad you could make it. Didn't Ellen come with you?"

My poor ex-roomie's shoulders dropped. "She's auditioning for a part in some stupid new soap opera in Berlin."

"Is she getting into acting now?"

"It's more like a cameo role. They're looking for a model for a scene."

"Goooooaaal!" cheered Erdie, which earned him the evil

eye from Rhashmi. And away Toby went, his bad mood all forgotten as he and the other guys discussed the score.

Rhashmi turned back to her family, who were taking turns hugging and petting her. Her mother's pride in her daughter was clearly written on her face, which somehow hurt my soul, even though I was really happy for both of them. Only—I would've also loved to celebrate with my parents today.

Ben slipped his arm around my waist; he must have noticed me staring at Rhashmi.

"We'll celebrate with your father in Atlanta," he whispered in my ear and kissed me on the lips.

I smiled bravely and nodded, even though we both knew it wasn't going to be the same.

Erdie came to greet me with the obligatory swipe at my chin. "Hey, Shorty, looking good tonight." He bent down. "But your eye makeup is a little smudged, though. Maybe you should fix that."

That made Ben laugh softly. "You've never heard of smoky eyes, you hillbilly?"

"Smoky what?"

"Lucrezia," I heard a deep voice behind me call out, and spun around. Who dared to shout my stupid name out in public? My heart nearly stopped when I recognized the person in front of me.

Rhashmi giggled. "Lucrezia?"

"Dad!" I could not believe my eyes. "What are you doing here? I thought…"

He spread his arms, his red-and-black striped tie hanging askew; his crumpled suit seemed to have suffered in the suitcase.

"Surprise!"

Tears welled up in my eyes, only the fear of ruining my smoky eyes kept me from crying on the spot. There was no way I was going to look like a raccoon when I accepted my diploma, so I swallowed them back and threw myself into his arms. He smelled of his usual Old Spice, and I soaked up his familiar scent; it felt like home. "I'm so happy you made it."

"I'm happy I managed to surprise you," he muttered. "It feels so good to hug you again." Then he broke the embrace and gave me a quizzical look. "I'd like you to meet someone," he said after a heartbeat. Only now did I notice the attractive, middle-aged blonde woman standing next to him. Wow.

"This is Grace."

That name definitely suited her.

"Grace, I want you to meet my daughter, Lucrezia." There was pride in his voice.

I, on the other hand, was surprised. It was palpable how comfortable they were with each other.

"Please, call me Luca," I finally managed, shaking her hand.

Smiling warmly, she said. "Nice to meet you, Luca."

We stood facing each other, me feeling uncomfortable and tongue-tied.

"I love your smoky eyes," Grace said eventually, studying my face. "You look beautiful."

"Thank you. It's nice to meet you, Grace." I decided to give her a chance. Never before had I seen my father this happy; his radiant face was unfamiliar. He was obviously doing great, and that was wonderful to see.

My heart tingled with joy when I introduced them to Ben. My Ben. They shook hands, and my father gave him a thorough once-over, as if he were recruiting him for the army. "So, you're Lucrezia's new boyfriend?"

"Not so brand new anymore. I've passed my probation period so far."

My dad laughed, and I saw with relief that he seemed to genuinely like him.

"What's your major?"

"Computer science. I work as an IT consultant now with Siemens."

My father seemed to approve of this. "So, you know your way around computers?"

Ben didn't bat an eye and nodded, smiling politely. "You could say that."

"My computer at home crashes all the time. Do you think that could be fixed?" My father launched into a consultation right away, and Ben tried his best to explain what the problem could be. The question marks on my father's face grew bigger and bigger.

"You know what? Why don't I take a look when we come to Atlanta? It's probably just a few outdated drivers that need updating."

My dad beamed. I could tell that Ben had just been upgraded to the position of "Favorite Future Son-in-Law Ever."

A voice echoed from the microphone, requesting everyone to take a seat. The front rows were reserved for the graduates.

After we had received our diplomas—and Martin, as expected, snatched up the award for outstanding achievements in the master's degree class for Cellular and Molecular Biology, we moved on to the casual part of the evening, which consisted of a reception with a champagne bar and an eccentric band of professors playing live music. My dad and Grace joined us, and offered their congratulations. She was a genuinely lovely person, as I found out after we'd talked some more.

Erdie was a bit bummed, because Rhashmi would soon be leaving for Mumbai for her six-month program to help implement a project on sustainable drinking water abstraction. I was just about to cheer him up with a stupid joke when Rhashmi nudged me excitedly.

"Look at that."

"What?"

Her hands were shaking as if she were hyper or

something. "Check out Martin's girlfriend," she said under her breath, pointing to the side.

My eyes nearly popped out of my head. Psycho-Johanna was standing about five yards away, her belly visibly rounded under her sand-colored tunic. That was clearly a baby bump. I couldn't believe it. Rhashmi pressed a hand to her mouth while I gaped at Martin and his girlfriend in a mixture of embarrassment and fascination.

"I don't believe it," I finally muttered, nearly choking on my own breath. Martin had reproduced. I couldn't even imagine what this meant for the world. In my thoughts, I felt deeply sorry for the future generation.

"Don't believe what?" Ben asked next to me.

"Martin's girlfriend is pregnant," I said, nodding to the side.

A broad grin grew on Ben's lips. "It could've been you if you hadn't been so cocky back then."

I shuddered. "In that case, I'm better off with you," I quipped with a mischievous grin, which caused Ben to put one hand around the back of my neck.

"I'm the best thing that could've ever happened to you." He made clear.

"A bullseye, so to speak." I snuggled up to his chest.

"You hit the jackpot," he agreed.

Rhashmi tapped me on the shoulder. "Shall we go over to say hi to Martin?"

I forgot all my reservations at once. "Back in a bit." Waving to Ben, I let my curiosity win over and carry me the short distance across the linoleum floor. To be on the safe side, I let Rhashmi take the lead, arriving two steps ahead of me. Better safe than sorry.

"Hey, Martin." She tapped him on the shoulder. "Congratulations on the award."

"Yes, congratulations," I agreed, raising my champagne glass and putting as much enthusiasm into these two words as I could manage.

"Thanks." He seemed genuinely happy, his ears turning pink, as if someone had pressed a hot iron on them. "But I knew I was gonna get that award."

"Who else," said Rhashmi, giving a pointed look at Johanna's stomach. "Looks like there's another award coming up too."

"Two, actually." He beamed like the August sun, but there was a tenderness in his eyes when his gaze lingered on Johanna.

She seemed extremely reserved and had even moved a step away from me, which almost made me feel guilty. I planned to get out of there, asap.

"Wow, you're having twins—that's great." I smiled at Johanna despite myself. I couldn't help it. She was a pregnant woman carrying two babies under her heart. I just couldn't stay mad at her any longer.

"Yeah, we're all really excited." She finally joined in the conversation, reaching for Martin's hand. "Next week, we're moving to Vienna."

"I'm going to get my PhD at the University of Vienna," Martin added. "Why don't you come see us sometime?" He cocked his head and smiled at me.

Sometimes I really didn't know what was going through this guy's strange brain. "Maybe one day. You guys need to get settled first." Now I really needed to get away from them. I felt like I was walking into a minefield again. "Well, you guys take care and have a nice delivery and all that."

I pulled Rhashmi away by her sleeve, who was still shaking her head in disbelief.

"At least they're moving to another country," she whispered, and I nodded in assent. Then she returned to her extended family, and I noticed that my dad and Ben were talking amicably. Nice!

"Ben invited us over for breakfast tomorrow," my dad told me, holding hands with Grace. "And now, we're going back to the hotel. It's getting late, and the jet lag is kicking in."

It was lovely to see my dad so happy after all these years. To my relief, there wasn't even a twinge of jealousy inside of me. On the contrary, I felt he absolutely deserved being in love with this wonderful woman. We had both found our dream partners. "Looking forward to seeing you tomorrow."

Then Ben leaned over to whisper in my ear, "Let's go home too." With a wink, he added, "Anything Martin can do, we can do better!"

THE END